MW00758382

Shir Azgoth
Erehalle
Morin Mountains
Medric
N
W
E
S
Ren Noctis
Glooms Wood
The Red Peaks
River Wood
Icebarrow River
Red Acre Wood
Springcrest River
ELARION
Hrothgale
ENORMĖTEREN
Dridion
The Moaning Wood
Kazakmuir
Deavorás
Ravelon
Cauldarím
Arena
Nundric

The Keeper of Fates

The City of Night

By

Nicholas T. Daniele

Layout and design by Ryan Twomey-Allaire
Cover images provided by Shutterstock

ISBN: 978-1-936476-13-8

For Papa, Grandfather Extraordinaire.
For the lessons.
For the laughter.
For the love.

May you be my light in dark places,
when all other lights go out.

Contents

The Keeper of Fates

THE CITY OF NIGHT

PREFACE

Greetings readers, and welcome once more to the journey. I consider it an honor that you've chosen my tale to transport you—if only for a brief while—to somewhere far away. I thoroughly enjoyed writing this volume of The Keeper of Fates series, mostly because it allowed me to add to the development of the main characters while introducing interesting additions to the exciting cast. It's a pleasure having you back! Now get comfortable, grab a nice hot drink, and, as always, enjoy the journey.

Prologue

Search for the Rider

Rolan Weatherstead peered deep into the gray dawn over Hrothgale, marking this the third consecutive morning the ghostly shroud of dense fog clung to the yellowing horizon. It had been long since a Lord of that land had taken it upon himself to carry out the king's orders. It would have served him better to choose able men for the cause while he turned his mind to more prevalent matters. But Mascorea had made it clear that this was as important a trek as any, upon which hung the very fate of the world, and he would neither entrust nor burden any of his men with the task of seeking out the rider who, four months ago yesterday, set out from Adoram.

A chill wind rustled the folds of his thick, fur-lined cloak and his rain-wet locks of gold as he scoured the distance through his looking glass. The lands north of the Elarian— the great river that spilled out of the Blue Mountains in the upper Northeast and bent to cut the southwestern lands in two—seemed to be growing quieter by the day, and what was more, it seemed as though winter would be arriving early this year, unless he was off his mark. His mind would often stray to such absent thoughts as he studied the unmoving lands beyond Hrothgale's walls. Not even a sea-going bird or a family of beasts crossed his line of sight for nearly a week now. He could not remember the last time he saw a ship passing along the wide, gray bend of the river flowing under him . . .

I will not mark them dead until I see their bodies, he

constantly told himself. *There is yet hope . . . There must be . . .* However, the passing of so many empty hours made even the Lord of Hrothgale's unwavering heart succumb to a whispering doubt. He was growing edgy upon the high stalk of the north tower. Not since his first days as a soldier had such angst welled up inside him, such need for something to happen. Anything.

He had waited five weeks before setting a watch for the rider—Gamaréa, son of Gladris, most recently a resident of the coastal town of Titingale. He would have waited longer had the vessel bearing him east not been captained by Gawaire and propelled by the rowers of his acclaimed crew. They could cross the Mid Sea in half the time it took other galleys to do so, which was perhaps the main cause for his concern. *Four months gone . . .* he told himself. *Four months.* Word would have been sent from Adoram had the rider and his companions arrived by another route, but even Medric's other sectors remained silent as the fog-bathed fields before him.

Rolan remained at his post throughout the day, despite constant suggestions from those closest to him to select another Morok to take watch for a while so that he may at least eat. Ever the stubborn sort, however, he refused every separate offer. This was not received quietly. As the walled-in town supped, Captain Lem Avroinon strode through the doorway on the tower's peak with a plate of bread, salted meat, and a horn of ale.

"You look terrible," Lem grumbled, setting the tray atop one of the tower's merlons and handing over the horn. Gray was beginning to fletch his black, bristly beard, and also started to show in streaks along his temples. His frame seemed double that of its true stature with the great, horsehide cloak wrapped around him. As he stamped upon the stone, Rolan heard his mail jingling beneath the layers of hide and fur. Lem's philosophy was to always dress as though an engagement could arise at any moment. In such an instance, one would want to look his best. Of course, the Captain regarded a proper engagement to be a clash of swords.

Looking into the horn as though the idea of ale was new to him, Rolan answered, "It is but a glimpse of how I am beginning to feel."

Lem rested two thick hands atop the nearest merlons and swayed a bit within the open crenel. He had fired many an arrow from this post defending Hrothgale from advancing Fairy hordes who sought open passage across the river and into Medric. Rolan had stood beside him for nearly every one that flew. Yet the fear that was beginning to cling to his bones was the strangest he ever felt atop that tower. Looking upon Lem's hard profile—the jutting, frequently-broken nose; the angular, bearded jaw; the eyes like a crow's—he sensed that he likely felt the same.

"There is still no sign of the rider," said Lem. Rolan thought he might have meant to phrase it as a question, but it came out as firm a statement as any he had ever spoken.

"None," Rolan answered, bringing the black-streaked ale-horn to his lips before setting it back down without drinking. He could not fathom putting anything in his stomach just yet. The worry would not allow it.

"It must be close to four months now," said Lem, as if to himself.

"Four months and a day."

Lem's brow furrowed slightly, and his posture slackened somewhat, yet he remained silent as they both continued peering absently into the bleak and quiet distance. For Rolan it was more out of habit than anything. He knew, even with the gifted sight of Moroks, that he would be hard pressed to see anything scurrying across the foggy expanse of folds stretching beyond the gates of Hrothgale.

After a time Lem spoke. "Nothing has passed along the river?" Though his words were spoken softly, the sound of his voice woke Rolan as if from a daydream. The Elarian stretched west for a long way before making a sharp bend and running directly beneath the arches of Hrothgale, which was built over it—a raised town of slate and stone beneath which the river passed, long serving as a bridge for paying passerby, and long sought by enemies of Medric as a shortcut to glory.

"Nothing," answered Rolan grimly. Loose strands of his damp, golden hair clung to his forehead and flitted around in front of his eyes, though he had stopped bothering to move them. "They set out in Gawaire's old galley from Stormbeard, yet I have seen no sign of *The Sojourn* along this river."

"It is likely they returned to Stormbeard, then," said Lem. "The Elarian flows too close to Dridion in some spots. Gawaire would never risk a course so close to our enemies."

Rolan shook his head and frowned. "There has been no word from Stormbeard. Mascorea's errand runners have had about as little sleep as I of late. Had *The Sojourn* come to port we would have known about it within two days of its first sighting. Yet Adoram is quiet. Dwén Alil, Titingale— silent as the lands before us."

He could see Lem looking at him out of the corner of his eye as he gazed beyond at nothing in particular. Along the shaft of his ale-horn he tapped his fingers anxiously, but said nothing. He knew the way that Lem was looking at him, this man who knew him as well as he knew himself.

"What do you mean to do?" Lem asked.

For the first time in many hours, and only the second or third time that entire day, Rolan stood. His back ached, and his legs were stiff and weary, but his face was hard, and his heart was resolved. "Look for them," he said at last.

* * *

His mind decided and unable to be swayed, Lem followed in Rolan's wake down the winding stairs of the north tower and into the scantily populated courtyard. In random corners he could hear muffled music and crowds chattering, but there were few wandering, and none who would question their Lord or his Captain. Thus they passed unhindered to the stables, where Lem understood instantly what Rolan was about.

"You mean to go *now*?" he asked. Though he ever considered himself the daring sort, even he knew it was far too big a risk to wander outside the gates of Hrothgale past dusk. Packs of Fairies were said to be searching the hills for wandering Moroks. He heard, in some cases, that they were starting to even capture and imprison them. But to what end he neither knew nor wanted to imagine.

Rolan was already inside one of the stables and saddling a muscled bay, who twitched nervously for a moment or so before the Lord of Hrothgale calmed her. Rolan always had a way with horses, and fared much better with their sort than Lem ever had. It was a skill that required patience, which was a virtue he unfortunately lacked.

"I cannot wait any longer," Rolan said, now busying with the bay's bridle.

"And what do you hope to find out there?" Lem demanded. He heard the firmness of his own tone, yet did not think to recoil. Someone had to talk some sense into Rolan. Hrothgale could not afford its Lord to be captured by Fairies, or worse. Medric could not afford it. Mascorea hadn't any sons, and rumors had begun to spread that his health was slowly failing. Should he die his crown would pass to one of his appointed Lords, and Lem could think of none more able than the Morok before him, readying the mount upon which he would risk his very life.

"Answers," said Rolan plainly.

Lem shook his head. "And you think your answers will simply rise up out of the hills?" He was all but shouting at Rolan now. Had someone been walking by to witness this, he or she would have been startled at seeing their Lord, whom no other resident of Hrothgale was above, being reprimanded so openly. But Lem cast aside Rolan's title and that of his own for a moment, speaking candidly not to the Lord whom he served but to the boy beside whom he learned his first steps. "What makes you think you will be so fortunate?" he continued. "What makes you think that your search will fare any better than it has atop that tower? Just because Rolan Weatherstead, Lord of Hrothgale, comes down from his walls, the long-sought rider will suddenly emerge? Pay this the thought it warrants."

He might as well have been wishing Rolan a happy

name day for the subtle nod his reprimand yielded. "If I have not returned by this time tomorrow, do not attempt to rally a search party," was all Rolan said. Lem had never remembered a time when Rolan seemed so wrought with worry. His face was grizzled stone, flecked by a thick, yellow goatee and a patchy beard. Lem could barely see his blue eyes for the shaggy, golden mane that framed his newly gaunt, prickly cheeks, but through the strands of his hair he saw weary things, once-bright orbs whose lights were fading. "If five days come to pass, tell Jaine . . . Tell her I have done all I can."

Such audacity Lem never thought Rolan was capable of displaying. Did he truly think that he could depart in front of him without expecting him to follow? "Appoint someone else the duty, Weatherstead. I would not be from your side."

"No." Rolan's response was quick and final, the unwavering firmness of a command.

"I am no commoner seeking funds—" Lem began.

"But I *am* the Lord of Hrothgale," answered Rolan resolutely. "And you will address me as such. Do not forget your place, Captain. I have given you an order. No search parties. If after five days I have not returned . . . you know what you must do."

This was not the Rolan Weatherstead he once knew. This was the Lord of Hrothgale, the Lord the folk of this fortress above the river knew and loved. He knew what he was doing; he had seen Rolan do it before. He was severing their bond—instating a barrier between them so that Lem would be disinclined to follow. Clearly, Rolan failed to realize how stubborn he could truly be. "Rolan—my . . . Lord—please . . . " It was strange indeed, calling him that.

"My word is final; my mind is decided. I would have no other defend Hrothgale in my stead should my search go ill."

Lem felt his mouth fumbling soundlessly for a word. For any sort of sound. The all too finite feeling of farewell swept over him like a winter's chill. This was his command, his duty. He would see it done to the best of his ability, or die in the attempt. It was a responsibility he was ready for.

What he was not ready for was explaining to Lady Jaine Weatherstead that her husband fell beyond the gates, and it had been his own hands that opened them.

Rolan was mounted now, looking down upon Lem with hard eyes—a bear's eyes. Eyes that not only welcomed death, but taunted it. Lem nearly strained his neck to look upon his face; such was the figure he struck upon horseback. In his best attempt at reserve, Lem nodded and stepped aside, the heaviest steps he ever took or would take. The shod hooves of Rolan's bay clacked slowly past him, and Lem followed all the way to Hrothgale's gate. After working the mechanisms to see it opened, he stood there frowning.

As if seeing the lands beyond Hrothgale for the first time, Rolan sat hesitantly, peering hard into the gathering, foggy darkness beyond. After a time he nodded, as if reaching some sort of conclusion silently among his own thoughts. Then he turned his gaze to Lem, who stood beside him with errant fingers stroking the neck of his horse. A light rain fell almost soundlessly—more of a mist than anything— but the cold winds that accompanied it made even Lem shiver in his layers.

Suddenly his attention was drawn by Rolan's voice. They had been standing quietly for so long that Lem had almost forgotten he was present. "You are a good Captain, Lemdrig Avroinon; yet one would be hard pressed to find a better friend. Lead our people well should I not return through the mists."

And then he was gone. Lem watched as Rolan and his bay were swallowed by the dense white mouth of the fog ahead before turning aside to close the gate. That night Lem himself manned the north tower, seeking two riders where Rolan had so tirelessly sought one, and trying to pry his mind from the thought that his search would turn up doubly empty.

It took Tryxók nine days to descend the stairs of Cór Burndal, the largest of Nundric's seven obsidian towers, and the only one with a passage directly into the bowels of Parthaleon. Such was the depth of the sorcerer's underworld realm; such was the force and ferocity with which he was banished from Zynys high above. Despicable Zynys. Horrid Zynys. It served Ation right for how arrogant he became, how complacent with his creations . . . *How foolish, maybe. Never mind all that. Never mind. Mustn't even think of him down here. Even in his slumber the Dark One can read our thoughts. Can feel our emotions . . . Must the way be so long, and so far down, down, down . . . ?*

Sometimes he wished he had never succeeded Dyseus, Sorcerian's former first officer. It was unwise for him to order his band of Matarhim to the eastern shores, where not even Nundric's forces were comfortable going. Somehow, he believed that Sorcerian would have advised him to wait until it was certain that it truly was Kal Glamarig that had surfaced there, and the prophecy's true Keeper that had found it. His rashness had spelled his end indeed, at the hands of a Morok—a Morok!—no less. *The fool . . . and now Tryxók must clean up all his mess. Poor Tryxók.* He wondered how The Great Lord Sorcerian would react to the news that Dyseus had fallen, along with at least fifty other Matarhim warriors of good stock. The fact that he alone would have to break the news to him was enough to make even his own vile heart shudder in his molten chest. His new composition was not something one can easily get used to. Being comprised mainly of fire and brimstone had more disadvantages than perks, but he had learned to accept it over the last three thousand years. Sorcerian preached destruction, and his form, though grotesque, made such things easily achievable.

It did not, however, speed up the traveling process. The descent into Parthaleon from the top of Cór Burndal's stair covered forty-five-thousand spiraling leagues, directly to the bottom of the earth itself where the Dark Sage rested, feasting on the souls of the dead and gathering strength until the day that he was replenished enough to rise again and finish what he started upon Zynys—completing his ultimate destruction of the Sages and claiming all three sectors of the world for his own: sky, earth, and all the fathoms below.

It would have been easier could he have taken the Spirit Route, as it had come to be known throughout Nundric—the way by which the spirits were funneled into Parthaleon, the gaping crater blown through the wide, ashen bailey around which Nundric's fortress was built. It was the only remnant of Sorcerian's banishment from Zynys—the very location where his body broke through the earth after his brother hurled him from on high. But that path was reserved only for the dead now. No living soul could pass through that portal without instantly succumbing to the spirit world themselves. Flocks of green-tinged, wispy tendrils of things thinner than clouds made their way into that peculiar vacuum by the hour. The dead. His spell was working. His curse, some called it. They were drawn to him now, bound by the Chamber he stole from the Mountain long ago. The Chamber of Fates. It was meant to call all souls to Zynys upon a time, but no longer. Tryxók believed it to be a work of genius, if someone asked him. No one ever did. The Matarhim were not particularly fond of communicating with each other no more than was necessary, unless it involved plotting destruction or bringing death upon unsuspecting victims. Though, the suspecting ones proved to provide more sport.

It was a quiet land, largely, built into the black rock of the Kazakmuír, a range of sharp hills that spanned vertically across the southeast folds of Enorméteren. East of those hills was the blight of Surullinen, where no soul dared venture. A permanent darkness eclipsed that land when the dominion of Sorcerian began, and only fell things came to live there, though they made their presence scarce. Next to nothing could be heard amidst those wastes or within the thick confines of Cór Burndal. Aside from the strange, low-rumble of Parthaleon's portal, there was not much to be heard save the crows that lingered just outside the walls.

The gates seldom opened but for the occasional escort from Dridion. Tryxók always thought the Fairies were an odd race—the way they poked their noses about with their white features, glamorous raiment, and polished blades. *The pretties. No dirt, no grime, all shine . . .* Yet none were as mad as their king. A child would have asked more questions upon swearing fealty to Sorcerian than Melinta, son of Viridus, and even then they might have been unconvinced at Nundric's outrageous terms. He truly thought a share of the world would be his when all was said and done . . . The look in his eye upon leaving the fortress was priceless. Like he accomplished the feat of all feats. *How senile.*

It was no matter. The more wars Melinta waged in the name of Nundric, the more souls on which his master would be able to feed. And that was a good thing. For where there was war, there was always death; and death meant life for the Lord of Nundric.

At long last Tryxók reached the floor of Cór Burndal, a place seen by but a handful. It was darker than the blackest night there upon the floor of the world. Torches had stopped lighting his way three days ago, at least. A simple, stone door opened out into the surreal landscape outside— a vast, purplish-gray plain that made even those comprised of fire cold. A constant mist clung to the land before him that never seemed to lift. Spokes of sharp stone rose up in several places, around which distorted figures like peculiar shapes of men lingered frowning. They would be consumed before long, no doubt.

Beyond, in the center of that wide and sorrowful realm— even Tryxók found it sorrowful—the body of Sorcerian lay beneath the spotlight of the portal above. Somehow there was light there. It was not sunlight. Not even at its strongest could the sun bring light to that forsaken realm. Yet there he was highlighted, a grand monument displayed in a gallery of cloud and dust and despair. His black shroud had not moved since last Tryxók saw him, his hands had not twitched. The Great Lord of Nundric was just as he left him several months ago, like the stone figure of a sleeping giant. He was the only one of that realm to have not changed in appearance. Like the others, Tryxók had been a Sage as well. The Sage of Shepherds. And, like other Matarhim soldiers, he had been cursed with his new savage form. But not Sorcerian. Not his Lord. His mane of pitch-black hair was still soft and smooth atop his head, and his face was yet as firm and hard as ever. There was no weariness wrought upon it, no concern. Just a wizened look, a patient look—the look of one who knew his time was near . . .

Tryxók had not realized how close he had gotten to Sorcerian's mount until a voice sounded from behind him. "Don't stand so close, cur." It was Xef, the Watcher of the Portal. It was his job to assure all souls made their way into Sorcerian's mouth, or at least most of them. "You'll disturb the spirits' trajectories."

Tryxók hissed in response. He had never been fond of Xef. None were, really. That was one of the reasons he was given his current occupation. Out of sight, out of mind.

"How long?" asked Tryxók, looming over the Sorcerer and studying his features as though anticipating him to wake at any moment.

"Longer still," answered Xef, almost defensively. He clutched a staff of thorny wood in his clawed, reddish hand, and bore into Tryxók with eyes of gleaming yellow. "Though we got a good one this morning."

"A good one?"

"Spirits, fool. *Spirits!* Each one is worth something, of course—but you knew that."

"Of course I knew that." He had not known that, but he was intrigued nonetheless.

Then Xef began singing and tapping his staff excitedly:

> *The strong of heart make strong his heart,*
> *The keen of mind make keen his mind,*
> *The fierce and mean, the pure and clean,*
> *In time, in time, in time!*

Even Tryxók, who had grown to like horrible things, found Xef's singing a horrible sound. But it made sense to him. If your meat came from a strong beast, then it would work to give you strength as well. At least, that was what he thought Xef was getting at.

"What are you blabbering on about?" he snarled at the still-tapping Watcher.

"The *spirits,* blind one. The *spirits.* Some are more potent than others. The vile, the wicked, the noble, the strong—all of them work to make him stronger! He needs them. And he got a good one not long before you turned up. The Lord Rolan Weatherstead of Hrothgale—"

"Dead?" Tryxók was surprised to hear the high-pitched note of excitement in his own voice. Hrothgale was a fortified enclosure that provided Medric's capital with an elite fighting force, and also worked to defend against enemies who sought passage across the river. Without Rolan Weatherstead to defend it . . . "How? When?"

"Yestereve," answered Xef jovially, something like a smile playing with the corners of his jagged mouth. "Captured in the hills on the borders of Dridion, he was. Imprisoned, tortured, hanged—the whole bit!"

"By the Fair Folk?" asked Tryxók, not bothering to mask his confusion. Their stock had never been known to show such hostility. But curious rumors had been spreading through Nundric over the past year that Melinta had built prison barracks over marshlands south of Deavorás. It was widely believed that he had hired scouting parties to capture wandering Moroks and imprison them there. Cauldarím, he thought he heard it called. Every now and then a prisoner would be selected at random and executed; Melinta's offerings to Sorcerian's rejuvenation campaign.

"They've got hundreds locked up in those prisons," said Xef. "All pigs being fattened for slaughter. And when all is said and done, my friend, when all is said and done . . . "

Xef let his words trail off, and fixed his yellow, fiendish eyes widely upon his dormant Lord. His laugh was enough to make even Tryxók, First Officer of the Matarhim, quiver.

Part 1

"Faithless is he who says farewell when the road darkens,"

— J.R.R. Tolkien

1

Melinta

He had been known as "Gamaréa Ironfist" in the dusty alleys of Titingale, and though he had certainly lived up to the name, he would have preferred not to be known only by the deft capabilities of his hands.

It was a better name, however, than those his captors frequently spat at him.

"On with you, rat!" one snapped.

"Move your legs!" another shouted. "If you *truly* want to move like a cripple, it can be arranged."

Insults and threats such as these had become so consistent during the hours he had been in transport that he barely felt the sting of them anymore. Too many troubled thoughts were racing through his mind to pay undivided heed to what his oppressors were squabbling on about. Lucian was out there somewhere, he thought with frightened incredulity. And he was here, his arms intertwined with the mailed sleeves of two Fairy soldiers of Dridion's infantry, which had stormed Ravelon that morning and scattered his company.

It seemed a new discouraging thought ran through his mind with each glance he dared over his shoulder, glances that were often turned away by a swift punch to the stomach or an elbow to the ribs. They had begun to leave his face alone, at least, though it had been their primary target earlier in their pursuit. He could feel the cold numbness of swelling around his eyes, and the tickle of a streak of blood down his face from an open wound on the right side of his forehead. Yet, despite how battered and bruised his face might have been, he tried to maintain some kind of dignified expression, as though being held prisoner in the arms of Fairies hadn't any effect on his morale. But it became all too evident that he was only fooling himself.

The afternoon sky could not be rightly seen through the cluttered boughs above, and as much as he tried, he could not begin to estimate the time that must have elapsed since his company separated. It was also difficult to determine the distance that must have been wedged between him and the path where he was taken from his friends. In some ways, it seemed as though they had been traveling for minutes, putting only a matter of meters behind them; in others it felt like hours, with several leagues having unraveled at their backs.

Unlike the path by which he had led Lucian, the trees here were now condensed and without splendor, their boughs drooping down like frozen tears. It was fitting, he thought, for if trees in fact could weep, who else better to weep for than him? After all, his fate indeed now seemed decided. An image of Mascorea flashed across his mind just then, sitting in his hidden chamber deep within Magnis Abitaz, or maybe even standing upon the highest stalk of that tower, scouring the breadth of his kingdom for the Sage-chosen rider who would not return.

His thoughts ceased abruptly just then, as he was thrown down to the leafy floor by the Fairies who held him in their grasp.

"How much further?" one of them asked impatiently. "We have never gone this way before. We are well off the straightaway path."

The one whom he was speaking to seemed taller than the others, his shoulders of a greater breadth than theirs.

"I know this well enough," he said, turning. He could have passed for a Sage had it not been for the white talons wrought upon the gold of his breastplate. A bold cape of emerald was fastened across his shoulders by a golden broach of the same likeness, dragging behind him on the forest floor. His gloved hand rested upon the pommel of his sword, which dangled in a bejeweled scabbard off his waist. Gamaréa wondered for a moment what he meant to do with that blade, but somehow did not expect him to brandish it against him. Had he wanted to, he would have done so hours ago.

"Captain Faldrus," said the other who had carried Gamaréa. "Will His Grace be so disinclined to the idea of us smiting him here in this wood? He is a heavy haul, and we've still a ways to go."

The captain's eyes seemed to consider, green eyes so dark they seemed almost black. He had a strong nose, which Gamaréa could see was moderately hooked, and his hair was nearly a rich shade of black, exaggerated against the golden armor he donned, short and curled much like Didrebelle's had been. "Then pass him to another pair," he answered coolly. The softness of his words seemed not to match the firmness in his voice.

"Forgive me," said Gamaréa from the ground. It was a pleasure indeed to be off his feet without his arms crimped by those of the soldiers, or his body beaten by their numerous hands. "I know I must be heavy for a folk so frail."

The kick came from the right of him, a swift, booted stroke that landed flush upon his cheekbone and sent him twirling from a leaning position and flat on to his stomach. He lay there until the lights in his eyes faded and the salty taste of blood no longer made him cringe.

"Pick him up," he heard the captain command. Faldrus, he heard the others call him.

Just like that he was drawn up between two mailed arms, the captain of the small gathering the only thing in his blotchy sight.

"Forgive me," Faldrus said softly, his nose nearly flush with Gamaréa's own. "I might not have heard you rightly. I thought you said my folk was *frail*. I must have been mistaken."

"On the contrary, Captain," Gamaréa replied. "You seem to have heard me well enough."

Faldrus issued a white-toothed smile that would have

seemed flattering on anyone else. He turned his emerald back to Gamaréa and nodded approvingly to one of his men who had come to stand around them. Gamaréa saw the blow coming this time, at least. Though he had time to tense the muscles of his stomach, it was a shattering punch that managed to knock the wind out of him. The soldiers' arms tightened to support him as he wilted on his feet.

"I thought so," he heard Faldrus' voice say when he returned to stand before him, though with his head bowed, Gamaréa saw only the captain's brown leather boots. "Do not think that I won't kill you here, Morok," he continued. "My king would pay for your head with gold enough to fill a flagon, but I have been commanded to deliver you alive, if it can be managed."

"*My* head?" said Gamaréa, genuinely surprised. How could Melinta possibly have known he had a hand in this? "Why?"

"Not another word," Faldrus answered sternly. "Or I will take your head myself and claim you forced my hand. As I see it, seven witnesses stand around me."

"But—" he did not entirely mean to speak again. When the kick came, it brought him to his knees. The soldiers released his arms, letting him catch his breath upon all fours. His sweat-matted locks drooped down around his face when he bent his head to the ground, lurching and heaving for air.

That was when he felt the kiss of cold steel on the back of his neck.

"Please," he strained, his voice now half of what it had been. "Forgive me. I will comply." Slowly he worked his way to his knees, the edge of the soldier's blade never lifting off his flesh. Raising his hands, he looked upon the captain imploringly. *I cannot meet my end here,* he told himself. *So secluded. So alone.*

It began to seem surreal to him, that scene within the dense wood: he upon his knees gesturing for mercy, eight soldiers of Dridion holding him at sword point, Lucian and Didrebelle so far from him now that they might as well

have been on the other side of the world. It did not feel
as though they had been together that morning. In many
ways, that morning seemed ages past.

He closed his eyes, and there was Détremon rising high
above him, its gray face thick and bold. There were the
three great towers of Adoram raised tall before the scarlet
dawn: Tormoríl, with eyes upon the western fields all the
way to the mountains beyond; Magnis Abitaz, from whose
stalk one could see far across the southern plains all the
way to Hrothgale under which the river flowed; Rheulár,
which kept watch upon the coastal towns to the east and
all the ports in Stormbeard Bay. There was Mascorea robed
in blue silks, his crown adorned with sapphires glinting
in the unveiled Medric sun. There were the dusty streets
of Titingale, and the laughter rising out from The Adder's
Nest. As if it wafted on the breeze itself, he could smell the
pungent scent of the hard whiskey Prig was wont to serve.
But most of all there was Lucian, and the look he had been
wearing the day he introduced him to this horror. There
was Mary Rolfe, who out of the Elderland crowd came
forward to beg that he kept the boy safe.

And he had failed them all.

The soft chuckling of Faldrus woke him from his trance.
"Well then," he said, "*this* is frailty, if I have ever seen it."
A ripple of laughter spread throughout his men. "Sheath
your blade," he ordered the soldier at Gamaréa's back. "If
he says he will comply, it falls upon us to deliver him to His
Grace. Get him up."

The city of Deavorás beamed fervently that afternoon,
sprouting like a white forest out of the four emerald hills
over which it had been built. Sentries manning the high
gates spat curses at him when his captors led him through,
and the folk close enough to recognize him as a Morok
added their own insults as he passed.

Avenues of various widths crossed throughout the city.
The wider streets hosted the most traffic. These were the
busy roads leading into the market squares, Gamaréa
suspected, or perhaps even to Melinta's courtyard upon

the highest hill. Some roads required deft movements in order to dodge oncoming horses or merchant carts; on others they were allowed to pass without hinder.

A sweet fragrance filled the air. He could not register a guess as to what it was, but it was a delicate, floral scent that worked to make his breathing easier. The folk of Dridion had indeed been eloquent once, long ago when Viridus reigned before the dominion of his son. Shades of that eloquence he could find in the alleys through which they passed, where Fairy women strolled about in decorative raiment of various pastel hues. He heard music out of some of the buildings, beautiful melodies upon lyre and flute. Yet every time they worked to soothe him, another curse or insult would make him recall again that he was among enemies.

Above him he saw flocks of white eagles gathered in the sky, circling away west of the city. It was in their likeness the sigil of Dridion had been fashioned long ago: the white talons ready to grip, standing boldly amidst an emerald field. A crowd seemed to be flooding that way as well, moving in groups as if to the same location.

"Is it happening *today*?" asked one of the soldiers.

"It is long overdue," answered Faldrus. "The hangings have been infrequent of late. The Dark Sage cannot afford long respites between offerings."

Hangings? Gamaréa thought suddenly. *Offerings?* Surely they did not mean what he thought they meant.

"Make way!" shouted Faldrus to the thickening crowd as they turned on to a main avenue. "On with you!"

Far away, Gamaréa saw the glint of steel, shining fervently against the sun. It was bright on this road; no buildings stood tall enough to blot out the blinding light ahead. Thus he heard the horsemen approach before he saw them.

"They will hang him today, then?" Faldrus asked the lead rider.

"Within the hour, I think," he answered. His horse was white and speckled here and there with silver, and his golden armor sparkled as he swayed within its saddle.

"What's this?" he asked, bending his sight upon Gamaréa. Underneath the shadows of the helm he wore, Gamaréa could see only the faint glimmer of his eyes.

"A token for His Grace," answered Faldrus proudly, "found among the company of the alleged Keeper."

"Then you are returning from Ravelon," replied the horseman knowingly. "A slew of our men passed through not long ago with tales of our triumph there, yet without a token to match yours. And a *Morok*, no less. Gallows Hill will be busy in the weeks to come, I suspect. Farewell, Captain."

With that he trotted off alongside the throng, and Gamaréa's company pressed onward. *Gallows Hill,* he thought frantically. Were they truly conducting . . . *hangings?* Public executions? He had heard the madness of Melinta was beyond the point of recall, but he would never have guessed the severity of it.

In much too short a time, however, he knew he would witness it first hand, for after another rightward bend in the road, they passed along the steep, white lane to the king's tower. The lay of the courtyard was decked in emerald lawns and white pillars, with wide basins scattered throughout into which elaborate fountains poured. The sun had fallen behind the great tower, and a heavy shadow was cast over the company in pursuit of its doors.

Once within Melinta's stronghold, they walked down a long, fair hall, with a floor of marble and white-stone walls that rose up to the high rafters blackened by shadow. Tall white pedestals led down the path to where Melinta was sitting in his golden throne, having his nails filed by a smug-looking little servant. Above the sheen of his long black locks, a glowing emerald stone crested the throne like a green crown. The Emerald Throne was alive, despite the filth that occupied it. He knew that in Medric the Sapphire Throne thrived as well, decked in blue and furnished with a blazing sapphire upon its crest. *If only the Ruby Throne would blaze* . . . somehow became his first thought.

"Leave us," he heard the king's voice say. Though he spoke softly, his voice seemed to carry throughout the cavernous hall, sending the soldiers shuffling and his servant scampering down the stairwell leading down from the throne. "Not you, Faldrus," Melinta added. Before long, Gamaréa felt the captain's presence behind him again. As if from far away, he heard the latching of the mighty doors, which seemed to echo long after they closed.

"What is this?" Melinta asked with a hint of distaste. Gamaréa's gaze was bent to the glossy floor, or else the king might have recognized him.

"This is the Morok whom captained the alleged Keeper's company, Your Grace," answered Faldrus.

"And the others?"

"Scattered, Your Grace. Our men yet patrol the breadth of Ravelon in search of them. I wished to bring you this token of our efforts before the day was through."

That was when Gamaréa looked upon him for the first time. Not an ounce of his person had changed since their last meeting. The soft black waves of his hair ran beyond his shoulders to settle on his breast, and he wore the same smug expression upon his ageless face that Gamaréa remembered plainly from long ago. Only then he had seen it in his council chamber, the night Melinta charged him with the murder of his daughter, one of the few he had ever loved. Rising, Melinta bent his gaze upon him, a black stare that seemed to have the power to see through him. Like fragments of obsidian, they shone within the paleness of his face. They seemed not to be . . . natural eyes. Yet, when he moved out of the shadows and stepped into a streak of sunlight blazing through his hall, they seemed to reclaim the state he remembered: a deep green, with little flecks of gold wrought within his irises.

"I thank you, good captain," Melinta said as he took one step down the stair, his eyes bent hard upon Gamaréa as if fighting to recall the image of a sight long removed. "You have my leave."

Out of the corner of his eye, Gamaréa saw the golden form of Faldrus issue a bow before stamping toward the door. When they shut again, Melinta came down to him.

"So *you* are the one they hold in high regard, I see."

he said curiously. He wore a padded evergreen doublet wrought with white swooping eagles, and a bold cloth-of-gold cape that shimmered as he strolled in and out of the strands of sunlight projecting through the thin windows of his tower. The crown he wore upon his head was a thin circlet of gold, decked all around with emeralds. Standing before Gamaréa now, Melinta seemed to truly see him for the first time, though what image he beheld, Gamaréa could only guess. His face felt heavy and swollen, and was certainly distorted by bruises and blood.

"It cannot be," he whispered at last. "I know your face. Fate has proven a dexterous seamstress, it would seem."

Gamaréa said nothing.

"I have tracked your small company since you washed up on shore two mornings prior," he continued. "You carried something that is of great worth to me. Tell me: who were the others, and where are they now?"

Again, Gamaréa kept his silence.

"It would seem your tongue has escaped you," continued the king. "That is no bother. I have more to say as it is, and you can listen. It is not my desire to chastise you this day, Morok. Instead I seek only to offer terms. Though tidings of your triumphs on the long road from the east angered me deeply, they indeed warrant great merit. A sword as deft as yours should not be so sadly wasted, and a soldier with as much skill to lead should not be so rashly fed to the noose. So it is, I offer to yield your penalty on the sole condition that you join with me. You were in my service once, as I recall. And though you brought great pain to my house, you can repay that debt by taking arms among my generals in the war that soon will spread. The darkness that shall encompass the world will not envelop you or me." Leaning in closely, Melinta then spoke in a voice that seemed different from his own. In its stead now was a vile, sinister sound that said, "What say you?"

Gamaréa could not help but chuckle; such was the madness Melinta exuded. "The rumors are warranted, then," he answered. "You truly have lost your wits."

Melinta for a moment chuckled also, and it seemed, at

least to Gamaréa, that sincere amusement was flooding through him. But then his genial expression abruptly turned grim. "In a month, or perhaps two, no banners will wave but Dridion's and Nundric's. The walls of Adoram will crumble; its high towers will fall. It will become a ruin like the Mortal realm of old. When the Great Sage reclaims his strength, there will be none able to oppose him. My fathers were never inclined to side with a losing cause, and thus I will not be. You seek an end of fire and rubble; I seek only the chance for new beginnings, in a world more vast and prosperous than ever before. I ask you now, whose wits are truly lost to them?"

"Still yours," answered Gamaréa firmly. "I thought the King of the Emerald Throne capable of making a wiser choice than this. You could have been the one to reestablish the alliance of the Three Realms—"

At this Melinta sneered. "You speak of an alliance long forgotten," he said shortly. "The Three Realms are no more. It began with the fall of Dredoway, when the Mortals fled east. The pathetic lot that remain are cave dwellers and wanderers. Tell me, do their sharpened branches and stone clubs attract you more than my ranks of thousands? Do they stand a better chance than I? And Medric is no different. Do you truly believe that Détremon will stand against the force Sorcerian will bring? It will crumble like all else in his path. No alliance I agree to will change that."

"If you would just open your eyes and see—"

"MY EYES ARE OPENED WIDE ENOUGH!" Melinta snapped, his voice a dense cloud that filled even the vastness of his long hall. Gamaréa had given a start at his outburst, but only slightly. As the dregs of his echoing scream faded, Melinta continued to speak more collectedly. "No," he said, turning to climb the stair to his throne. Over his head, the emerald blazed fervently, its gleam meshing with the streams of sunlight in the quiet air. "I will not be the weak link in the chain of my fathers," he said, sitting. "None of them needed your people, and neither do I. I will do away with them, once and for all. They are but a barrier—all that is left to oppose me. When I fatten enough of them for the

Great Sage's ingestion, you will see. Then you might wish you spoke differently here."

"Listen to yourself," Gamaréa said pleadingly. "You have gone *mad!*"

"*Impatient* is what I am," the king answered quickly, rubbing his temples with the tips of his fingers. "The offer is still available. Either you are with me, or against me. It does not require much thought."

It would be here, he knew, that it all would end. Though he did not voice it, he thought of himself donning the golden armor of Dridion, and the flowing emerald cape of the infantry, and the glinting helms that seemed so fair beneath the morning. He imagined the emerald banner in his hand, the white talons flapping in the westerly breeze from off the sea. He thought of all the trials his countrymen had put him through, the beatings of Jax and Stór, the harsh names his kith had called him long ago. But then he thought of Lucian and Mascorea, and the dependency their eyes had housed in the times they had looked upon him, and all his prior thoughts were dispelled. Quietly, he was ashamed to have ever thought them.

"I would not join you if you were my own king," Gamaréa heard himself say. "Nor would I wave your banner in war."

From atop the mounted throne, Melinta seemed to eye him curiously. Gamaréa wondered what thoughts festered in his mind as he registered his refusal, wondered what he might have said next or what he had in store for him. But in time he only answered, "So be it."

2

Imprisoned

Melinta had spoken for the final time. He summoned his guards, and after a moment of grappling, pushing, and shoving, Gamaréa was being forcefully escorted away from the great tower and back toward the gates at the head of the city. The biting chill of the wind prickled his skin as he walked off, bound by the grasp of the mighty captain and his company down the road to wherever they were going—perhaps to the gallows, perhaps elsewhere, but most certainly to death.

In time they left the city and tread on to the thin, green grass of Deavorás into the direction of the foul, decaying fields Gamaréa had noticed once leaving Ravelon. His mind could not make sense out of how this fair land now harbored such evil and deception, but of late it was clear that thorns riddled even the most lustrous rose, and Dridion was no exception. With inward desperation, he looked back toward Ravelon, looming sorrowfully now east of them atop the large cliffs, bending west away from the city, and he wondered what had become of Lucian. *Didrebelle is probably in search of him now. Go with haste, brother. Do not leave Lucian to suffer the dread and malice of this forsaken place.*

Soon the cliffs were behind him, shrinking off into the veil that would perhaps never be opened again, and the company pressed on through the river in the center of the plain, the soldiers' shoves challenging their prisoner's steadfast feet. The cool water, in spite of the weight fallen upon him from its current, was rejuvenating as it rushed against his lower legs, but it did not last long, for soon the outer banks were upon them, and a reek of something awful pierced the wind, and the phantom soldiers of the Matarhim walked passed them like long shadows.

They seemed larger than they ever had to Gamaréa. Their new armor was thick and broad, and, for the first time in all his years, he found himself intimidated by them. Grunting and hissing, they went storming in and out of the gates of a small, barren stronghold, in whose direction Gamaréa was being transported. As he was led through the gloomy entrapment of rusted iron, he noted that Melinta's city had grown small in the distance.

The gates wailed closed and latched shut, and he was left only to the road before him now, which was nothing of high regard. Ragged, run-down buildings stood here and there, without much upkeep, and the air was stale and stank of decay. He thought back to Titingale, and how this place made even that shabby little village seem glamorous.

It was darker here, though the sun still shone readily. Dust hung in every crevice, and their way was shrouded by a dense mist. The stronghold took on the feel of a separate realm altogether, one merciless enough to rival even that of Sorcerian himself. To Gamaréa's dismay, he soon found that the further reaches of this place were no more promising than those that came before it. A prison of sorts now loomed over them, stark and downtrodden, and from within issued the groans of its prisoners.

Being forced into the prison, dark and damp and dreary, he took the slow walk to what would be his cell, viewing the disgruntled, sorry forms of life that were caged along his way. Some were lying lifeless in the shadowed corners of their compartments, some clung to the bars as they passed, gazing up at him with wide, helpless eyes, as though he could save them in an instant, as though in one blink of an eye he could dismember the band that led him there and free them all. But this only worked to add to the guilt that had been building since he was captured in Ravelon, a guilt that now bound his body greater than any shackles his enemies applied. Lowering his head in grief, he could but let himself be led.

Darkness and only darkness. Gamaréa remembered being seized by the arms and no more. Perhaps they had struck his head with something. He felt heavy in all parts of his body. His head felt thick and his temples throbbed, beating at the sides of his skull like a muted drum. It took many moments for him to be able to feel the rest of his body, and when he did he felt his stomach first, aching in wretched pain. Had he been struck there as well? Poisoned? There was a cold numbness in his shoulders, and a gripping chill at his wrists and ankles. He slipped away again, his surroundings fading briefly into darkness before he forced himself into consciousness.

He noted then the moist, warm-iron taste swelling in his mouth and he spat almost involuntarily. The blood spewed from his lips and sprayed across what part of the dirty stone floor he could see. He knew now that it was stone. His eyes were beginning to focus somewhat. Stone floor. Stone walls. A small rectangular window perched above on the left-hand side. *Why the numbness in my shoulders?* he wondered again in frustration. It was not until then he realized his arms had been chained at the wrists, and were now stretched upward toward the ceiling into iron clasps that were fastened high upon the wall. His ankles were shackled also. He could move nowhere, could do nothing but sway subtly forwards and back, and even then he cringed in biting pain, as though nails were being hammered into his body.

Across his face his sweat-moist hair fell loosely, the tips of his locks dripping with some of the blood that he had spat away. He could not put an estimate on the time that elapsed before he reached full consciousness. His limbs were numb and bereft of feeling except for an occasional tickle when a nerve twitched, but he could feel his stretched-out diaphragm completely, struggling to breathe as too much of an inhale resulted in the excruciating sensation that he would somehow split in two.

Then he remembered Melinta, and the premise of their conversation before darkness took him. *The naïveté,* he thought. *The audacity.* How desperate could Melinta have been? Did his army really lack leadership to the extent that he would make him such an offer?

He thought of such things between the intense surges of pain. It seemed every separate instant that he moved one way or another, a new jolt of agony attacked him. Lucian passed in and out of his thoughts. Where was he? What had happened to the boy after the Fairies seized him and dragged him away? He could not know. He feared, among other things, that he may never know. For with the boy traveled the fate of the world, and he could only hope that neither was lost or worse. Then his mind would wander to Didrebelle, who was beside him up until the end in Ravelon, and wondered also what became of him. What path had he chosen? Was he able to lead Lucian out of that compromising circumstance deep within the wood . . . ?

The chains seemed to be more of a nuisance now. He was regaining strength and longed desperately to be free of his bonds so that he may venture out and salvage his mission. But it was no use. No matter the effort he put forth to rid himself of the lowly bowels of whatever building he was under, his chains would not weather or break. Instead he could only sulk within their grasp and bow his head in blood and shame.

Emmanuelle lay pale in her grave, eyes heavenward and closed, and every aspect of her seemed at peace. He could not watch her lying there in her woman-sized hole of delicate earth. Instead he watched her ceremony from the wood through which he was to flee back to Medric. Though his mind urged him onward, his heart lingered there in that sorrowful place underneath the looming overcast sky that made the grass seem pale, and nearly as dead as the woman beneath.

He saw her father mounted over her, leaning on his spade,, his head bowed in counterfeit grief. The last suitor too was there—Demetrious as he was called—and he had also been digging. Twelve maidens stood solemnly round her grave, singing a melancholy song that carried softly on the wind and reached his attentive ears far away where he watched, and he wept at its sound. Tartalion stood beside the king, and of all their number was the only one to avert his gaze. Upon doing so he met Gamaréa's eyes, and subtly urged him away; though in their hearts, both knew he would attend the funeral.

You must go by the road that is open, *Tartalion had said amidst the uproar of Emmanuelle's death.* The nation will fall into mourning for three days, and in that time no Fairy will leave Dridion. This is your time to flee and be gone.

And so, too baffled to speak, he left without further word or question, only to stay within the wood the entire night and lament the loss of his love until the following morning when the nation would partake in grieving. But now he stole away as ordered and returned at long length to Medric.

The forest emptied him onto the last length of Enorméteren, just a mile or so from the gates of Hrothgale where the forts of the infantry had been built long ago—hundreds of feet of iron and brawn behind the towering walls and gates of stone. When he reached the sentry at the nearest post, the guard stood upright and wary, as though Gamaréa's presence frightened him. It was only then that Gamaréa realized the tears still filtering down his face. Embarrassed, he fought back his surging sorrow and conjured a stone-like countenance as quick as could be mustered.

But the sentry was not startled by his tears, nor even noticed them, perhaps; and as the two figures stood a yard apart there in the midst of the pouring rain, each recognized the other wholly.

And Gamaréa said, "You gave me directions to the city once."

And the sentry answered, "I did."

"Will you allow me passage?"

The sentry's lips shivered. "Hrothgale accommodates no foreigner."

"I am of Medric."

"They say you are of other places."

"Do you believe them?"

"I think." *Then the guard's voice sunk.* "But I am not sure what to believe."

"Will you have me stand here in the rain, having tread so many miles?"

"You stand in the rain as I."

But then the sentry stood considering a moment. His gaze had changed, as Gamaréa noticed, as though he acquired deep recognition of something he had long regarded differently, and his movements were slow and solemn as he stepped down to open the gates. Without a word Gamaréa walked through, but the call of the guard drew his attention back. "I guess I don't believe them after all."

He knew his eyes were closed. For a moment he thought he could conjure his brain to send some sort of impulse in order to open them, but when he tried his eyelids seemed weighted and he thought better of it. In the darkened cell he dangled, his near-lifeless frame softly rocking in its iron bonds. He did not feel like a member of the strongest physical race the world had ever known. Nor could he recount the last time he felt something like strength. He wore armor once, and fought in many battles, but those memories were distant now; and so too were memories of times he believed himself insurmountable—invincible even in the face of his most daring adversaries.

He heard the constant shifting of people outside his cell. *Guards,* he thought. He did not encounter them directly. Through the cracks of the small barred window, he could hear the soft stammering of an owl and discerned that it was night. In time, he was able to stir himself awake. He was unsure what he preferred more. In the night it was nearly as dark with his eyes open as with them closed, but at least when they were closed he had the opportunity to dream and psychologically venture to other places far from his wretched enclosure.

But his dreams grew progressively worse with every wave of consciousness that departed from him. Though he thought he had left his memories of Emmanuelle in that strange Queen's Mountain, she frequented his dreams. Not one was without Lucian either, or the Key. In his nightmares he saw Lucian begin carried away by enemy forces, bound, tortured, and even killed in some instances. He often dreamt of the Key being found and returned to Sorcerian, and Gamaréa watched omnisciently as the Sorcerer's power intensified and he grew to an epic, horrid stature, razing all the reaches of the world with a thrust of his hand or a nod of his head.

In another dream, Gamaréa was at the command of the entire sum of Medric's legions, yet not even all their amassed quantity of arrows could smite the beast that was the Dark Sage, and he watched as each individual soldier evaporated into dust when Sorcerian countered.

Yet he preferred that world of dreams over the black void that was his cell. At least his eyes could perceive things there. Outside of dreams it was only nothingness—eyes opened and closed.

* * *

He was startled awake by the shrill screeching of his cell door being slid open. The guard was yanking it wildly, as the rusted door was old and hard to maneuver along the hinges. Again, he had momentarily forgotten his predicament, as he had been encapsulated by another dream outside of his conscious state but could not remember it. He saw only glimpses of the guard who had entered, and discerned only colors—shades of white and gold flickering, as he was unable to maintain a consistent manner of keeping his eyes wide enough to behold much of anything. His inability to do this, however, was not on account of his deteriorating physical condition. It was morning, and the bright rays of the sun were filtering in from outside and nearly blinding him.

Gamaréa felt the presence of the guard alongside him now, but before he could ask what he was doing, his own left arm came crashing down at his side, and soon after was followed by his right. At once he toppled upon the hard, dusty floor, and when he gathered enough strength, turned over to see his empty shackles dangling from the rafters of the cell. He looked around incredulously. The guard left without a word, but had set a tray with an old clay bowl and cup in the corner by the door.

Gamaréa erected himself as best he could, and pressed his back against the cold stone wall underneath the barred window. For a long while he sat just staring out into the corridor outside of the cell. He could not perceive much from the angle where he had been bound, but now he caught a firm glimpse of what was outside. Across the corridor was another cell alike to his, but he could not see the prisoner. Perhaps he was elsewhere doing whatever it was that prisoners did—or perhaps some worse fate had befallen him. Aside from the cell he could see nothing else.

Lifting his left arm slowly he held his hand out in front of his face, and then did the same with his right. It was almost some sort of surreal experience to perform this simple act. It had been so long since he was able to move his arms freely that had someone saw the wonder in his eyes they would have thought his arms were recently acquired gifts. There were deep, red imprints on each of his wrists from the bonds he had just been freed of. His elbows were extremely sore, and for a long while it felt as though everything from there down to his hands was detached from him.

Never in his life had he felt this weak. He longed for a fresh slab of meat, but the steaming bowl the guard had left would suffice for now. If only he could muster the strength to bring himself over to the tray. Though it sat not even ten feet from him, the thought of any movement seemed impractical. But, after a long while of intense contemplation, he managed somehow to reach a crawling position and slug his way across the cell to the bowl and cup.

He could barely lift the tray to set it on his lap, and when he was finally able to, he wished he had not bothered. There was a thick, ill-green muck inside the bowl that he supposed was the guard's idea of ample sustenance for prisoners. The lukewarm goo reeked of old decay, and the steam rose upward and smothered his face even as he looked away in disgust. But as appalled as he was, he was also quite famished.

Gamaréa nearly vomited after his first intake. There was a rancid, sour taste to whatever it was that he was eating, and on top of the terrible flavor, it felt unnatural being on the threshold of hot and cold. He waited a moment before he took to eating, and when he did so it was in quickly shoveled spoonfuls. *Best to get it over with . . .* When he finished he kicked the tray away from him in disgust and set himself back against the wall, grimacing. His stomach was aching, and his throat was sore now from the thick, potent muck that slowly crept its way down.

How did I get here, he constantly pondered. Of course he recollected the actual process by which he wound up in his cell, but he could not forgive himself for allowing it to happen. He remembered Ravelon, but then from there all events were clustered in a relentless whirlwind spiraling down, down, down and out of control. He returned many times to that area in the woods where his company was divided, whether through thought or dream, and every time his mind returned, the expression on Lucian's face came more into focus—afraid, lost, confused, periled. So too were his memories of Didrebelle—determined, hoping upon all hope that he may free Gamaréa before he was completely taken away from the group. Gamaréa could recount them shrinking into the distance as he was carried off all too plainly.

He lay down then, curling his legs up against his chest. In this way he kept warm, but it also soothed his aching diaphragm, which had been stretched to its limit when he was bound. He did not care the floor was dirty, though he could feel every individual dust and dirt particle tickling his face and latching on to his beard as he lay. Even in his current state he wondered if he could perhaps wake from this moment to have everything that came to fruition be just elements of another nightmare. But he knew not to be naïve. He knew this was reality, and he knew there was no way out of reality—no way out but through. And he would do what it required to get through, even if the mechanism by which to take him through was death. A bigger thing than himself was in motion now . . .

Outside his cell there was a crow cawing. Its calls were sporadic at first but gradually progressed to excessiveness. Eventually it perched upon the sill outside his barred window and peered in. Its shadow lay long across the sun-streaked floor and stretched out into the hallway.

"Get out of here, you!" Gamaréa called. "There will be no carrion for you today." But the bird was stubborn and remained where it was. It would obey no prisoner—it did not have to. It was free, and could do whatever it pleased. He somehow felt that its caws were not caws at all, but bits of laughter at his expense. Thus, to those sounds of mockery, Gamaréa closed his eyes and tried harder than he ever had to fall asleep.

He woke again at dusk. There was an eerie orange-and-pink glow radiating through the cell. It almost seemed surreal. Every time he woke from whatever state of slumber he was in, he seemed to momentarily forget that he was imprisoned. But his forgetfulness quickly faded. He had begun to grow accustomed to the hard, cold, dirty floor, and the decrepit, rotting walls enclosing him.

Looking across the hall into the adjacent cell, he was startled to find a prisoner staring back at him. He perhaps had been watching him for some time now. The prisoner sat with one leg outstretched across the floor and the other bent upward so that his arm rested upon his knee. There was a blank stare across his dirty, bearded face, and after a moment staring back into his dark eyes, Gamaréa wondered if he even comprehended that he was there.

Still, he felt awkward sitting in the other prisoner's line of sight. But as he was too tired and weak to move away, he pressed his back against his own wall and stared back. At long length Gamaréa said, "How long have you been sitting there?"

It almost seemed as though the slightest bit of light came alive in the prisoner's eyes, like he was suddenly drawn to attention. "What does it matter?" he asked softly. His voice seemed old and weathered, though his appearance was that of a middle-aged man.

"You weren't there earlier," replied Gamaréa.

The prisoner now drew his attention to his cuticles, which he fussed with on the hand of the arm that rested atop his knee. "No, I wasn't."

What is the use? Gamaréa thought. This man obviously did not have much to say, and if he did it wasn't meant to be said to him. Still, somehow, Gamaréa was comforted just by hearing the sound of his own voice. It provided a reminder that he was still somewhat sane.

"So where were you?" Gamaréa ventured to ask at length.

The prisoner straightened out his other leg and shifted his body into a position he must have felt was a bit more comfortable. "Outside," he responded.

Outside? Gamaréa wondered. It was not the word that vexed him, but the subtly foreboding way that it was said.

"You mean to say you were outside of this prison?"

The prisoner gave three very deep coughs, then spat a wad of saliva aside. "You haven't been here long, have you?" he asked.

Gamaréa tried to estimate an exact duration of his stay up until that point, but could not. "No," he finally answered, almost questioning himself as he spoke. "No I haven't."

The prisoner shifted a final time to rest on his left elbow. Though his body was stacked with coils of hard muscle, his eyes gave him a very tired and fatigued look. "You'll go outside soon enough," he muttered, a sound like the grumble of a sleeping lion.

He did not speak to the prisoner for the remainder of that night or much of the next day. Gamaréa fell asleep shortly after their brief conversation, and when he woke the next morning the prisoner was not in his cell. Gamaréa figured he must have been "outside," as he had mentioned so mysteriously an evening ago.

Sometime in the afternoon a guard came into his cell with another tray. This time the clay bowl was filled with some sort of stew that was lukewarm yet again, and the cup contained water. It was oddly good, he thought—perhaps too good for prison food. But, then again, he regarded this tastefulness only on account of his growing famine.

That evening his body began to feel decent enough. Now he was able to actually stand and pace about, when before he thought he would never be able to do so again. It would perhaps take another day or so of nourishment and rest, he suspected, but in less than a week he determined he might return again to fighting shape. *Not that I will ever need to fight again, by the looks of things,* he surmised.

It was nearly dusk when the prisoner across the hall was led back into his cell by two guards—armored soldiers of Dridion. Gamaréa caught a better glimpse of him now in the bright light of the setting sun. His head was shaved, but a thick, brown beard grew upon his face. His eyes were stern and hard, and seemed to remain so—he didn't seem the type to show much emotion. Draped over his large body was a brown cloth, tied at the waist by a rope band. His arms, locked together by iron shackles at his wrists, were thick like a blacksmith's, yet worked with muscle as a statue's might be.

Why does he not counter them? Gamaréa wondered when he saw him, for he seemed as though he could stifle an entire army in his lonesome. Yet he was strangely obedient and calm in the presence of the guards. They slid open his cell and unbound him and that was the end of it. Then he sulked into his corner, just outside of the light emitting through Gamaréa's barred window, and sat quietly in shadow.

Gamaréa wondered who he was then. Was he some hero of war? Or was his story much more humble and honest? Perhaps he had been a locksmith or a potter in his previous life. Perhaps he had a wife and children who were now missing him. All these things Gamaréa ventured to ask but refrained. Instead he too faded into his own shadows, rested his back against the wall, and continued wondering.

It felt good to stand now. He was unsure if he would ever

sit again. To feel blood circulating through his legs and down into his feet was almost a foreign sensation. But in time his eyes grew heavy, and when it became dark within the prison he lay back against the wall and fell once more into slumber.

That night he had vivid dreams but could not remember them when he awoke. He was dismayed at first, for it was still dark within his cell and he knew that it was night still. How deep he was into the night, however, he did not know. It was darker now than he had ever remembered it being since he had been there. Suddenly he recounted what he had dreamt of. Voices. Low, monotonous voices chanting, singing something in some unearthly rhythm to some unearthly tune. Phantoms. They had found him. All those quietly amassing phantoms had gathered and located him in that deepest of all nights—in that loneliest of all places. *Shh!* he commanded himself. *They will hear you if you shuffle! They will hear you if you shift!* But there was nothing. Not even the smallest sound of any kind.

Then he heard it, and he knew he was not dreaming. A low voice, like a grown man's, humming from across the darkened corridor. It was the other prisoner. Gamaréa was sure of it. Soon he began to sing a song that Gamaréa had never heard. It was a simple tune about a young boy— simply written and simply sung, but it was its simplicity that made it beautiful. Or perhaps it was the sincerity with which the singer gave it voice, though he had no singing talent to boast about. *But the sincerity,* he thought. The sincerity would win over any crowd, most certainly. It was a song that was clearly dear to him. Gamaréa could tell by the strike of the first note. The emphasis on the word *Oliver.* No doubt it was a name that was etched upon him in some way. *But how?* he wondered. *How on earth?*

Then he heard something he never thought he would hear out of a man of that stature, for at the conclusion of the song the prisoner across the hall began weeping. It was not the sort of weeping that is loud and dramatic, but the kind of weeping that is much more real—the deep, sporadic intakes of breath; the hissing, saliva-filled inhales through the nose. *The man is weeping!* he thought. Weeping! How surreal: a man who personified brawn, weeping only ten yards or so away from him.

He felt as though it was his place to say something. But what? The prisoner probably assumed he was asleep, thus chose this forsaken hour to conduct his small, whispered concert. Gamaréa thought he might embarrass him by saying something. But the silence that now took over the cells was too heavy to ignore, and so, against his better judgment, Gamaréa cleared his throat, and said, "That was a heartfelt song indeed, my friend."

For what seemed like many moments, the prisoner was silent. Perhaps he *was* embarrassed after all, and for his embarrassment, Gamaréa felt extremely guilty. But at long length the prisoner pulled himself together, and answered, "It is indeed."

It was a more composed response than Gamaréa had expected. He nodded as if in answer, but did not know what else to say. Then, to his surprise, the other prisoner continued, "It's a song about my son."

"Oliver?" said Gamaréa, who for a long while was unsure how to respond.

The other prisoner's voice wavered. "Yes."

"You are a good father to have composed a song about your boy."

For many moments the other prisoner said nothing, but when he collected himself he replied, "I composed a song about him, yes—but I was not a good father."

Gamaréa felt now that he was meddling in places in which he had no business. He had never fathered a child, nor planned to. Thus, he felt it was improper for him to concern himself with affairs of that sort. Thankfully, he thought, the other prisoner was not forcing the conversation. Gamaréa did, however, enjoy the other prisoner's company somewhat. The prison was so dark and forlorn in the night that it was quite pleasant to hear someone else's voice and hold a conversation. "What are you here for?" Gamaréa continued. But there was no response. The other prisoner had either fallen asleep or simply chose to speak no more.

3

The Broken Path

As the pace of the Matarhim quickened, Lucian closed his eyes. He could not recall when the sounds of the battle died away, or when the breaking branches stopped snapping. All he knew was that it was likely over.

It won't be long now, he told himself with sad acceptance. *Now you've done it, Lucian Rolfe.*

There was no way of telling whether they had been in stride for minutes or hours. In many ways it seemed like both. Yet time, somehow, no longer seemed relevant.

The Matarhim horde smelled of old, burning sewage, and the heat emitting from their hides stifled the forest air. On a normal day the temperature would have been comfortable, suitable for a nice walk or picnic. Thus his thoughts strayed to what he would have done today had his life been left alone—had the Key not found him and Gamaréa never sailed to the Eastern Shore.

I probably would have been fishing, he thought. *With Jem. At the creek.* Then he remembered that, had he not gone fishing that fateful April afternoon, he would not have been in this predicament at all. *I don't even like fish all that much, come to think of it.*

Then his thoughts passed to MaDungal, whose bellowing laugh he recalled as plainly as if he were standing near him. *Oh, Mac,* he thought sadly. *I'd give anything to see the pub again. To go home again . . . Who am I kidding? I'd give anything for a pint of Eveland Cherry.*

Thoughts like this always made him laugh. They made

him feel older, more sophisticated, important. When he looked around the pub on Friday or Saturday nights he saw only adults. Men with small businesses, for example, who in terms of the Amarian villagers were modestly successful. They were men who fathered children, and in many cases saw them through school and guided them in obtaining longstanding occupations. They were men who worked with their bodies for modest pay, upon whose hardened faces and rough hands was strewn the wear of their toilsome professions. But their merriment was never dampered.

And women. He had been bending a great deal of thought upon them, too, and more so than usual since the Enchantress locked him in her snare. Fully developed, beautiful, strong women. Women who were not afraid to put a man in his place, stand up for herself, or sound her voice above the din of men. The respect they showed themselves commanded others to follow suit, demanding respect not with words but actions, so that they were treated as queens even by drunkards. These were not the swooning, gossiping—not to mention confusing—girls he had become acquainted with at the schoolhouse. These women had standards and morals—dreams beyond twirling their hair and laughing at boys and sneaking drinks of bourbon in the latrines before lessons.

He would have given anything to have them laugh at him again, though. For although they clucked like a flock of chickens when gathered, it was a sound sweeter than music compared to the hoarse chants and grunts of the demon army that was presently hauling him away. He might even have kissed one, given the chance. And that was a strange thought indeed.

After a great distance the pace of the Matarhim slowed to a halt, and the black band looked around anxiously as though waiting for something to occur. Sure enough, not far from the east, a host of Dridion soldiers emerged. Lucian, who had been thrown upon the ground like a rag doll, crawled away as both armies began conversing.

One of the Matarhim soldiers initiated the exchange,

and he spoke to whom Lucian presumed to be the leader of the Fairy soldiers.

"Remove yourselves from the path," he hissed, his voice gruff and menacing. "The mortal is to be delivered to Nundric directly."

Viewing the scene for the better now, Lucian saw that this Matarhai was larger than the others. His shoulders were broad where the others were lanky, and his red-and-black face was much more round and monstrous, with little spiky horns rising up in ridges on the sides.

But the leader of the Fairies was unfazed by the horrid figure the creature possessed. "You will speak when bid, creature," he retorted sternly. He was tall, and his armor was gold from his boots to his helm, through which his beady eyes peered fiercely. "My lord is mighty in Dridion, and his order was most forward. It is to Deavorás the boy shall go."

Deavorás? thought Lucian with a nervous start. *I wish I had a map.*

The beast scowled, lurching as though prepared to pounce, inching closer to the soldier. "We answer to none but Sorcerian."

At these words his cronies hooted and hissed excitedly, revealing their daunting weapons, preparing for confrontation. But the captain of the Fairies remained reserved. "Consider my master's words equal, for they are in league."

The Matarhim chief guffawed. A vault within Lucian's mind swung open just then. *I know that laugh,* he thought frantically. In fact, he had never forgotten it. Not since the night Amar came down.

"Purebloods!" he shouted in his beastly manner. "Nundric will never be in league with your sort." The horde's taunting laughter continued.

Without a verbal retort, the Fairy captain drew his blade, and his fair companions followed suit. For a brief moment, the forest came alive with a shrill chorus of unsheathing steel. Their swords reminded Lucian of Didrebelle's— slender, with a thin, wispy curve of a blade. The hilts were different, however—broader, and etched with Fairy runes—and their diamond-shaped pommels were crested with fine white jewels.

By a trick of the morning light it was as though every blade emitted radiant beams, as if from their waists they had drawn rays of the sun itself. They were a harsh complement to the weaponry of Sorcerian's men—broadswords, battleaxes, scimitars, and maces all black as soot.

Those would do the trick as fine as any, though, Lucian rationalized. With the two forces ready to engage, he began to wish for that drink a little harder.

Soon the glade was filled with a maelstrom of arguing voices. The Matarhim warriors waved their arms around excitedly, yelling and cursing the Fairies, while the Fairies stood poised, with smug grins on their faces, insulting the host of Nundric. Not one set of eyes were on Lucian.

They forgot I'm even here . . .

Above the ruckus, the captain of the Fairies shouted, "The Keeper of Fates will go to Deavorás. That is final!"

This time, there was no verbal retort from the Matarhim. This time, they brandished their weapons and swung them, roaring and snarling and leaping and clawing. Soon a great battle was raging, greater even than the one from which Lucian had escaped.

Whining swords dashed through the air, shields and breastplates crunched, and Lucian hadn't the slightest idea what to do. Heeding his instincts, he broke away, scampering down the forward path and away from the fury. Carrying himself as quickly as his weary legs would take him, he ran with one thought in mind: to put as much distance between him and his captors as possible.

He ran tirelessly, until the battle could only be heard through blotches of muffled sound. Though he felt it remained just inches away, he in fact had managed a good distance. Yet he pressed on nonetheless, his quick and heavy breaths blotting out the battle cries and ringing swords altogether. It was not motivation that urged him away so much as the utter terror burning within him.

No rest, he ordered himself. *Can't rest. Won't rest. No time. They'll . . . break . . . through. Someone will!*

His mind wandered back to the line Gamaréa and Didrebelle had fought to hold. It had been two against nearly forty strong. As he frantically fled, he wondered what kind of bravery must possess someone to stand and fight against such odds.

I surely don't have it, he reasoned sadly, and quite embarrassed despite his solitude.

How could someone give up their life so rashly? he wondered. *What was it that inspired someone to sacrifice themselves for an uncertain cause?*

They . . . died . . . for this? Lucian thought, feeling foolish as he ran for his life when a stronger man would have stood and fought. A horrible sense of incompetency and inadequacy reigned supreme within his soul.

But his fear of being recaptured propelled him onward. *They'll . . . break through . . . soon. Only . . . matter . . . time . . .*

It was no doubt mid-afternoon. He could tell by the boldness of the sun gleaming down through the canopy above, bathing the evergreen-and-auburn display before him in gold. In a twisted way it reminded him of Elderland, and sadness overcame him at the memory of his last meetings with Mary and Jem.

Of course I'm fixing to come back, Jem, he had said. *Anyone would be fixing to come back. It's just . . . unlikely.*

The image of Jem's watering blue eyes, long ignorant of the world's evils, remained a hammer driving a thick nail of guilt into his heart.

So that's it, then? Jem had said. *This is goodbye?*

Just like that, in that microscopic minute within that miniscule hour, the only life he had ever known ended. With those first steps out of Elderland, a new chapter of his life opened—a darker chapter, and perilous beyond anything he could have ever imagined.

It's bound to be a short one, though, he surmised.

Soon his body lurched, and he knew he could not withstand another step. Propping himself against a nearby tree, he leaned gasping. *Water,* he thought. *I need water.* But it had been many hours since he had seen a water source. Though the ground he managed to cover was extensive indeed, he felt as though he would never be able to distance himself as far as he wished.

After several moments he resumed his flight. *Run.* Even his thoughts were panting. *Run . . . run . . . never . . . look—*

Suddenly his boot smacked off of something protruding from the ground, sending him tumbling wildly. His downward, spinning plummet ended against a tree at the foot of a steep, leaf-laden hill. There, on the hard, earthen floor of Ravelon, he lay in pain and weariness as if resting. His heart thundered like a stampeding destrier against his chest. At the sides of his head his temples beat like vicious drums.

And all the while his right foot burned with pain. When he regained most of his wits, he felt it throbbing relentlessly. Sitting up slowly, he felt a warm streak of blood trickle down the side of his cheek. He attempted to stand, but the pain in his foot caused him to crumple back into the leaves.

Perfect, he thought. He was ever wary of the surroundings now. It was quiet. And in the silence his fears began to stew. Above, he saw the high ridge down which he had fallen, imagining the Matarhim horde racing to reclaim him. It was in fact this image that spurred Lucian to rise and hobble on at length, though speed was no longer his.

Then he heard it—that old, familiar sound. The cry of the Matarhim chief rose up from behind, and his companions wailed in answer. Lucian spun frantically, and in time their black shapes emerged through the trees a hundred yards back, their black silhouettes racing disorderedly his way. Even across the distance between them Lucian caught their sulfuric scent.

Breaking into as much of a run as his throbbing foot would allow, he scampered on. It was not long, however, before he found that there would be no escape; the speed of the advancing horde was too great.

Risking a quicker pace, he fell a second time. His injured

foot had been worked to its end.

Crawling backwards, he could only watch them gain on him. The shrieking black host paraded down the hillside, each Matarhai redder and more fiendish than the one at its back. Yellowish eyes gleamed haughtily from each skeletal face. A hundred slits of cat-like pupils blazed excitedly at the sight of their surrendering quarry. Rallying by the dozens, they sped on, shaking the ground as they flew.

Lucian's face became damp with tears. It was over. His mission, failed. A nearby tree brought his meager backpedalling retreat to an end.

I'm sorry, Mary . . . he thought sadly, wiping some tears away with his sleeve.

The Matarhim charged fervently, wailing and hissing.

I'm sorry, my brave friends . . .

The first few were nearly on him. Sweat mixed with his tears as the hellish heat emitting from their bodies strangled the air and choked him.

I'm sorry, Jem!

Then he closed his eyes for what he thought would be the final time. He could feel the shadows of his attackers closing in. A clawed hand grasped him, searing the cloth of his shirt—

When suddenly it sent up a shrill cry and released him. Opening his eyes, Lucian was startled to find the beast standing directly over him, a blank expression on its hideous face and the devilish fire in its eyes all but extinguished. His companions stopped their pursuit and stood confusedly around him.

What's happened? Lucian wondered.

But then he saw it. Buried to the fletching it the Matarhai's smoking chest was a blue-feathered arrow. Gamaréa must have broken free! He was saved.

Just then the sound of heavy sprinting steps thundered from behind him, and the great figure of Gamaréa leapt over Lucian from the trail beyond. He had resorted to his bow, which thrummed wildly. Arrows whined and thumped into their targets in rapid succession, sending them to leafy graves. Lucian was overcome with joy, until the light afforded him new knowledge: this archer was a stranger. Gamaréa and Didrebelle were still at large.

A great helm of dazzling silver was atop his head, such as Lucian could not see his face beneath. From it sprouted a thick, blue-velvet plume. His raiment was kingly, though he wore only sparse war-suited gear. A plate of thin armor covered his torso and back, but his arms were left exposed (perhaps to make archery easiest), and they were made of lean muscle. Yet of all the equipment Lucian had seen, the archer's was surpassingly magnificent. The silver plate was without dent or blemish, though Matarhim attacks landed every now and then, and shone flawlessly even in the dim shade beneath the forest roof.

The archer was faring well against the odds opposing him, but turned dismayed when the great horn of Dridion bellowed from beyond. Soon a throng of Fairies came swarming down the hill like a gold storm. Lucian cried out, having become enthralled by the fighter's display. It would be a regrettable waste to see it amount to nothing. With his quiver emptied the archer cast his bow aside and drew his beaming sword, and it rang like a great chime against the weapons of the beasts. But the odds were now against him more than ever, and he would soon be overcome.

That was when two more figures entered the maelstrom from a westerly trail, clad in the archer's likeness and wielding great weapons of their own, scintillating even in the gloom.

Nearest Lucian fought a swordsman, whose blade was long and broad and etched with strange runes. In his left arm he carried a glimmering steel shield, shaped like an elongated crown. It was so polished and untarnished that it reflected the meager light of the sun as though it shone directly on it, blinding the first of his many assailants. Its edges were etched in pure gold, and in the exact center was the sigil of a prancing golden lion.

Remarkable! Lucian gaped inwardly, as though a child watching a magician.

The swordsman made quick work of his enemies, ducking and dodging the beasts' tactless attacks, slaying them with his blade, and swatting off their advances with his shield. Most of his victims fell hewn in two.

The other fighter had vanished into the wild, ringing fray, but eventually crossed Lucian's vision on the right side of the battle. Fluently twirling like a dancer, he wielded a great silver hammer that made itself known to Matarhai and Fairy alike. It was a beautiful brute of an instrument, with a bold head of blue stone in the likeness of a ram that sat atop a long, slender shaft. Lucian's own bones seemed to crush as he watched it repel enemies.

Now a violent threesome, the fighters went on swinging, firing, and shouting curses at their adversaries. To Lucian's bewilderment, they seemed to find great joy in their doings. Soon the loudest sound of all was their laughter, as though they were participating in some monstrous game of which they were very fond.

It was not long before the din subsided. The few survivors attempted a meager retreat up the great hill at their back, only to be run down when the archer retrieved some arrows. Now the path was left to four, and the three warriors stood panting and gazing proudly at what they had done. It was only then that Lucian realized his back was digging into the bark of the tree, as though he sought a hiding place within its trunk.

The bodies of the slain Matarhai hissed like dying fires, and the sulfuric odor emitting from them was succeeded by those of rot and decay. Yet the fighters stood poised. Bowing their heads in weary glory, they seemed rather to seek air than praise. The black blood of the Matarhim oozed and dripped from their gleaming plates. The archer's arms were rank with it.

Lucian too found himself panting, as though having participated himself. He had been snatched from the clutches of death so quickly that he did not have time to react to what had occurred so abruptly before him. Relief flooded through him like a rampant deluge—that is until the archer turned his piercing gaze toward him. After stooping to retrieve the last of his arrows, he turned his head casually, as though he had known Lucian's whereabouts all along. Though his countenance suggested that he was friendly, terror welded Lucian to the tree against which he sat.

Now that the battle was over Lucian was able to survey these fighters for the better. The fair-faced archer was indeed the most slender of the three, but that is not to say he was without brawn. His face was fair yet smudged with dirt, and if there was any age upon it, it was in his eyes, which peered intently like blue crystals. When he removed his helm, Lucian saw that his auburn hair was shorn before his jawline, and was well kempt. His brow seemed to furrow when he beheld Lucian on the ground, but his look was more grave than stern.

Soon the swordsman and hammer-wielder came forward. Their raiment was decorative and kingly, and of sparkling silver and gold.

The swordsman struck the greatest figure Lucian had ever seen. His helmet, which he still wore atop his head, was similar to the bowman's. Though his face was largely shadowed by it, Lucian saw that his skin was bronze and blanketed by a grisly black beard, braided in a long strand past his chin. Wary and dark, his eyes perceived every inch that was around him, but settled on Lucian with particular interest. His arms were exposed as well, and were perhaps as thick as a grown man's thighs, wrought with taut ropes of solid muscle.

The hammer-wielder had set his weapon to rest on its ram-head and folded his hands atop the base of its shaft. He was neither as hulking as the swordsman nor as slender as the archer, but could be measured somewhere in the middle. Out of his helmet his locks spilled down in golden tendrils. Beardless and youthful, he appeared fairer than his sword-wielding companion. A cold and wild fire was in his crystalline eyes, which shone like beacons out of the shadows on his face. Still on his lips a wide smile lingered for the beautiful destruction his company had caused.

The archer made as if to speak when suddenly every set of eyes was drawn eastward. Voices of a new contingent of Dridion soldiers could be heard faintly over the hill. The archer stepped toward Lucian in earnest.

"Lucian Rolfe," he said, stating his name knowingly. This was much to Lucian's bewilderment.

Thus he stammered uncomfortably. "I . . . I . . . I am." His face flushed at how childish he sounded.

"That was not a question. Stand, friend." He reached out a bloodstained hand to Lucian, who grimaced.

"What is it?" asked the archer concernedly.

"I took a fall, back that way." Lucian gestured to the hillside over which the Fairies would soon swarm. "I think I did something to my foot."

The archer nodded. "Leonysus." At his call the hulking swordsman slid his great blade into the sheath upon his back, and it was as if a light in the forest had been snuffed. Now he stood towering over Lucian like a flesh-riddled battlement.

There was no formal introduction given. Instead, Leonysus threw Lucian over his shoulder effortlessly and awaited further instruction. "What now, Orion?" he asked, Lucian's head now dangling uncomfortably close to his buttocks.

"The host of Dridion advances quickly," answered Orion. "Their numbers are greater than the first wave, I think. We may not be able to overcome them so easily."

"And with the boy injured," the hammer-wielder added.

Orion looked down the path where the advancing voices were shouting and singing. Now his gaze passed down the road yet traveled. "That is another factor, my good Aries," he said at length. "Though it pains me to say this, we must break for the steeds."

The steeds?! Lucian gaped in thought.

"Run from a fight?" said Leonysus gravely.

"Toward a greater cause, no doubt," replied Orion. "Dridion will have its war indeed, but our orders are long in the giving. We must get Lucian to safety."

Well, what are we waiting for? Lucian wanted to exclaim. Yet he remained impatiently silent as his boots and arms dangled over Leonysus's mighty shoulder.

His silent pleas were shortly answered, however, for

in that moment their flight began, and was achieved in time after a period of great haste. Need fueled their pace swiftly onward. Lucian did not think men could speed so vehemently on two feet. So it was the question of their makeup came to his mind. *Are these Men?* he wondered, bobbing up and down. Last he knew, there were no Men on the western shores of the Mid Sea. Yet they did not bear the features of Moroks, and Fairies were easily distinguishable among the Three Races. Not to mention they would be delivering him to Deavorás rather than safety.

The pursuit died down after a long haul. Behind them the path was quiet. Leonysus set Lucian down, asking if he preferred to walk or be carried, to which he obliged to walking the way's remainder. Now that his small intestine was wrapped around his large one and his liver was somewhere near his throat, his foot became the least of his ailments.

In time Orion led them through the eaves of Ravelon's western face, and Lucian could see vast rays of sunlight peering through. He was looking out now across the stretch of a far golden field that ran out into the distance to the end of sight.

"Ravelon is ending?" Lucian asked to anyone who would answer. It felt like years since he entered the forest with Gamaréa and Didrebelle, and on many occasions he felt as though he would never make it out the other side.

"Indeed it is, Lucian," answered Orion from the front of the small line they had formed on the green ledge.

Lucian gaped. "I thought for sure we would not reach the end for another day or so."

Orion, Aries, and Leonysus each laughed.

"If we stayed on the path we would have," said Aries smugly.

Leonysus, who was walking beside Lucian, peered down at him harshly. "Took a little shortcut," he said, his voice deep and raspy like an old horn of war. Now that he had taken his helmet off, Lucian saw that an old purple scar, perhaps six or seven inches long, ran down his left cheek, and his brow was wrought with sweat.

"Where are you taking me?" Lucian tried not to sound as frightened as he felt, but he feared the wavering of his voice betrayed his attempt.

"No need to fear, my friend," said Orion hurriedly, his fiery gaze spreading over the far field ahead. "You will get your answers soon enough."

4

The Protectors

Lucian passed on through the trees with his company, and what he found there seemed to dispel any feeling of urgency he still possessed. There on the rock shelf, like living and breathing statues, were two great stallions, one coated in pure white, the other in pitch black. Walking casually around the grassy sward, they grazed peacefully, seemingly ignorant to all the evils from which Lucian and his three rescuers were fleeing.

Yet Lucian soon found that it was not ignorance which brought them comfort, but the creature sitting at the hill's edge. It resembled a lion in every facet possible—a magnificent, golden lion whose mane seemed to kindle with red flame in the light of the sun peering over the valley. Calmly it sat like a wizened shepherd, as if scouting the vast, empty plain below. Although it was not drawn to its full height Lucian could tell that it was perhaps larger than lions were supposed to be, and that when it stood it would equal the stallions in measure.

Suddenly Orion whistled, and Lucian, who for a moment forgot he was in the company of others, gave a start. As if in answer the white stallion lifted its fair head, and the pail wisps of its mane swayed in the light breeze as it came up from feeding. Trotting over with a proud gait, it stood a hair's breadth from Lucian so that it towered over him like a great pillar.

"This is Godspeed," said Orion, his voice so filled with admiration that it was as though he beheld the stallion for the first time himself. "I have raised him from a foal, and his bravery has seen me through many perils." Godspeed, as if in response, began to whinny, and bowed his head as if in thanks.

Lucian raised a hand almost involuntarily to stroke the soft, white coat upon the stallion's muscled frame. He abruptly recoiled, however, at the last moment.

"Do not fear, my friend!" exclaimed Orion assuredly. "Godspeed is eager to bear you on, and taste the thrill of the chase once more."

"I'm not sure I would say that it's thrilling to be chased," said Lucian, as if to himself. "And I don't think that my heart can withstand another scare like the one I had before you three showed up. This is a beautiful horse, but I'm not much for horse riding as it is, though I've done my share." Then he bent his sight upon the valley below, and the leagues of wilderness that lay between them and the unknown horizon. "And that's quite a distance to go," he finished, discouraged.

Just then, to his right, Aries's stallion brayed eagerly. The hammer-wielder was mounted, and seemed as though a living statue of old, a tribute to warriors past. "This is Night-Treader!" he exclaimed proudly, and at the mention of his name the black stallion bounced upon his forelegs excitedly. "Alike in speed and size to his brother, though I must say he inherited whatever personality descended through that line."

Orion made as if to retort when suddenly a coarse bellow filled the air that seemed to stop the world. Lucian's bones quaked as it rang and echoed in the hollows beyond, and all turned to behold Leonysus mounted atop the great, saddleless lion. Lucian's former guess was accurate: it stood as tall, if not taller, than Godspeed and Night-Treader, and as it walked its great mane wafted and its lean muscles flexed.

"I'd say Goldbearer's had just about enough talking," said Leonysus smugly. "Now's the time, I think. Yet whatever secrecy we hoped to achieve may well be set aside across wide Enorméteren. Melinta's spies will be dispatched before long, if they're not already, and there is little shelter across these plains."

"Unfortunately your account is accurate, Leonysus," answered Orion gravely. "I fear we cannot go the way we came. Whereas before we snuck past Deavorás as sheep creep past a sleeping wolf, I fear that same path will undoubtedly be watched now. Thus we must take a western route across the plain, though it will become dank and marshy before long, and follow those foul roads to the Redacre Woods at the western skirts of the Red Peaks."

"Marshes and bogs!" laughed Leonysus "Goldbearer can weather those with ease if given the chance."

"He will have it before the end," replied Orion, looking warily over his shoulder. Then, without much preamble, Orion helped Lucian onto Godspeed's back. "You will be riding with me," he said. "Surely Godspeed can bear us both with ease." The stallion snorted, as if to suggest otherwise was laughable.

"The western road will be hard, as I have said," Orion continued. "The woods of Redacre may be our first chance for true shelter—twenty-six leagues from this ledge, as the eagle goes. We shall race until nightfall, and perhaps through if we draw attention to our trail. Let us hope we go unnoticed."

Aries the hammer-wielder gripped the shaft of his weapon. "Let *them* hope we go unnoticed," he said menacingly. Beneath him Night-Treader whinnied.

Thus all were set to embark. To where, Lucian did not know. He had never heard of Enorméteren, or the Redacre Woods, or the Red Peaks before. To him they seemed as daunting as The Black Forest once had, or the Provinus Path. And he recalled all too vaguely what befell him on those dark and dangerous roads. But now that the hard voices of Fairies and the shrill wails of Matarhim horns rose up behind them, Orion and his fellows could have been leading him to the moon for all he cared. For there was certainly no road ahead worse than the one from which he had just been rescued.

Atop Godspeed's back he felt as though a giant. The

sward from which Orion lifted him now seemed many leagues below, as though he looked upon it from atop a great white hill. He could not be certain what frightened him more: the pursuing enemy, or the thought of the flight that he would have to endure. But now the moment was upon him.

Orion hopped gracefully into the saddle and stroked Godspeed's soft neck. Lucian could hear him whispering something softly into the stallion's twitching ear, and the words seemed to rile him. Suddenly Godspeed's rough voice rose up anxiously, and the others became roused as he brayed, so that the green ledge came alive with the din of excited beasts. Then, much too soon for Lucian's liking, the white stallion sprung away, and at length it seemed as though the world around them was vacuumed into an unknown portal at their back.

As though he built the land himself Godspeed found a winding path that spilled down into the golden field below. It was by this way he led his companions, and soon the four riders were splayed across the plain charging out into the open. Bounding sharply westward, they raced intrepidly while the plain was soft and passable. Lucian felt a strange comfort in the saddle. He thought back to his flight from Marshal Crowley's quarters long ago, and how sore he was after he endured his speeding horse's frightful retreat. Now Godspeed raced at nearly twice that speed, yet Lucian felt as though he simply strolled.

Barren wilderness wheeled before them under the vast blue sky. The plains of Enorméteren indeed proved flat and soft for a great distance, rising and falling in soft folds every so often, and lacerated here and there by trickling streams of white. Lucian felt as though the entire world was before them, wide and open and untouched by the hands of men or any other being. It was not sullen emptiness, for there was certainly promise present. As they raced he could imagine great homesteads plotted out in long blocks and tall white towers of kings.

He wondered curiously why none had tried their hands at establishing their people there, and that was not the sort of thing he usually bent his mind upon. Nor did he often ponder the concept of a league. Geography was never his favorite subject, though he had never given any of them their fair chance. Thus he had heard the term used quite often, but failed to understand what it meant or what it felt like to travel one from end to end. It was a hollow term to him, such as he thought all those who used it did so wantonly. Twenty-six leagues did not sound like much to his ignorant mind, for twenty-six is not a large number in itself. Thus he was flabbergasted to find that their journey was not even half complete by time dusk rolled up from the east to meet them.

"Ten leagues is a fair bit of traveling in such a short time," said Orion sharply. "I should like to see how long it takes beasts from your lands to travel such distances."

The riders yielded their pursuit somewhat. Godspeed, Night-Treader, and Goldbearer took to walking. Beneath them the land had indeed grown marshy, as Orion promised, and there was a foul scent following the wind from the road ahead.

"Bogs," said Aries. "Haven't missed those, I must say."

"One of the inconveniences of the westward road," added Leonysus. "Goldbearer doesn't like them, I don't doubt." The great lion grumbled throatily. Lucian became uneasy.

"I wonder what the road ahead yields," said Orion thoughtfully. Suddenly, without warning, he urged Godspeed into a gallop and mounted a solitary hilltop peeking out of the marsh not far ahead. From there they could see well over the plain. The yellow marshes stretched on into the shadows of the coming night, and the amethyst sunset glittered off the veins of foul water winding along the fields. As far as trouble they saw nothing, yet nothing of shelter either.

Godspeed turned as if to pass back down the hill when a raven suddenly alighted on Orion's shoulder. Lucian, having nearly been startled out of his saddle, gave a cry, yet Orion seemed unfazed. In fact, he began speaking to the menacing, croaking bird. "What news, Eap?" he asked.

To Lucian's surprise, the raven answered. "Scout," it

said. "Scout ahead. Scout ahead. Scout ahead."

Peering out across the plain, mingling with the shadows of the coming night, Lucian could see a moving shape nearly the size of a pebble. Without word or warning, Orion notched one of his great arrows and took aim, preparing for what Lucian imagined was an impossible shot. *He'll do nothing but give away our position,* he thought. *That arrow won't reach halfway across this marsh.*

Then Orion loosed his whistling missile, and in a moment or so it disappeared into the darkening sky. It came down seconds later, stuck between the eyes of his target still far away.

Lucian gaped. "What!" he exclaimed aloud, though he meant to keep it in his thoughts. "How did you . . . What did . . . Can we just go now? Please?"

Just then the raven began squawking from Orion's shoulder. "Please? Go now! Please? Go now!"

Lucian eyed the foul bird menacingly. "You wouldn't have a second arrow by any chance, would you?" he asked.

Orion laughed. "Eap is an essential component to our team," he said. "He must like you to quip with you so."

Soon Godspeed bore Orion and Lucian down the hill where they met with Aries and Leonysus.

"What was that about?" asked Leonysus sternly. "We saw you loose an arrow."

"Scout," answered Orion plainly. "The westward trail is being watched. I cannot be certain of what lies ahead, and what we may find in places beyond. Be one your guard, all of you. There may be business yet for mettle."

Thus the party cantered on as the moon climbed up the rungs of night. Dense clouds cast it in a dreary veil, though it peeked out every so often to apply meager light to their path. Largely the night was starless, much to the solemnity of the riders. This Lucian found strange. He had heard of travelers relying on the maps of the stars for navigation, but there were other ways to wander darkened roads. Yet the riders seemed to lament their absence.

"I want to at least put the marshes behind us," said Orion, breaking a long silence that had fallen over the riders. "Though I don't think we will go much further tonight."

"Unless I am mistaken," said Aries from behind. "The Elarian is but an hour's tread from here at a leisurely pace. The river might be a good place to rest."

"Rest!" squawked Eap. "Rest!"

"Yet Elarian does not yield many spots to ford," said Leonysus. "We may have a good deal more to travel when we take up our journey again, and not straightaway."

"Nevertheless, our brave mounts need water," said Orion thoughtfully, "and Elarian may be the only source for miles, until at least we meet the Springcrest running out of Redacre."

"It would be a punishment to keep them from water so long," said Aries concernedly. "Their deeds since Ravelon are worthy only of reward."

"Reward! Reward!" croaked the bird on Orion's shoulder. Lucian looked at him disconcertedly in the dark.

So it was talk ceased, and the riders resumed their journey across the marshes. By now the heavy, foul-smelling air alleviated somewhat—or perhaps Lucian had just become accustomed to its reek. Nevertheless it was behind them before an hour was up, and the field became hilly and soft. The landscape was black beneath an ashen sky in which the ghost of the moon lingered passively behind thick clouds. It was impossible for Lucian to discern any sort of detail, though he had a strange notion that his companions perceived the world before them as if it were day.

Unhindered by the fresh fields, Godspeed burst once more into a gallop, followed eagerly by his brother Night-Treader. With Goldbearer bringing up the rear, the riders stole across the nightly plain. It was not long before their pursuit halted, and they came upon a great hill overlooking the breadth of a wide river. Lucian could see this much, though there was little discrepancy between the water's adjacent edge and what lay beyond. Only the shadows of spiky hills could be seen there, crowned scantily by moonlight.

"Elarian," said Orion. "The Great Swan Lane, as my forefathers called it."

Even beneath the sheer blackness of night's bowels, Lucian sensed a great beauty before him. Elarian somehow caught what meager light the moon could offer so that it seemed adorned here and there with glittering diamonds. Yet its eastern and western arms were swallowed by the darkness, and Lucian wondered what evil things lurked in those desolate, mysterious places, which seemed to grow larger by the minute. Fear enveloped him.

"Are we agreed that this spot will do?" asked Orion.

The others gave their consent. One by one each rider led his mount to drink. Leonysus went first, and when Goldbearer finished his long consumption he was sent on ahead to patrol the area, for his vision suited him best at night, he was told. Lucian longed for a fire, though Orion ordered against it. He was becoming much too bossy for Lucian's liking. Yet he supposed the odd archer was right. It would have been unwise to draw unnecessary attention to themselves.

"We cannot be sure who patrols the river these days," he said. "If there was one scout on the range then there are certainly many others; and they will pay close heed to watery roads."

They set about constructing a small camp, modest though it was. There was a small delve in the hill beside them that proved an ample area for those who wished to be unseen at night. It was there they set their blankets, all thick and lined with fur—much to Lucian's pleasure. Though the trail through the marshes had been muggy, a distinct chill hung within the air by the river.

Orion, Aries, and Leonysus settled down, grumbling and fidgeting to find a suitable position in which to sleep, but Lucian was not prepared for slumber. Now that he was able to lie still for a moment, a maelstrom of thoughts bombarded his mind. The day seemed fragmented, like a wild dream of which only segments could be recalled. Not even a day had passed since he was in the company of Gamaréa and Didrebelle, yet it felt as though a year since he had seen them. Sadness filled his heart for the fate they must have met.

Fate, he thought with frustration, and consequently thought about the Key. He had nearly forgotten that it was still lodged in his pocket. *If I had only stayed home that day. If I really had forgotten Jem's birthday . . .*

He revealed the Key from his pocket, and suddenly the world was ablaze with piercing lights of emerald and sapphire. His companions gave a start. Suddenly Orion's hand was on it, yet not even his grasp could stifle the gems' radiant lights. A sound like thunder seemed to envelop the world. Then all went quiet. The Key was back in Lucian's pocket, and Orion faced him angrily.

"No fires," he said, panting. "No lights whatsoever. If you were going to do that, I would have staked signs in the ground all the way from Ravelon telling where to find us."

"I'm sorry!" said Lucian, genuinely unnerved. "I . . . I wasn't thinking—"

"We could tell that much," said Aries. Leonysus snored loudly nearby.

"Now sleep," said Orion, sternly. "Another outburst like that will have even our brave steeds break for the Red Peaks, and it is a long walk from here. Shed no lights."

No part of Lucian wanted further conversation with Orion, moody now as he was, but he found himself doing so. "Speaking of shedding light," he said, trying to sound as polite as possible, though anger began to fill him too, "would you mind shedding some on what the meaning of all this is? I've followed you this far, regardless of whether or not I had a choice, and I haven't pestered you with questions. But now that we're here, I'd like some answers."

"We saved you," said Aries plainly. "What further answers are needed?"

"He probably means a bit of formal introduction is in order." The voice was Leonysus's, and he was not happy to have been woken. "I suppose I'll begin, then. The name's Leonysus, lad, though my kindred call me Leo. You can call me either or."

"And I am Aries, friend Lucian."

"Leo and Aries," said Lucian. "Pleased to meet you." Though even as he said this he was not sure if he truly meant it. He then turned his gaze to Orion. "We've already been introduced formally enough. But you said I would get my answers in due time. I'd like to have them sooner rather than later."

"True enough," said Orion. "Those were indeed my words. And you will know all in good time. It is much too long a tale to tell in one sitting, especially when time is pressing."

"Can you at least tell me the important parts?"

"To tell you the important parts would still take some time, more time than is given us tonight. You are an intuitive fellow. That is good. Always hold firm to that trait! Never stop seeking answers, for there is no strength more powerful than knowledge. I will answer your question with one of my own." Then his gaze grew hard, and even in the darkness they seemed to house a long suppressed flame. "What do you know of your family?"

Lucian started, then hesitated for a moment, unsure of how to begin. "Mary is an innkeep—"

"Your blood family," Orion interjected, not unkindly. "Your mother, father—what do you know of them?"

A small wave of embarrassment washed over him then. He could not tell three men of such apparent status that he never knew his mother or father. These men were probably descendants of royal lineages—the sons of kings, perhaps. He was unable to think of a quick enough lie, though Orion seemed to know the truth already. "I suppose my mother left me in Mary's keep when I was just a baby. I don't know anything of her, really. And nothing of my father either."

Lucian did not expect the three men to look as if they understood, but somehow their eyes suggested that they related to Lucian in some way, as if they had expected his account.

Orion leaned in, his face mysterious and hard. "What if I could tell you *why?*"

There was silence.

Lucian was unsure now if this was some game they were

all playing—some means of keeping themselves occupied in the dark and quiet reaches of the night. But none of their countenances changed even slightly. All of them looked on, curious and anticipating.

"Tell me why I don't know my parents?" Lucian asked, trying not to sound as confused as he was.

Orion nodded.

"I would welcome the information, definitely," continued Lucian. "But I don't see what that has to do with my initial question, nor how it's relevant to what I have to do."

"We all have origins, Master Rolfe; and yours, I think, is less ordinary than you can imagine."

Lucian grew nervous. The presence of the three riders now felt heavy and daunting. Now more than ever, he felt scrutinized and tiny—exposed and vulnerable. "Who are you?" It was the only question that came to his reeling mind.

"We have given you no false information," said Leo.

"True enough," said Aries. "But I believe Lucian wants to know our purpose. He has a right to, I imagine."

"I think I do!" answered Lucian hotly. "Start with this: how did you know to find me in Ravelon? What led you there?"

"Master Rolfe," said Orion, with purpose in his sonorous voice. "What I am about to tell you may be difficult for you to understand initially. But you must trust us."

There was an urgency and fierceness present in Orion's voice, though outwardly he used a gentle tone. Nevertheless, Lucian's bones shivered with anticipation and anxiety. Something was wrong. He could feel it. The words Orion was about to utter bore the power of change, and he almost wanted to beg him to refrain from speaking. He wished now that he had never revealed the Key and upset his companions. But, to his own surprise, he straightened his posture and employed his ears to listen. "Alright," he murmured feebly.

Thus Orion began: "The Mortal Realm was destroyed many ages ago. You might have heard a skeletal account of this in your lessons"—(Lucian cringed)— "The accounts are largely true; for it *was* destroyed, but not entirely. That had been a violent day, that which the records refer to as the Mortal Damnation. A deluge of fire razed the great Mortal realm of Dredoway to ruin; lightning flashes toppled great walls of stone; and when the destruction was finished, the Mortal world was no more.

"For Ation had come down from his High Seat, and the Great Lord of the Mountain dealt his final judgment. A great number perished. Many who survived the Renting of the Realm (as it is called) were damned. Understand, Lucian"— (Here Orion must have noticed the horror in the boy's eyes)—"Dredoway had become littered with filth. In those vile days, it was shameful to wave the banners of Men. The numbers of the guilty ruled so greatly that a pure soul became as rare a sight as dragons. Murderers, traitors, adulterers, and worse—such folk did the Mortal realm boast. It was a mockery of the Great Sage's plan, and thus he wiped them away to begin anew.

"Yet he found no punishment suitable enough for some of the most evil men, and thus he cast upon them a hideous spell. They are bound to live as beasts in the ruins of their fallen city. Daylight is their bane, just as they fear all else that is good and bright. I will not speak of them so openly, however, for such talk is disquieting in the deepening night.

"There were others, however,"—and here his voice trailed off for a moment, and his eyes passed over his companions, who sat listening attentively like children round a fire—"others that he spared. We are three out of the number exempt from his wrath, Lucian. Yet our reward was not given freely. The Great Sage bestowed upon us a weighty task—an errand to which he would entrust no others.

> *"Brotherhood of dark and light*
> *Severed bonds of day and night*
> *He who from the East has come*
> *From shadows will reveal the sun,*

"He who from the East has come," continued Orion, "And it became our tireless errand to find him. Thus here we are. Eap here tracked your company since you arrived on the shores of the west." Only now did Lucian see the raven perched upon Orion's shoulder, as the dim light of the moon reflected subtly off his pitch sheen.

"As I'm sure you know," said Leo, "no mortal seafarer has crossed the sea from end to end since the Banishment. Not until you, that is. *He who from the East has come*, the prophecy states. As far as fulfilling it, we liked our chances."

Lucian started. "Prophecy?" he asked. Since taking up his burden, he had heard a great deal about prophecies. Everything seemed to be a prophecy, or a tale from a song, or an ancient relic of some forgotten land. But he was never told outright what any of it meant.

"Sure enough," continued Orion, "the prophecy has taken many forms. The Bard of Zynys put it into song thousands of years ago. I have recited an excerpt of it for you already, though in its entirety its verses are numerous.

"Yet you question how we came upon you in Ravelon, and I will provide an answer at long last. Eap's tidings brought us great promise. The pieces of the puzzle seemed to fit together too well to cast aside. Thus we set off at once from Ren Talam, our home tucked under the inner arm of the Red Peaks. From there we followed the eastern road through the mountains and down into Redwood, a small forest in their eastern foothills. We slipped by unnoticed along Elarian's outer bank and crossed at the Ford of Summerhill. Ravelon on its tall cliffs shielded us against the eyes of Deavorás, which looms not far beyond the edge of the wood in those sad and dying lands.

"We came upon your company just as you entered the Enchanted Wood, though we kept our distance. Your companions seemed loyal and stout of heart, and thus I found no need to interject. Yet I knew we had been called there for a reason, and that a great peril was likely to befall you before you reached the forest's end, for not even then were we aware that Melinta held Ravelon.

"Thus I made the mistake of going on ahead. It was my plan to meet with you, as if by coincidence, at the edge of the wood, and lead your company the way we now tread.

Had I not been so rash, perhaps our number would be greater tonight."

A harsh silence fell. Lucian felt his eyes brim with tears at the thought of his companions left for dead, and the harsher realization that it could have been avoided. Something like cold fire swelled within him, and a small hatred for Orion danced at the edges of his heart. But the searing emotion subsided as quickly as it mounted, and he looked out into the dark and listened to the sound of slow-trudging Elarian as it flowed west into the black and eerie night.

"That's a great story," said Lucian coldly. The vulnerable feeling of being toyed with overcame him. "You expect me to believe that you three, who claim to be mortal, were present at the time of Dredoway's fall? I'm not a scholar, or a reader of many books, or an attender of many lessons, but even I know that this 'Mortal Damnation' you speak of occurred over—"

"Three thousand years ago," said all three riders at once.

Lucian thought for a moment, though his weariness and confusion united to bewilder him. "But that would make you . . . immortal," he said contemplatively.

"The Great Sage could not subject his message to the wearing nature of time. Words become lost when generations hand them off. Fact passes to legend, and some legends are too often forgotten. He would not permit his message to suffer such a fate. Thus he granted us immortal lives, for it was to us that he entrusted this task. We have been alive, Lucian, for sixty lives of men, and have said hello and farewell to two ages. But this age will be different. This could be the age of replenishment and promise, if you will make it so. And we, as your sworn protectors, will help you, if we can."

"And I hope you are able to," said Lucian at length. "But, as it stands, I don't even know what you would be helping me do. I feel so lost now. Everything has happened so quickly. Part of me just wants to stay on this hillside and hide, though I know I can't."

"Not at all," said Orion.

Than Aries leaned in. "I would advise you to think of your journey as a large meal," he said. "You do enjoy eating, don't you?"

"Not by the looks of him," said Leo.

Lucian passed the hulking swordsman a stern glance. "I do like to eat, yes," he answered.

"I thought so. And, let me ask you, when there is a fine roast in front of you, do you try to consume it in one mouthful, or in several helpings?"

"Obviously multiple helpings," Lucian replied. "I can't finish a roast in one bite."

"No indeed! It takes many small bites to get to the end. And that is what I'm playing at. Think of your journey as a huge scrap of meat. In order to finish it off, you need to take it bite by bite."

"No doubt you must be riddled with famine," Leo quipped at Aries, who scowled.

"I'm trying to make a point!"

"I guess I see what you're saying," said Lucian, although he felt Aries's analogy would make more sense if he was hungry. At the moment he was conscious of nothing but his fear. "So what do you suggest my 'first bite' should be?"

"Leave that to us," said Orion. "For now, all you need to do is ride with us. We will take care of the rest. Our journey to Ren Talam will resume before daybreak, so I suggest you find what sleep you can."

Orion's was the final word that night. It passed quietly, without so much as a whisper. An hour or two after the company took rest, Lucian heard Goldbearer return from wherever he had roamed. At first he heard what he thought to be an advancing warhorse approaching their camp, yet was oddly comforted when the head of the giant lion peered over the hilltop to the coursing river below. Then, with a grunt and a thump, the mighty beast found slumber of his own.

Lucian woke some hours later alone on the hillside. It was cold and dark and soundless. Never before had he felt so alone, though he somehow felt Orion, Aries, and Leo were close by. Risking a look over his shoulder, he even thought to see Orion's silhouette standing on the hill's crest. Thus he turned over and tried to find sleep once more, yet he could not find any comfort. After a while he gave up, and made for where Orion stood.

At once his breath left him. The figure on the hilltop was not Orion but a vile creature, one his perilous journey had yet revealed to him. Venomously it peered at him through eyes of flame, its every feature darkened but the ridges of its face. Icy horror paralyzed Lucian where he stood, stilling his blood, forcing his heart into a rapid cadence.

Suddenly it swept forward and towered over him, revealing behind it all that its shadow had blotted out. There, lifeless and cold were the bodies of his three protectors and their mounts, all smote, their own weapons turned against them.

The creature loomed over him, hissing and growling, and without a word reached a head-sized hand for Lucian and shrouded him in utter darkness.

He woke screaming, his grip white upon the hilt of Excebellus. The nightmare vanished instantly from his memory. Only vague images remained. The black figure was still present in his mind, but he knew he was safe now. Some paces beside him slept Orion, his face skyward and his hands folded atop his chest. Leo was nearby in a crevice of the hill, his deep snoring cutting through the still night. Aries was absent, and Lucian gave a nervous start before he saw the hammer-wielder's silhouette further down by the bank of the Elarian.

I'll go down to him, I think, Lucian surmised. *Don't think I'll be finding much more sleep tonight as it is.*

Aries had taken to smoking a long pipe, and was humming a soft song to himself when Lucian approached. He had set his hammer to rest on its great head beside him, and was glaring hard at the flowing current of the river.

"Lucian!" he exclaimed when he saw the boy approach. "What could possibly have awoken you?" He passed his bright eyes over the spot where Leo was snoring relentlessly.

"I had a dream, believe it or not," replied Lucian. "More

of a nightmare really."

"I'm surprised you managed to find sleep with the old Lion trying to suck the world in through his nostrils." Aries laughed softly, and it was a sound like music. Now and then he would take a puff of his pipe and send a wisp of blue smoke up to the heavens. "They're beautiful, aren't they?" he asked after a moment of silence. "The stars?"

Lucian had not even realized, but the storm clouds had been lifted, and the moon and hundreds of beaming stars were revealed. Thus he followed Aries's gaze into the vast expanse of blue midnight where the stars twinkled like gems. "They are indeed," he answered absently.

"It's an old legend of men that those whose lives were of worth would one day find their likeness wrought within the stars. We used to have games as children to see who could find the most star-figures. There was a time when I believed that great men and women alike were honored by the heavens, but now I'm not so sure, Lucian. Now it is only a beautiful mess, pieces of a diamond necklace strewn across a wide blue floor.

"We believed it to be the work of the Sages. They are cunning and crafty, after all. It would be just like them to create figures out of starlight. But that was when things were joyful, and Nundric was a quiet place, and green things still grew in the distant reaches of Surullinen. Now there isn't much to be joyful for."

"There may yet be," said Lucian, but his voice seemed faint and small. His near-silent words danced upon the edge of sound, so that even Aries's keen hearing strained to hear them.

"What was that, my friend?" he asked.

"Nothing," said Lucian. "I wonder: how did you and Leo come to be grouped with Orion? He seems to be your captain, or at least the leader of your company, if I'm to guess."

"He was my highlord once," said Aries reminiscently, "though he constantly reminds us that we are equals now."

"Highlord?"

"A First Man of the king. There were seven highlords

when Dredoway fell. Orion was the only one spared."

"Why?"

"Because the other six were greatly tainted. Orion lived his life by the codes, and upheld his honor until those last days, never dismissing the oaths to which he swore. The others were gluttonous and murderous, concerned more with vanity than valor."

"And the—uh—Great Sage—recognized this?"

"Of course he did." Aries spoke as though the answer should have been obvious. "He spoke to Orion without the glimmer of a doubt that day."

Lucian could not help but think back to when Orion shot the scout across the gap of Enorméteren earlier that day. "That shot today," Lucian began, "when he took down that scout across the fields—I've never seen anything like it. I still don't understand how he managed it."

"He had a bit of help, mind you. Not to discredit his natural skill, of course; he has always been a master archer. But Ation left us other things besides our immortality. The smithies of Mount Zynys forged for us sacred weapons designed especially to enhance the qualities with which we fight best. It was no secret that Orion was the best archer in the realm. Men from all reaches used to travel to Dredoway to challenge him, and return with their hearts heavy. Thus the Great Sage awarded him the mighty Zynian bow to greaten even his accuracy. It is made of ageless, unbreakable yew, native to the Mountain itself, and the arrowheads are crafted of Zynian steel—the strongest and lightest metal forged. You will find Leo's shield and sword comprised of it as well, as is the shaft of my great hammer."

Lucian looked to the hammer sitting idly on its head beside Aries. In the starlight, it seemed to possess an eerily fervent, blue gleam.

"You might have noticed his shield is without blemish or dent," continued Aries. "That is a testament to the metal's impregnability. Would that all things meant to keep evil at bay were crafted of such stock."

"That's incredible," said Lucian in awe. "What about the head of your hammer?"

"I beg your pardon?"

"The head of your hammer. You said the shaft is made of Zynian steel, but what about the head?"

"Ah," said Aries, understanding now. "The head is comprised of another element found only in those climes. Moonstone! You see, Lucian, when the hammer was crafted, it was made so that only I could lift it. Not even the mighty Leo, with all his strength, can lift this instrument from the ground!"

"But why?"

"Because these weapons are extensions of ourselves. Orion's arrows, for example, are bound to his mind and eyes. He only needs to lock his desired target in his sights and the arrow will see his will done. As long as the target is visible, it is doomed; and Orion's gaze reaches far and wide. Much in this way is my hammer only able to be wielded by me—and Sages of the Mountain, of course, for it was they who forged it."

"I wish I had a weapon like those," said Lucian. "I like my sword, don't get me wrong, but it doesn't have the stories tied to it like your weapons do."

"Yours is a good blade. I've glanced at it once or twice. It is named Excebellus, and all blades with names have stories tied to them, whether good or evil. You've inherited it, I don't doubt, and so may not know all there is to know about its past. But in time, I suspect, all will be revealed to you. And who's to say that in that time you won't forge a story of your own? Excebellus's finest hour may yet be before it."

"I suppose," said Lucian, somehow unconvinced, though Aries's words did soothe him somewhat. He was no longer troubled by the nightmare that initially woke him.

"I suggest you find some sleep, Lucian," said Aries after a time. "Dawn will be upon us soon, and then we will fly."

So it was Lucian returned to the spot where he had laid, but sleep did not find him again. Instead he lay wide-eyed thinking of his loved ones far away and the journey ahead with this odd assortment of strangers, until the chill of dawn came up over the riverside.

5

Cauldarím

At dawn the next morning, Gamaréa was woken by a guard. As he tried to shake off his weariness, he noticed that the prisoner from across the hall was merging into a fray of many other captives bunching into the corridor. Finding little point in resisting, Gamaréa obediently joined the dirty, reeking, muttering crowd.

This was the first time he was able to see down the entire length of the grim corridor. Despite the bright morning, the only hint of light within was that which reflected off the armor of the Fairy guards. The blank-faced, battered assembly they funneled into the passage was grunting and grimacing. As the passageway condensed, the air became thick, inheriting a stale and sour smell. As such, Gamaréa reflected back on those dark, spider-riddled tunnels leading into the Mountain of Dreams.

Yet after a fervent shove he became one of them—those pale and sluggish captives—and passed amidst their number into the blinding light of morning. It was time now, he thought to himself—it was time to go outside. Not long after meshing into the crowd, Gamaréa noticed his neighbor, and a moment later their eyes locked on each other. But Gamaréa's line was moving more steadily than the other, and as he began to move on ahead, his neighbor urgently grabbed him by the wrist.

"What?" Gamaréa heard himself exclaim.

But before his neighbor could answer, his hand was struck away by the nearest soldier. What could he have wanted? What was that dire look in his eyes? Gamaréa risked a look behind him to see what they were doing with the man who had been singing that solemn song, but it was no use; the traffic within that corridor soon thickened even more, and they marched on, until the unbearable light of morning spilled over them.

Presently Melinta's guard led Didrebelle through the tower; along the ramps, down the corridors, and up the endless spirals of stairwells, until at length he reached the door that would present him to his father—the one who for a countless age was little more than an entity in his mind; so long removed from his heart and memory that he felt as though on the cusp of encountering a stranger. But Didrebelle had not forgotten his father entirely, nor could he. When his thoughts lingered upon the King of Dridion he did not see the image of his face or recall any wisdom-riddled words he may have once said to his only son. Instead he recollected only his malice and severely poor judgment.

In much too short a time the doors to Melinta's hall were upon him and the guards were leading him in. It was as he always remembered: white, wide, lofty and shining, the high-set rafters issuing a boundless quality, as though the hall itself reached up to the heavens. From above draped the emerald banners of Dridion, the solid sigil of the white talons embroidered in their midsections. Glossy and black, the floor seemed like a nightly sea, over which the great emerald cresting Melinta's throne shone like a green sun.

Now Didrebelle was brought before the high seat where his father could look down on him, and was left there to face him alone. In a moment or so he heard the great doors close in the far distance across the room, and the closing panels echoed when indeed they shut at last.

There Melinta sat without expression. Didrebelle realized his father hadn't a clue who he was or why he was there. Slouching in his seat, Melinta rested his head in his long hand as though at the peak of boredom. In Didrebelle's years away from Dridion, he had seen bastions of many powers, but he could not recall a time a ruler seemed more extraneous in a throne. It was fitting at least, Didrebelle thought. After all, his father had given up his right to rule when he joined with Sorcerian and signed the contract to be his puppet, to be the shepherd that would lead flocks of souls to Parthaleon so that he may feast and grow stronger. Even now it seemed like the sorcerer's strings were tugging at his father's white robes as he looked down on the son he did not recognize.

It seemed as though a year passed as they stared silently at each other—the returned son well postured before the high steps to his father's throne; Melinta bent, resting his unimpressed, black-locked head on his fist.

Finally, it was Didrebelle's voice to sound first throughout that cold, open hall. "Do you not know who I am?" he asked plainly.

Melinta sat up, as though hearing the sound of his lost son's voice brought him to attention, making him curious. "How should I know this stranger?"

His father's voice initially unnerved Didrebelle. There was a serpentine tone lingering within it that had not been present when last he saw him.

"You might find my *arrival* here strange," replied Didrebelle, his tone hardening. "But I am far from a stranger. Look hard—strain your eyes; tell me who stands before you."

He could tell Melinta was attempting to remember, straining his dark eyes to combine a name with the face capped by golden locks. Melinta straightened his posture in his throne and was now sitting at the edge of his seat in angst, as though Didrebelle had presented him some sort of game in which he must compete. But after a moment he sat back again, and the temporary light that had blazed within him faded.

"Speak lively, stranger, and with haste," said Melinta lazily, having obviously grown tired of guessing who Didrebelle actually was. "I've important matters at hand today, and it was against protocol for my guards to have delivered you here unannounced. But I can see you are of Fairy stock, at least, and their reason must have been legitimate. Enough of these games—tell me who you are and be done with it."

Though it nearly made him ill to hear himself say it, Didrebelle replied, "I am Didrebelle, your son."

When the light faded and his eyes were able to perceive the surroundings once again, Gamaréa noticed that he was in the middle of a mass gathering. Completely surrounding him was a horde of prisoners in the same dress as his neighbor from across the corridor. He wondered who they were and how they had gotten there, but there were too many to even fathom, let alone count. Some bore such resemblance to the other that it was hard to tell them apart in some instances, and it was as though a swelled quantity of the same imprisoned man stood there staring blankly; the dirty, thick beards; the pale scars upon flesh; the eyes of hopelessness. Had he been able to see his own face Gamaréa did not doubt that he now bore the same appearance: blank and afraid, yet too weak to show fear. But was he really afraid? Did he really think this was the end? Not even he could say.

There was a guard at the front of the gathered horde pacing back and forth, his hands clasped behind his back, shouting orders sternly. He looked young, but so did all Fairies. That is when Gamaréa remembered for the better how he had come to be in this place. The last image he could recollect since the days before his imprisonment was Melinta's face, yet even that was in shadow now, as though he recalled some vague dream from long ago. He remembered his serpent-like voice accurately enough, however, as he spoke of his allegiance with Sorcerian. Then he woke in his cell and that had been the end of it. Even now he could see the white tower in the distance, like a far off white mountain, solidifying his belief that he was in some prison camp of Dridion on the outskirts of the capital city of Deavorás in the reeking marshlands not tended for centuries.

And there he stood, his sandaled feet now sinking in

the stench-filled, moldy earth, listening to orders he could not hear had he bent his ears upon all ability to listen. The prisoners had been led to stand in a wide, square rank—a formation similar to soldiers in preparation for battle. In the distance to his left and right Gamaréa could see old brick buildings, so rundown and weathered that they had become a grotesque hue of brown, and from their midst came more flocks of prisoners who eventually took up ranks of their own beside Gamaréa's.

More cellblocks, he thought. *Surely the king's madness has exceeded perception.* In his little cell he had not realized the buildings were so numerous, nor did he think that there could have been more than one. There was also a larger structure centered in the middle of the sodden yellow field—a fortress of iron and stone with high walls over which peered the henchmen of the Dark Sage. Some Matarhim legionaries were present upon the battlements, and their sulfuric scent pierced through the already-horrid air and made it difficult for him to breathe. To compound matters, he noticed that more creatures had joined forces with them—beasts of an ancient age. *Morgue* was the name the former generations had given them, passed down to children so they could learn it and forget it all in an instant. Hideous, horned brutes like legged boulders, and twice that size when armored. Atop their massive mantles sat heads like bulls, and if actual descendants of bulls, or within the same genetic framework, then the most wicked and awful of any ancestor of that genealogy. Like men they walked upon two legs. Some carried maces, some spears; some wielded bows ten feet in length, with arrows fletched by the feathers of crows. Gamaréa had seen them once in an older time, armored and war-ready as they were now, but he had not been present long enough to physically encounter them. This time, he feared, he would not have a choice.

The headman finished shouting his orders, and the prisoners then broke off into sections. It seemed every two rows were to separate and follow three guards to a designated area of the field. While taking in his surroundings, Gamaréa neglected to realize that he was actually standing beside his neighbor. And as their row moved elsewhere, he locked eyes with him somewhat, and he could tell that the man was pleased he was with him as well.

There were perhaps fifty men in Gamaréa's group. The guard led them to a section of the camp where large, white stones were piled on top of one another. His neighbor then explained to him what their duty would be. "We are to carry each stone to the tool tent," he began, "then we are to craft them according to the blueprint supplied by the contractor. We are then to drag the stones to Deavorás where they are constructing the king's new monument."

His neighbor spoke as though he had been programmed to say those words. Gamaréa's stomach lurched. "Melinta," he said sternly and softly, as if to himself.

He looked to where the other prisoner had directed his attention, and, some twenty feet from the pile of stones, he saw a small station that had been provided for them with tools for sculpting.

"If that's his right name, then yes," answered the other prisoner. "It's being crafted in his likeness."

Gamaréa then followed his neighbor to the stone pile and watched as he bent with both legs, wrapped his large arms around one of the stones, and struggled to his feet. Then he staggered back over to the tool tent and slammed it down upon the crafting table.

"You're not going to take yours?" he asked as he saw Gamaréa standing curiously still and without intent.

Then the Morok walked hesitantly to the stone pile and flipped one on its side so that it sat vertically upon the ground. Cupping a hand underneath it, he brought it up to his side and took to carrying it in one arm, like a child, to the table. It was not until he prepared his tools that he noticed the other prisoner's bewildered expression. Gamaréa wondered for a moment if he had forgotten his breeches.

"What is it with *you?*" asked Gamaréa, becoming a bit uncomfortable.

After stammering for a word, the other prisoner answered, "These stones exceed a hundred pounds in weight, yet you carried yours like a sleeping child! Unless I'm mistaken, the question at hand is: what is it with you?"

Gamaréa stood up looking for the blueprint. "This is not the first time I've been imprisoned," he said searching about.

The other prisoner then stood, curious as to what Gamaréa may have been searching for. "That doesn't explain the strength you just displayed," he said, sitting back down again.

"What is heavy for one man may be light for another." Then he realized the blueprint under the other prisoner's arm. "Will you hand me that?"

The other handed Gamaréa the blueprint. "Don't hedge or feed me coy excuses," he replied. "You interrogated me last night; now I'm the questioner."

The other prisoner's argument was fair and honest, and Gamaréa could not help but explain the truth. "I am of Medric," he answered softly, "of Mascorea's people."

"Another Morok?" answered the other prisoner. "I had never met a member of the Sapphire Sons until I was taken here."

Gamaréa gave a puzzled expression.

"It's the name taught to me by my father," explained the other prisoner. "It wasn't until my later years that I learned the true name of your people."

Gamaréa focused on the blueprint and began chiseling.

"What brings you this far east?" asked the other prisoner.

"An errand for my king," answered Gamarea, "but I will say no more of that. I was westward bound when captured."

"I would venture to guess that Cauldarím was not part of your errand?"

"Cauldarím?"

"Indeed—it is where we are; the name of this forsaken place, if such places can have names."

Gamaréa was learned in Fairy dialects—enough so to realize that the term *Caulda* translated loosely to "ruin" or "destruction," and that for *Rím* was "enclosure" or, in this case, he guessed, "camp."

He grew inwardly anxious, but maintained his poise.

"How long have you been held here?" he asked the man.

The other prisoner thought for several moments before he responded. "I'm not really sure," he answered finally. "I've lost count of how many suns I've seen since coming here."

So there is time, Gamaréa determined. But he would not linger in plotting his escape, if escape was even fathomable—even possible.

"What do they call you?" asked the other.

"I am Gamaréa, son of Gladris. And you?"

"Daxau," he answered, almost sadly, as though he said the name of someone he had forgotten or lost.

"Good to meet you, Daxau. It seems our paths have crossed by unfortunate means."

"Indeed," answered the other, but a smile flirted with the edge of his mouth. "But who's to say where they will go from here?"

Just then a prisoner came running through their tent shouting that the time for the first shipment of stones was nearly upon them.

"It's probably for the best that I warn you now," said Daxau plainly, he might have been telling Gamaréa that they were not serving his favorite lunch item. "They make us drag these to the construction site."

Gamaréa looked puzzled. "Drag, you say?"

Then Daxau lifted his frayed shirt of roughspun and showed Gamaréa his waistline, around which a thick, pink band of scar tissue was wound.

" . . . into the city?" asked Gamaréa incredulously.

But before Daxau could respond, a guard appeared, forcing the prisoners to move with their crafts into the center of the yellow field. There they were provided ropes with which to tie around their stones, and eventually wrap around their waists. Then, like one massive multitude of mindless creatures, they walked slowly and painfully onward, dragging their stones behind them into the city of Deavorás.

* * *

A light blazed in Melinta's eyes, and he sat up attentively. From the bottom of the steps, Didrebelle could see that his lips were quivering, perhaps from searching for the proper words or approaching tears. It seemed an age since Didrebelle had revealed himself to his father—for a long while there was silence, broken only by Melinta's wavering voice, "And you have . . . returned?"

"Indeed, Father . . . " said Didrebelle, quite proudly.

"And after so long a self-exile?"

"Are you not pleased that I am here, Father?"

Melinta stood then, and advanced slowly down to Didrebelle, until he was on the step above where his son was standing. There was a studious gaze in his dark, emerald eyes, such as though Didrebelle instantly felt scrutinized. But Didrebelle also observed his father carefully. Though his kindred bore no hint of age upon their faces, Didrebelle clearly saw age within his tired, weathered eyes. *What have they seen?* he wondered.

"Damn all deceptive hallucinations," said the king softly, never straying his eyes from his son's. "My eyes have conjured some mirage—some image of a lost time—and delivered it to my hall. Yet your face," he said, reaching out and gently sliding his hand down the side of Didrebelle's soft cheek, "it—it does not vanish. What is this? You are authentic?"

Didrebelle had expected an outrage, expected it so much that he was on the brink of hoping for it. But there was only surprise in his father's voice.

"I am no hallucination or mirage, Father," said Didrebelle. "I am very much of flesh and bone and stand before you now at long last."

It was then as though Melinta was overcome by reality, like he had just been in a daze or under a spell. "Oh, my son!" he exclaimed. "I thought you dead! The world out there is savage, and you being of royal lineage . . . Right then! There is much to discuss! Much has developed in your absence. We must talk over lunch and wine, you and I. You must be starving, having come so far."

The idea of dining with his father nauseated Didrebelle. How could he maintain an appetite when having lunch with the one person he loathed most?

"A meal is certainly much needed," Didrebelle lied. "I have much to report as well."

Jovially, Melinta summoned one of his attendants to see to the preparation of a table in the dining hall for him and his son, and that a fine, warm lunch be readied as well. They sat across from each other, one at each end of the long table, which was decorated in emerald and gold. Soon the trays of food were set before them, and large glass jugs of wine placed at each end.

Melinta clasped his hands loudly together. "Now," he said delightedly, "we shall speak of many things. But where in the name of all things shall we begin?" His voice was disgustingly genial, and he smiled as he poured himself a glass and took a small sip. Then he set the chalice down again, the blood-red wine rippling softly within it until it all went still.

"Certainly there are many things to say," answered Didrebelle, trying his hardest to feign the same level of enthusiasm his father was exhibiting. "Allow me to first commend you on this marvelous room. I do not remember it being quite so decorative. I am nearly blinded by the shining jewels and various trappings of silver and gold."

"Yes indeed!" replied Melinta. "So kind of you to take notice. You have always boasted a keen eye. In fact, it pleases me that you remember this room at all, seeing as how you've been so long departed. Even the immortal mind cannot store everything that filters into it."

"Mine has chambered the memories dearest to me." Didrebelle nearly choked on his next sip.

To that Melinta raised his glass to his son and drank again. When he set the chalice down he said, "You have not taken a drink."

"Forgive me, Father,"—he uttered that last word as if he had to physically throw it up—"I am so encapsulated by this moment that I have nearly forgotten my manners." He raised his chalice to the king and sipped lightly, but when his father bent his head to eat he spit it back into the glass.

Melinta then swallowed his food and raised his cloth to wipe his mouth before setting it back on his lap again. "Much has changed since last I saw you," he said. "Much has changed indeed."

"Then you must tell me of this nation's good fortune," said Didrebelle, feigning his interest quite believably, he thought.

Melinta waved one of his long, bony hands. "I wish for fewer words on my part and more on yours. Being so long removed from Dridion, I would not fill your ears with dry tales of my endeavors or those of this country, though both include many. There will be time for us to obtain all the information needed to fill the void in which we lost contact. But now, for you! Tell me of your ventures since last I saw you."

Didrebelle, now backed into a corner, filled his face with something like a smile. He would say nothing of Elderland or his brotherhood with Tartalion Ignómiel, once beloved general of his father's legion. But the gap of time he had to fill was indeed spacious, and he felt no story would be entirely believable. Nevertheless, he attempted. "I was . . . in the east," he said, and he knew his tone was hesitant and uncertain, and he could see his father's brow rise slightly, as though the statement puzzled him, and the only sound in the room for a while was that of chewing.

"The east, you say?" replied Melinta at length.

"Yes indeed. The Far East. Very far from here."

Something more complete than silence fell over the table then. Didrebelle's blood began revving, and his heart hammered relentlessly in his chest. Melinta had picked up his chalice without much of an expression on his face. After finishing the wine within, he took to pouring himself another glass. "And what brought you out that way?"

Didrebelle finally gave in, taking his first sip of wine and finding that it was a nice deterrent from the conversation, and also a way by which to stall. "Well, it was a gradual progression," he said, without leaving any reason for disbelief. "First I became a porter on the western shores, and then a friend of mine there taught me how to sail, which led to my time as a waterman. It was an honest living and a humble atmosphere, but ultimately deprived me of reaching my true potential."

"Yes indeed," said Melinta, laughing a bit. "That work is entirely mundane."

Didrebelle chuckled, and sipped again. "Mundane would be referring to it lightly," he said, with an air of arrogance he thought his father would be proud of. "From there I purchased a decent ship of my own and sailed across the sea with a small crew. It took nearly a year to reach the Far East, but when I arrived I was able to utilize my gifts of the Mountain as a bounty hunter. There was a very convenient dragon infestation that I consequently fell into, and, seeing as how I was the only resident of that hemisphere with the ability to tame them, the jobs became mine alone. I made a handsome fortune during my stay there."

At this point, Didrebelle could not read his father's expression. He neither appeared to believe nor disbelieve his account. "Then why did you come back?" he asked, not unkindly. "Dragon bounties are extremely high. You are being humble even by saying your fortune was handsome."

Didrebelle, nearly out of breath from forging his tale from nothing, took another sip of wine, annoyed at his father's prodding.

"In time," he said, setting his glass down, "I managed to tame them all, and there was no wild dragon left to be seen in that part of the world."

His father sat, staring. Upon his face was no emotion, and out of need to avoid awkward staring, Didrebelle began to eat his lunch for the first time. It was dry, and now lukewarm. He wasn't sure what it was, but it was meat. Perhaps some sort of pheasant or another type of fowl.

Then he looked up and saw his father raising his glass to him, a small smile upon his face. "Well done, my son," he said. "I commend you. Not only did you take your life into your own hands, but tried to make something of yourself in the process. There is something now that I must ask you; something that has been the cause of my withering innards. Why did you feel as though you had to leave to begin with? Why was your departure so final and full of haste? I was sure that it was out of hatred towards me."

He had asked the very question Didrebelle wanted to evade. Of course he wished now to throw the table aside and send all the glassware, food, and gaudy decorations shattering onto the floor and walls. Of course he longed to pronounce his true reasons for abandoning his father and his father's nation: his irreversible descent into madness, his allegiance with darkness, the murder of Emmanuelle, his hatred of the Moroks and all residents and descendants of Medric. He would assure him that those were the reasons his departure was so final and so filled with haste; and also that his original perception of his departure was accurate— that it was out of the utmost hatred toward him. But he took another sip of wine. It was cold atop his tongue, and scratched his throat as it traversed down and fell warm upon the top of his stomach. "Never, Father," he answered softly, and against every last measure of his controllable will. "Your son could never come to hate his father; nor your prince his king."

Melinta smiled then, wider than he had yet smiled during their luncheon, and in that smile was something deeper than evil. "Splendid," he said. "Now there is something I must show you."

The thick rope around Gamaréa's waist dug into his hips as he walked slowly on, dragging the heavy stone. All around him the men were grimacing and moaning in pain. Guards flanked the rank of prisoners who traversed across the swampy fields to maintain order, carrying whips and shouting in their disturbing tongues.

A man not far ahead of him toppled over onto his face, whether by weakness or other means. Promptly a guard fell upon him and seized him, and when it was found the prisoner could not rise by his own strength, he was whipped until his shirt was nearly ripped off. The group could only carry on as the sounds of whip striking cloth, then whip striking flesh, and the cries of the prisoner rang aloud and lingered in their ears even after they were out of earshot.

The walls of Deavorás were upon them in time, and a beastly sentry, whom perhaps was employed by Melinta or a deeper, darker authority, opened the immense, heavy doors of iron before them with just its bare hands and brawn. Gamaréa wondered what it was, so brutally muscled and of rotting-green colored flesh. Perhaps it was a descendent of the swamp itself, imprisoned as he was, forced now to help further the duty of prisoners. It hissed and snarled and snorted through an iron mask crafted in the shape of a demon, and steam sprang from the cage concealing its mouth. Those closest to it shuddered and cried out, and some even tried to run despite their haul.

Onward. It was not long before they were trudging along the polished streets of Dridion's capital. The scraping of the sliding stones filled the air with a sound like a hoarse wind. The guards were leading them down alleyways where the streets were slightly sloped, perhaps to instill more agony upon them. The weight at his back now tugged more intensely against the bottom of his stomach and the sides of his hips. What was worse were the civilians of Deavorás who had come out of their homes or stood atop their balconies to taunt and ridicule them. In time it became as though walking through a storm of household products and food. Gamaréa was struck several times by objects— mostly vegetables.

It took nearly an hour for them to be able to see where they were going, as the alleyways were behind them and there were no more back-roads by which the guards could take them. Now they had reached the centermost portion of the city where buildings towered over them, aligned neatly on their city blocks. In the distance, perhaps another quarter of a mile, they saw the king's tower, and other prisoners who had previously endeavored there with their stones leaving to return to Cauldarím.

Daxau, whom Gamaréa had forgotten was next to him, leaned in as the march began to slow up. "This is where we go every day," he whispered, "two or three times."

Gamaréa surveyed what was ahead, and noticed now the

white structure being built behind the wooden scaffolding. Though the bust of Melinta was completed only to the shoulders, it still stood nearly a hundred feet high. Farther upward, within the shadows of the high tower, Gamaréa could see Melinta himself peering from his balcony, an attendant at his side, scrutinizing every last detail of the building process.

Melinta led Didrebelle to the balcony of his tower and bid him peer out across Deavorás. From there he could see many things. They were high enough so that the city beyond seemed as but a maze of rooftops. It truly was a magnificent city in a once magnificent nation. The late-morning sky was cloudless and blue, and the unveiled sun splintered down atop the white buildings for miles on end. It seemed as though someone had emptied jewels across a wide floor and left them there to glitter. It was the first time in many centuries that he beheld his homeland from that high balcony, and he remembered doing so as a young child—young even by mortal standards—when his grandfather showed him all there was to see from that height.

But standing there with his father did not merit the same effect, an effect that indeed once left him breathless and inspired. For now he beheld the massive structure to his left, and the captives who tirelessly filtered their strength and health into constructing the bust of their captor. Even from the height at which he stood, Didrebelle could hear their cries of agony as whips lashed them and guards cursed. This was not Deavorás. This was not Dridion. Despair filled him, and the fire of his hatred fueled to a new level.

Melinta, however, enjoyed a deep inhale of breath, closing his eyes and raising his head to the sky. "Can you feel that, my son?" he said. "The winds of change arrive upon the breeze. Dridion shall be ever prosperous."

Didrebelle perceived what was below him for the better now: Morgues and Matarhim legionnaires. Melinta was now employing the henchmen of Nundric. The king was in deeper league with Sorcerian than he could ever have imagined.

"I . . . can feel it," said Didrebelle, trying hard to feign a believable sound of approval. "Your soldiers down there," he said after a while, "what are they?"

"Forgive me! I am so enveloped by this construction work that I nearly forgot to explain what I have been up to in your absence." Melinta might have been describing a new birdhouse he had built.

Don't worry, Didrebelle thought to himself, *I know all about it.*

"Dark times are nearly upon us," began Melinta. "Every day they inch closer! The malice of Sorcerian cannot be matched by any who dwell on this earth."

"The Sorcerer of Nundric?"

"Shh!" cried Melinta, and he faced his son for the first time since standing upon the balcony. There was genuine fear in his dark eyes when his son looked into them, and for a moment he nearly felt pity for his father. "We must not speak his name," he continued. "He may be listening. His spies are here."

"Those creatures below?"

"Indeed."

"But they are armored as though your own soldiers. Have you not employed them yourself?"

"Well . . . yes, but not—" then his voice shrunk to an even softer whisper, "—by my own will."

"Then by whose?"

Melinta's eyes widened, black beaded balls without discrepancy between iris and pupil, the whites bloodshot and weary. "There is no hope now," he said coldly, and his voice seemed not his own. "What's done is done and hope is lost. See? See how they parade about, the monsters? See how he has deceived me? See how he has deceived your father?"

Melinta had grabbed hold of Didrebelle's wrists so hard that he nearly thought they would break. "Release me, Father!" shouted Didrebelle. "Release me!"

Then, as though coming out of a deep sleep, Melinta's

eyes gained a bit of life, and his grip subsided upon the wrists of his son. Then he looked away, out across the vast breadth of Deavorás. "Yes," he whispered lightly, "yes, hope is lost indeed."

Didrebelle wanted nothing more than to explain the truth about his fairings since he fled his father's homeland. But Melinta had been corrupt long before his allegiance to Sorcerian. His lust for power buried him in the hole he was now trying to wriggle out of. But the hole was much too deep now for him to rise again, and it seemed he was beginning to realize that very fact. Didrebelle knew there was nowhere to go for his father but forward; thus there was no one for Didrebelle to focus his hatred on but him.

Just then Didrebelle noticed the prisoners who had been laboring over the already-towering statue filed away behind the guards, and a new band of them coming up the main road with more stones.

"Here comes a new wave," said Melinta. "Ever since we added new prisoners to Cauldarím, the quality of the work has lessened. It is my belief that the guards whom I have appointed are not completely seeing to their jobs."

Then he saw what he had ventured all that way to see— found whom he had risked all hope to find. For coming up the path, enclosed among a hundred captives, was Gamaréa, dragging, like the rest of them, a heavy stone in his wake.

Now to his mind came the father of all ideas, so well planned in such a quick moment that Didrebelle nearly smiled at his own cunning. "Then you must allow me to stand in the stead of the present disciplinarian," he offered. "I have spent nearly two hundred years relocating dragons; a community of prisoners will be as though apprentice work."

He could tell his father was considering. "Cauldarím is no place for a prince," he said at last. "Your job is here with me, learning how to run this country in the days that I am gone. Not in those forsaken fields with that forsaken lot."

"I insist, father," he said intently. "There will be time for me to learn the job of a king. But for now there is other work that needs tending. Look at this lot, they are haggard and sluggish, and lack discipline. I daresay a change is in order indeed."

Melinta again considered, and was quiet for many moments. Finally, he said, "I suppose there would be no harm in seeing a new disciplinarian in Cauldarím. I will send word to the warden's fortress. It is he whom you must consult before you begin your duties. And when you speak with him, have him send the present disciplinarian to me."

Didrebelle was nearly in shock. Could his father be so easily deceived? But then he thought upon that question for the better and answered it himself. The time was soon that Gamaréa and he would be able to set about their true mission and head back upon their true path. He just hoped upon hope that his plan would not be foiled.

6

Beyond the Great Swan Lane

Dawn proved bleak and cold. Lucian, who had just begun to doze off, was suddenly brought to attention when Leo's heavy foot smashed against his side and the hulking swordsman went tumbling over him.

"Apologies, my friend," he said, standing up and looking around embarrassedly. "Glad to see you're awake."

I am now, Lucian wanted to say. Instead he only feigned a smile. Yawning, he cast his squinting eyes upon the rising sun. Beneath the dreary orange globe the horizon seemed wispy and blue, like a layout of oddly shaped storm clouds. Far away he could see the plain figures of great mountains at the end of a distant rolling road.

Somewhere behind him he heard the voice of Orion preparing Godspeed for another day's journey. Every so often the grumbling voice of Goldbearer would come up over the hill, and Leo would answer as though the two were engaged in an articulate conversation.

Aries already had Night-Treader saddled and ready. The great black steed was now enjoying a fresh drink from Elarian's bank, the current of which was moving swiftly this morning. Atop his back the silver etchings of his saddle glittered under the modest dawn's gleam.

Soon Orion appeared, leading Godspeed in his wake. The white stallion gave a start when he saw the sunrise, and even in the dimness his coat shined as though made of diamonds.

"Get yourself some water," Orion said to his stallion.

"We've many miles to put behind us today, and you will need your strength since your load is doubled. If no peril greets us perhaps we may make for the Springcrest further east, though I fear the river flowing out of the mountains may now be garrisoned. Drink heartily!"

With that Godspeed trotted off for the river to drink beside his brother, who neighed in greeting. Then Orion turned to Lucian. "You should take care to drink up as well," he said, "though Aries certainly has the water skins filled by now. Still, it would be wise to provision them for as long as possible. Are you hungry?"

Though the burning sensation of hunger was present in Lucian's stomach, the thought of a meal nearly made him cringe. It was now over two days since he had anything to eat, but the events of those days expelled any want of food he might have entertained. Somewhere in his heart it saddened him to think that Gamaréa and Didrebelle were alive when a morsel last crossed his lips.

"Never mind that," said Orion suddenly. "You will eat—you must eat. The ride ahead is long and without promise of respite. Eap has flown ahead to scout the plains, but he may not return to us for many hours. It may be your only chance to eat for a long while."

"Then I'll have some," said Lucian sheepishly. *He's bossier than Gamaréa for sure.* Yet this thought only added more weight to his grief-laden heart.

Breakfast was a thin slab of jerked meat, lightly salted and very tough. "This is food fit for travel," Orion had said. "Easy to store, light to carry, and made for quick consumption." After the third bite or so Lucian felt as though his jaw was on the verge of unhinging. Nevertheless, the sensation of food in his mouth alerted him to how hungry he had truly been, and before long he was putting away his second helping.

In time the foursome converged at Elarian's edge where Godspeed and Night-Treader stood readied. Goldbearer, meanwhile, remained lapping his long tongue in the passing current. The dawn had yet succumbed to morning. Aries, whose sight was keenest, stood gazing eastward for a great distance, following the river's current until he could see it no more. Far away it passed in a winding white strand before it vanished round a bend of the plain.

Leo, Orion, and Lucian stood awaiting him. Before long he returned. "We can cross at the Knobb, it seems," he said confidently. "It lies not more than a mile westward. From what I could see, there is no garrison or sign of trouble. We will go unnoticed, most likely."

"Good," said Leo gruffly. "Then let's get this party moving. I'd like to feel my own bed beneath me again, and wrap myself in some fur blankets. If I never sleep outdoors again it would be too soon."

Together they mounted. Aries and Night-Treader helmed the small line. Godspeed bore Orion and Lucian behind his steadfast brother, and in his wake Goldbearer wandered vigilant. They passed westward, following the twists and turns of the river for a good while at a slow pace. In no more than half an hour they approached what Aries referred to as "the Knobb." There the river sloped swiftly downward, and upon flattening again became pinched by two gravelly banks. Here its depth was reduced to a matter of inches, and the mounts made quick work of fording it before dashing out into the plains beyond.

"Good, good," said Orion. Whether he was speaking to Lucian or himself, the boy could not tell. "That was easier than I thought," he said after a while. "No doubt Aries's eyes have served us well, and not for the first time. I feared we would meet some obstacles at the Knobb, but it seems as though these reaches of the Elarian are yet under the enemy's command. That is good news! Though I fear passage may only be granted to servants of Deavorás and Nundric—and perhaps other dark places—before long. But never mind that now, Mr. Rolfe! Our business lies on this side of the river."

Their trek across the wide plain of Enorméteren was long and tiring. The faraway mountains Lucian glimpsed at dawn came in and out of view as the land rose and fell beneath them. For many miles it seemed as though they ran in place, although in truth the steeds swallowed many leagues.

In their pursuit they put many fields of gold and green behind them, lone riders across an empty land. Now and then they slipped along a dell where red-leafed trees stood like old sentinels, their knobby branches open as if allowing the travelers passage to places beyond. In the yellow glens and wide sloping meadows, mighty spruces scattered to greet them like the remains of great green spear-points from a battle long ago.

It indeed was a vast and beautiful frontier, a place Lucian thought he might like to revisit one day to walk along those fields and maybe camp beneath the stars. But then he wondered indeed if he would come back at all, and the grim impracticality of his return disheartened him. Such things and more Lucian thought of as they rode, and all the while Godspeed devoured miles with his hooves.

Eventually the afternoon waned, and the sun began to dip earnestly into the west. Soon the cloudless blue sky that had unfolded above them became blotched with rumors of dusk. From the western horizon, red and pink licks of color peered up over the folds like pastel flames below a layout of star-riddled amethyst. There in the foreground a great range of mountains sprouted and bent away eastward until their eyes could see them no more. Under the warring sun and stars, their peaks glinted with a fiery red.

"The Red Peaks," said Lucian, as if to himself. The company had slowed to a brisk walking gait.

"Very good, Master Rolfe," said Orion. "Though I thought you would first comment on the time we have made, but never mind that. Now you understand how the mountains acquired their name. They are a marvelous sight, if I do say so myself. I have looked on them for ages, under the rise of sun and moon, yet their beauty grows each time I lay my eyes on them."

"I can see why," replied Lucian, unable to look away from the vast mountain range ahead of them. "It seems like there's some magic at work in their slopes."

Orion laughed. "Magic," he said, as though recounting the punch line of a memorable quip. "You could assemble the staves of every Sage to cast a single spell, yet would fail to see more magic than what lies before you. The world, my friend, is the greatest wizard. Indeed we would be surprised beyond measure had we attended her shows more often. The days are now spent stripping her beauty away, yet still she boasts her splendor. That is magic indeed."

Lucian sighed. "I don't think I want to leave this place," he said. "I wish I could stay here and look at the mountains. I'm sure they must be beautiful under the sunrise."

"Indeed they are, Master Rolfe. But you need not worry, for it is into the mountains we go, after all. Yes, there our dwelling lies: Ren Talam—and you won't find another place like it. Surely you will hold it equally breathtaking, as it is built within the range's highest peak. Shír Azgóth, the Red Giant, as the songs often name it. But we've still many miles to go before your eyes can feast on the sight, and night will be upon us soon."

Godspeed, Night-Treader, and Goldbearer sped on again before long, trying to cover as much ground as possible before the full arrival of night, and even when the moon was high above them the company passed on, for the world below was lit well enough for travel. Soon they came upon the eaves of a small forest at the feet of the Red Peaks looming high above. A clear spring trickled out and bent southwards, no doubt for a good distance until it converged with the Elarian.

"The Springcrest," said Aries when the company halted. "You would be hard-pressed to find water more fit for drinking. It is fed by the mountain snows, and can replenish even the most weathered traveler. Drink up! I will refill these skins, though it may be some time before they bear a purer load."

"Another night in the wilderness," barked Leo grumpily as he made for the stream to refill his own skin.

Lucian had taken to sitting by Springcrest's edge, listening to the calming sound of the water trickling by. Looking westward beyond the mountains and into the wilderness, he gaped at how plentiful and bright the stars appeared. To him it seemed like he was viewing a battle from above, with thousands of bright-plated soldiers defending their shining, spherical keep. Together they lit the distant golden reeds as though it were day, and seemed even to make them glow. Lucian wondered if something could be haunting and beautiful all at once. Then Goldbearer came and stood beside him, bending his horse-sized head into the stream to drink. Suddenly his heart froze.

"Pretty friendly, that lad." The voice was Leo's. Stooping beside Lucian, he sat down and laid his long, bright sword across his lap, and with a whetstone began scraping at its edges. The wide, polished blade reflected the starlight, and Lucian soon found himself squinting.

"I'm referring to that brute, of course," continued Leo, gesturing toward Goldbearer, who had now taken to sprawling out in the trickling stream and groaning very lion-like for the pleasure it brought him. Pride gleamed in the massive man's dark eyes as he watched his companion frolic in the stream, as though he beheld a child of his own at play.

"I've—uh—never seen a lion before," said Lucian, still wary of the great beast, however preoccupied he might have been. "I was led to believe that they were . . . smaller . . . than that, though."

Leo scraped the whetstone along the edges of his blade several times before he answered. "And you weren't mistaken," he said at last, with a strange heaviness in his voice. "The new breeds are half his size, and the females even smaller. But Goldbearer there is of an ancient kind, the last of his kin that once roamed the northern jungles of Greydale and Ironden. The Nammen-Maso folk named them—the Takers of Flesh." Then his every motion ceased, and he looked unseeingly into the glowing fields beyond. When he spoke again his voice was troubled. "And they took it where they could find it, if you could imagine."

Hard not to picture it. Lucian made as if to ask how Leo had come to befriend such a beast, but when he turned he was already on his way to converse with Aries, who was feeding Night-Treader from a leather sack. At the sound of his whistle, Goldbearer abruptly sat up in the water and followed in his wake like a well-trained hound. He emerged much too close to Lucian for his comfort, and shook enough wetness from his hide to drown a small village. Lucian was not spared from this shower, and voiced his feelings when the beast was out of earshot.

Takers of Flesh—more like Givers of Baths! Foul thing—

"I see you could not resist the fresh waters of the Springcrest," said Orion, who showed up unexpectedly behind Lucian. "I hope I did not startle you."

"No, I was just—"

"Taking a bath, I would say."

Lucian tried to suppress a scowl.

"Forgive me, my friend, but I could not resist. Goldbearer, it seems, is tamed in all but his manners, though they have gotten better over the last century or so."

"I can imagine," said Lucian, cringing at the blatant air of annoyance in his own voice. Orion sat beside him. "I'm sorry," Lucian continued. "I was tired and hungry, but now I'm wet and freezing. I didn't mean to be so—"

"Uncouth?" laughed Orion. "Hardly, my friend. You are not the first among men to find yourself in—what would you call it?—a mood. Our journey was long for those not used to traveling, and even for some of the most skilled wanderers. I did not entirely expect to find you in bright spirits. That is why I have sought you, of course, and here I find you washed and clean."

"And angry."

"Of course! We mustn't be forgetting. But you will no doubt grow to love Goldbearer as much as Lionsbane. He is a loveable beast when all is said and done, though the look of him fills even the stoutest hearts with fear. The endurance of a horse and twice an ox's strength, not to mention a mouth of daggers that yearn for the taste of Morgue and Fairy alike. He is not overly fond of those fiery fellows, however. Prefers his food to be room temperature. Picky, but we cope with him as best we can."

"He can eat them all, for all I care. And we'd be better for it."

Orion smiled. It was Lucian who spoke after a brief

silence. "What's a Lionsbane?" he asked curiously. "You mentioned it a minute ago."

"Forgive me," replied Orion. "I was speaking too casually and forgot you are new amongst us. Lionsbane is how we used to refer to Leonysus sometimes."

"Like a nickname?"

"No, I'm afraid I do not know any Nicks."

Lucian suppressed a laugh. "No—a nickname. It's . . . well . . . it's a name for someone, but it's not their real name. The girls at school used to call me Greaseshanks."

"Ah, an epithet," said Orion, beginning to understand. "Yes indeed, it is an epithet for Leonysus. And, if I may add, your shanks bear not even the slightest—*grease*, did you say it was?" Lucian nodded his thanks. "Long ago, before the fall of Dredoway even, Leonysus lived in a village on the outskirts of the northern jungles of Ironden. It was a land of turmoil, long plagued by a horde of beasts known as the Nammen-Maso. It grieves me to think of how many men, women, and children lost their lives to those creatures. Hundreds, perhaps. Sadly the founders of Ironden built their villages in the midst of the Nammen-Maso feeding grounds, and as such were subjected to their vengeance."

Orion's tale kindled a spark of fear in Lucian's heart, and his brow furrowed. At once he became very wary of Goldbearer's whereabouts, peering over his shoulder as often as he could as though worried the great beast was lurking.

"Why didn't they just move?" he came to ask worriedly, as though he watched the hardships of Ironden unfold before his very eyes. "If they knew those things were out there, why didn't they just up and leave?"

Orion sighed. "Such questions I have often pondered," he said. "Hubris has ever been man's greatest flaw, and the men of Ironden were no different. Theirs was a culture brimming with ferocious pride. They felt the land they claimed was theirs and theirs alone, and no beast, however native, would force them elsewhere. This logic nearly brought them to ruin. Instead of migrating, Ironden's armies waged war against the Great Lions, invading their dens in the jungles as their villages had been invaded. It was a great malice they brought with them: husbands avenging wives, wives avenging husbands, parents avenging children. Thus their strength could not be counted merely by bodies alone.

"He will tell you it was a hard few days, passing through the jungle under the heat and cleansing it of the murderous beasts that roamed within. Their errand brought them far, and when all was finished a fraction of their sum made the journey home. It was while returning that Leo came across Goldbearer, lying nestled in his den. His life had been spared by a sliver of weeds that conspired to hide him from the soldiers. And their work proved cunning indeed, for beside him his mother lay slain in the open. Perhaps she set the shelter about her child, knowing well the fate that awaited her. I cannot say.

"I do know, however, that Leonysus, whose kills numbered more than any soldier, was prodded to slay him, yet chose to spare his life. His choice was the one thread of light to pierce through those dark few days. Leonysus recognized that Goldbearer was yet marred by the ways of his kin, and was in no way responsible for the grievance his brethren had caused. So it was he brought him to his village, and raised Goldbearer amongst his children, and he grew to be as loyal and friendly as any of them.

"Yet there were none who forgot Leonysus's tale. The total of his kills was thrice that of the next largest tally, thus he was given the name Lionsbane by the Lord of Ironden, who was most valiant. Goldbearer has accompanied Leonysus on all of his exploits, and has brought his mouth of daggers to every battle since."

Lucian looked over to where Leo and Aries had been talking. Night-Treader was loitering by the stream in his lonesome, but not far from him Aries was taking rest. Some yards away sat Leo in the pale, golden grass, and on his lap was the massive head of Goldbearer, who lay beside him like a brutish hound.

"I was wrong to get so angry with him," said Lucian finally. "It's just that he scares me, I guess. I've never seen a lion before, let alone one the size of a horse. My nerves got the best of me."

"I do not ask for apologies," said Orion kindly. "When I first set eyes on Goldbearer I made to shoot him with an arrow. Imagine how that would have turned out. Leo is not someone you want as an enemy."

"Somehow I don't doubt that," Lucian laughed, casting his gaze beyond his idling companions to the eaves of the nearby forest. "What's in there?" he asked. All that talk of lions and great beasts of the forests had begun to rouse his nerves.

"Trees," answered Orion smugly. "Though to articulate further would be to say that you look upon the Redacre Wood, and in that wood lies the westward path through the mountains."

"Will we continue tonight?"

"I think not. No, I rather like it out here by this stream. I do not sense trouble, and our mounts are so sure-footed that they will have left no discernible trail for others to follow, believe it or not. These woods have not been known to house evil. Beyond them we have enjoyed peace for countless years whilst our neighbors' days grow dark. Rest well tonight, Lucian. I don't doubt your body yearns for a good sleep."

Orion could not have hit nearer the mark. Weariness had overcome Lucian more than it ever had. Never before had he thought that a long day of riding could bring someone the exhaustion he now felt. Lying in the soft reeds he was consumed by heaviness, and in no time at all fell into a deep and unhampered slumber.

It was Aries who woke him. Lucian felt immediate disappointment, for it was mid-morning and he had wanted to see the sunrise. But the morning proved a spectacle in itself: a deep field of indigo with a splay of wispy, loitering clouds spread far over the golden field around them.

"Take some breakfast," he said. "Another long march today, through the forest and up the stairs of the mountain. Can't count on speed on the trails ahead, I daresay."

"How much longer will we have to journey?" asked Lucian, taking a strip of jerk.

"Orion knows trails that are safe to travel by night," said Aries, "and that is not common for mountain passes these days. Should we choose to travel by the moon we may reach Ren Talam in two days' time, maybe three depending on respites. However, who knows what we may meet on the trail? It has been long since we came this way."

After refilling the water skins for the last time, the foursome made their way into the Redacre Wood. Lucian did not need a history lesson to understand how it had gotten its name. The high sun set the forest roof ablaze in a burst of crimson, and the leaves reflected the red light upon the path at their feet.

They followed the trail along the Springcrest as long as possible. Within the wood its breadth was narrowed, and in some spots was no wider than a modest brook winding around the trees and knees of the forest floor. Lucian wondered how the paths were made and who took the time to make them. So were his thoughts regarding all trails and paths in places that seemed largely forgotten or abandoned. But there was always a story, he found—always some sort of lengthy history belonging to even the smallest road.

It was pleasant, at least, to travel the calm and quiet paths of Redacre. Lucian recalled his previous forest-ventures with disdain. He thought he had surely met his end in the Black Forest, and would have had Didrebelle and the folk of Elderland not come to his aid. Marshal Crowley's laughter still darkened his dreams every now and then, and his first meeting with the Matarhim was as present in his memory as his most recent. Yet it was Ravelon indeed that had yielded the most peril. He thought of its great, enchanted door only as a portal to doom, and would forever remain a vision of woe recalled only to recount the world's most treacherous reaches.

Thoughts such as these seemed to darken the path ahead, though in truth it was beautifully lit by the high sun. As for food they ate sparingly. Lucian helped himself to another strand of jerk, glad to find that it alleviated his hunger as though it were a large meal. The water from the Springcrest had the same effect on thirst: he had not felt urged to tap his drink supply since the start of the day's journey.

The dregs of the red-and-gold afternoon were fleeting when the company arrived at what Aries had referred to as "the stairs of the mountain." In passing Orion mentioned that it was formally known by a similar name: The Mountain's Stair. Sure enough it resembled a stairwell as closely as anything built by nature could. Great mountain stones sprouted from the earth in high layers. The ages had turned them dark and gray, yet there was a beauty about them specific to ancient things that grow. Lichen, moss, and ferns clung to them in patches of green. Steep and sure they rose, and so it was the Redacre path climbed with it, coiling around the bends of the rock like a great snake.

Godspeed whinnied and began the climb. His eager companions followed in his wake: first the steadfast Night-Treader, followed by Goldbearer the Mighty. It took much longer than Lucian thought to mount the winding stair. Its true height had deceived them all from below, but none more than Lucian, for it seemed to rise with every ascent of his company. Soon the air became thin and cold and still half their climb remained.

To their far left the Springcrest sloped steeply down a great slide of stone. Here its current passed swiftly, spurred on by the great height from which it fell. For a while its descent was among the only sounds heard. Additionally there were the cautious footfalls of the three mounts and the tapping of random packs as they bumped lightly against their hides. Somewhere abreast of them (for they had now climbed high), they heard the genial twittering of small forest birds, and some even flew out of their perches to get a better look at the odd company passing through their realm. Surely their attention—and no doubt alertness— settled mostly on Goldbearer. Such a beast perhaps had never crossed the trails of Redacre in this age or the last, and it would not be surprising had they wished never to see the like of his kind again.

At the crown of the stair's height was a wide plateau, and

moving eastward from there was a road of stone winding narrowly into the further reaches of the mountains. Far above, the opening between great towers of stone revealed a deep-pink sparkling twilight. Yet where they passed below, the megaliths seemed to shroud them in greater darkness than had fallen over the outer valleys. It was not, however, the perilous darkness that Lucian had often felt on the foul roads he had somehow weathered. It was a darkness he compared to the midnight hours in which he walked home from MaDungal's, full and in high spirits. Suddenly and unlooked for, a sliver of that feeling began to reawaken in his heart, and he sat more comfortably in Godspeed's saddle reminiscing of a simpler life long ago and across the sea.

How long they traveled the narrow mountain road Lucian had no way of knowing. It seemed like ages. Looking behind him now and again, the nether ways seemed more unfamiliar. At one point the great crimson roof of the Redacre Woods seemed but a wide splay of shadow far below them, yet when he looked now they were gone. In their stead was a valley far below, much too far for Lucian's liking. He wondered if Godspeed or Orion feared these lofty heights as much as he, though they gave no inkling of such fright.

Thus along the nightly scaffolding of the mountains they passed. Whatever rest Aries believed Orion might take seemed not to be had. It was a leisurely pass, regardless. If the flight across Enorméteren had not exhausted these mounts beyond measure, Lucian was sure a light stroll down mountain trails would prove an easy errand.

So it was the night passed overhead. After some time the eastward trail bent northward around a knee of high stone, and they followed this bend into the stomach of the range.

"We have passed too long on the outside of the mountain," said Orion. Lucian was not sure if he was speaking to him, for he had been quiet a long while as though he were asleep. "My heart is yet unsettled, for there is no promise that we have passed unseen."

"Who may have seen us?" asked Lucian. Orion's head jerked slightly, as though the small voice of Lucian so deep within the night startled him somewhat.

"Morgues," he said grimly. "They are known to patrol the stony reaches of the world. That is where they were recruited from, after all. At least most of them. They were once a peaceful race, and better left alone. Now Sorcerian and Melinta have teamed to arm them and teach them the ways of sword and arrow, washing their brains with deceitful tales of white-skinned evildoers whose lone purpose is to destroy their homes. Thus they have joined their league, until these days are done."

Lucian shifted nervously. "Have they seen us?" he asked warily.

"I cannot rightly say," answered Orion. "Though it is likely that they haven't. Stealth is not a trait that belongs to them, nor are they overly witty when it comes to battle. You would hear a throng of Morgues long before you saw one. Yet there is a foul smell on the air, such that is foreign to these climes, or at least to me. And I have lived here long."

"I don't smell anything," said Lucian, straining his nostrils to pick up the slightest morsel of a scent.

"Then you may find unhindered sleep," said Orion after a moment in which he gazed alertly around him. "And now would be the time to take it."

So he did, and it was not long before he found himself in a deep dream. He was in the meadows of Amar on a bright afternoon with his friends. Jem was there, and they were laughing, and he saw Sam Fryer's farm in the distance and heard the animals roaming within the fences. Then it was suddenly evening, and Lucian made as if to leave. Suddenly Jem stopped him.

You are fixing to come back, aren't you? he asked, his eyes pleading and his voice desperate, as though he knew some peril of Lucian's road he was yet to know himself.

Of course I'm fixing to come back, Lucian heard himself say, but his words were slowly drained from him, stretched out as if time itself was careering to a halt. *It's just . . .*

unlikely . . .

And that last word echoed as though he had shouted in a chasm, and rang in Lucian's ears until he woke to see the pale light of dawn over the unchanged setting.

"I don't doubt that," he heard the voice of Aries say. "Unlikely is right. You see, Orion, he has been tuning in to us the whole time, or at least for most of it. Not a simple thing to find slumber on horseback; not even in in the comfort of Godspeed's saddle, I daresay."

It was then that Lucian realized he had spoken that final word aloud, if not his dream's entire dialogue. Flushing, he sat back embarrassedly.

"I still say Eap would have been here by now," grumbled Leo. "Truancy has never been a habit of his."

"He is wise," said Orion. "His delay no doubt signifies that there has indeed been trouble abroad. Every winged messenger will certainly be taken into account, even if they are impartial to the business of the war. Thus perhaps he was followed, and so flew astray to lead enemies off our trail. If so, I will be first to express my gratitude when he returns."

"Let us pray he does so," said Aries.

From here they journeyed on in silence. Orion perhaps was wariest of the skies, constantly lifting his gaze into the bright gray field above in hope to glimpse the odd raven. Yet his crucible proved fruitless.

They followed an upward slope of the trail through the late morning and into early afternoon. Lucian could tell that they were passing almost due east now, yet the mountains gave no inkling that they would soon yield to open terrain or some grand city such as Orion had described. Boredom consumed him. He had never been one to sit still and silent for so long a time. His instructors often reported that he had some sort of attention deficiency, but such was their report of nearly all their pupils. Yet he had sat in the saddle so long that his legs were aching uncomfortably, and the small of his back was throbbing with a very annoying pain.

"Would it be alright if I walked?" he asked at long last. "I'm starting to get a bit uncomfortable, and this journey is showing no signs of ending at any near hour."

"Very well," said Orion. "In fact I think we all could do with a bit of rest."

The others agreed. Wedged within those towers of stone they found that night came swiftly. Long shadows were cast over their campground, and a very stiff coldness passed through and troubled them.

"Is it always this cold up here?" asked Lucian, wrapping himself in his now-weathered cloak.

"We have climbed high," said Orion. "Very high indeed. We are upon one of the range's many northerly roads. It will be some miles before the path winds down again, yet when it does we will be home, and your bones may find warmth."

Had Lucian not been so weary he would have found great difficulty falling asleep. Yet it seemed that once his eyes were closed he was lost within another dream in which his sight was somehow blurred. Tall images surrounded him, but he could not distinguish them clearly. He felt as though he was being held or carried. Soon he discerned three human shapes, all distorted as though they appeared through a dense fog. Somewhere it seemed a light was shining. From an unknown location he heard his name, faint and whispered, yet it soothed him. Soon all he felt was comfort. Gently he felt himself being lowered, and when he was set down the three figures stepped back and fleeted away. Only one of them returned. The part of Lucian closest to the waking world strained to bring the figure into focus, but it was not to be. It stooped again, and might have said something, though Lucian could not hear.

Then he woke. The pass was dark and he was cold again. Had he ever been warm? Around him his companions slept peacefully. Goldbearer lay sprawled on his back with Leo resting on one of his outstretched limbs. Both were snoring. The stallions were quiet, perhaps asleep themselves. Sleep did not return to Lucian again, though he tried his best to reclaim it. He was too aware now of the darkened pass and the deep midnight of the mountains. Through the crevices of stone the wind howled ghoulishly, and he thought to hear footsteps nearby, though he dismissed them for scattering stones.

The shadows toyed with the corners of his eyes. Every time he turned his gaze away they seemed to be in motion. At one point he thought to see the shape of a person standing in the pass, leaning against the mountain wall. But as soon as he made to wake Orion the shape dissolved and became nothing.

Finally Lucian could stand the dark no longer. His wits had all but reached their end. There he sat huddled wishing for light when he had the greatest light of all tucked away in his pocket.

It will only be this once, he thought to himself. *They're sleeping as it is. For all I know I might be saving us from some foul mountain beast, though I don't know what I would do except scream and wake them to defend me. Just this once. Nice and slow. Best not to wake them unless at need.*

Stepping beyond his companions, he removed the Key slowly from his pocket. Boldly the light of the sapphire and emerald jewels pierced the pent blackness, revealing a great distance behind and in front. Both ways were empty.

Trick of the eyes, Lucian Rolfe, he told himself. *I don't know why you're scared. And you had such a nice dream too, whatever that was about.*

Dawn came red, bringing cold light to the pass ahead. Orion woke with it, and prepared Godspeed with the energy of one who had been awake for hours. It was not long before the company set off again.

"Won't be long now," said Aries from behind Lucian and Orion. "I can almost smell them breakfasting in Ehrehalle. If we cover good ground perhaps we may join them for dinner!"

Leo grumbled inaudibly from behind. Orion smiled, but said nothing. Lucian, for one, was becoming fond of this group. He was starting to feel comforted by their company, for his trust in them was growing. Not even Goldbearer frightened him that much anymore.

The talk of dinner excited him, and having it alluded to as a feast rose his spirits even more. He meant to question

Aries about Ehrehalle's various dishes, but just then a raven swept down the pass and drew everyone's attention.

Then Lucian beheld one of the strangest occurrences he ever saw. In mid-flight the raven's shape began to change. Somehow its wings became elongated, and much denser as though riddled with bone. Now its tail feathers drooped downwards in long shadowy tendrils, and seemed to Lucian to resemble the lower folds of a dark shroud. Almost at once the raven was gone, and landing upon the pass with a brisk walking gait was a scraggly, pale-faced man with sallow cheeks and stringy black hair. A dark shroud indeed was over him, so large it seemed to double the size of his skeletal frame. His eyes were beady and black, as though they were the only features that remained of the bird from which he transformed. Striding earnestly toward them, he seemed ready to express something urgent.

"Eap," said Orion. "We expected to meet you on the plains."

All the while the company passed on. Eap skulked beside Godspeed, who of the three mounts was calmest. The strange news-bringer drew a gaunt, skeletal hand from his cloak and caressed the white horse's reign as if to lead him forward. Night-Treader snorted at this, perhaps urging the odd man away from his older brother. Meanwhile Goldbearer issued low grumbling growls that stretched until his utmost need of breath.

"You more than any should know not to expect *anything* from a raven," Eap replied smugly, his voice high and shrill as only a raven's might sound when using human speech.

"Right foul the lot of them," barked Leo from Goldbearer's back, whose lips were furled to reveal his clenched fangs. Perhaps the spectacle of seeing Eap become man unnerved the lion as well.

"Now, now, Lionsbane," said Eap, "it is all in good fun, I daresay. No need to get snippy, though your love of traveling is known to all. No doubt you'd want to bend a strong ear to my news, though."

"Then let us have it," said Leo impatiently. "Enough of this idle chatter." Goldbearer, whose growls intensified, seemed to agree with his master.

"Indeed, Eap," said Orion, softly and patiently. "I would have news of your experience over Enorméteren."

Lucian saw Eap nodding for many moments, as though recounting whatever he had seen before voicing himself. A look of strain came over his sunken face, and if at all possible, he seemed to grow paler.

At length he spoke. "Such experiences I have never had over those plains," he said. "Morgues were issuing from their caves in these mountains, flying south in great hordes."

"To Deavorás, no doubt," said Aries.

"Indeed, indeed," said Eap. "It seems the Fairy King's strength is mounting. Though Morgues are not keen of sight I worried they might glimpse your party fording the river. So it was I made myself present, like a flitting shadow over their assembly. They followed me, as I expected, perhaps thinking me a favorable omen. You know how they favor all things dark.

"So it was I ventured further west than I had planned, decoying them until they were forced to follow the Elarian to its nearest ford. This brought them many miles off their course, for they had been breaking with all speed toward the Ford of Six Marches and would have crossed the river in no time at all.

"One duty aside, I followed the Elarian to the Knobb and saw that your company had passed many hours before. That was when I caught wind of something fouler than I ever smelt as man or bird. From it I could conclude nothing save that it was evil, and perhaps the vilest thing to cross those plains in this age or the last. My search brought me southwest, almost to the base of the Ravelon cliffs, but it was worth the flight. There I saw, in a great file, Fairies, Morgues, and a slew of Fire Warriors bearing great carriages across the fields, upon which were some of the most perilous beasts yet known to this corner of the world.

"All of them lay limp, and I would have thought them dead if not for the direction in which they traveled. It is unlikely that Melinta seeks the pelts of five such creatures for the many cavernous halls of his tower. They are joining his ranks, Orion. A Wolf of Nine Tails there was, and a Minotaur, and two others unknown to my eyes. Yet there were none more horrible than the beast at the line's end, for he was the herald of all woeful creatures. Even in his slumber he seemed an instrument of death. His length exceeded four carriages, and the smells emitting from him were of sulfur and brimstone. Those vapors choked the air, and would have cast me from my flight had I not hastened away north with all speed.

"It was Ignis, Orion,"—and here his voice dropped to a shrill whisper, such as to avoid the wind carrying his words to the caravan from which he had scurried—"Sorcerian's Drake. The guardian of Parthaleon's very gates!"

Orion tensed in Godspeed's saddle. "You are sure of this?" Lucian had never thought his voice was capable of issuing such fear.

"There he lay before me," said Eap, as though he himself did not believe his own account. "Massive, bright, and red. His very scales were veined with cracks of flame. Drakes of Fire passed out of existence two ages ago—"

"Aye," Aries proudly interjected. "We helped expel them."

"And indeed you rid the world of their entire number," said Eap. "All, that is, but one. Something wicked is at work in Dridion, I warn you. Sorcerian must sense his victory is near at hand to dispatch his greatest servant so freely."

"Indeed," said Orion, as if to himself. "And where should his fury strike first, I wonder?"

"Adoram seems his likeliest course," Eap replied. "Mascorea's people pose the largest threat; this is no secret. It is told no foe has ever stepped foot beyond Détremon under the watch of the Sapphire Sons."

Lucian's heart leapt at these tidings, and his heart filled with worry for Gamaréa's people. Would they be warned? Would they be able to prepare?

"Drakes and beasts from all corners of the west, and Ignis amidst their number," muttered Orion. "I suspect Détremon's impregnability will be challenged in short time. The days have grown dark indeed."

"What do you mean to do?" asked Eap. Urgency flowed plainly in his voice.

Orion did not hesitate to answer. "We must get Lucian to Ren Talam at once. In Ehrehalle he can regain his strength, and we can rally ours. Sorcerian will not have taken the Ancient Order into account. Surely he is expecting resistance from Medric; this is to be expected. But from Ren Talam? He will not have counted us amongst his enemies."

"If he's counted us at all," said Aries.

"Precisely. In the meantime, Eap, I bid you watch the skies, and alert me of anything you find unusual. If an owl hoots strangely, I would have word."

Orion's voice had assumed a tone so stern and hardy that Lucian had no trouble visualizing him as the highlord he once had been. Upon Godspeed's back he seemed to sit taller, and his posture now seemed much prouder than it had a moment prior. Eap's beady eyes brimmed with admiration, and a subtle smirk played with the edges of his lips.

"My lord," he said, and nodded. "I will make it a point to alert every one of my order to this cause. Together we shall search the skies tirelessly, like an unwavering lidless eye."

Just then Leo's voice sounded from the rear of the line. "Not a good idea, Orion," he said sharply. "Right foul the lot of these shape-shifters. Never can tell who's to be trusted and who would sell you for a sack of gold in an eye-blink."

"I can," said Eap pointedly, raising an eyebrow in Leo's direction. "And I will call on them now, if it is your bidding, Orion."

"Do so," Orion answered. "If you can vouch for them they will be welcomed into my service. Send your crews skyward. I want the Elarian under constant surveillance from end to end, and I want eyes on Deavorás as well. Report to me weekly."

With that Eap went running up the pass, and with a deft leap reclaimed his raven form. Lucian still gave a start despite having expected it. He sat silent for many moments watching Eap bound towards the clouds.

"Yes, Eap takes some getting used to," said Orion, who

might have felt him twitch. "But he is an asset, and may prove a very pivotal one at that."

Lucian did not speak until several twists of the mountain pass were behind them. "Will you go to Medric?" he asked at random.

Orion gave a start. Lucian thought his question may have surprised him. Yet Orion gave no answer for some time. At length he said, "It may yet be so. I have long believed that our road would somehow lead to the gates of Adoram. Mascorea's people cannot stand alone against the storm that is coming."

"That's where I was going," said Lucian heavily. "That's where Gamaréa intended to lead me."

"And he was wise to do so, for I know of only one location that could offer you more shelter than Adoram, and we are nearly there."

7

The Prisoner's Tale

Gamaréa and his group made three such trips into Deavorás before dusk. They were not immediately escorted back to their prison, but instead were led into the main fortress for what he heard some of the prisoner's refer to as "muck hour"—also commonly known as supper. The gates were made of iron, blackened perhaps from the weathering years since they were forged, and they squealed when opened. Gamaréa was the only one of them to look up to the battlements, seeing for the better now the Matarhim legionnaires and the massive, bulky Morgues, their horns like thick, winding tree roots with sharpened edges.

The courtyard was a relatively square area, floored by the same decaying, swampy grass as was in the fields. The fortress rose up ahead of them, withering and grimy. Surrounding the courtyard entirely were low-hanging, metal roofs held up by old, gray pillars. They concealed the atriums in so much shadow Gamaréa had to squint to realize they were even there, but he saw them nonetheless—dimly lit mess halls, weaponries, and rooms clad with devises of torture, it seemed. *Wouldn't want to go in there,* he thought decidedly to himself.

But the mess hall proved to be their only stop, at least for now. They were brought to the eating area where each prisoner was issued the same thick, bubbly stew that Gamaréa was served earlier in his cell. The day's work, however, had instilled within him such an appetite that he consumed it in nearly one breath, neglecting the sour taste and rancid smell. Not long after he had finished eating, they were ordered to rise and form a line in which to march back to the barracks, and they did so in that very fashion.

In the night he lay across the floor so that he could stare into the small gleam of moonlight creeping in through his window. He heard Daxau humming a soft, melancholy song to himself, which would have lulled him right to sleep had it not been for his budding curiosity. Who was this man? What was his true story?

He stood up then and went to the forefront of his cell, clasping a hand upon one of the bars. "What song are you singing tonight?" he asked.

Daxau, whose back was turned, stopped singing, and Gamaréa thought to hear him sigh. "It is an old song," he answered, almost sadly. "My father taught it to me, and his to him, he said."

"Did you teach it to your son? Oliver is his name, right?"

Daxau was silent for many moments, and Gamaréa wondered if somehow his question offended him. "You don't sleep much, do you?" said Daxau at length.

Gamaréa took a good, hard look around him. "The sleeping arrangements aren't exactly ideal."

Daxau released something like a laugh. "Fair enough."

After a quiet moment, intercepted only by the distant chirps of crickets, Gamaréa said, "I might ask you the same question."

"I might give you the same answer."

Gamaréa was beginning to grow quite frustrated. "And so we're right back to where we started," he said.

"Started what?"

"Do you not have any friends or acquaintances? Shouldn't it thrill you to hear the voice of someone else inside this place?"

Daxau chuckled under his breath. "It quite possibly should."

"Yet it does not."

"I never said that."

"Then you imply it."

"Alright, then," said Daxau, who had clearly become as

frustrated as Gamaréa. "You really want to know about my son, is that it? Will it satisfy you to hear me speak of him?"

Indeed it would, Gamaréa wanted to say. But instead, he said only, "I think it would satisfy *you,* my friend."

And Gamaréa would not have known it, but deep within the soul of his brooding neighbor he struck a chord not touched for years. Daxau was starting to become content with his inner anguish. He had forced his thoughts to stray from his son for so long that he had forgotten what it felt like to think of him. It brought a smile to his face there in the sullen moonlight, though Gamaréa could not have known this either.

Daxau said nothing aloud, however. Instead he stood, and the moonlight shrouded his body in shadow. But when he removed his robe and shifted in such a way that his body was touched by the light, Gamaréa discerned multiple scars across his wide back. Some were small, almost unnoticeable red lines; others were long and swollen, and of a color distorted from his own skin. Then Daxau turned and took to sitting again, facing Gamaréa, his back pressed against the cold wall. Now Gamaréa saw scars across his muscled chest and abdomen—fierce wounds perhaps from battle, or perhaps from something else.

Gamaréa knew well that his inquiries were pricking Daxau's last nerve, but the man's numerous scars nearly stupefied him. He leaned forward eagerly, and whispered into the darkness almost involuntarily, "Your scars . . . "

"They are nothing," Daxau said shortly. "They are from a past life."

Gamaréa was quiet for a moment, much to the apparent satisfaction of the scarred man. But he was quiet with contemplation. Never before had he met someone so clouded in mystery. In a strange way it nearly made him realize how he himself was publicly perceived in his younger days. But for all his contemplation and speculation, he could think of no right answer, and so, though he wished to leave the man at peace, said, "Were you a soldier once?"

He heard Daxau sigh, like someone antagonized. "For a

time," he answered. "But if you are trying to inquire about my scars, I must tell you their tales are less honorable."

Gamaréa raised an eyebrow. "I'm not sure I understand."

"You will in time, neighbor."

"And what if I have none left?"

"Pardon?"

"Time. What if I have none left?"

"Are you ill?"

Gamaréa could tell that Daxau was a bit more attentive now. His posture against the wall straightened somewhat when it had been slouched; his voice was now clearer.

"No, no, nothing of that sort," assured Gamarea. "But I certainly am fixing to flee this place in the days to come. If I am successful our paths perhaps will never meet again. If I fail I will surely hang. Thus I ask you to tell me your story while you can! From one ship passing in the night to the other, I will hear of your tale or go to a restless grave."

Daxau seemed content now to speak of his scars. His voice gave no hint, and his mannerisms bore no sign, but Gamaréa felt as though hearing about his plot to leave saddened Daxau somehow. Perhaps he knew the unavoidable fate of those who tried to flee Cauldarím. That day among the other captives, Gamaréa heard countless stories of those who tried to flee and failed. Hundreds had attempted and every trial ended in ruin. Perhaps Daxau knew that Gamaréa's attempt would be no different.

Daxau cleared his throat. "Then I too would be restless should you fall without knowing. But I must tell you: it is a frightening tale."

"Speak as you will. I have had my share of frights."

Daxau began: "When I was brought to Cauldarím they conducted many fights at the arena a couple leagues east—"

"Arena? Its existence is true, then?"

"It is," answered Daxau, "but it is forbidden to even speak of. It's there, alright. You've never seen anything like it in all your long years, Son of Medric, however long your years may be. A vast entrapment made of stone-grey rock that looks as though it was freighted from the Darklands itself, with towering decks upon which spectators sit and watch and shout and jeer.

"They held a betting circuit there, where their strongest prisoners were forced to fight the most unearthly beasts the king had introduced to this side of the world—beasts of claw and fang; beasts of wing and talon; beasts of slime and thick, slithering coils . . . and dragons. I was one of the prisoners sentenced there. The king, I suppose, thought I would give good sport—"

"And did you?"

"I won the king much gold, and so, for a time, I was prized. I was the only one to outlast the games."

"And so they no longer wage these battles?" asked Gamaréa.

"Only on occasion. Lately they've occurred when representatives from other provinces of Dridion come to visit the king. He uses the fights as a form of entertainment. But no one has come to see him for a long time."

"And when they do, will you be called on to fight again?"

"Perhaps, and perhaps not. I think they may have shifted their focus to . . . others. In fact, perhaps you *would* do well to flee, as you've said was your plan."

Gamaréa's heart gave a start. "You imagine they would call on me?" he said dubiously.

"They are not the predictable sort, but I would say they are likely to. I have witnessed your strength, and from their high walls I'm sure they have as well. It would be easy to risk gold on the odds of your victory. After all, my time in the arena was successful, and I am just a common man."

Gamaréa thought to himself that Melinta would indeed fix to call on him to fight in the arena, should fights ever be waged there again. The king's dull mind was filled with hatred for him and all his kin; why would he pass up the chance to publicly humiliate him, and execute him at the same time?

But he excluded the matter from his mind. While it seemed somewhat practical, he minded a subject more at hand and dearer to him than battle. Who was the man he had been talking to this long? Where did he come from?

Such were the questions he asked himself and pondered in his lonesome when his neighbor was asleep, or when he dragged his heavy stone across the plains to Deavorás and was left with nothing but his pain and thoughts.

Daxau said he was a common man, but that was odd to Gamaréa. Though he was far from scholarly on the history of mortals in the West, he knew enough to recall their entire population crumbling during the reign of their last official king, and that was nearly two centuries prior. The remaining mortals were said to have either perished of famine and other diseases, or sojourned east to establish small villages, as did Lucian's family. But to encounter a mortal west of the Mid Sea was as rare as encountering a polar animal in the jungle. It simply did not make sense. *Why hadn't I thought of that before?* Gamaréa wondered to himself. Then he remembered why. He was too overwhelmed by his sudden predicament to completely comprehend anything, let alone mortal timelines and rises and falls of empires. But he was coherent now, and his thoughts were free to flow through him, and as much as he tried to refrain, his mind was bent upon this riddle.

"What army were you part of?" asked Gamaréa, breaking a moment of silence between them.

For a moment Daxau hesitated, not out of reluctance to speak the truth but out of inability to formulate his proper tale. "It wasn't exactly an army like you're thinking," he said at length. "I fought for myself, mainly."

Gamaréa was perplexed. "For yourself?"

"Yes."

"How do you mean?"

"It is hard to explain, literally and emotionally." He spoke with a manner that seemed weathered and exhausted. The deep bass of his voice rumbled gently from the adjacent cell like soft rolls of distant thunder, almost soothing.

"You don't have to speak of it, my friend," said Gamaréa. "I was curious is all."

"No," replied Daxau, almost contemplatively. "When I spoke to you about my son it—it made me feel at ease, almost. It's important, I think, to talk about these things .

. . so I am going to try talking. You and I are alike in many ways, and I feel if there is one set of ears worthy of my tale, it's yours.

"I'm not sure where to begin, so I suppose I shall start by stating that I never knew my mother. I was born into the only life I knew and raised by my father. Our life was hermitage. At the time it was the only life I knew, and so I was content and grateful above all else. We lived in the depths of some wood many hundreds of miles from here. I do not know its name. I may have heard it once but the name is lost to memory. Our small, makeshift cabin was rudimentary at best, but large enough for my father and me to fit in rather comfortably. We didn't have much in it save a small table my father built; so small that you had to kneel at it to eat anything. I preferred sitting outside on a stone by our fire-pit. At least that way my knees wouldn't burn from being pressed against the wood.

"Anyway, that is how we went on living. When I was old enough he showed me how to hunt and how to wield a bow. He also fastened long spears out of wood from the forest and showed me how to thrust properly. I developed quite a good one.

"I'm not sure how old I was at the time—I don't even know how old I am now—but before I was a man my father fell ill and died shortly thereafter. His death was difficult for me to bear. It was the first time I encountered such a thing, that I could remember, at least. I heard of my mother's passing, but only through stories my father shared. Now I was witnessing it before me, and I couldn't bear it. He coughed and wheezed for a week or so, spitting up blood and cursing his fate. He wouldn't eat, even though I managed to hunt well while caring for him.

"I'll never forget when he called me to his side before he finally passed away. It was sunrise, and I was preparing myself to hunt; hoping that my father would finally show some sort of appetite and eat so that strength would seize him again. Instead he grabbed on to my dirty, worn rags and pulled me close as if he had something of dire importance to say—one final word before he fell away into another realm of life—but his grasp subsided and his hand fell limp and the words he never said were left for me to forever ponder.

"The whole of that day I sat by his body and surveyed it intently. I wondered how a person, once they've died, seems artificial. I had heard mentioning of the 'spirit' of a person, but I never knew what that was or what it meant. I determined at that moment that I realized its meaning. While he was living, it seemed like everything else in the room was living. But once he died in that little old cabin, it seemed as though the room was darker, as if with his death came that of all else—the wood, the table, the fire-pit, the blankets; everything. It baffled me. It troubled me. I couldn't sleep. I couldn't eat. I didn't hunt for days after. After the day I spent by his corpse, I remained by the fire-pit for a long while without returning indoors. When I did his corpse was parchment-colored and his cheeks were sunken, and so I carried him atop my shoulder off into the distant wood. The one thing I remember vividly is his weight atop my shoulder. He was so light. I hadn't thought a grown man would be that light. But he was. I felt as though I was carrying a child.

"I suppose I was fixing to bury him. Where, and with what tools, I guess I hadn't considered, but it was no matter. I came upon a wide stream with a steady current and decided to cast him away by that watery road. I had brought the spear he had crafted for me when I was younger—the spear with which I learned to thrust and defend myself. But then I realized that he should be carried away on something—some sort of platform or mantle so that whoever perceived him flowing past their banks regarded him as he should have been regarded: as a passed king flowing on towards a kingdom of higher promise. And so I returned to the cabin with haste, where I broke off the top of the table he had built and laid his body upon it. Then over the spear I folded his cold, frail hands, and his body bore all the trappings of one sleeping. Then I set him adrift and watched until his makeshift barge was carried out of sight for my eyes to never see again."

Gamaréa had not noticed, but tears were beginning to run a slow course down his cheek. In all his long years, he had no account of his own father, yet Daxau had shared a special bond with his, and the story of his passing filled the Morok with grief. "My heart is broken for your loss," he said softly.

"Don't fill your heart with woe, my friend," answered Daxau firmly. "But allow me to continue: From then on I lived a reclusive life—or more reclusive, I should say. I went years without saying a word. There was no one to whom I could speak, thus making speech superfluous. Until one day, maybe some years later, a young boy wandered into my territory. He too could not speak a word. I'm not sure what stage of infancy he was in, but he could walk. He was dressed rather plainly. The tiniest woolen outfit I had ever seen before. I had not thought of the grandeur of human growth. *Was I once that small?* I asked myself. His face was a bit puffy, with little rosy cheeks. *What is this?* his little eyes seemed to be asking, innocent and ever inquisitive. *What is that?*

"In time I showed him everything my father showed me. As he got bigger, I named him and called him Oliver. I thought of him as my son. At the time, I could feel the beard upon my face and thought that I was man enough to accept the responsibility. It is an unfortunate decision I made. I was a man, but I wasn't ready. It was much too soon to emotionally commit myself to another bond. My love for Oliver developed in such a way that I actually believed I was his true father. It had to have been true, I kept telling myself. I was this boy's father. And one day, when I died, he too would cast me adrift in the stream through the woods—as all good fathers should be commemorated. It was like a dream for me—a dream that I had not realized I had dreamed, but nevertheless came true.

"Then one unfortunate day I decided to show him that stream. I felt as though he should have understood how important it was to me. But Oliver, ever curious, strayed into the water. On that particular morning, the current was oddly swift. I had never before seen it that cunning. I should have stopped the boy from wading in. I thought it would be nice for him to feel the cool stream on his ankles. Instead it swept him up from underneath and toppled him over violently. When I realized what was happening I leapt in after him and grabbed hold of his tiny wrist. But the boy's wrist was too slick to grip firmly enough, and soon the stream claimed him. I chased after his crying voice until I too was knocked off my feet and fell. The stream, however, subsided then, and I sat in the now slow-moving current listening as the cries of the boy faded into the distance and then ceased entirely.

"I mourned my son until I lost track of the days since he had perished. Then, after a time, it pained me so much to remember that day that I forced it out of my memory altogether. I did not reminisce on it again until I was first brought here. You have time to think about all sorts of things in here; things you didn't even know were in your mind. And so think I did."

When Daxau stopped talking Gamaréa noticed the way he himself was sitting: cross-legged, like a child listening to a riveting tale round a campfire. The man was an uncanny storyteller. There was something remarkable about his voice—that soft, deep, rumbling tone. Its reserve is what called him to attention, and its fervor held him there like some spell was cast over him, as the teller told his poignant tale to his audience of one.

"If I may," began Gamaréa softly, and through his wavering voice he could discern that he had remained very emotional. "How did you get here?"

"In time I lost touch with my home," answered Daxau sadly. "I was there and it was there, but I felt as though my heart was absent. Instead of security I felt only heartache. It reeked of tragedy and represented despair. In time I decided I needed to move on and go elsewhere. On a nomadic adventure I moved westward, without clue or recognition as to where I was going. In time, when the forest ended, I fell upon a small, outlying stronghold of Medric that spanned the Elarian. I cannot remember its name—"

"Hrothgale, surely," Gamaréa cut in. Though he had only been there once long ago, he knew no other Medran stronghold that had been built within range of the great river.

"It may be so, then," continued Daxau contemplatively. "The folk there were very generous and hospitable. At a boarding house of sorts I was able to sleep and eat for a while. The fact that I carried no coin on my person was no matter to them; I repaid them in service to their Lord. It was upon a routine surveillance mission that a small company of ours were flanked by Dridion troops and forced to surrender our horses and weapons. Then the lot of us were bound, man to man, and brought here in wagons."

Gamaréa wondered for a moment. Daxau's account was only growing stranger. He was a mortal, certainly. A mortal among nearly a thousand Moroks. It was a thing that Melinta could have easily overlooked. Daxau certainly blended in with folk of Medric: the broad shoulders, the hard facial features, the muscle-bound arms, torso, back, and legs. Having been captured among a company of Hrothgale soldiers worked to hide his identity further. But how such a thing could be was yet odd to Gamaréa. How could Daxau be all that remained of a race long exiled from this side of the world? *How indeed?*

It seemed like many moments passed before Gamaréa spoke again. "It is odd to me," he began, "that you are, assumedly, the last living western man. Do you understand that possibility?"

"If that is what you say, then I will not disagree," answered Daxau, as though speaking of a thing of as little concern to him as the flavor of his tea. "You perhaps hold better knowledge of those matters than I. But I will say that I do not care about that statistic. I am the last of several things."

A sudden thought attacked Gamaréa's mind, but it was so impractical that he dismissed it entirely with a small chuckle. *Impossible,* he thought to himself.

"You have no recollection of your family beyond your father, you said?" asked Gamaréa.

"None."

Gamaréa sighed. Daxau in time said he was exhausted from having spoken so much, for he hadn't spoken like that in many years; and so he retired, leaving Gamaréa to his lonesome.

Then the Morok crept away into the shadows of his cell and lay upon his back, resting a hand behind his head. He looked up at the ceiling, though it was pitch black. *I wonder what tomorrow will bring?* he thought to himself. He was pleased with the progress he and Daxau had made, and was glad that his neighbor felt comfortable sharing such a personal account with him.

He grimaced, though, for now that it was quiet he realized how sharply his waistline burned from the constant grip of the thick ropes with which he dragged his stones into the city. A wide, red-velvet imprint had formed along his pelvic area; yet as painful as it felt, it was all the more displeasing to behold. It took a long time to find a comfortable position, and even longer to find sleep.

8

Ren Talam

It was nearly dusk when the mountain trail opened before them. Once out of the shadows of the megaliths a fervent light bathed them, as though dark curtains had been thrown back to reveal the light of day. They had come to stand upon a wide plateau overlooking a rich, golden valley flanked by both arms of the Red Peaks. Scattered upon the valley's many folds were small streets of pavilions and cottages. Several passageways ran between them, branching off into other clumps of little dwellings, and on these small roads people were busying about their daily lives. It was truly the oddest place Lucian would have expected to find a fully functional community, but he welcomed the assuring feeling of company all the same. In many ways he was reminded of Amar, and he soon fell into the clutch of nostalgia. And though within range of the mountains' chilly night-winds, a great sense of warmth overcame him.

He could not explain it, but he felt no harm would find him here. Wandering the wilds for so long nearly made him forget how it felt to feel secure. Only in this moment did he realize how grave his heart had become, programmed almost irrevocably to see things for their potential evil uses or intentions. Yet this valley seemed to know only richness, growth, and hearth, as though it was secluded from all the trials of the world outside. It was as if the winding crescent of the peaks warded off any sense of danger, a cloak shrouding them from evil eyes. A long forgotten sensation made itself present in Lucian's heart, similar to being able to stretch your limbs after being cramped for so long.

The plateau gave way to a path on their right and delved down into the yellow-green foothills of the mountains. Godspeed whinnied as he approached the home he no doubt missed, and the others followed him briskly like hungry children called at last to supper. There amidst great bulging boulders they picked up a winding road that coursed along the outer arm of the Red Peaks. It was only then that Lucian saw yet another spectacle. Before his eyes was the unmistakable sight of Shír Azgoth, whose summit was highest. Like a general amidst his soldiers it stood tall, proud, and daring. Yet as Lucian's eyes coursed down its girth, he noticed there was more to behold. Filed from its very rock were two towering bastions of stone connected by an arching causeway. Beneath its cover was a high doorway from which issued the flicker of flames, and a smell rose through the open doors so mouthwatering that Lucian nearly began salivating.

"That must be Ehrehalle," he said, his voice quieted by rising astonishment.

"Right you are," said Orion proudly. "The Great Hall."

"And dinner smells like it's just about ready," added Aries wistfully.

In the light of the fading sun the Red Peaks seemed ablaze, like licks of flame made stone, and the road they followed brought them ever closer to Ehrehalle. Soon they were close enough that Lucian thought to hear many voices issuing from within, all filled with merriment.

"There are others here?" he asked at one point.

"Several," answered Orion. "Not including the folk of the valley, though we often welcome them amongst us."

"You mean to say you live here? In the mountain, I mean?" It had been Lucian's notion that Ehrehalle was only a congregational establishment. In measurement it was large, but how deep it delved was yet unknown to him. He was certain, however, that it could not possibly contain an inner community.

Yet Orion dismissed his theory fervently. "Of course, Mr. Rolfe!" he exclaimed. "Where else should we live? Ehrehalle was not built to serve as a mere kitchen. There is much you will find inside."

At once Lucian recalled the Mountain of Dreams, though in many ways it seemed a forgotten memory of someone else's haunted past. This was the first moment that he felt disquieted since entering the great valley, yet it quickly subsided—if it had been there at all—when a sweet song lifted from Aries's voice.

In mountain steep, o'er valley deep,
Within Shír Azgoth's crimson keep,
Through rocky shelves, a hall they delved
With golden vales outspread beneath.

Stones in wonder rent asunder,
Never seen o'er earth or under
Sage or Man a sight so grand
Than when high Azgoth roared with thunder.

Tools of old and hammers cold
Drove far into Azgoth the Bold.
In caverns dim and darkness grim
They lit their lightless paths with gold.

Their crafts were lent, and deep they went,
And well into the mountain rent
A hall so fair beyond the stair,
With every heart within content.

"There's more to it, mind you," he said as his song trailed off. "I always forget it though. Those are probably the best verses. I wouldn't have held on to them so long if they weren't."

"A collector of verses, he is," said Leo, not unkindly. "You'll find none more learned in song-lore than Aries here."

Lucian in truth never thought he would hear a song

of mirth again. As segmented as Aries's might have been, it soothed him as though it were at full length and given voice by fair maidens. Meanwhile the company passed on. Lucian found that the road to Ehrehalle was longer than he expected. It had seemed close enough from the plateau when he first set eyes on the Great Hall, yet heights and lengths conspired to deceive his perception. It was some time before they were close enough for Lucian to perceive any true detail. He could now see gray-clad watchers manning the bastions' crests. Some walked about the causeway directing the attention of their companions to the approaching riders. Soon a sound lifted mightier even than Goldbearer's roar, and it spread across the lower valley like wind in a wide field.

"The Horn of Ehrehalle," said Orion. "It feels like an eternity since I heard it last. The Knights Eternal call us home."

"The Knights Eternal?" said Lucian, not entirely sure that he meant to phrase it as a question. As their line drew closer he could see bright armor twinkling beneath their thick gray cloaks. Some stood with bows nearly equal to their height; others carried silver-pointed spears that glinted under the fading sun. Yet all looked down on them with pride in their stern faces. In unison they brought their free hand to their breast and swung it outward as though welcoming the newcomers into an embrace. So it was Orion gestured alike in answer.

"They are the heralded members of my order," said Orion. "Men so righteous have never grasped a hilt before, and perhaps never will again. Their number is few, yet I would call them to my aid before any army of hundreds."

And so under their watchful eyes they passed until they reached a high stair of many steep and lofty steps. It was here the company dismounted. Several people ran to greet them, and Lucian immediately noticed that they were dressed in tattered clothes. Some wore old tunics and frayed breeches. Their faces were age-worn and grim, though only joy could be detected in their eyes.

"My lords! My lords!" they shouted as they came, like

children welcoming their fathers home.

"Ah, my good men!" said Orion genially. "At long last we have come, and it smells as though you all have been busy in Ehrehalle."

"Indeed we have, milord," answered a skinny balding man. Sweat was beaded upon his brow and there was dirt in the small crevices of his wrinkles. "Wanted to have the feast prepared a'fore milords returned, but that's been botched. Almost ready though, it is."

"Do not trouble yourself with haste," said Orion kindly. "It is enough that you have come up from Dwén Marnié to lend your learned hands to our kitchen, Halag."

Halag's face brimmed with delight, and he groped to receive the first packs.

"Now, now," said Leo gruffly. "Plenty here to go round, mind you. And we've got arms too, you know."

"Our lords have had a long journey," said a scrawny, young-looking man. "It would be a great discourtesy to leave them to their own packs." He issued a crooked-toothed, yellow smile and blew some greasy golden locks out of his eyes.

Soon Halag and the others scampered up the high stairs laden with the baggage of the riders. In their ascent they passed two handsome looking men that Lucian noticed to be dressed alike to the watchers above, if not of their company themselves. Yet their cloaks were unveiled to display glittering plates of silver and gold. Upon their hands were fair glinting gauntlets and on their breast was the white sigil of a four-pointed star that seemed to be exploding.

"Highlord Orion," said the first with a bow of his head. His stare was sterner than the other's, and the features of his face more square. To his shoulders his dark-brown hair flowed smoothly, some tendrils of which were garnished with gold braids.

"My good Camien," answered Orion. "And I see Bravos is among the first to greet us."

"Indeed, highlord," answered Bravos with a bow. His golden hair was of a darker hue than Aries's, and though his face was ageless like the rest of his kindred, something about him suggested to Lucian that he was young and less careworn than the others. "I would not miss your return, valiant as it is, and from so perilous a road."

Then Bravos turned to Aries and Leo and smiled. "I see the extra baggage you brought did not hinder your task."

"Come now, good Bravos," said Aries, locking arms with the other, "jealousy is a trait best left to recruits."

"I'd watch that tone, young Bravos," said Leo. "It's been long since Goldbearer had a sufficient meal." At the mention of his name, the lion grumbled.

Camien laughed. "Indeed he will have his chance to claim it, if he wishes," he said. "We have come to show your fine mounts to their lodgings, if you would permit us."

"Indeed," said Orion. "Be sure to see that they are rewarded food and drink enough to fill them. They have endured a tireless flight from Ravelon with little respite."

"Of course," answered Camien, bowing. Then he gently took the rein of Godspeed, who fidgeted briefly before consenting to be borne. His allowance of Camien's guidance seemed to reassure Night-Treader that all would be well in his master's absence, and he followed his brother willingly. Leo, however, had to walk with Bravos halfway down the hill to the path leading to the lodging of the steeds. All the while he spoke to Goldbearer like a father reprimanding a child. "You be good now, you hear? Or you'll have me to answer to." Before long Leo deemed it safe to leave him to his temporary keeper, and they passed away and out of sight without trouble.

There at the base of the steps stood Lucian, who in the company of Camien and Bravos had felt small and quite ordinary. It was reassuring to know that there were more men like Orion and his companions, but they were a stern folk, and he soon longed for the company of Gamaréa. Within moments the stair was teeming with folk filing out from within. In time they lined the thick stone banisters excitedly, both in praise of the three riders' return and in welcome of Lucian's coming. As he walked up beside Orion he heard the din of their many voices, but he could distinguish some words among the maelstrom. "From the East," some were saying. "He has come," others whispered. Suddenly a chill enveloped him. He felt exposed and naked before their eyes, and he could feel blood rush to his face in embarrassment. All eyes fell on him unblinkingly, and it felt as though an unwavering spotlight held him captive in its sight.

Despite the heaviness that was welling up inside him, it in truth was a joyous moment. The folk of Ehrehalle did not mean him harm at all, and expected nothing more from him than his company at their feast. Yet a nagging sense of duty boiled in his blood, as though the many watching eyes expected something more, something wonderful, some spectacle he was incapable of showing them. Perhaps it was because he walked in the great shadow of Orion, who was loved by all, and looked on as a king returned from war. Or maybe it was the reality that he was unaware of any melodies outside of poorly written pub songs, and could not hold a candle to Aries's love of music and poetry. There were indeed many contributing factors to Lucian's sense of inadequacy, but he carried up Ehrehalle's many steps nonetheless, and the folk within celebrated his coming.

Their climb was slow and delayed by excited guests. Some of Orion's men came forward out of the bustle and welcomed the three riders home. Men and women from the valley below were present also, and some even threw roses at their feet as they passed. Children ran and played, excited to be at such an altitude looking at their little homes from above. Orion and his men always infatuated them, and some took up sticks and twigs and fought with them like swords.

When at last they reached the doorway Lucian peered into Ehrehalle for the first time. He saw a lofty, cavernous room, filled with blocks of long tables. Small wooden streets ran between these and joined the main passage in the center. Thrice the amount of people who had come to greet them were present now. Many were tending unlaid tables or carrying great casks or platters of cooked or uncooked meats. Along the perimeter of the room were several tables laden with fine-smelling delicacies. It was the most food Lucian had ever seen gathered in one place, more even than at Mary's inn during holidays, and yet more was spread out by the minute.

Several musicians were scattered about. Men and women with viols stood together in a far corner and tuned their instruments while the chirping flutists played sweet tunes on theirs. Ladies were singing, gentlemen were chanting, children were playing or taking up verses. It was the most cheerful place Lucian had ever seen, and he soon forgot his prior woes as if they had never been. A sense of belonging abruptly fell over him like a warm blanket, and for the first time since Ehrehalle came in his sights, he smiled.

"That's what I like to see!" said Aries, patting Lucian on the back rather roughly. "I was beginning to wonder if you would show *any* sign of emotion. Ehrehalle can brighten the gloomiest spirit. And if it doesn't, well, I daresay you don't have one!"

Together the foursome traversed the length of the Great Hall down the main aisle. Soon Aries and Leo parted from them, falling into conversations or songs with friends long missed. Lucian was not sure of Ehrehalle's true length, but it felt like a great while before he reached the opposite end with Orion. Here were filed many busy ovens and blazing furnaces. Butchers chanted in an assembly line of knife-wielders, sending their filets down the rows to be cooked. The traffic from here was heaviest. Men both of Orion's order and the valley below were walking in with raw meats and out with sizzling platters to add to the long buffets.

"There will be a time for feasting," said Orion when he finally had a moment to speak. "But first we must get you out of those clothes and into something new. You are our guest of honor, after all."

At the very end of the Great Hall were three high archways that opened to branching corridors. Orion opted the leftward pass, and Lucian soon found himself in a long corridor of blue stone, lit by braziers alive with blue flame. It was not as Lucian expected an artery of a mountain to look or feel. The braziers boasted a great, pale light, and as such he soon forgot that evening was approaching. Beneath them the floor seemed made of fine marble, and Lucian wondered if a grand palace of old had stood here only to be overrun by the sprouting of the mountain.

In time the long corridor widened and the doorways of many rooms flanked them. All doors were made of heavy oak and plated with gold, and in and out hurried guests, knights, and other strange folk either going to or coming from the preparations in the Great Hall. All smiled or said hello as Orion and Lucian passed together, but neither made a point to break for conversation, until at long last Orion reached his destination and turned to Lucian. "I have brought you to my chambers," he said. "You have my leave to treat it as your own, though you will be given lodging soon enough."

With that they entered, and the room was wide and decorative and garnished with many fine furnishings. Against one wall was a sturdy four-poster bed, the feet of which were shaped to resemble the clawed paws of a lion. Thick blankets of various furs were nestled neatly and tightly over the mattress, and Lucian longed immediately to wrap himself inside one, for they had delved deep into the heart of Azgoth where the warmth of Ehrehalle could not go. The floor was made of gray stone, gleaming blue for the light of the braziers on the wall. In the midst was a wide-open hearth laden with fresh wood ready to burn, and Orion was quick to set it ablaze. As it grew, Lucian came to stand before it, spreading his hands over the flames and wishing the cold away.

"Fire at last," said Orion. He had gone to stand beside his bed.

"At last is right," said Lucian. "I thought I'd never be warm again when we were up in those mountains, and I was reminded of that feeling when we stepped foot in here."

Orion laughed. "It takes some time to get acquainted. Being native to these climes, I sometimes forget the affect the height of Azgoth has on outsiders."

Then Orion came to stand across from him, and Lucian

saw that his clothes were different. The breastplate he had worn was replaced by a well-fitting crimson tunic, brandished with the same emblem from Camien's and Bravos's armor. Also he wore a pair of black breeches and boots to match. Lucian gaped at how different he appeared now that his battle-attire was cast aside. Now be believed he gazed upon Orion, the man, as his children might once have seen him, rather than Orion the highlord.

"I have set out clothes for you to wear," he said happily. "You may wear whatever you find comfortable. Tomorrow we will walk in the vale of Dwén Marnié and see if we can't have your own clothes washed. For now, my wardrobe is yours. You will find I have acquired quite the collection over the years."

There was in fact a closet the size of Mary's kitchen for Orion's wardrobe alone. Lucian would not have been surprised if he owned more articles of clothing than all the girls in Amar put together.

"It is a marvel, is it not?" said Orion when Lucian walked out of his closet with a wide-eyed expression. "I do have far too many clothes, despite often handing them down to citizens of the valley, who welcome them as kingly gifts. You will find many of them dressed valiantly this evening, I presume, and you will match them!"

Before long Orion returned to the Great Hall and Lucian had privacy at last. He could have cared less about clothes at that moment. In the warmth of the bellowing hearth he was overcome with heavy weariness, and he hopped on Orion's bed and lay there on his back. He had almost forgotten what it was like to have a mattress under him. Not since Elderland had he known such comfort, but Elderland was now a distant memory.

The hearth warmed the chamber sufficiently. As he lay, Lucian watched the tendrils of gray-blue smoke climb to the rafters before rising through a vent in the ceiling. The calming ambience of the dancing flames nearly lulled him right to sleep, and he desired in his heart to remain there forever. Now again a foreboding feeling played with his nerves. He did not wish to be the guest of honor at this feast, to have all eyes on him again. It made him uncomfortable, though his companions seemed to encourage it.

"There's nothing for it," he said to himself. "I might as well get dressed and be off. Otherwise I'll probably have a search-party come knocking at the door, and that would be much more embarrassing than going off on my own."

Sitting up was difficult after so much comfort. Standing now upon the warm floor he looked at the bed like a dear friend he was to leave behind. Unclasping Excebellus from his belt he lay the sword upon the mattress in its gold-etched sheath. Even in the faint gleam of the far-off blaze its bright hilt glinted, and the crescent of gems along the pommel seemed as though little balls of flame themselves. A strange feeling came over him then, and he took up the sword at once and unsheathed it. The scream of revealed steel briefly echoed through the room, and Lucian looked on the fine blade in wonder and awe as though noticing it for the first time. It felt like a feather in his hand, yet bore as much brawn as any other lordly weapon. In the polished steel he saw a blurry reflection of himself and the throbbing fire, and he caressed a finger along the fuller as one might stroke the cheek of a loved one.

When he sheathed Excebellus at last it felt as though the world stopped, or that a great light had been extinguished. As his hands were clasped around its hilt he felt worthy even of Orion's company. Now that feeling seemed as though a dream on the cusp of recollection, and he looked at his empty hands with the same insecurity as he had since his departure from home.

He undressed quickly and with frustration. First came his green travel cloak, the bottom lip of which was worn away, then his frayed and tattered shirt, which had once been long-sleeved. There were now weatherworn holes in the left shoulder, and the sleeve of the right arm had been ripped off, and ended in wispy frays at the elbow. His collar was burnt and tattered from when the Matarhai soldier grasped him in Ravelon. Aside from this it was stained awfully. Blood and dirt and grime were everywhere, so that he nearly forgot what color it had been when he first put it on.

"Mary would have a thing or two to say if she could see this now," he said to himself. A small smile came to his face as he folded the shirt as best he could and set it down on the floor. Next came his breeches, which were equally worn. A vast majority of their travel-wear came from his escape from the Matarhim. The bottoms were ripped and jagged now, and the cloth over his right knee was completely gone. Being made of brown fabric, dirt smudges and things of that sort were not as noticeable. However there were streaks of blood, and soiled spots from bogs and mud.

Making as if to cast these to the floor, a sudden realization came into his head. "I almost forgot," he whispered. Then from the right pocket of his breeches he brandished the Key, and suddenly the red-orange blaze from the hearth was overthrown by radiant lights of emerald and sapphire. Lucian quickly turned it over, smothering the Key into the mattress. Despite being stifled the lights fought to shine, leaking out of the infinitesimal gap between them and the bed.

"That was wise," said a voice from the doorway. Lucian gave a start, and released his grip on the Key. Now that the pressure of his hold subsided, the lights shone from under the pillow a little more fervently.

There, lit by the gleam of the hearth, stood a short woman dressed in a fine purple robe. Plumes of white fur lined her collar and the cuffs of her sleeves. Her face was hard yet fair, and her eyes were keen and searching, such as Lucian felt strangely that she had the power to see through him. In a strange way that stern glance reminded him of Mary, and how her eyes would bore into him when he was up to mischief. Across her brow she wore a circlet of silver flowers, beyond which her black and shining hair flowed back into a tight braid.

It had been a great while since Lucian saw a woman face-to-face, though for all his recollection he could not remember one so breathtaking. He felt oddly cold, like the woman's very presence chilled him to the bone as her dark and questioning eyes unblinkingly pierced him. It was not long, however, before he remembered he was naked.

"I must say I presumed Orion Highlord would have chosen a better outfit for you to wear this evening," she said sharply.

Lucian scuffled on the bed for something to cover himself with, and found the shirt Orion laid out for him.

"I'm sorry, miss," stammered Lucian, embarrassed nearly to breathlessness. "I didn't expect company."

"Clearly."

An awkward silence fell between them in which only the sporadic crackle of the hearth was heard. "I'm Lucian," said Lucian at length.

"Pleasure," said the woman shortly. "I am Ursa. The celebratory event will be underway within the hour, and I have been asked by Orion to seek you out and lead you to the bath chambers, if you will."

"The bath chambers?"

"Indeed. You have been traveling for four months or more, I don't doubt, with nothing to cleanse yourself but a modest spring where you could find it. You stink, I daresay."

Not much for subtlety, are you? "I guess I could use a nice bath," said Lucian contemplatively. He had been so used to open roads, fresh air, and the stench of horses and other creatures that he had not even become aware of his own lack of cleanliness.

"You guess correctly," said Ursa, in a manner much too snippy for Lucian's taste. "I have procured these for you to wear on our way." She tossed him a robe of rough cotton, with which he was quick to cover himself. "Now, if you would follow me—and at a distance, please."

Ursa walked at a haughty pace, sweeping round the bends of the corridor deeper into the mountain. Lucian could not help but wonder if there was some magic at work, for the corridor seemed to unfold before them as they passed. Whenever he thought it was sure to end there was more ground laid before them, and more bright braziers affording them wonderful light by which to walk.

At length he heard the sound of fountains and saw arms of clear steam flowing towards them.

"You will find all you need in here," said Ursa, standing at the entrance of a wide room. "Choose any bath you prefer, but do make it quick. These pools will cleanse you in seconds, though the longer one lingers the more difficult it is to leave. Do not defy these instructions, Lucian. It would be a great hassle to come and fetch you. Ehrehalle is far from here. I do not desire to make the journey more times than necessary."

With that Ursa left him and swept off briskly down toward the Great Hall. Lucian was alone. Stepping cautiously into the bath chamber, he looked around him. The room was indeed wider than he thought. Blue stone encompassed it from the floor to the arching ceiling, and beyond it fell away into shadow. Row upon row of circular marble pools stretched beyond and into the gloom. In the midst of every pool was a great fountain, fashioned in the likeness of some beast or person. The one nearest him was of a massive, bearded man holding a staff aloft in his left hand and brandishing an indomitable sword in the other. Though blank, Lucian could not help but feel as though his eyes contained a thriving flame, and that beneath his bulging chest a fierce desire was housed.

How long he stood gaping at this display he did not know, but soon he gave a start and remembered the reason he had come. Thus removing his robe he stepped into the pool. Instantaneously a replenishing sensation of warmth enveloped him. He felt all his aches, pains, and weariness dissolve from his body as though they had been great weights suppressing his limbs. And all the while his eyes still bore into the fountain-figure, just as the figure's eyes bore into him.

Suddenly a voice rose up from the entranceway. "Best not to tarry now!" Lucian spun round quickly, as though startled out of a dream. There stood Aries leaning against the wall, arms folded and a smile on his face. "I see Ursa has left you unattended."

"Yeah," said Lucian. "I think that was for the best."

Aries chuckled. "She grows on you, if you let her. I've been sent to fetch you. When we heard that she left you alone Orion sent me to make sure you were still afloat. And here I find you alive and well, however pruned. Feast is nearly underway. Best get yourself situated and join us. They'll be looking for you, after all."

"Who's *they?*" asked Lucian wearily.

"Well *every*body, of course! I'd be glad to escort you down, if you'd like."

Lucian thought for a moment. "I think so," he answered. "I left my clothes in Orion's chamber. I'll have to go there to get dressed. If you don't mind—" Lucian made to get out of the pool, and Aries quickly turned round. Now Lucian wrapped himself in his robe and was ready.

Together they carried on down the corridor, busy now with folk filing toward the Great Hall. Many were singing or talking lively. Sometimes Aries would join in when he heard a melody to his liking. All but Lucian seemed to be in high spirits, though he tried not to let it show. It was not entirely his nerves upsetting him anymore. This time it was something different: something he could not explain. The only vision in his mind was the tall figure in his pool, yet he was uncertain why it was troubling him so.

"You look sickly," said Aries suddenly. "Are you going to be alright?"

Lucian flushed. "I'll be fine," he said shortly. Then for a brief moment he made as if to inquire about the fountain and the room of many baths, but he concealed his question and remained silent.

"Have it your own way," said Aries as they came to the doors of Orion's chamber. "I'll wait here."

So it was Lucian dressed in the attire Orion provided. There was a tunic of soft red silk, embroidered across the chest with the white star of his order, as well as a pair of fresh and sturdy brown breeches. A pair of light boots made of soft velvet was standing near the bedside, and beside these sat a sturdy leather belt, which Lucian fastened across his waist. Dressed and ready, he made as if to depart, when suddenly he remembered the Key. Still its lights were moderately stifled between mattress and pillow, but he did not think it wise to leave it out in the open."Best keep it on my person, then," he surmised. "That way I won't have to worry about it being snatched or anything like that."

Thus with it pocketed he met Aries outside the doorway, and the two brought up the rear of the last line into Ehrehalle.

9

A Change of Wardens

"I have a surprise in store for you, my son," Melinta had said when he left his balcony with Didrebelle as evening approached. The last groups of prisoners had finally unloaded their shipment and were staggering back across the city to Cauldarim, and a red sun was beginning to drag the pink-velvet sky slowly to the depths of the world beyond the mountains.

The surprise was indeed nothing worthy of praise. In fact, if anything, it was quite predictable. Once Melinta had said, "Follow me!" Didrebelle knew where he was going to lead him.

Now he stood inside his old bedroom alone. The only surprise for Didrebelle was that it had remained untouched, except for the areas that were obviously cleaned regularly as to not accumulate dust. His large, ovular window was brighter than ever, displaying for him the entire splendor that Dridion was. He saw the evening sky painted over the emerald fields outside the city, and the glistening stream, glinting with crimson every so often as its ripples caught the light of the fading sun. It was undoubtedly the best view in the palace.

His large bed with white sheets draped over the sides was as he remembered, and the golden frame upon which the thick, fluffy mattress sat had been polished and shined regularly, it seemed. He could not touch it, however. He longed not even to go near it. But he was direly exhausted. His eyes were perhaps heavier than they had ever been, and, though attempting to refrain, he fell upon the bed and sunk within the sheets and the soft pillows until he was overcome by dream.

The next morning, before his father could fetch him for breakfast, Didrebelle ordered a horse be saddled and ready in the courtyard so that he may ride into Cauldarím and inform the warden of the change that was about to be made. It was a dank fortress and smelled rotten, but he maintained a high chin as his hard, blue eyes scanned the perimeter for the room where the so-called warden might be sitting. A guard led him to his sought location, and he came upon arguably the most grotesque creature he had seen to that point in his life—aside from dragons, of course—sitting in a creaking chair.

It looked more like an insect than any living being he had ever beheld, its neck long and segmented like a centipede—only a seven-foot tall centipede with muscular arms and legs that made a squishing sound when they moved. It wore an armor-plated vest with leather flaps over where its genital region would be, and when it stood it towered over him, menacing and proud, and abhorrently reeking.

The guard introduced Didrebelle meekly. "Warden," he said, his voice quivering, "the—er— Prince of Dridion, Didrebelle son of Melinta, brings word from the king in Deavorás." With that he hastily left the small cell of a room, and Didrebelle and the creature stood alone an arm's length apart, its stature overwhelmingly broad as it loomed over Didrebelle's lean and lanky frame, peering down on him with attentive, beady eyes.

So this is it, Didrebelle thought. He had fallen into his father's trap and thought he could fool a fool. But that fool had been foolish a lot longer than he, and knew how to devise treacherous plots to net those trying to defy him. He would not be tricked by anyone, most certainly his long-lost son, and none would stand in the way of his ultimate goal. How could he have expected Melinta to believe his makeshift tale? Not even he could believe it now that he reran it through his mind in the moments before he would be ripped in half by this brute.

This was it. The beast approached and lifted its huge, green-muscled arm—

And gently moved Didrebelle aside. Moving passed him now, the creature stooped to the ground to pick up something small that must have fallen before Didrebelle's arrival. His heart sat racing in his chest as the creature turned around. "Well?" he said, not impatiently, a voice like the low buzzing of a hundred wasps. "You bring word from Deavorás?"

"I do," answered Didrebelle reluctantly. Then he tried to muster a way he would relieve this monster of its duties without causing it to act rashly. "It seems as though the king is making a change in this camp's leadership," he continued, nearly stammering.

He could discern upon the beast's expression (for what expression was visible on its distorted, insect-face) a hint of confusion.

"The king requests your presence in Deavorás," he continued. "For the time being, I will take over as warden."

The beast laughed. "You?" it jeered. "The young prince, come to relieve an old prison warden of his duties? I must say, you didn't seem like the joking type. How fooled was I?"

"I do not joke, Warden. This matter is of serious business. The king requests your presence at once."

"Is that so, then?" The beast came closer, apparently agitated. Didrebelle gulped, but his feet stayed put as the warden drew up to him, its large chest nearly flush against his own. "The wandering son returns and Father suddenly sees fit that he takes the job of a veteran. How appropriate. How appropriate Melinta gives this order, the fool that he is."

Didrebelle said nothing, and the warden noticed his expression hadn't changed. "Yet you say nothing to defend your father, while here I insult him? Are you afraid, son of Deavorás? Do you fear I would rip you in two?"

Didrebelle, though completely against backing down from challenges, said nothing, and stepped aside as to allow the warden passage out of the room. "Deavorás," he said softly, and not unkindly, "requests you."

The warden was appalled at Didrebelle's composure, hoping for him to either break and crumble at his feet or pose a challenge. But the prince did neither. Instead he simply opened the way for his departure, and, without much knowledge of what else to do, the beast hissed and snickered his way out the door until his large frame disappeared through the main gate to never be seen in that side of the west again.

Then Didrebelle was left to his office alone, though it was not much of an office. It was a small room with gray walls and a small barred window carved into the upper right wall. The chair, sticky with residue where the warden had sat, remained a few feet away from him. He decided to venture out into the main hall to take in his surroundings. A small number of Dridion soldiers were busying about. He was glad to see that no members of the Matarhim were present, but he could smell them plainly as if they had been. They were perhaps patrolling the perimeter of the fortress and the battlements. Some Morgue officers were walking about in the mess hall through the overhang left of the main hall.

Disgusting, he thought. He remembered when Cauldarím was an open expanse of glistening emerald fields where life was plentiful. There was once a great artery of the Elarian that ran along the base of the cliffs to the east, but it was swallowed up by the earth long ago, and was now nothing more than an overstretched, barren ditch. It was in those fields now cluttered with prisoners that he learned how to ride his first horse and shoot his first arrow. Now it was a deteriorated mass of yellow, dirty grasses, corroded by iron-shod feet and evildoings.

What am I in for? he thought to himself. His current position suddenly seemed overwhelming. He was the acting warden; therefore he had to do what wardens typically did. But what was that? He knew nothing about the work of wardens, except of course that they were the overseers of large prisons. Was he supposed to walk around the fields and inspect the separate stations or the separate buildings? Was he supposed to assure that everything was running smoothly? He didn't even know *what* was "running" and how it would look when running "smoothly" compared to disorderly.

Suddenly the voice of a guard woke him from his moment of deep contemplation, and waking from his thoughts he looked upon the speaker. He had never seen this guard before, but then again he hardly recognized any of the Fairy soldiers present. "Shall I take you round the prisoners' quarters, Warden?"

Didrebelle almost did not realize he was the one the speaker was addressing. "Yes, soldier," he replied hesitantly. "Take me there indeed."

There was a white tower, far but glinting under a sweltering sun around which were no clouds—no remnant of anything save an eagle flock stretching across the sky, their bodies but shadows against the pounding rays, their motions slick and calm and smooth as they flew beyond the tower. And their shadows upon the ground seemed too large to be natural, yet they were natural, or could have been. Loud and triumphant stretched their fleeting song, and in the far distance he heard the faintest of voices. It was the voice of memory, and, perhaps, of reason too. And the familiarity of it brought him to attention, for he was no longer in that place but another place—a dark place, a place of musty stench and blank expressions; a place as far from serene as the tips of East and West. Yet the voice was steady and melodic and provided hope even in that most forsaken of places.

Gamaréa suddenly shook himself awake, trying to recall his dream. But he could recount only images—pointless, faceless images—and his mind became riddled with thoughts and questions. The one constant recollection coursing through him was the voice he had heard. He knew he had heard it before. But where? *Wait!* he thought. *Is that it again? But surely I am not still dreaming.*

It in fact was not a dream, for in time he heard the voice rise in both volume and relevance, and to his utmost bewilderment he saw Didrebelle pass through the corridor, clad in the emerald, gold-embroidered raiment of Dridion, flanked by two other Fairy guards as they crossed the hall laughing merrily.

Gamaréa's initial reaction was not one of anger but of sympathy. He knew the rebellious Fairy well enough to know how much he hated his father. He knew also that he disagreed entirely with every theory and philosophy in which his father believed, and in every law he enforced. He pondered then the unfathomable toil Didrebelle had to endure whenever the thought of his father presented itself.

Didrebelle walked on down the hall, his voice carrying off until it faded entirely. Perhaps a half hour or so later he heard it approaching again, and like an enclosed pup crawled over to the door of his cell and wrung his hands around the bars so that he could see his companion for the better. He looked the same, though Gamaréa was not entirely sure what change he expected to see in his friend. He forgot then that it was not an eternity since they separated, but merely felt like one.

Though a matter of seconds, it seemed like one frozen instant that the two locked eyes. And Didrebelle Dragontamer noticed the pleading in his companion's gaze as he knelt there on the dirty, disgusting floor looking up at him solemnly, condemned to the filth and rotten realm of the prison camp. So too did Gamaréa notice the sternness in his friend's glare as he tried to maintain cover so that his colleagues would not discover his true allegiance. But for a moment it seemed so authentic—the hatred between the two countries, separated by war and petty differences. In that long, surreal moment, Gamaréa believed the hatred and understood it, knowing why the two realms could never come to peace. He no longer saw Didrebelle before him but a reflection of Melinta, and had the bars not been so thick—had most of his strength not been depleted—he perhaps would have leapt at him. But he could only watch as Didrebelle passed him by and walked back into the fields, the large doors of the quarters closing loudly behind him. He crept back into the shadows of his cell, depressed and unable to think. An overwhelming sadness consumed him, and the realization that he was alone and left to die there in that cell became all too real.

It took nearly half the day for Didrebelle's colleagues to give him the tour of the entire prison camp, and his mind was flustered for nearly the entirety of it. He was unable to think or perceive anything clearly, for the very first barrack he visited was Gamaréa's. The building was shaped in a horseshoe fashion and was dark even in the midst of morning. Sunlight was molested by the little windows in each cell, and only a small fragment of light was able to peer through each one. It was dank and quiet, for the majority of the prisoners were out in the fields. But there were some that had yet been summoned, such as the prisoners in Gamaréa's block. Thus, to his sorrow, his companion was present when Didrebelle walked by, and he saw him staring helplessly like a child, his eyes brimming with tears, his beard and hair disheveled; a deteriorated shell of the unrivaled warlord he had come to know. But with difficulty he maintained his poise—or tried to—and acted as one in his father's league, so that the guards flanking him would not suspect his fell intentions. More than anything he wanted to slip back behind them and assure his companion that all was well and that he was even fixing to free him. But the guards never left his side, and he could only gaze sternly at the Morok trapped helplessly in his cell with a face alike to the guards. Into the light he carried on, visiting the other barracks throughout the morning and into the afternoon. But the image of Gamaréa never left his mind or heart, and worked to peril him. When his tour concluded he returned to the fortress and sat in the slime-covered chair, weeping behind his closed door.

10

The Warden's Whip

For the remainder of that day, Gamaréa could not feel the tug of the rope pulling at him. Seeing Didrebelle had disheartened him for many reasons. Firstly, his presence there meant Lucian was alone somewhere in the forest, which was probably being watched more keenly since they had been discovered; and secondly, of course, it meant that Melinta was not holding a grudge against his son for having exiled himself long ago.

The mission could not afford to lose Didrebelle's allegiance. He knew too much information about their itinerary, and could easily reveal their true plan to his father. Then the entire mission would be undone. The thought of such things racked his mind as he walked along, worrying him to the extent that he hardly felt the burning of the heavy rope against his chafed waistline.

Every now and then, Gamaréa would snap back to reality. The sun was flowing freely through a cloudless sky, and the fields below were unbearably humid. He was drenched in sweat, his meager rag of a shirt clinging to his body as though he had just emerged from a pond. But he did not make a sound. At times, it felt like he was not even breathing. Like a newly risen undead body he slugged toward the white city, adding his freight to the others when he arrived.

On each trip he looked up to Melinta's tower, the shadow of which hung over the prisoners like a cloud. But this time he saw him standing there, proud and tall, his glowering dark eyes observing them. But Melinta's presence did not unnerve him, and he stood alone when all others had started back, planting his feet and meeting Melinta's gaze. No word was spoken, but there was a distinct hatred in Gamaréa's eyes, raging more hotly than the unveiled sun. Melinta, he thought to see, simply smiled.

During muck hour Gamaréa ate little. His stomach would simply not accept food, let alone the insufficient crud served to the prisoners. That is not to say, however, that he was not hungry; he was staving, in fact. His emotions were simply too riled to take in any kind of meal. Thus, Gamaréa retired to his cell, hungry and cold, and crept up into the shadows away from the moonlight etching in from his little barred slit of a window.

Never in his wildest dreams could he have imagined the impact seeing Didrebelle would have on him. At one point he wondered if he would ever see him again at all. Gamaréa felt as though he should have been excited, ecstatic, relieved—but he found himself only vengeful and upset.

Why would he dare leave Lucian alone? he constantly asked himself. *He is smarter than that.*

But then his heart dropped into the pit of his stomach when he thought of the possibility that Lucian may already be dead. Perhaps Didrebelle *had* tried to rescue him, but the numbers of Dridion and Nundric were too overwhelming. That would mean the Key was well on its way to Nundric . . .

No, Gamaréa told himself. *You cannot think that way. Lucian is alive. He is pressing toward Medric this very instant . . .*

They were empty thoughts. In the shadows he mused over the impracticalities of Lucian making the trip to Medric alone. *It was foolhardy even with Didrebelle and me accompanying him . . .* The thought of a seventeen year old boy from across the sea navigating his way through most of the western frontier was almost laughable. Didrebelle knew this. He had to have known it. For him to leave

Lucian, Gamaréa determined, meant only one thing, but he refused to admit or accept it.

The warm tickle of a slow-moving tear snuck down the side of his cheek as a foul and troubling thought crossed his mind. *Could Didrebelle have been false all along? What if he devised that plan for the ambush in Ravelon? What if he killed Lucian himself once I was captured?* As if waking from a dream his eyes widened in the shadows, and he heard the low rumble of Daxau's voice.

"Are you alright?"

It was a short while before Gamaréa answered. "Yes . . . " But it was not until he heard himself speak that he realized how gripped his voice was by emotion.

"You were shuffling over there, and panting," said Daxau contemplatively. "I thought you must have been having a nightmare."

Gamaréa was thankful for the excuse that Daxau provided. "Yes . . . " he answered shakily, "I was."

"What did you dream of?"

For some strange reason, Gamaréa longed to tell him everything—everything that had occurred since he retrieved Lucian from the east and brought him west. But instead he answered vaguely, "Terrible things."

Silence fell. Down the corridor, something like a stone dropped, and its echo rippled past them.

"Care to elaborate, my friend?" Daxau asked through the silence.

"Not now . . . not here."

"Is it what was on your mind today? Something about you seemed off . . . "

"Not here," said Gamaréa, and Daxau must have caught the finality in his voice, for he did not speak again after saying goodnight.

Gamaréa, however, did not sleep at all.

Didrebelle had never been subject to such sadness before. Cauldarím was a pitiful environment indeed. The madness of his father had certainly reached an extremity that not even he thought was attainable. From the high ledge of his enclosure, he could see the decaying fields were littered with an uncountable mass of captives. There might have been a thousand. Sounds of hammering, chiseling, grunting, and moaning filled the sweltering air from among the multitude of work-tents along the perimeter of the field, and it nearly ripped his soul in two to know that Gamaréa was laboring somewhere amongst that sorry lot.

Several guards passed by him on the wall, and before long he stopped one questioningly.

"You there," he said, "these prisoners—where has the king found so many? Surely the arm of Dridion is stretching further and further these days."

"Indeed," answered the guard, with an air of pride in his voice. "Moroks, the lot of them. They have proven to be an easy folk to catch. Mostly nomads, I think. We have caught a great many of them wandering across our border, or close to it at least. Some are failed rebels who have tried to oppose us. Came up in a frenzy one day, waving Mascorea's flags and all. They were repelled, as you can imagine. The lucky ones perished. The others, well,"—then the guard's gaze shifted toward the captive-riddled field—"you take my meaning, of course. Rumor has it a mortal stands among them as well, though none have been able to locate him. It is no matter to us. All below share the same fate. They will be disposed of eventually. Sacrifices to the Great Lord of Nundric. He needs them, you know . . . "

Didrebelle stopped listening to the soldier, who if anything spoke as if programmed. All clones of his father, they were, at least in mind now. But the guard mentioned something in passing that worked to vex him, and as he turned to leave, a sudden realization sprung into Didrebelle's mind. *Mortal?!* Thoughts of Lucian cascaded through his mind. Had he too fallen into the clutches of Dridion? Had another assembly of Dridion's ground forces scoured Ravelon and found him?

"Guard!" he called after him, trying with effort to keep the tone of his voice neutral. "I'm terribly sorry, but I thought I heard you say *mortal*."

"You heard me correctly, Warden," replied the guard.

"Mortal. Just a rumor, mind you. Nigh on a year since the rumors began,"—at this Didrebelle tried to suppress his sigh of relief. It could not have been Lucian, and this returned the slimmest sliver of hope to his heart. "Talk originally spread among the captives before reaching our ears," the guard continued, "but such words have dwindled of late. If he ever was here, he has no doubt perished by now. Basest form of life, if you ask me—Man, I mean. More two-legged animal, in my opinion. I cannot remember what they said his name was, but they reported he was as beastly as they come."

Didrebelle could not help but draw a perplexed expression. "You are aware of the tales of the fall of the mortal race?" he asked conversationally. "Excuse my prodding, but the stories have always fascinated me."

"I suppose they are *interesting* accounts, Warden, but I cannot say I have heard them entirely, and certainly not enough to hold a conversation regarding them."

"Then allow me to assure you that it is widely understood that mortals have been entirely expelled from the west—"

"Perhaps, sir," said the guard noncommittally. "Again, I heard only rumor. But if I may be so bold, why should such a bland subject interest someone of your prestige?"

"It quite possibly should not," answered Didrebelle, scrunching his nose as though detecting a horrid scent, as was the presentation of most Fairies these days. "I do apologize, but when you mentioned the subject of mortals I could not help but grow curious." The guard shifted as if to turn away—he certainly was becoming antsy—but Didrebelle spoke again. "These prisoners," he asked, "what is their charge? Surely they cannot all be here for having broken the same laws?"

"Yet most of them are," answered the guard. "Defilers of the Border Laws set long ago, if I have heard it right. They do not give us much information—Deavorás, I mean. Ours is the duty to establish order among the captives; we do not meddle in other business. One can find himself in trouble for asking questions around here. I take my orders and fulfill them; that is the extent of it."

Didrebelle nodded. "Fair enough, guard. I thank you for your time."

The guard nodded and walked off briskly. His tidings certainly unnerved Didrebelle to the utmost extent. How could one civilization, such as Dridion, completely undo others? What kind of vain pride made them think they had the right to stand above everyone else? Inside, Didrebelle was beginning to writhe with an anger toward his motherland that was almost nauseating. The thought that his father, his own flesh and blood, was captaining such an inhumane operation, only swelled his fury.

It was now, despite being in the same location as Gamaréa, that he felt miles removed. Though he had ultimate access to his friend's enclosure, he felt that reaching him was impossible. Ideally, he would take the keys to Gamaréa's cell in the middle of the night and free him, then make for the path in Ravelon where their search for Lucian would commence. But there was no route of escape that did not require them to cut across Cauldarím and Deavorás. *How can I free him and escape Dridion unscathed?*

He would certainly have the element of surprise, at least. Melinta seemed all too convinced that Didrebelle was home for good, and that his allegiance to Dridion was as strong as ever. The king would not be expecting such a daring maneuver from his son whom he believed to be loyal. *Or would he?*

He needed time, he knew—time enough to concoct a feasible plan that could be executed successfully. *But how much time will I have? How much time does Gamaréa have?* Though the thought of Gamaréa's potential fate agonized him, he tried to remain positive. It was hard to do, however, what with thinking of the "sacrifices" being made regularly to the Lord of Nundric. But he was resolved at least in this: if it was in his power to prevent Gamaréa's death at the hands of his father, he would see it done, or fall in the attempt. *My father has spared him this long,* he reasoned, *perhaps he will continue to do so. All I need is a few more days . . .*

Just then a guard bounded toward him excitedly.

"Warden," he panted, "His Grace is on his way from Deavorás unannounced. A small infantry accompanies him."

Though the news made his heart leap, Didrebelle maintained an almost-bored tone. "Very well," he replied. "I will—er—surely see to him then . . . "

From there Didrebelle reported to his office, and in half-an-hour's time he heard bustling within the guards' quarters preceding the serpentine voice of his father, who promptly flung the door of the office open and strode in with his arms wide as if to embrace.

"My son!" he exclaimed. "The new warden! I commend you on a fine first day at your new post."

Didrebelle was certainly puzzled. *I have not done anything . . .* But he played along.

"Indeed, Father," he said, fighting hard to retain the hatred that must have been at least somewhat present in his voice. "I have just toured the entire camp, and I must say, it is an unrivaled disciplinary facility."

Melinta laughed his venomous, vile laugh. "Indeed, indeed! But, Diddy,"—he had hated being called this as a child, and even more so as an adult— "you must not get Cauldarím confused with other camps of its like. I have something unforeseen in store for our guests!"

Didrebelle ignored the smirks of the guards after Melinta referred to him as "Diddy", returning only a puzzled glance to his father. "You must elaborate, I'm afraid."

"Disciplinary facilities," began Melinta, "correct with the intention of releasing the corrected subjects back into society. We have no intention of doing so! No, not these subjects. It is only a matter of time before my monument is complete and standing above the city. When this task is finished the scum you see in those fields will be dealt with as all Moroks should be . . . "

Melinta unfolded his plan to Didrebelle so casually that he might as well have been talking about tending his lawn. His savage words poured from his tongue so freely that Didrebelle nearly wanted to beg someone to make him stop speaking. But at least the information was had at last; the most important thing Didrebelle needed to hear yet the very thing he feared most. It was indeed a race against time. Once Melinta no longer had use for the captives of Cauldarím, he would dispose of them all. How, Didrebelle did not even want to guess. But they were all destined for Sorcerian's innards, and in turn would make him whole again.

All the while that Didrebelle was running these thoughts through his mind, his eyes had been cast to the floor for fear that the expression on his face would betray his true allegiance.

"You mean to murder them all?" he said finally, and with great heaviness.

Melinta laughed. "Oh, Diddy,"—the guards smirked again; Didrebelle again ignored them—"do not say it like that! With such . . . moroseness. You appreciate responsibility—after all, you are *my* son. Do not fear that the ruin of these prisoners will leave you unemployed. You will always have a place in my kingdom. After all, it will be yours one day! Do not think of it as *murder*—that is such a harsh word after all. Think of it as . . . *cleansing!* Yes, cleansing."

Didrebelle thought it would be impossible to loathe his father any more than he did before returning to Dridion, but it seemed that every word he uttered only worked to strengthen his hatred.

"Well! Look at the sun!" Melinta continued. "I must be getting back to Deavorás before the next wave of prisoners arrives with the stones. Good day, Diddy, and keep up the good work!"

With that Melinta swept away abruptly, swarmed by his guards. Didrebelle watched him leave with a sour taste filling his mouth and his stomach twisted in all sorts of inconceivable knots. *Of all the vile savagery!* he thought coldly as he watched his father's carriage pass back into the city. But there was little time to let his newly risen hatred toward his father fester. The monument would be completed in a week's time. A plan needed to be devised quickly. And as much as he refused to admit defeat, he knew he was in a hole that was becoming too deep to climb out of.

The radiating arms of dawn came reaching into Gamaréa's cell. He shook himself upright as if he had been sleeping, though it had not felt like it. Whatever sleep he did receive did not play an active role in replenishing his body; he was still very weary, and had little desire to stand when the guards came calling. As was routine, he was led out of his cell into the groaning masses, and came to stand beside Daxau in the crammed corridor as the light of morning blinded them through the opening doorway.

The day began normally enough, yet for some reason Gamaréa felt strange. An odd sensation coursed through his veins, mingling with his blood and making him sweat. Subtly, he was panting with something like exhaustion, but it was not due to weariness that he began to feel discomfort. It felt as though a warm river of aggression diffused throughout his body—aggression that he had not felt in a long while. Daxau noticed it too; he must have. Even without looking at his neighbor Gamaréa knew that he was giving him odd stares.

And indeed it was as if Daxau was witnessing a new Gamaréa, dissimilar to the broken Morok he met only several nights ago. There was a definite swagger in the way Gamaréa walked today; when once he had moved sulkily, he now carried his head higher and stood with a posture proud and daring. He noticed the veins throughout Gamaréa's sinewy arms protruding from the surface of his tawny, war-scarred skin, and his muscles flexed more noticeably as he lifted his stone as effortlessly as ever and slammed it on to the table in front of them. Today, his actions were deft, when all the while they had been methodical at best. But the thing that Daxau noticed the most was the look in his eyes—a strange look, a possessed look; though what possessed Gamaréa, Daxau could not venture to guess.

And yet he would not have to. As Gamaréa set about sculpting his stone, a guard with troublesome intentions strolled by in his glinting armor. A decorated sword dangled from his waist in its gaudy, jewel-riddled scabbard, and he lay his hand upon the hilt with a smug little smile upon his face, as though the sword itself were a beast-infested moat beyond which he stood out of harm's reach. When he came through Gamaréa and Daxau's station, he stuck his long, pointed nose almost in Gamaréa's ear, peering directly over his shoulder like a flea upon a heap of dung.

"You do not seem to be following the blueprint," said the guard, his voice nasal and quite annoying.

Daxau noticed Gamaréa's eyes flare, as though a long dormant light had been rekindled within them. Turning his head slightly, his nose nearly met the guard's. Standing upright, and backing away almost involuntarily, the guard's eyes widened.

"I think I am reading it just fine," said Gamaréa with the softness of a distant storm.

After turning his attention away from the guard, Gamaréa continued working, but the Fairy—clearly against his better judgment—spoke again. "Prisoner, I tell you your reading is incorrect . . . "

The next sound to lift into the stale, midday air was the wailing of the guard as Gamaréa, in one swift, violent motion, swung his arms around and flung the guard away. When the guard finally stopped rolling, Gamaréa fell upon him with a fiery rage. Pressing his knees against the guard's shoulders, he began to punch with ferocity not even he knew existed inside him. Not even in the undergrounds of Titingale did he unleash himself upon an opponent with such reckless abandon.

Including Daxau's brute strength, it took three pairs of arms to restrain him, and after a very toiling struggle Gamaréa was escorted back to his work station. Against his chest his heart pounded with fury, and the hair atop his brow was covered in the blood sprayed up from the guard's face, with more splotched on his forehead and cheeks. It was salty and warm, but the fact that it was a Fairy's worked to ease his spirits.

Daxau came to sit beside him on the ground, and

together they watched as other prisoners stopped to stare at the scene that had unfolded in that corner of the field. Guards from across the grounds came speeding over to tend to their wounded colleague, who now lay almost motionless there in the yellow field. When they were done taking in the defeated soldier, their eyes transitioned to Gamaréa.

Daxau, who had been searching eagerly to find something to say, cleared his throat. "That was perhaps . . . ill advised, friend," he said plainly, though there was a twinge of amusement in his voice.

Gamaréa said nothing. Instead he lifted both of his knees and rested his wrists on top of them, and in his right hand began fingering a thistle he had picked up from the ground. To say the least, Daxau could somehow foresee an incident such as this occurring, but he had kept that to himself. Gamaréa's look was fierce and frightening, even as he sat still and calm upon the ground, and he felt as though the slightest judgmental remark would set him off again. So it was he remained silent, simply sitting beside his friend in case he did finally decide to say something— anything.

But Daxau noticed something then that Gamaréa did not. Coming across the field, among the mass of onlookers, was a small caravan, flanked by guards and helmed by the warden.

Didrebelle had returned to the disgusting chair and sat hunched over, his golden head wrapped in his slender hands. Time was a tricky thing indeed. He scoffed at how some people complained they had too much of it, when he would give anything to have an abundance of minutes and hours at his disposal. But now that Didrebelle understood just how little time he did have, he felt as though all the heavy weights of the world's greatest burdens had gathered into one force and pressed down upon his shoulders.

His attention was drawn quickly by a guard whom he had not heard enter. "Warden?" he said hesitantly, seeing that Didrebelle was sitting as though in pain.

Startled, Didrebelle shot his head up to acknowledge him. "Soldier."

"I request a word of you, if I may?"

Didrebelle stood and allowed the soldier entrance. "What word do you bring?" he asked, genuine interest filling him. A mad hope gripped his heart that the soldier's tidings bore news of Gamaréa, or even Lucian.

The soldier stammered as though having not anticipated the awkwardness of the exchange. "Well, it is just . . . and forgive me if I am being blunt, but . . . "

"Quickly now," said Didrebelle impatiently. "I do not have all day."

"It is the topic of discussion throughout the grounds that . . . Oh, but I am stammering, just listen . . . "

"Stammering indeed. I must urge you to get to your point."

"The truth is, Warden, that I have not come here on my own behalf. The others have chosen me . . . I think it is because I am new . . . "

"Yes, well never mind who sent you; share your words."

The soldier's face contorted with an expression of utter discomfort, and he clasped his hands together as though it would help quell his growing worry. "My lord," he began, "some of the soldiers appear to have overheard you weeping the day you toured the grounds . . . "

Didrebelle returned a perplexed stare. "Weeping, you say?" *I was too open with my emotions . . .*

"Indeed, sir. I did not hear you myself, so I cannot say. In this case I am merely a messenger. But it seems to be widely known around this fortress, and I must inquire on behalf of my colleagues—"

"I am not sure exactly what your colleagues think they have heard, but I can assure you that no one was weeping in my chambers. Perhaps a soldier used this room to express his despair privately, but as far as I am concerned, I have not wept in a great while."

The soldier looked away, embarrassed for being there. Didrebelle's lie was so firm that he was beginning to feel genuine anger. Yet the soldier persisted, though his mannerisms suggested that it was the last thing he wanted to do.

"Warden," he began sheepishly, "it is said that your voice was heard distinctly . . . and upon peeking through one of the openings above your door, a soldier saw you plainly grieving."

The soldier, his hands behind his back and a grave look on his paling face, stood like a child caught in a wrongdoing. Didrebelle wondered who he was, and how old he might have been. He wondered who his parents were and in what region of vast Dridion they made their home. How much did the soldier truly want to be there in his chambers, practically imploring him to admit his false allegiance to Dridion? But Didrebelle would not blink or flinch, despite the substantial evidence heaved against him.

Though no words had been spoken, the soldier said through the silence, "I hold your words true, Warden. Forgive me for accusing you of such acts on the basis of hearsay. It is not in my make to do so."

"See to your duties, soldier."

He opened the door to leave, and as he did another soldier stormed passed him into the chamber. "Warden!" he exclaimed. "There has been an incident in the fields! One of the prisoners nearly killed a guard—he is being contained as we speak."

The soldier who had questioned Didrebelle was still present in the doorway, and Didrebelle noticed an inquisitive look brush over his young face, as if to ask him how he would respond to the situation. *You have said your allegiance is true,* his eyes seemed to say. *Now do what needs to be done . . .*

"Prepare a caravan," replied Didrebelle. "I will see to this prisoner. Come! Rally an escort."

Arming himself with his swords, Didrebelle walked out to the courtyard where the caravan he requested was waiting for him, helmed by decrepit, black steeds imported from Nundric that seemed death made flesh and bone. Snorting and hissing and spewing white phlegm, they stood fidgeting and groaning as Didrebelle mounted the carriage, and when all was readied the party moved out toward the fields.

A guard to his right leaned over to him, reaching out his hand in which he held a long, black flagellum.

"What need is there for this?" Didrebelle asked over the sound of the creaking, wooden wheels of the carriage and the hissing of the pressing steeds.

"It is the Warden's Whip," said the soldier instructively. "Forty lashes—the penalty for raising a hand to an authority."

Didrebelle said nothing. This was his test, as well he knew. He could have handed the Warden's Whip back to the guard and commanded him to carry out the procedure himself, but he knew that would only rally more suspicion toward him. He could not afford more components to thwart him further.

In time the speed of their pursuit subsided as the grounds became cluttered, the sea of solemn-faced prisoners parting before Didrebelle's caravan as if hesitant to allow him passage.

"They know the punishment well," one of Didrebelle's five guards said. "You can see it on their faces. Some have endured it before; many have died on its account. I wonder how this one will fare."

Even the captives who had been there longest could not remember a time when they saw such a crime committed. Guards were struck every so often—but toppled completely? Beaten to the brink of death? It was too bold, they knew—a bold act that would not go unanswered. They saw the stern faces of the guards atop the coming carriage, all their faces as though of stone, and their leader between them—the new warden, feared for his relation to the heinous king.

But those closest thought to see something strange in the warden's eyes—something warm and, could it be, compassionate, as though for a minor instant he was taken by empathy in their presence. The carriage passed. Now only the backs of their heads could be seen fading into the afternoon sunlight toward where the condemned waited patiently for his executioner.

Didrebelle was the last to leave the carriage. His guards had filed out in order and were now circling the prisoner who was to be punished. As he turned the corner so that the carriage was not blocking his view, he saw Gamaréa, and at that moment Gamaréa saw him. In that infinitesimal moment of realization, Gamaréa's expression did not change; it remained passive yet defiant, as though he knew his fate and accepted it fully. And though his heart gave a start, Didrebelle's expression also remained steady, despite knowing that it was his longtime friend he would have to lash.

It could not change. Any discrepancy in his face would trigger the guards to seize him and accuse him of treason. If but for a moment his eyes suggested that he knew Gamaréa, both would be sent to the gallows once Melinta received word.

Both companions knew there was no other way—both knew what had to be done.

"Are you the prisoner?" Didrebelle asked, finding it difficult beyond measure to feign a steadfast tone.

But Gamaréa did not answer. Instead he raised his head to Didrebelle, a melancholy look in his eyes.

In his mind, Gamaréa knew his road had ended. In that small moment, he understood that he had forced his companion into a situation from which he could not be pried. A surge of sadness filled his heart as he thought of all the things he should have done differently. It could not be changed. No matter how much he fought the urge to stand and run as fast as his legs would carry him, he knew it was hopeless. There was no escape possible in that long expanse of field in the middle of the day beneath that merciless sun.

He let himself be seized, not bothering to retaliate. Binding him to the post against which he sat, they tied his hands over his head and made him kneel. Somewhere out of view, Daxau had to be restrained, but Gamaréa could not hear his neighbor yelling for him, could not see him trying to break through the hold of the guards in attempt to rescue him, did not notice when he was knocked unconscious with the pommel of one of their swords.

Before Didrebelle approached, one of the soldiers stuck his cold-steeled blade down the back of Gamaréa's shirt, and in one smooth swipe cut the garments from him, exposing the already-scarred flesh. Then that same guard read from the list of accusations for which he was to be punished. Though he tried to tune him out, Gamaréa could not help but hear bits and pieces of his charges: "assault of authority" and "defilement of Deavorás property" among them.

When the reading ceased, Gamaréa saw the shadow of Didrebelle loom over him from behind, then the shadow of his hand raising, the whip dangling from his fist. In a black streak it came down, and the CRACK that ensued hissed throughout the grounds, and Gamaréa could hear the gasps of all the onlookers behind him.

CRACK.

It came down a second time, then a third, and then a fourth. Yet, some time after the fifth lash, Gamaréa became encapsulated by a dimension of consciousness he had previously been foreign to. His thoughts took him to a time when he was a young boy, and as though a spectator he watched himself being reprimanded by Stór. Then the same sort of wheeling dream took hold of him a second time, and he was watching himself being beaten by Jax— watched himself as he spun around, snapped the general's rod over his leg, and thrust a sharp fragment through his heart.

But soon he saw only shadows. Vaguely, his senses strained to understand what was happening. The touch of dirt was warm and moist upon his cheek; when a soft breeze brushed by, he felt the slashing sting on his back from where the forty lashes had fallen. His hands were placed awkwardly, yet bound above him, though the rest of his body had slumped to the ground.

Didrebelle had done what needed to be done, though it was the most strife he ever had to endure, as though he also lashed himself with each individual crack of his whip. It was all he could manage not to weep openly during the process. Had it not been for the audience of guards he would have at least whipped him lightly, but he was pressured into striking him with the force that prisoners were meant to be struck. Though it had concluded, the entire scene replayed itself through his mind: Gamaréa bending beneath his every lash; his body jerking upon being struck; his frame sliding down the post forty times until his face was pressed upon the ground; his bleeding back when the episode was over.

The guards commended him on a job well done upon returning to the fortress, though their congratulatory words did not offer him any solace. Instead, being among them only compounded his grief. He could no longer perceive the day, feeling as removed from the world as the souls lost in the chasms of Parthaleon itself. His only concern was the medical treatment Gamaréa would receive, if any. Would he be left tied to the post, or offered a sanctuary to heal?

It was a stupid question, and he knew it; in all likelihood he would be left out there for days. *And what of that prisoner beside him?* he wondered, thinking of Daxau, who lay now unconscious beside Gamaréa. The passion he had expressed for Gamaréa's release was that of a brother's. *Who was he, I wonder?*

Such questions riddled Didrebelle all the way back to his chambers, where he barred the door, clogged the miniscule vermin-holes between the wall and ceiling, and wept bitterly for hours without care of who may be listening.

11

Ehrehalle

Lucian was not entirely sure what to expect as he coursed down the corridor with Aries, but it certainly was not the display before him. Ehrehalle was now alive with boisterous activities. Jesters manned every corner, juggling plates, knives, torches—seemingly whatever was in reach. The children took particular interest in their antics, though they drew the attention of nearly everyone in their vicinity. Exuberant melodies rose up from the viols and the flutes, joined by men and women singing.

The floor of the Great Hall was teeming with dancers, and thus boasted a sea of ravishing color. Were it not for the age-touched faces of the folk from Dwén Marnié, Lucian would not have been able to tell them from those of Orion's stock. Women wore fine gowns of all hues: pink, purple, lilac, rose, and evergreen. The folds of their raiment flashed dazzlingly as they twirled. Many of the men were also dressed fashionably, clad in likeness to Orion, as he had predicted.

Lucian followed Aries through the bustle warily, as one trying to prevent losing his way. It took quite some time before they made it to a long table in one of the rightward ranks. There sat Orion and Leo, along with several other well-dressed men from Orion's order. Folk from the valley were sitting there also—men, women, and their children.

"Lucian!" Orion exclaimed when he saw him. "Looking refreshed and fine as ever. I trust the baths were to your liking?"

"Yeah, they were great," said Lucian, still somewhat perplexed by the figure in the pool.

"Get the boy some food, will you?" barked Leo, who was already half-finished with one plate. "That bag of bones is going to need some filling."

Aries released a bellowing laugh. "And so do I," he said. "Come, friend Lucian! Now you may relish in the delicacies of my house."

So it was Lucian accompanied Aries to one of the numerous buffet tables. Before him was a platter of fresh-roasted pork, potatoes, carrots, squash, and a plump golden turkey.

"This table seems to have slipped by unnoticed," said Aries, noting the platters before them that seemed to have gone untouched. "It was never long for this world, however."

With that he dug in, shoveling mounds of meat and vegetables onto his plate. Lucian followed suit. He was hungry enough that he felt as though he could finish off the entire table if given the chance.

"That's the spirit now," said Aries. "And plenty more where that came from, mind you. That's just the tip of the mountain. They'll be replenishing these tables all night."

Together they returned to where Orion and the others were sitting, and men raised their glasses as they sat. For a while Lucian was silent, busying himself with eating. The meat was as tender as he could have wished, and the scrumptious flavor seeped out of it with each new bite. Scattered about his plate, the potatoes and other vegetables absorbed the juices left behind so that they nearly fell apart in his mouth when their time came. It was delightful, and though his stomach felt full, he did not want to stop eating.

Meanwhile several conversations were being had around him. In the time that Lucian was getting food Camien and Bravos had joined the benches, and were sharing their accounts of stabling Godspeed, Night-Treader, and Goldbearer.

"Godspeed was a bit edgy," said Camien. "Though I count it a moral victory to have left with all my fingers."

Those who understood Camien's quip laughed; others

perhaps wondered who or what Godspeed truly was, for Orion and his knights seldom rode their mounts in the open unless at need.

"He has been friendly enough to most strangers," said Orion. "Yet he is stubborn when it comes to being ordered and handled. It has ever been my affair, but he must let down at least some of his walls."

"If they haven't come down yet, I reckon they're impregnable," said Leo, gnawing the remaining morsels from a brown leg of turkey.

"It was a wonder to us all," said Bravos, "when we saw you coming up the road, what with Godspeed bearing Lucian so willingly." Here he directed his attention to Lucian, who was continuing to ingest supper at an inhuman pace. "You have a way with kindly beasts, do you?" Now all were looking at Lucian, who had not heard the question over his ravenous chewing.

Suddenly the feeling of scrutiny began to weigh heavily on him, and he risked a look up from his plate and met the whites of all the onlookers. "Sorry?" he said, his mouth full of pork and carrots.

The table burst with laughter, and Aries, who found this moment particularly funny, smacked Lucian on the back none too gently.

"He'll be as big as Leo before long, I'll warrant!" he exclaimed.

Leo grumbled into his mug as the others chuckled. "Big as me," those closest heard him mutter. "I'll give him 'big as me.'"

"Godspeed had no problem bearing you," Bravos continued. "I thought you might have a history of horse-whispering."

Lucian laughed involuntarily. "Horse-whispering?" he said. "Me? No, I don't think I've ever spoken to a horse, or felt comfortable getting close enough to one to whisper. In truth I never really enjoyed riding, and only did so back home when we traveled into the North Country, up in Eveland or beyond to the Marshal's hill. I prefer walking when I can."

"Could have deceived us," said Camien. "That horse was foaled in our very stables, and he barely lets us near him."

Lucian found this strange, but did not think on it for very long, dismissing Godspeed's tolerance of him as the result of Orion having been present.

Suddenly Halag appeared at the tableside with whom Lucian believed was his son, or one of them at least. He might have been of an age with Lucian, if not older or younger by a year or two. Lanky and blemish-faced, he stood nearly a head taller than Halag, and had the same joyous light in his eyes. Both of them carried three pints of ale in each hand, pinched together by the handles and overflowing with brown foam. Halag was first to set his down and slide them across to their respective owners.

"Saved you a trip, we did," he laughed, distributing the mugs before finally sliding one to Lucian. "Won't find no ale like that in your country, milord. No sir! Finest brew, that is. Grow the barley not far from here our own selves, we do. Halax here, and me of course, and plenty others. Finest grains and plants you'll ever find put in a boil. Then when it's nice and hot we let it chill up in the mountain. Reckon you'd be hard pressed to find a colder ale."

Lucian's first sip bewildered his pallet. The ale indeed was rich and full, with a fragrant aroma that smelt almost like honey. Its time spent chilling in the lofty climes of the mountains had done wonders for its flavor and appeal. Though he did not speak aloud, he was sad to admit to himself that this was indeed the best mug of ale that ever passed his lips. MaDungal's had proven adequate in his ignorance of other worldly brews, but now that the ale of Ren Talam was known to him he wondered if he would ever enjoy another pint like this again.

Maybe one day, when the world is well and good, we can have casks of this shipped over, he thought as he drank. But then he remembered the night the pub was sundered, and the mirth that had arisen in him fled. Thus he buried his nose in his mug and drank. When he lowered the rim and revealed his eyes he was startled to see everyone at the table looking at him studiously yet again.

Leo broke the astonished silence. "Well, he can drink just fine," he said.

"Aye," said Halag. "You'll want to go easy with those, you will. Otherwise one of these lordlings is gonna have to carry you up to bed."

The feast carried well into the night. Every time Lucian looked around him the number of guests seemed to have swelled. The music grew livelier; the ale flowed more freely; and the food tables were replenished with a mind-boggling rapidity. The young children were yet without weariness, and ran around the hall in boisterous assemblies. Their jovial laughter filled the busy air. Dancers brushed by them on several occasions, bumping into their table every so often. Aries joined the fray many times. Even Orion fell into a dance or two. Lucian was still much too timid, and remained at the table feasting with Leo and the others.

He filled his plate on two more occasions. Each time he visited the buffet table a new assortment of selections was before him. At one point there were golden-brown hens, and at another, thick and steaming sides of beef. He filled himself well beyond capacity, and washed his supper down with several more pints of ale. As the night passed swiftly on he could recall no time sweeter spent than in that lofty hall inside the mountain.

Their mirth spurred the telling of great tales, and it seemed each knight had a valiant account to share. Thus Bravos, who by his kith was called The Noble, told of his captaincy during the War of Six Marches. In that battle he helmed the force that drove Melinta's ranks back across the river and thus barred his straightaway passage across the Elarian forever.

"Five times he sent his ranks across the ford," said Bravos. "Fairies and Morgues, and some bólgs were also among his lines. Yes, even they were in his service for a time. Hundreds were in his formations altogether; mine barely outnumbered a score. Yet the passage was narrow, and thus his numbers failed to overwhelm us. We held fast for three days, withstanding four of his advances. His losses were terrible; ours few. When the fifth march came our numbers were nearly equal, yet it was a shell of the strength we met at the start. There were only sad oaths driving his servants at that point. They were destroyed, and the sixth march was ours, and passing unchallenged we barred Dridion's way across the river.

"Thus a great victory was won for our people. There is no ford now within thirty leagues of Dridion in either direction, though I don't doubt Melinta will order his men to those crossings at need. But that need is far away, I think, and his business lies with his greedy crucible for Moroks trespassing on his borders, though I can't imagine what need would drive them so far. The existence of our realm is yet unknown to him."

Lucian, who had been listening intently, looked on with wonder. "But didn't the king know who he sent his men to fight?" he asked. "Didn't he know who you were?"

"There was no true knowledge for him to tap," answered Bravos. "Our order has ever remained hidden from the lands to the south, and those north of here with whom we once had dealings are gone, and our secret with them. It is my belief that he understood us to be of Medric. Mascorea has been known to send small contingents across Enorméteren to scout the river, though they seldom follow it so far down. I have come in contact with parties from Medric once or twice, as it happens, and every time was greeted warmly."

It lifted Lucian's heart to hear tidings of Medric, and of King Mascorea whom he remembered Gamaréa mention. To hear Bravos say they sometimes crossed the same territories he recently passed made him feel secure. Perhaps his route to the Morok lands would resume sooner than he thought.

Bravos's was one of many tales shared. Camien, called The Valiant, spoke of a quest in which he slew the head from a sea serpent that had been periling the southeast shores.

"Though many tales suggest I came too late," he said gravely, "for it had already reproduced and sent its spawn into open waters to carry out its deeds. The male is dead, if there ever was one. It may be fell enough to create hatchlings without a mate. Whatever shores came under its shadow I do not know, but I pity the folk of those beaches if the songs are true."

Thus Lucian shared the fragment of his tale in which Beelcibur attacked *The Sojourn* and was smote by the many hands aboard. The listeners marveled at his account of Didrebelle's prowess with sword and bow and Gamaréa's might and the bravery of the doomed vessel's crew.

"Riveting!" exclaimed Halax, gripping his father's sleeve tightly. "I wish I could've been there."

"No you don't," said Lucian, not unkindly. "It was one of the scariest things I've encountered so far. I felt so helpless out there. I don't remember nights ever being so dark as out at sea. We couldn't see where Beelcibur would strike next until it was too late. Then the ship was destroyed, and we were at the mercy of the Mid Sea with nothing under us but the ocean floor."

Then Halax inquired how they made it to shore, and Lucian touched on the heroics of the Aquilum, and though many of the younger children looked on dubiously there were some present who seemed to understand.

"Aquilus, then, still watches the waves," said Orion distantly. Then he smiled. "I believed him to have led his folk to less troubled depths. It is good to know that they are near."

"Aquilus?" said Lucian.

"The Lord of the Aquilum, of course," replied Orion. "His is a fascinating race, long overlooked by folk of the shores. I can only imagine they have dwelled between these coasts for moments just like the one you have described."

"They definitely proved handy," said Lucian, who for a moment was dampened by grief at the thought of Gawaire and his valiant crew.

"And may prove handier still—"

Just then violists and flutists sprung up beside the table and played a vibrant tune. Aries and the others raised their mugs and cheered, and some of the smaller children leapt up onto the table and danced. Lucian was thankful only that it was wide enough for them to do so without kicking any of the plates or mugs over.

Recounting the night of Beelcibur's onslaught had worked to dampen his spirits. Though he never got to know the crew of The Sojourn, he lamented their losses dearly. These were men who would never get to see their families again, or enjoy another meal as he was now. Thus he was not entirely in the mood for having children stomping around merrily in his personal space. Thinking up a way to deter his attention, he decided to revisit the buffet tables one last time. *Maybe there will be some desert now,* he wondered. Desert always seemed to bring warm thoughts to his mind even when it teemed with troubles. He could not help but reminisce on Mary's wonderful pies and cakes, and by doing so a somewhat logical notion came to him: If the beer here was better than MaDungal's, perhaps the pies, cakes, and pastries were better than—

Suddenly, as though being reprimanded for allowing such blasphemy into his mind, his plate was knocked out of his hand and shattered on the floor. The mere sound of this resulted in cheers from anyone close enough to have heard it. But there was no cheer in this moment for Lucian: he no longer had control of his hands. Looking on incredulously, he realized with dismay that his fingers were locked with a dancing girl's. Whether her strength or his shock bound him there he did not know, but he found himself following her every movement.

Almost instantly he stepped on her feet, and she gasped momentarily before giggling at Lucian's flushed cheeks. He was so embarrassed and afraid that he did not even dare to look at her. She seemed to like this, and used it to her advantage. When they flitted through the narrow alley between the tables and reached the open floor, their dance enlivened with the tunes that fueled it. First she led him rightward in somewhat of a darting fashion, then (he was not sure how she managed it), she made him spin her, and her gown seemed to burst with lavish strobes of lilac and white. Then she spun back into his keep again, and when their fingers reunited she brought him leftward.

Not even when Ursa saw him naked did Lucian feel

more awkward and exposed. He felt all eyes were on him, but none more particularly than the folk at his table. And indeed they relished in the sight of seeing Lucian pried out of his shell (though he had not truly emerged just yet).

"I was worried he would become a spitting image of Leo," Aries whispered in Orion's ear. Leo grunted, though his eyes never strayed from Lucian and his partner.

Orion laughed. "He may yet in body, should he continue eating like he did tonight."

Lucian and the girl twirled on. Frightened and embarrassed, he took this moment to closely study all the features of the Great Hall—the lofty ceiling, the dark-wooded floor, the high walls of stone, the long narrow benches; anything but her—yet it seemed the dance intensified with each new effort he employed to avert his gaze. At a rapid pace they bolted one way, then abruptly spun another. Her vice-like grip tightened to the point where Lucian felt the blood leave his fingers and his wrists tense up. He wished he had not eaten that third helping, or drank that seventh pint. A storm-like maelstrom seemed to fester in the midst of his diaphragm. This could not be happening. It could not happen. Not here. Not now. Sweat began to bead upon his brow and seep through the gaps between their fingers. It was coming. He felt like everyone knew it.

Then suddenly the music stopped, and her grip slackened but did not let go, and the discomfort he had felt began to subside. Mildly gasping he dared a look into her eyes, and suddenly the feeling of sickness welled up once more, for there before him was without question the most beautiful girl or woman that his eyes ever had the privilege to behold. Her golden hair draped over her shoulders in soft folds; yet to say that it was merely golden is a slight. It was the perfect hue of gold, neither darker than a nugget from the depths of mountain mines, nor brighter than a pale winter sun in the first hours of the day. His embarrassment began to subside when he looked upon her face. It seemed that she too was blushing, as though all the daring qualities she exhibited when forcing Lucian into a dance were fleeting, or might never have been hers at all.

There he stood as though transfixed. Her eyes were blue like adamant when touched by mountain snows. Whether by a trick of the light or some inner magic housed within, they sparkled with a fervent light. Then she smiled, and it seemed like all other lights subsided. Lucian's heart flushed and seemed to plummet into his bowels. The cheers and quips from the throng around them faded, and there was only her. The urgent thought that he might kiss her there stormed boldly into his mind, until the music lifted once more. Then, with a subtle twitch, she made as if to smile before she suddenly flitted away to wherever she had come from. The thickening crowd swallowed up her fleeting figure, and though in the midst of many, a cold and lonely feeling settled over Lucian like a wintry wind.

12

Bigger Things

Gamaréa's mind had become full of dark images. He was lying on a hard surface, but whether it was the ground where he had fallen or another place he did not know. Vague visions of events that had recently come to pass crossed his mind. Upon his wrists he could still feel the jagged edges of the post he had been tied to, and the coarse coils of the heavy rope that had bound him to it. His knees burned from having knelt for such a long time, and under such strenuous circumstances, and the relentless cracking of Didrebelle's whip was still ever present in his ears. His throbbing back stung more intensely at the memory of it.

Opening his eyes for the first time, he found himself in a room both dark and unfamiliar. A stale, reeking smell like that of old sweat filled the air, and for a long while he lay taking short breaths in his lonesome. It was not until moments later that he saw shapes of bodies in the dimness of the chamber. Most did not stir.

Gamaréa fought to sit upright, but this sort of pain was new to him, and so he remained on his side for a long while. From there it seemed he faded in and out of deep sleep for hours. By doing so he was offered a respite from the pain, finding himself in the sunbathed province of Guinard, sparring with Tartalion.

"Feet planted! Back straight. Yes, yes, that's it!"

The sound of the waves washing up on shore beyond them was soothing, and remained in the background with Tartalion's voice even after the images faded. "Tell me, have you heard any stories of heroes who have ventured down the street and back?"

Gamaréa saw his young face pondering.

"Come now, the night grows old! Have you? Good, for you would be caught in a lie. You and I know well indeed that the only stories written—the only ones worth telling—are those of individuals who defy impossibilities, who meet their destinies though gripped by fear."

Tartalion reached a hand out as if to help Gamaréa up from his seat. "Come," he said. "There is much yet to be done."

And so, opening his eyes, Gamaréa reached to clasp his hand, only to find himself groping at the darkness of the dungeon.

Didrebelle found no rest that night; the memory of that afternoon haunted him beyond recognition. At first light, he saddled the most able horse and rode into Deavorás where he sought to question his father.

He found Melinta poring over yellow parchment upon a cluttered table in his study, not far from the main hall. A white raven was perched upon his shoulder that flapped its wings and took to hovering over their heads when Didrebelle entered. The room was dark still, for the light of dawn was yet to reach the center of the city.

"Away with you," Melinta said to the raven, who squawked in response. "Do not return unless with worthy tidings."

Didrebelle watched the raven fly away and out into the bleak predawn. Meanwhile Melinta turned his usual smug smile to his son. "To what do I owe this visit, Diddy?"

You really need to stop calling me that.

Stepping out from behind his table, Melinta cast two firm hands upon his son's shoulders.

"I merely sought a visit," answered Didrebelle, putting effort into masking his grief.

His father chuckled. "Well, of course!" Releasing his grasp on Didrebelle, Melinta strode back behind the clutter of papers. "I just thought you would be resting! If the rumors are true, I understand you had quite the eventful afternoon yesterday."

Didrebelle swallowed a large clump of despair. "I did indeed," he said, nearly under his breath.

Melinta raised an eyebrow, perhaps sensing the odd tone issuing from the voice of his son. "Does it trouble you?"

Didrebelle came to attention so fast Melinta might have slapped him. "No, no," he replied hastily. "Not in the least."

"I see."

Curiosity seemed to fill Melinta's eyes, and he stepped out from behind the table once more to sit at its edge. "Such is the duty of the warden," he began. "You are the disciplinarian of the grounds now—the overseer of justice. The savages outnumber our guards four to one. Without discipline—the constant threat of our power—we would be overrun. Gamaréa perhaps looked to serve as a sign of hope yesterday, a symbol of the promise the others have of overtaking us. It was imperative that he was brought down—made an example of. And you did so beautifully, Diddy. They will not be raising a hand to any of my men any time soon, I can assure you.

"He is unpredictable, and almost incapable of being tamed by any whip or method of discipline we might possess. It is crucial that we control him above all others. I thought you would find solace in your deeds. He is the reason your sister is lost to us, after all. My dear, sweet Emmanuelle."

Didrebelle could say nothing. Instead he bit his tongue with a force that nearly severed it.

Melinta went back behind the table and took up his drink that had been sitting idly atop some dusty pieces of tattered documents.

"Yes," he said, as if to himself, taking a small drink and looking out through the tall windows at the coming sunrise. "You did what was necessary."

Didrebelle stepped closer. "Indeed, Father," he said unpretentiously. "But I wonder what became of him? I left him lying on the ground unattended. A guard suggested I leave him tethered to the post, as is customary."

"Customary indeed," chuckled Melinta, as though speaking of a childish game. "Let him serve as an example to all others who may harbor foul intentions, as I have said. Normally, the prisoner would not be fetched until noon today, but I have special plans for the Morok. Yes, special plans indeed."

Melinta grew keen to his son's perplexed expression. "Ah, yes, how forgetful of me!" he exclaimed. "I forget sometimes how long you have been absent. I must share great news with you then! Not two centuries ago—this being shortly in the wake of your . . . departure—I had an arena constructed in the name of your grandfather, who quite enjoyed battle and sport. In those days, lords and noblemen from all corners of Dridion were coming to Deavorás seeking my favor and hospitality. Those who were awarded it I brought to the arena to be entertained by the games."

"Games?"

"Yes, Diddy! Games! The strongest prisoners were summoned to fight whatever champion I called upon. Not only were they tests of brawn for my champions, but a rather . . . *creative* . . . way of offering sacrifices to the Great Lord Sorcerian."—Didrebelle could not help but cringe upon mentioning of the Sorcerer's name—"Though games have not been held there for many years, I feel as though it would be splendid to call it back to action. Yes, an honorary event in the name of my son who has returned. The new warden! It is there, I think, the Morok is destined to fall. In fact I am quite sure."

"And which of your captains will you call upon to face him?"

The laugh Melinta issued was sinister and vile, filled with something more terrible than evil. "No captain of Dridion will oppose him, my son. No, no, no! I have bigger things in store for him. Yes, bigger things indeed."

Didrebelle felt only fear in the presence of his father now, but could not bear to be left to guess what "bigger things" meant.

"Will you show me?" Didrebelle asked, trying to sound eager.

Melinta drew that vile, noxious smile. "I thought you would never ask."

Didrebelle had no way of telling how far beneath the tower his father was leading him. It seemed he had been descending for hours. Deep within the foul blackness, it seemed not even the mounted torches gave off adequate light. The surroundings grew cold and quiet, their soft, descending footsteps echoing into the upper reaches of the cylindrical tower before vanishing from their ability to hear.

Strange sounds issued from down below. Bellowing, shrieking, gargling sounds, such as made Didrebelle's stomach feel a bit queasy. Countless times he thought to inquire as to where Melinta was leading him, but thought that doing so would suggest he was afraid, and ultimately weak. His father passed before him without the slightest reluctance, holding his torch aloft and feeling as way along the stone wall.

The smell was awful, comprised of so many foul components that Didrebelle did not even want to begin wondering what they were. When at long last they reached the bottom, Didrebelle had to retain the urge to rush back up the spiral mountain of stairs.

"Is it not the most glorious assembly you have ever seen?" said Melinta, feasting his eyes on the sight before them.

For the life of him, Didrebelle could not think of what to say. He was supposed to sound pleased, infatuated even; yet at this moment, all he knew was horror. "Mag— magnificent," he answered sheepishly.

"Do not fear, Diddy, do not fear. They are fascinating creatures, one and all."

Together they walked along the nethermost reaches of Melinta's tower, where not even Didrebelle himself had gone before. There before him, in heavy chains and countless tethers, were the most enormous, terrifying, horribly beautiful creatures he had ever laid his eyes upon.

Melinta, with the mannerisms of a young boy, grabbed Didrebelle's hand excitedly. "Come on!" he said enthusiastically. "Do not be timid! They are drugged at the moment; won't be roused until I give the order."

Jerking Didrebelle to the nearest creature, both father and son stared on in wonder. "Is this a—"

"A Minotaur, yes," said Melinta. He may have been showing off a new toy he procured in a market square. "I know what you are thinking, my boy, and I too thought them to be extinct. Not an easy brute to find, mind you—a shadow scattered throughout historical records for the expanse of two thousand years."

"They are a damned species," said Didrebelle absently.

"Indeed, indeed, Diddy; forced from the northern mountains during the Great Storms. The only records I have of them track their migration to large agricultural territories, where they began crossbreeding with common cattle—"

"Morgues," was the only word that Didrebelle could muster.

"Yes, of course! That does explain the origins of those brutes. You are as sharp-witted as they come. Chip off the old block, if you ask me." Melinta gave him a little bit of a nudge.

Didrebelle took in the creature before him, savage even in its sedated state, its broad back heaving slowly as it filled its lungs with air, its thick horns like ivory-plated pythons coiling. For a long while, only its steady, rumbling breathing sounded throughout the dungeon.

"Where did your men find it?" Didrebelle asked at last.

"In a cave many leagues from here," answered Melinta matter-of-factly. "Took nearly five poison-tipped arrows to sedate it, but they managed."

"And this is what you have in store for Gam—for the Morok?"

Melinta's eyes had flickered briefly even at the near mentioning of Gamaréa's name. "No," he said softly. "There is much, much more."

Just then an older Fairy—an adviser, Didrebelle guessed—raced over to Melinta. Age was evident on his face: His brows were wrinkled, and his hair was sooty-gray and fletched with white. In his long and bony hand he carried small sheets of parchment, which were fastened to a slate as to make writing easier.

"Ah, my dear Thaldrid," said Melinta, embracing the approaching Fairy. When the king's hands clasped the adviser on the back, dust and soot sprang up from his robes in a dense cloud. Everyone coughed.

"Your Grace," replied Thaldrid in a nasally voice. "I had not expected you for some time." His weary eyes then fell upon Didrebelle, still gaping at the creatures before him.

"Forgive me," said Melinta. "Thaldrid, meet my son Didrebelle."

"The *prince?* I thought—"

"Pleasure," said Didrebelle, taking Thaldrid's hand.

"The pleasure is mine, I trust," he answered. Whatever the adviser had meant to say was stifled as Thaldrid turned his gaze back to the king. "The preparations are all but set, Your Grace. Took a great while to secure the brutes, but we have managed to do so, though at great cost."

"How many?" asked Melinta.

"Almost three hundred in all," replied Thaldrid heavily. "Most of them on the last job."

"Ah, yes. It is a sad price to pay for victory. Now it is our duty to make sure that it was well spent."

Didrebelle had only caught bits and pieces of this conversation, busying his eyes upon the station of the creature that came after the Minotaur. Thaldrid's voice startled him to attention. "Taking a fancy to the wolf, are you?" he asked. "She is a rare beauty, if I do say so myself. Not easy to find these nine-tails anymore; most of them being extinct. Had to brave the snowstorms of the Far East to nab her. Nature's damn near cast that territory into an endless winter."

"I have heard that these are the only creatures to have survived the malice of those storms," said Didrebelle thoughtfully. "And even then only a handful remain."

"She was the last of her pack when we found her," replied Thaldrid, a hint of remorse in his frail voice. "Theirs is a rare breed, dear boy—as immortal as you and I. Its tails, as I'm sure you know, are why it is considered one of the most lethal predators in the world."

"They are powerful enough to whip flesh clean from the bone," he answered.

"Indeed! Very whip-like, very fine, and very deadly. And that is just one tail. Adults her age have most certainly managed to utilize all nine at once, making her defeat nearly impossible."

Didrebelle stood, marveling at how something so beautiful could be so deadly. The golden wolf lay so quietly and peacefully that he almost longed to curl up beside her for a nap of his own, had the nasally voice of Thaldrid not been ringing in his ears, eagerly leading him to the next paddock.

"Gracious me!" exclaimed Melinta, in genuine awe at the sight before him. "Those etchings in my study do not nearly do this one justice."

Didrebelle, who refused to go any nearer than where he stood about ten yards away, cringed. "Is that a—but, of course that can't be . . . "

"Oh yes!" replied Thaldrid. "You thought them myth, my prince, I know. I was also ignorant to their existence. But the criosphinx, as you can see, is as real as any of us. You see, when the Fairies of Flordrien—and this is many years ago, mind you, before even my time—crossed the North Sea from their cities in the icecaps, they brought with them this mischievous species."

Thaldrid then began an annoying history lesson as to the origins of the beast, saying that they started off as wooly, blubbery beings, whose bodies were designed to endure the frigid temperatures of the northern territories, and how, after over three thousand years of evolution, the beast's stature had shrunk, and in turn made it more mobile and cunning than its ancestors. Didrebelle did take particular interest in the eagle-like wings in which it wrapped itself while sleeping. Thaldrid was quick to mention that they had taken the place of fins along the course of its evolutionary progression. It's body—once like that of a mammoth's, according to the adviser—was now lean and muscled, its coat sleek like a lion's. "And, of course, as you can see, it has something like a ram's head," Thaldrid pointed out. "Excellent for battering down enemies, very much like what we use to hammer down gates!"

"It is truly odd," said Didrebelle. "Though I do not doubt its power."

"Nor do I," answered Melinta. "It will be a very valuable asset in our future endeavors. Perhaps with its help we can be the first to breach Détremon."

Didrebelle's brow furrowed slightly. "The Great Wall of Adoram?" he asked curiously. "You mean to march upon Medric?"

"Not now, Diddy, not now," said Melinta. "All will be answered in due time. It would be rude to interrupt Thaldrid, though. He really is encapsulated by these creatures."

Thaldrid released something like a giggle. "Truer words were never spoken, Your Grace! Follow me, follow me! Look here!"

The trio reached a fourth paddock in which six guards were stationed with spears at the ready. In their midst, the king of all wild predators.

"One cannot be too careful with a kórog," whispered Thaldrid, as though speaking any louder would wake the beast.

Didrebelle looked on incredulously. "This is not—but, how . . . "

"The arm of Dridion is long, my son, as you have no doubt come to learn," said Melinta plainly. "Even the most savage beast can be subdued and broken, as you can see here."

"Respectfully, Your Grace," said Thaldrid timidly, "I must advise you to use caution, even with your words, around a kórog. This is not your usual predator."

"It is nearly the size of a horse," observed Didrebelle.

"And nearly as fast," answered Thaldrid.

Each of the kórog's four legs was wrapped in thick muscle, every head-sized paw edged with dagger-like claws. The qualities of its face were strikingly feline, though not even Thaldrid was certain if it was truly in the same genealogy of the modern jungle cats. Certainly its most intriguing feature, aside from its sheer size, was its tail. Longer and thicker than a proportional tail would have been, this wound behind it for nearly two yards, two sharp-edged shafts of something like ivory tusks protruding from the tip, which, Thaldrid was quick to mention, scholars claimed to be an abnormal growth of bone.

It seemed a lifetime before someone spoke, and Didrebelle's gut twisted at the sound of his father's voice. "Splendid!" he said proudly. "Just magnificent. You all have truly exceeded expectations. I only wish that we could see all of them in action in the arena."

Didrebelle's heart gave a start. "These are the creatures you mean to unleash on Gam—on the . . . prisoner?" he asked.

"As I said, Diddy, I wish I could. But I doubt the Morok would outlast any one of these creatures. I was thinking about selecting the Minotaur to combat him. I feel as though the crowd would take to that splendidly."

"But—" Didrebelle began.

"Not now, son. Later, perhaps. Thaldrid, what about the fifth?"

If at all possible, Thaldrid's face took on a paler shade of white. "Ah, Your Grace," he stammered. "The fifth is indeed present. We have exceeded great lengths to retrieve him, but it seems as though the sedation is wearing off."

This was the first time since entering the dungeon that Melinta seemed disquieted at all. "What? How is that possible? My very own necromancers have seen to the sedative; it was made to wear off only at my bidding. How can this be?"

"I am only guessing," said Thaldrid sheepishly, "but it may be that our earthly concoctions take a different hold on creatures of such magnitude. We have doubled the dosage he was originally given in hopes of subduing him. I daresay it will be successful. Nevertheless, if such a strong dose tapered off already, I can only assume that it will do so again, no matter the quantity Ignis is given."

Ignis? thought Didrebelle. *They have named the fifth?*

"See that it is done," said Melinta sternly. "Pity. I would have loved for Diddy to see him."

"Ignis is a spectacle indeed," said Thaldrid, his tone harboring something quite like fear.

Melinta turned his back on Thaldrid then, and swept off toward the towering stairwell. "Come then, my son, now that your eyes have feasted," he called to Didrebelle, who was standing and looking into Thaldrid's worried face. The adviser's eyes seemed to be imploring something of him, but Didrebelle did not dare ask what.

"Didrebelle," his father called again, his serpentine voice echoing across the voluminous dungeon. As if in answer, a cry rose up, something shrill and unbearable, from the deep places of the dungeon beyond, and the temperature rose almost immediately.

"Ignis grows restless," Thaldrid whispered, as if to himself. "You should go now, my prince. This is a malice that was never meant to be tampered with."

13

A Lesser Man's Fear

In three days' time Gamaréa was able to sit up. He ate lightly and sparingly, and was given a splash or two of water every three to four hours. What he did with it was his choosing. Usually he drank, but being as his face had become dry and hot, he used it to cool down every so often as well. But the coolness was only temporary, as luxuries tend to be, and he continued to sulk in frequent pain.

He still hadn't a clue where he was, but, looking around at the unchanging surroundings, part of him did not care to learn. Now that his senses were beginning to strengthen he saw that the walls were made of thick concrete, and the thing upon which he lay was nothing more than a slate slab propped upon wooden planks that were bolted into the ground. A thin sheet was the only thing between his shredded back and the cold stone. The muffled moans of the others in the room were all that sounded in that forsaken place. Sealing off the entrapment were celled doors of rusted iron, outside of which a slew of dim torches revealed a corridor leading to nowhere.

Casting his legs off one side of the slate, he let his feet dangle. They were cold for lack of circulation, and began to itch when the blood slowly filtered back into them. *Is this it?* he asked himself. *Is this where I am to die at last?*

It indeed was the most horrid of imaginable places, more horrid even than his cell and the prison camp combined. Perhaps it was the sheer reek that stifled the air; perhaps it was the realization that this was a place of misery and death lost within the bowels of some accursed fortress. But there was not a category of agony strong enough to match that already inflicted by the realization of his failure.

Suddenly the screech of the opening door startled him from his thoughts, and he turned to see a hooded medic enter with a tray upon which sat two clay mugs. The physician brought them to the two shadowy patients opposite Gamaréa, and in time the Morok saw their movements falter before ceasing entirely as they dropped their mugs onto the floor where they shattered. Turning now to Gamaréa, the medic, cast in shadow by his hood, set aside his tray and revealed himself.

"Didrebelle?" whispered Gamaréa incredulously.

"Quiet," said Didrebelle. "We cannot allow others to hear."

"Your friends, you mean?" The look on Didrebelle's face suggested that he did not understand Gamaréa's comment. "You have brought the others mugs of poison, but what do you have for me? Twenty more lashes? Thirty?"

A flicker of sorrow was apparent in Didrebelle's light eyes, such as they seemed to lose some of their luster. Gamaréa nearly regretted speaking to him so rashly. Nearly.

"I have not come on behalf of others," Didrebelle answered softly. "And that was not poison; it was a sleeping mixture."

"Why are you here?" asked Gamaréa after a moment, making sure to speak as kindly as he was able, though his resentfulness toward Didrebelle was difficult to stifle.

Didrebelle accounted for the surroundings, looking alertly to and fro for any sign of an eavesdropper. When he was certain the coast was clear, he spoke.

"I have come to warn you," he said urgently.

Gamaréa chuckled. "Warn me? Against what? Bad things? *Very* bad things?" Didrebelle made as if to speak, as if to defend himself, but Gamaréa persisted hotly. "There is no fate that could undo me further, yet here you stand speaking of others that may arise. Tell me, friend, where was the alarm signaling your whip? When was the ceremony held initiating the new warden? But, then again, it all makes sense in the end. You move in shadow and darkness, always have. No ray of light can reveal your cunning ways . . . "

Didrebelle seemed to be fighting with his emotions. For a moment it seemed to Gamaréa that his words had indeed saddened him, but then a flare of anger flashed in his eyes and he leapt forward and clasped his hands around Gamaréa's shoulders. "Look at me!" he said desperately, abandoning his attempt at subtlety. "I did only what had to be done if I am to gain your freedom—if I am to gain ours. Forgive my actions, if you can find it in your heart, but know that it was not in vain. The road we have found ourselves upon is not without obstacles, and braving it successfully requires a bit of improvisation. I acted as I saw fit because they expected it of me, and the consequences, regrettably, are what they are. But there are bigger things at work here. You must hear me."

Didrebelle then seemed to note Gamaréa's back. The wounds had all but fully scabbed and were pale pink, outlined by a sickly yellow hue. "Your wounds," he said, aghast, "they are nearly healed. This is indeed master stitch-work."

"I was not awake for it," replied Gamaréa matter-of-factly. "They are still sore, however, but the pain is subsiding." Didrebelle saw that the anger in Gamaréa's face was slowly draining, the madness that had possessed his eyes was nearly relinquished now, and the voice that filtered from his companion was the one he had been ever used to.

"Speak now," said Gamaréa softly. "Tell me whatever you know. Is it news about Lucian? Those are the tidings most precious to me."

Didrebelle returned a grave expression. "I let Lucian go," he said, in a half-whisper, as though he himself could not believe it. "It was the Sage Charon who instructed me to do so."

"Then the Mountain is still at large," said Gamaréa, as if to himself, though not with anger as Didrebelle seemed to have expected.

"What?" asked the Fairy, apparently perplexed.

"The Mountain," answered Gamaréa. "I too have had visitations, though not since I crossed the Mid Sea months ago." Gamaréa's gaze was both worrisome and hopeful as he looked down at the floor in thought. "He may yet be alive."

It was a moment before Didrebelle said anything. "He may yet." Yet his words were absent depth, as though he doubted them in his heart.

"Is this what you have come here to tell me?" asked Gamaréa after a moment.

"No—I have come here to warn you that the king has delved deeper into madness. He seeks to reopen the arena two leagues south of here."

Gamaréa nodded as if in understanding. Daxau had mentioned the arena not too long ago, and for some reason he felt as though he would be directly acquainted with it soon enough.

Didrebelle's eyes fixed hard upon Gamaréa. "You know of this place?" he asked.

"I have heard rumors of the arena, nothing more. When you make a living fighting for coin as long as I have, you meet people whose knowledge of various venues is extensive. The man in the cell across from me holds a wealth of knowledge regarding it as well."

"Whatever rumors or tales you have heard, I assure you they are true, and Melinta seeks to use you as the centerpiece of entertainment. He has bent many champions to his will. Before long, all of them will yearn for the taste of blood, and the only source to quell their thirst will be yours. You stand alone, my friend. I have seen you in action, seen you outlast outstanding odds, yet I fear this will be the greatest challenge you have ever faced."

Gamaréa's mind did not host a single thought as he mustered only a half-spoken word. "Champions?"

"Beasts he has forced into submission, fetched from whatever reaches they may have once called home. I have seen them—"

Suddenly a muffled sound shuffled from without and Didrebelle reapplied his hood quickly. "You are the very image of a lesser man's fear," he said hastily. "Melinta will stop at nothing to rid himself of the threat you impose." Suddenly the sounds of shuffling grew louder. "I must go," Didrebelle finished quickly.

Fetching his tray, he reached the door, but turned back to Gamaréa once more. "Forgive me about . . . I meant no—"

"It's alright," said Gamaréa, dismissing Didrebelle's apology. "I think I am beginning to understand."

Nodding, a hint of a smile at the edge of his lips, Didrebelle slipped away and out of sight.

Part 2

"Tiger, tiger, burning bright,
In the forests of the night,
What immortal hand or eye
Could frame thy fearful symmetry."

— William Blake

14

The White Hawk

"Your Grace, the messenger Cormac seeks a word," said Lord Thrikon, one of Melinta's several hall-servants.

Rolling his eyes, Melinta issued his consent. It was not yet midday, and weariness had already cast its weight upon him. He had spent the last twelve hours directing errand runners to every corner of his realm, delivering advertisements for the spectacle with which he planned to reopen his grandfather's old arena. There had been fifteen in all, and none of them particularly sharp-witted. He just hoped the messages reached the outlying provinces in time. He expected all of Dridion's nobility to attend, after all—counted on it, at that. Their coin was needed if he was to strengthen his army for his . . . future endeavors.

Cormac sauntered in, the hem of his white robes streaked with brown from his many travels. His beady eyes were a thing Melinta had never taken a liking to, and his bald head was egg-shaped and flecked with pale spots.

"Your Grace," he said, folding his hands and bowing before the steps of the Emerald Throne. The palm-sized gem cresting it worked to reflect off Cormac's polished head.

"And what news do you bring this day, I wonder?" said Melinta impatiently. "If it involves the unseasonable flight patterns of owls again, I might just call for your head."

"Negative, Your Grace, though they have indeed proved unusual of late. I bear tidings more . . . relevant to your interests. Oh yes."

Melinta's posture straightened in his throne, and his eyes glowered upon Cormac curiously. "I'm listening . . . "

Cormac continued. "It was indeed the strange flight patterns of the owls that led me to this discovery. Lately they have frequented the skyways more often than is their wont, accompanied by ravens, hawks, and even eagles every now and then. No airborne creatures travel in such mixed company. They are creatures of territory and kinship, as you know."

Melinta hoped the newly kindled flare in his eyes spurred Cormac into the sharing of information that would actually be useful. "Cormac, my winged friend," he said crossly, "at this moment I am thinking of the proper stake on which to prop that bald little head of yours. Now, if the next words out of your mouth are not part of a worthy account, I will order you beheaded where you stand."

"I followed them, Your Grace," Cormac stammered suddenly. "The birds. I followed them to the inner crescent of the Red Peaks, and there I saw many things. An odd assortment of men there were, living within a great hall built into the mountain of Shír Azgoth, that range's storied peak. Below a wide, golden vale was splayed, and upon it a thriving village. The hall seemed to be welcoming a small party into it, four riders upon three mounts. Three were clad in knightly armor, the fourth a boy in weathered rags. I doubled back, and returned to the woods of Ravelon with all speed. There I studied the tracks from where the Keeper's company was intercepted. Evidence of the Morok's scuffle with your men was plain to see and follow. The Keeper's, however, branched off a separate way—a way that led toward the plains of Enorméteren. But on the path I found great carnage. A Matarhim horde lay slain, along with dozens from your infantry. Many had been pierced by arrows, it seemed, retrieved undoubtedly by the archer when his work was done. Some had been felled by a sword. But not just any sword. I have cause to believe that no blade of such magnitude has ever been brandished in the field. I counted fourteen slashed in two. Yet I cannot begin to wonder what other fate met some of those doomed souls.

There were many whose chests were staved in, as if some great boulder had been wielded to smash them . . .

"Nevertheless, I followed their tracks. They set off on mounts, two steeds and . . . and something else. I saw what I can only describe as paw-prints beside those of hooves. Unnaturally-sized paw prints, like those of a great bear—"

"Owls and bear-riders," said Melinta, rising from his throne. He had heard quite enough. If anything, Cormac's imaginative account only made him wearier.

"Your Grace, I implore you to listen. I know such tales seem . . . farfetched . . . but it is what I saw."

Melinta, though his fury was beginning to rise, looked down upon his messenger, and saw something like fear and pleading brimming in his little eyes, and against his better judgment, he sat again to listen.

"When I returned to the Red Peaks, and cast my eyes upon the display within the mountain's hall, I believe I saw the one you have so tirelessly sought. The boy who had shared one of the mount's saddles was none other than The Keeper of Fates."

"How can you be sure?" Melinta's stern question was out of his mouth before Cormac even finished speaking.

"Around the face of Azgoth I flew, Your Grace. What I hoped to find, I cannot say. But my flight yielded a telling sight. For I saw the boy in his chambers, brandishing Kal Glamarig. I saw the emerald and sapphire lights! And here I am now to tell you that it is across the breadth of Enorméteren—across the wide face of long Elarian—your spoils await."

A long while passed when a heavy silence filled the cavernous room. A great hall, built within Shír Azgoth. Men who rode bears. Swords that could slash a fully-armored soldier clean in two. But Cormac's words had never proven false before. Thus Melinta sat thinking deeply, too intrigued to dismiss his messenger on account of his impractical tidings. Instead he called upon Lord Thrikon again, and requested that he send for the captain of his infantry, Faldrus, son of Fladrielle.

He arrived moments later, swaggering into the hall in

his plates of polished gold. His gaze, if anything, was as stern as Melinta's own. He towered over Cormac when he came to stand beside him at the feet of the throne, looking up upon Melinta with his shorn locks of black and a gaze blacker still. Under his arm was nestled his golden helm, the white plume of which sprouted around his shoulder in thin tendrils.

"Faldrus, my good lad," Melinta began, spreading his arms in greeting. Faldrus had always been dear to him. His father, Fladrielle, had been as close to him as a brother before he fell, and Melinta took it upon himself to watch over Faldrus with a fatherly eye.

In due time, Cormac's account was shared again, and Faldrus's eyes seemed to brim with curiosity. "The Red Peaks, you say," he said contemplatively. "You are sure of this?"

The gaunt messenger seemed to shudder in his flowing, white robes. "Surer than I have ever been, good captain. I saw them, plain as could be. They're there. There to be had, I say."

"My father once said that it is unwise to dismiss the words of a messenger," said Faldrus at length. "Their eyes see far afield, and their wings bring them further still. I find truth in his claim, my lord, and will rally my men upon your word."

Melinta sat back in his throne, covering his face with his hands in weariness. There was no way he could fully commit to sending men into the mountains because of Cormac's account. "Gather five hundred of your best," he said at last, though heavily. "You will depart in two days' time. See that you accrue proper stores. And Cormac, you will accompany them, as you alone hold knowledge of the way."

Simultaneously, Faldrus and Cormac bowed. "My lord," they said.

"Dismissed."

When he was alone with his thoughts, Melinta reveled in the idea of holding Kal Glamarig in his hand. After all, he had only heard tell of it, and beheld mere etchings upon weathered parchments lost in the bowels of ancient archives. The thought that he might hold it in due time sent excited shivers throughout his body, pimpling his skin with beads of glee.

After two days' time, when Faldrus had lined his chosen men into formation, Melinta met them in his courtyard. Taking Faldrus aside, he said, "I do not care how many there are. I do not care who they may be. Your task is simple. Bring me Kal Glamarig, and kill all who stand in your way."

From the high loft of his tower, Melinta watched as Faldrus led his rank out of the city, under the watchful eyes of Cormac, who in hawk form guided them north and out of sight.

15

The Netherlings

"I must say, we haven't had a feast like that in a long while," said Aries later in the night.

Lucian had returned to the table glumly, and though Orion, Leo, and Aries tried to broach the subject of his mood, he elected silence.

"Probably the only dampened spirit in the hall," said Leo under his breath. "You'd think he'd have been enjoying himself. After all, it was a party in his honor."

"Leave it, will you?" scolded Aries. "He obviously isn't in the mood."

"I'm right here," said Lucian, who despised being talked about as though he was not present. Mary had done this quite often.

Many of the guests at their table had dispersed. Halag and Halax were still present; they were engaged in conversation with other folk from the valley nearby. Bravos and Camien had ventured off to other reaches of the hall, though more knights came to sit for a pint of ale or two and to introduce themselves to Lucian, who tried his best to feign enthusiasm.

The dregs of the feast were now upon them. In an hour's time it seemed the number of guests decreased by more than half. Large assemblies of folk made their way down the winding roads into the foothills and from there into the valley below. Many of the violists had set their instruments to rest, though some took up a harp and played soothing melodies nearby.

Beside them the buffet tables were being cleaned and stripped. The great hearth in the belly of the hall was fed for the last time. Lucian watched as men and women dispersed, filing out into the open air and down into the night. Beyond the archway he saw a wide starry sky illuminating the snow-capped peaks of the range's adjacent arm, and a gentle mountain breeze filtered through the doors and tickled the fire that was burning.

Lucian could not help but sit and brood. *A party in my honor,* he thought. *I don't know why it's in my honor after all. Unless these people praise keys or other silly trinkets.* It would have made more sense if the feast were in celebration of Orion's, Aries's, and Leo's return. But for him? These people would not have known him from any other villager of Amar.

Additionally, he could not get the vision of the girl's face out of his head. Now that he had time to collect his thoughts and settle his blood, he thought of all the things he could have said. *I think I would have started with hello; then I might have told her my name.*

It was useless, and the more he thought about it the more he realized the idiotic impression he must have made.

She's probably dumbfounded by my stupidity, he contemplated. *No doubt she'll be telling all her friends about what a clumsy dancer I am, and how awkward it is to try to talk to me.*

When the last of the guests departed Lucian ventured up the corridor with his three companions. Leo was the first to leave them, going off into his own bedroom and expressing his enthusiasm to be reunited with his furs. From there Lucian, Orion, and Aries moved on. Not far along the way they met Ursa, who was coming toward them with a blanket folded under her arm and a grim look upon her pale face.

She passed a grave look to Lucian. "And how did our guest enjoy the festivities?" she asked snidely.

"Just fine, thanks," said Lucian shortly. Orion passed him a subtle sidelong glance.

"I see," she answered, and her mouth formed what

Lucian believed was her attempt at a smile. "Though I daresay I could not detect a jovial expression, cherubic as your face might be." She passed a keen look to Orion before meeting Lucian's eyes again. "Perhaps this will brighten your spirits some," she continued, "your chambers have been prepared. You must forgive me: I could find no room available save the uppermost chamber of this passageway. I have provided extra furs for you; I do not doubt you will need them. Also the hearth is ablaze, and we have provided extra kindling should you wish it refueled. I trust this will suffice."

It was Orion who answered. "It will, Ursa," he said cordially, though Lucian detected a small jolt of anger in his voice.

At this she bore her hard eyes into Orion's, and with a slow, unblinking nod swept back down the corridor and out of sight. Orion lingered as Lucian and Aries carried on, watching the fleeting figure of the cold woman become smaller in the torchlight.

When Aries finally realized Orion had not followed, he turned back and called down the way. "Are you coming?"

Orion's gaze on the now-empty corridor never faltered. "You go on ahead," he said absently. "Show Lucian to his chamber. There is something I must see to."

Lucian saw Aries's brow furrow. "Are you sure this is the time?" he said nervously.

But Orion gave no answer. There was a moment when it seemed to Lucian that he stood mustering some sort of inner strength; a will power strong enough to propel him forward. Then, bravely though with no lack of caution, he proceeded in Ursa's wake.

"What is it with her?" said Lucian to Aries as they walked on toward his bedroom.

"She means well," Aries answered.

"I'm sure."

* * *

Ursa turned to face Orion the fourth time he shouted

after her. Her hair, normally well-kempt in a tight braid, was now frazzled, and the redness around her eyes betrayed the sorrow she tried to conceal. Noticing this, Orion, who had pursued her hotly, subdued the sternness in his voice and stepped away.

"You were calling me?" she said, lifting her chin proudly. Yet her brow furrowed and twitched as though she were on the verge of tears.

A moment of silence followed. Orion looked at Ursa, averted his eyes, and then looked at her again. "You know I was."

The passage was empty but for them, and even the slightest sounds seemed to echo off the walls. Tendrils of cold winds leaked in from the Great Hall and whistled dully as they passed.

Ursa stood caressing the jewel of her necklace absently. "And what words does the highlord desire to share at this late hour?"

"I think you know why I am here," said Orion at length, straining to keep his voice low enough so as not to attract attention. "It was only all too plain that you hold the boy in contempt."

"Oh, but highlord, surely you are mistaken. I withhold no contempt for the boy—"

Suddenly Orion sprung within a hair's length of the woman, but his words were collected. "Spare me your lies, Ursa. An eye less keen might have let your hints slip, but not mine. Whatever your vendetta is, it does not lie with Lucian."

"Yes, and how silly of me to forget how *keen* of sight you are, Orion Highlord. You see far, this is true, yet while your gaze tests the limits of its reach the things closest to you go unnoticed."

"Leave us out of this, Ursa—"

At this she guffawed. "Us?" she exclaimed. "Was there ever an 'us', Orion Highlord? I've often bent my mind on it, and cannot say there was."

A look of bewilderment came over Orion's face and his jaw clenched. "I married you—"

"Out of duty." Ursa shouted this, letting her jewel alone and straightening her posture. The final word she spoke echoed far down the corridor.

Orion stepped away, anger rising from the pit of his stomach. Yet he was uncertain if he was angrier at her words or his inability to deny the truth of them.

"How can you say that?" he said blankly.

"Because it is plain, highlord." Now Ursa, too, recoiled and backed into the wall of stone behind her. Her posture slackened, as though she had assumed a figure too painful to uphold, and her voice again was dismal and broken. "I was my father's eldest daughter, and you his greatest general. Your duty was to your country, and thus to him. Our betrothal was his desire, and so we were betrothed, and later married."

Orion made as if to retort, but said nothing. He had heard this all before, yet each new time rent his heart asunder.

"Duty brought you to the stand, highlord; not love for me," Ursa continued.

"And it was duty that bound you also. Do not hold me fully accountable for a deed I did not commit alone."

Ursa released a sigh of exhaustion and looked away from him. In the now-faint glimmer of the torches Orion saw plainly the gleam of tears. Yet after a moment she turned back to him resolutely. "Duty may also have extended my hand," she said sternly, "but it was love that twined my fingers with yours and my heart that spoke the vows."

"Now it is laid bare," Orion replied shortly.

"For me it has lain bare for countless years."

Neither spoke. In the shadows of the sleeping corridor one pair of eyes warred with the other to prove less faltering.

Finally Ursa looked away and spoke again with grief. "When the city fell—"

"Don't—"

"Long have I listened to you ramble on about your sorrows, highlord. While I have your ears I will speak freely of mine. Surely you have not sought me so tirelessly to scold me like a child." Then she recoiled, for she had erected herself again to speak fervently. She continued with a troubled voice. "When the city fell I rejoiced in solitude. I thought, *What worth is a man's love for his city if there is no city to love?* It was an end in which I saw only the promise of beginning. We were spared, highlord—from wrath, yes, but also from the burdens we once carried. Your service to Dredoway ended that day, but the devotion I thought you would transfer to me was deposited tenfold into some fool's errand given you by Ation himself, or so you say."

"How dare you doubt me—"

"I might have you entertain the same inquiry, Orion Highlord. Surely that is a complex question to ponder; for never has a husband doubted his wife more."

Eyes ablaze, Orion slipped back. A wide breadth of the corridor now lay between them. His mouth stammered wordlessly, confused, angered, and deeply grieved. There stood Ursa like a storm-bent tree, wavering and straining against uprooting. Her every word iced over the hollows of his heart, yet he could not combat them. To do so would mean to lie—not only to himself but to the woman he once called his wife. It was once held dishonorable to do either. Though many ages past, he never forgot the lessons learned in his service to Dredoway, or the codes he worked inexhaustibly to uphold.

"I have only ever been faithful to you," he said with somewhat of a sigh, as though the pressures imposed on him by this unexpected confrontation were causing him physical strain.

Ursa chuckled wryly. "How dense the heart of man," she said under her breath. "After all I have ever ventured to say, you respond as all complacent husbands do. No other woman has shared your bed, this is true; and for that I am grateful. Yet there are locations other than the bedroom to call forth your matrimonial fortitude."

"I fought to uphold your freedom, your life—"

"You fought to uphold your honor. And what grieves me is you know it." There was a moment when her eyes bore yet again into his. Neither harbored the care to keep their business private any longer. Orion stood erect, taller than even Ursa may have remembered him being, and he advanced from his section of the passageway with steady ferocity. She looked up on him, into his hard eyes with their blue flame, on the chiseled cheekbones and jaw-line that she once took pleasure in kissing, on the furrowing brow that once signaled her to inquire of his troubles, and felt only the chill air of night seeping between them. Then she shoved him, and for all his might he flew back against the adjacent wall and slumped there bewildered.

Now it was Ursa who advanced on him, and though brawn was not hers to boast, his already-bent figure slunk even more under her shadow. Darting his eyes away he looked down the empty passage gravely. Suddenly her icy, care-worn fingers jolted his head to look on her, and her face was hard and grim, with a fierceness he never thought she could express.

"Don't you ever confront me like that again," she said. Like a whetstone her tongue sharpened every last syllable.

"Ahem." Orion and Ursa jolted to attention. Beside them, in the direction of the Great Hall, stood Eap, who had recovered his human form. Draped in his black robes, he skulked barely visible in the shadows. Orion assumed his full height again and stood in front of Ursa, smoothing the wrinkles along his tunic.

"Nice to see you two out and about again," said Eap lazily. "Hope I'm not interrupting."

Ursa stuck out her sharp chin. "As it happens, I was just leaving," she said, shooting Orion a fiery look before storming off in the opposite direction. The torches blazed a little more fervently as she passed, as if to light her way.

"Glad to see the Lady is in high spirits," said Eap when he was certain Ursa was out of earshot.

"What is it?" asked Orion sharply.

Eap's eyes brimmed slightly at Orion's apparent agitation, but he seamlessly recovered his usual collected manner. "Bad," he answered.

Lucian's chamber was smaller than Orion's but twice

as spacious as his old bedroom at Mary's inn. There was even a balcony that could be accessed through solid oaken doors. It was a nice surprise, though he could not help but lament the absence of a rocking chair. *One day, if I have my own place, that's going to be the first thing I see to.*

A comfortable chair would have indeed served him well on this balcony. It saddened him to think that there were probably no others like it. The uppermost chamber of the corridor actually opened upon the outer face of Shír Azgoth, and looking out from the wide patio of stone Lucian was able to perceive much of the northern lands before him. A great stream forked around the summit of the peak and fell in sighing falls before converging out in front of him. As one they wound freely down the gray-white slopes and out into the far field beyond.

The moon was high above them, and the stars shone freely across the vast expanse of the blue-velvet night. Their ghostly light paled every hue below. Far away the stream twinkled as it threaded through the yellow field and bent east to where Aries said it would eventually merge with the Elarian. That plain, as Aries told him, was once called Dredrion. It was renamed Reznarion—The Forgotten Plains—by those who survived the wrath of the Great Sage.

"Yes," said Aries sadly as the two of them gaped from off the balcony. "This plain once teemed with luscious meadows, pastures, homesteads, towns—leagues of invaluable resources built along the banks of the Silverthread. Now it has nothing to boast but dusty folds and brackish waters. The great stronghold of Dredoway has long lay in ruin, and keeps its name no more. *Ren Noctis*, it is referred to now; *The City of Night,* in the modern tongue. Sometimes I still dream of when the walls came down."

As he said this Aries's gaze never strayed from some invisible place in the night seen only by his memory.

"It's out there, isn't it?" Lucian ventured to ask, though he did not entirely want to know the answer. "The City of Night, I mean; the ruins of your city."

"Former city," Aries corrected. "This is my home now. Dredoway has fallen to memory; but yes, what's left of it is out there." He issued a slight gesture with his golden head. Far away Lucian thought to see the sharp points of black mountains.

Silence fell between them. From below the tributaries of the Silverthread hissed as they sloped downward, and from all sides the night wind howled.

"Best go inside," said Aries at last. "It's cold for August, and your hearth seems inviting."

Once inside they each brought a chair up to the fire and basked in its warmth. After asking Lucian's permission, Aries lit his pipe. His leaf smelled sweet, almost as though it were some sort of fruit-laced blend. Lucian was not mindful of smokers; the pub had always been full of them. In fact, now that he was cooped up in one of the mountain's highest rooms, he welcomed anything that moderately reminded him of home.

For a long while they sat in silence. Lucian's eyes soon became heavy-lidded, a result of both the warmth and his full stomach. Yet there were several subjects he wished to broach with Aries, with whom he felt most comfortable speaking to of personal matters. Orion felt foreboding at times, almost like a father who expected too much of his son. Lucian was sure this was not the impression he wished to give off, but he could not help the insecurity he often felt around him. Leo was just plain grumpy.

Thus Lucian broke the silence. "Can I ask you something?" he asked.

Aries, as though coming out of a trance, released a puff of smoke and nodded. Lucian continued. "That chamber—where the baths are—what's all that about?"

"Ah," said Aries, running the butt of his pipe absently about his lower lip. "I was wondering when you might ask about that."

"It's a strange room, as I'm sure you know."

Aries blew another smoke cloud. "There are many mountains in the world that hold some inner magic," he answered. "They were made by the Sages to serve as strongholds in the event that Zynys ever fell, impregnable though it has proved. Shír Azgoth is among those. There is a reason Ehrehalle was built here after all."

"I *thought* there was something odd about this place." At this Aries raised an eyebrow. "No offense, of course! I don't mean strange like a bad strange, but a . . . well, a good (?) strange. I don't know what I'm saying."

"Relax," said Aries, laughing. "I know what you mean. These types of things are difficult to put into words. It's said one must see to believe, yet many things are not easy to register even when one sees them plainly."

Silence fell. At length Lucian spoke. "This isn't the first magic mountain I've been in since I left home," he said. "We were forced to pass through one in the east. The Mountain of Dreams, it was called. Yet there were . . . things . . . living in it. Vile things." Then a vivid image of the Enchantress clouded his vision, and he did not hear the words he spoke next. "Beautiful things."

"Magic sometimes begets magic," said Aries at length, and his voice seemed to pull Lucian out of his brief trance. "Unfortunately I don't have all the answers concerning those matters, and the one I've provided is vague at best. Orion is the one you should consult with such inquiries, if you really want to know how you came to see what you saw there."

"I'd rather just forget them, to be honest. I'm more interested in those baths, anyway. That room—it seemed, I don't know—"

"Boundless?" Aries suggested through a cloud of purple smoke.

"I guess," said Lucian unconfidently. "I don't really know how to put it into words. It's like you said before, I think. I saw it, but I'm having trouble understanding what I saw. There seemed to be hundreds of bath-pools, and each one had a fountain in the middle pouring water into them. From outside the pool the fountains were shapeless, yet when I sat down in the water I saw—well—I guess I'll just say the fountain had transformed."

Aries leaned in on his chair, his interest blatantly piqued. His eyes had come alive with a fire other than the hearth's reflection. "Into what?" he practically whispered.

"It was a man," said Lucian blankly. "A tall man, muscled yet old-looking. He had a mane of flowing hair and a long wavy beard. I can't get his eyes out of my head, though. They were blank, yeah, but it was almost as though I could tell how he was looking at me."

Lucian looked at Aries hopefully, wishing the account he provided was enough for Aries to develop some sort of definitive answer. But all he said was, "Go on. What else did you see?"

Lucian sat, remembering. "He held a staff in his hand, and he was holding it over his head like he was ready to strike someone. In the other he held a sword, that, well . . . wait—" Then he recalled the vision for the better, and though he had not made the connection in the pool, he realized suddenly that the sword the statue carried was Excebellus.

Fear consumed him. What could this mean? Was this even real? Could this mountain, much like the Mountain of Dreams, be deceiving his eyes? Resolute, he decided quite plainly that he would not bring himself to fall into the same trap. "I must have stayed in the water too long," he said faintly.

"What about the sword?" asked Aries, intrigued yet confused.

"It's nothing," said Lucian, thinking quickly to change the subject. "I guess my main question for you is: what is one looking at when he steps into those pools? Obviously the fountains are designed to trigger something in someone's mind. I understand that much. But what?"

Aries smiled. "You've become cleverer since you tumbled down that hill in Ravelon," he said. "They've been called many things—Dream Pools, mostly, though their eldest names are Luminai. What you bathed in was called a Luminos. Only the magic mountains have them, though they are difficult to locate once inside. It took nearly a century to find ours."

"So, are they supposed to get you clean quicker than a normal bath or something?"

Aries laughed. "They are handy in that way also," he

said. "But they have better uses. A Luminos can show you many things. It can see into the future and show you things that will come to fruition should the viewer choose one course of action over another. It can look into the past and show you what might have been had you chosen a different road. The most apt minds can even view loved ones from afar in the state they are currently in. I can look into one and spy on Leo snoring now, if I wished."

Lucian chuckled slightly, too mesmerized by Aries's account to register jabs of humor. "I didn't see any of that though," he said. "I only saw that the fountain had changed."

"That's because you weren't looking *into* the Luminos; you were viewing things from inside it. If one steps into the waters of such a basin, his or her mind is instantly altered. You can see a number of things while sitting in one. It has long been believed that one can even catch a glimpse of his or her destiny. Why you saw the fountain in the shape of that man I cannot say, Lucian, but it's not a thing to be ignored. Have you seen him before?"

Lucian racked his mind for all it was worth. "I think so," he said. "Only in dreams. I've been having them since I was young. But they're always so quick and vague that it's hard to say if it was him at all."

"Interesting," Aries said contemplatively. "Who do you think he might be?"

Lucian opened his mouth to speak when suddenly his chamber door burst open and they were startled out of their chairs. There in the doorway stood Leo panting. His eyes were intense and his mane of black hair was unkempt from sleeping. The massive blade he was carrying glinted in the firelight.

"They've come," he said gravely. "The Netherlings."

It seemed Aries had darted out the door before Leo finished speaking, leaving Leo behind in the doorway and Lucian puzzled as ever. Wrapped in his furs he seemed more bear than man, his great sword the only fang he would ever need. "You stay here," he barked, passing Lucian a swift, stern glance.

Leo was reaching to close the door when Lucian answered. "I want to come." For a moment both stood looking at each other incredulously, as though having heard the strange voice of an unseen third party.

The hulking man's fierce eyes bore into Lucian, standing feebly by the fire and swimming in Orion's hand-me-downs. Removing his thick fingers from the doorknob, he proceeded slowly into the room. There was a look of confusion and deep thought upon his face as he approached. Lucian's knees began to shudder and his heart seemed to palpitate. He figured this was how all of Leo's adversaries felt in his presence.

He came to stand just inches away, settling his sword down in front of him and resting his hands upon the pommel. Every so often a flicker of reflected firelight caused Lucian to squint. "You want to come, do you?" he asked, not unkindly, though the natural bestial properties of his voice made it difficult for anything he said to sound endearing.

Lucian thought he would cower under his shadow, in the face of his great sword that stood nearly as tall as him, but he remained steadfast. "I do," he said. "I want to see."

"You've no idea what you're *going* to see."

The foreboding nature of Leo's words caused Lucian to recoil almost involuntarily. He recovered almost as quickly, however, and looked back into the grim eyes of Lionsbane. "I don't care," he said softly. "I haven't known what I was going to see since I left home, and most of it's been bad. I'm used to seeing bad things. And I have a sword; a pretty good one, too. Let me come."

A small grin came to Leo's face, which appeared to Lucian to be the meshing of a snarl and a smile. "Maybe I was wrong about you," he said at length and with an air of surprise. Lucian did not understand why he felt so excited to get permission to see something horrible, but his spirits rose tenfold. Until Leo said, "That's not my decision to make, unfortunately."

Lucian's brow furrowed and a deluge of agitation crashed

over him. Another rally to protect him—another moment in which he cowered behind his betters and let them fight his battles. "But—let—I just—"

"Stay here."

Leo's words were final. Yanking the edge of his blade from the stone floor, he swept off, shutting the door forcefully on his way out. Lucian shouted angrily, and in a fury paced around the room just looking for something on which to release his aggression. Finally, taking up one of the chairs by the fire, he flung it against the door where it splintered into tethered pieces.

"I'm not a child!" he screamed, and his voice, feeble though he thought it was, echoed madly and seemed to shake the very walls of his chamber. With a roar the hearth briefly flared. A sudden wave of something like ice welled up inside him. Suddenly he felt strained—stretched and crammed all at once. A searing pain jolted from within, sending him to his knees, casting him to the floor. With a last-ditch effort he reached for the only thing within range, but Excebellus sat too high upon the bed to be grasped. Falling to the floor, he lay struggling until his every movement ceased.

As Leo raced down the corridor he came upon Aries, who must have stopped in his chamber to arm himself. Clad now in his steel plates and fur-lined cloak he advanced toward the Great Hall with his hammer over his shoulder. Leo came abreast of him, slowing to a walk and carrying his sword likewise. Passing among them were several other knights. Up ahead they glimpsed Camien shuffling through the throng with Bravos not far behind. Suddenly a gruff voice rattled their bones from behind them, and they both turned and looked upon the brutish figure of Streph the Summit. Nearly two heads taller than Leo he stood, and boasted perhaps double his brawn. Like Leo he was clad in furs, and carried with him his thick-bladed scimitar, the fuller of which was fashioned in the likeness of a lick of flame.

"I thought supper was over," was the first thing he said

in his rumbling manner. "Suppose I've some room left for Netherling, though."

"First time for everything, Summit," said Aries.

"Where's the boy?" asked Streph. "Had him removed from your hip, did you?" He released a laugh that made him sound like a panting bear.

"I told him to stay behind," said Leo frankly. "He wanted to come, too. Now *that* was a surprise. No need for him to see this though. Beasts are one thing; beasts that once were men are quite another. Could play with his mind in an unsavory way."

"Surely there's a beast in every man, Lionsbane," answered Streph.

"Right now the ones outside are the only ones I care about," Leo answered.

Soon the corridor opened into the wide breadth of Ehrehalle. Many of the tables had been removed; only the usual few remained. Four torches—one in each corner—shed the only light in the room. The steel of armor and weapons glinted in their meek gleam. A company of Orion's knights stood gathered in the center, waiting. Aries and Leo glimpsed him at the forefront of the fray, his fighting knives drawn and his posture unwavering, piercing the darkness with his gaze. Behind him everyone readied their arms and mustered their courage, for the howls penetrating the deepening night no longer belonged to the wind.

Leo and Aries joined Orion on either side. Upon the shaft of his moonstone hammer, Aries's grip tightened. Hands overlapped on the pommel of his sword, Leo stood leaning.

"Why don't we shut the doors on them?" Aries suggested. "There's still time."

"No," said Orion with fierce finality. "We will settle this tonight."

Leo smiled. "I hoped as much."

They caught a sound like thundering hooves rising up from the westward road, and soon heard activity on the stair, like many daggers slashing away at stones. An empty hush fell over them. Every grip tightened. Leo brought Lionsbane to his face and kissed the blade. Every set of eyes strained more alertly. Then several brutish shapes came into view. A row of gleaming eyes peered in at them. Warily they emerged from the shadows and stepped into the hall, a tangle of thirteen brutish men.

Nothing about them seemed right. The closer they approached, the less man-like they appeared. It had been long since Orion or his men had stood in their presence, the Netherlings of Ren Noctis. Most of them had nearly shriveled completely out of their former skins and appeared to them now as two-legged wolves. There were some, however, who still clung to man-like attributes. Their leader, for one, still grasped the remains of his fading human complexion. Coarse hair now sprouted from his chest and limbs, but it was not as thick as his companions' yet. Beneath those black thickets they could see the color his skin had once been. This was Amarog, Captain of the Netherlings. His brawn was still with him, though like his kith his limbs had become elongated, sharp at the joints, and bent somewhat awkwardly. Striding forward with much of his former, swaggering gait, he bore his yellow-tinged wolf-eyes into Orion's. The twelve at his back skulked forward in his wake, hunched like old beggars. Every mouth was contorted into a snarl. Some were even growling. Within their gaping, lipless mouths their teeth had been chiseled into fangs. Whatever noses they once had kept had been shorn away by their transformations. Only slits remained that throbbed as they breathed, releasing wisps of breath into the chill air. Amarog came so close that his own began misting over the tip of Orion's outstretched blade.

"Amarog," said Orion, his voice seeping with disdain.

"Highlord," answered Amarog mockingly, feigning as much of a bow as his distorted body could manage. A small, gurgling wave of laughter rippled through his cronies. Amarog's eyes studied every corner of the hall, which had been tended to the extent that no evidence of a feast remained. "A pity, gents," he continued. "Looks as though we've missed the festivities. I do loathe tardiness; don't you, highlord?"

Amarog then shifted away from Orion and began to

slowly circle the knights, running a clawed hand seductively along the head of Aries's hammer as he passed.

"You are trespassing, Amarog," said Orion sternly to the Netherling's back. "We had an agreement—an agreement you are now breaking. Never to—"

"—trespass upon the other's lands unless with dire need," finished Amarog lazily in his brutish, gritty tone. "A need that may only be deemed dire by the party whom is trespassed upon. Yes, of course; we've been through this."

Amarog had now reached the outer ring of the circle of knights and stopped before Streph the Summit.

"Ah, I see the Summit is yet to bear snow atop his high peak," he said. Orion turned, surprised to see that even Streph, the mightiest of all his knights, bore a look of terror.

"Now, now, Strephon," Amarog continued, "there's no need to get antsy. I'm just saying hello, after all. I'm glad to see you looking so well and youthful. It's been a long time, hasn't it? Too long, in fact. I thought for sure you'd look older—much, much older. But of course I'm forgetting. You've been given the same gift as the rest of your order, though whether you truly earned it is debatable—"

Suddenly, in one swift motion, the circle of knights parted for Orion, and Amarog yet again found himself at knife-point. Many of the Netherlings dropped to all fours at his back, preparing to defend their captain, but the knights were quicker, and held them outside their gate of weapons.

Had Leo moved his blade an inch forward it would have drawn blood from the throat of one of the beasts. "Move and Lionsbane gets a snack," he growled. The Netherling cowered under his shadow, whimpering like a wounded hound.

"You will leave my men out of this," said Orion, inching cautiously closer. Seeing his companions held at bay caused Amarog to subdue Streph, a clawed finger settled amply on his throat. The hulking giant of a man was bent back awkwardly now, as Amarog stood nearly a foot shorter and drew him below even his level. A trickle of blood coursed down the Summit's neck and disappeared beneath his furs. The look on his face was desperate.

"Oh, now, now, highlord," said Amarog, slowly backing away from Orion's cautious advancement. "No need to get angry, though I do *shudder* at your temper."

Orion's blade never lowered or shook. "Release him."

Amarog issued what could only have been a smile, grotesque and inhuman though it was. "Ah, well, you see, highlord, I would be glad to. However, there is a *bit* of a problem. Just the slightest *smidgen* of an issue. You see, as we speak my men are held captive by yours. Should I relinquish your man, I fear the lives of my own will be jeopardized."

Orion said nothing for many moments. Aries tucked his hammer under the chin of the nearest Netherling so that its horrid eyes could see his face.

"Stand down," said Orion at length.

"I'm sorry," said Amarog. "You must forgive me, highlord, but the hearing of a cur has its limits, you know."

"Stand down," Orion repeated fervently. Reluctantly, his men did so. Leo was the last to lower his blade.

"Your knife," said Amarog after making certain the knights had heeded Orion's order. Orion looked at his knife as though he had forgotten he held it outward. There was a moment of hesitation before he brought down his arm.

Amarog gave the same fangled smile, but his grip on Streph never relinquished. "Now that wasn't so hard," he said.

"Release him," said Orion sternly.

"Ah, yes, of course," said Amarog. "I must uphold my end of the bargain." Then Amarog lifted Streph from the ground and threw him across the room. Streph the Summit came crashing down nearly thirty yards away, bowling over some unsuspecting Netherlings as he passed.

Several knights raced to his aid, but Streph was more aggravated than hurt. "Get off!" Orion heard him shout. "I'm fine. Let me at him. I'll kill him!"

This resulted in the general rise from Amarog's cronies, though they were brought back into submission as Orion's men shot them stern glances.

"Enough, Streph," said Orion. Reluctantly, Streph

stepped back and meshed (as best he could) into the throng of knights.

"Ah, Strephon, no hard feelings. I see you've become obedient since last we met—"

"Why have you come?" said Orion sternly. There were none between them now. Knight and Netherling alike looked on in anticipation, wondering what would come of the exchange or hoping for a specific turn of events. "Do not forget: at hand is still the matter of your trespassing."

"Yes, of course!" said Amarog, who stood hunched and rattling some of his claws together. "My sincerest gratitude for reminding me, highlord. I was actually getting to that—"

"Speak!"

"Temper, temper," said the Netherling chidingly. "And after I come to do you a favor. After my men and I risk the horrors of Reznarion to bring you these tidings."

"You are the only horror that festers on Reznarion," said Leo from the assembly at Orion's back. "Your lot is the only thing worth dreading on the Forgotten Plains."

"Ah, Lionsbane speaks!" said Amarog. "I wondered where you were. Where's that little devil of yours? All snuggled in his den while daddy goes and disposes of his relatives?"

Leo started as if to advance, but Aries held him back.

"Such ferocity, such malice," said Amarog, moving closer and closer to where Leo stood, his sickly, yellow eyes never straying from the knight's. "Renowned, of course, and rightly so. Destroying an entire civilization because they fought to take back what was theirs is indeed honorable. But it is the sad plight of a usurper to think everything belongs to him, is it not? Of course you would agree, Lionsbane; perhaps you more than any. Do you ever look at your cub and wonder if this was the life he would have chosen? Do you think he ever wonders where his mother is, or remembers what she looked like? No, I don't think you do—"

"You speak plainly of emotions as if you bear them," said Leo after a moment. His voice was as broken as Aries or Orion ever heard it. "That's what got you *your* plight, vermin."

Amarog made as if to retort, when Orion spoke. "Amarog, you are trying my patience to its end," he said. "Speak and be gone. I will not suffer this hall to house you any longer."

"Of course, of course," answered the Netherling. "Then I will say what I have come here to say, and flee as you wish. Long have you taken shelter here with the notion that you are undiscoverable, yet whatever secrecy you've so long withheld is fleeting."

The knights mumbled amongst themselves. Some looked to the Netherlings as if to catch a hint that their captain was lying, though all of them stood steadfast and grave.

"You lie," said Orion at long last.

"Do I?" said Amarog. "Do you suspect I rose this morning with the idea in mind to seek you out for old time's sake? How many times have I stepped foot in your land, highlord? How many times before tonight have I cast our agreement aside?" There was silence, then Amarog rose to his full height, and his shrill wolfish voice rang throughout the hall. "ANSWER ME!"

Swords were drawn involuntarily. Orion cowered for the abruptness of Amarog's exclamation.

"Never," he said, a bit shaken.

"Too true," said Amarog, reclaiming his former lazy air. "Whether you believe me or not is your own business. You've ever been the stubborn sort, from what I've heard."

"Our location is known then?" asked Orion, not bothering to mask the gravity with which he spoke.

"Its secret has been told, certainly," said Amarog.

"To whom?"

Another fiendish smile. "I think you already know."

"Melinta."

Amarog's eyes brimmed. "Glad to see your genius is still with you," he said.

"How is this possible? A party of Fairies has not crossed the Elarian in years, not since their straightaway passage was barred. And it has been longer still since they traveled through the mountains."

"It wasn't discovered by Fairies, of course! Far be it for

them to stick their pretty little faces into the mountains. Frostbite is not an option for their kind, fragile as they are. And climbing might chip a nail, or worse, the poor dears."

"Then who? And how have you come by this knowledge?"

Amarog smiled again, and brought a hairy arm up over his shoulder to scratch his back. "Do excuse me," he said. "Fleas. Dreadful things. How do I know this, you ask? Well, I too have my little winged messengers, highlord. It would seem as though the skies are more cluttered than the plains these days."

"Then it could have been one of your own who told."

"It very well could have," answered Amarog, "though if my flyers meant to bring outside attention to this quaint little nook they'd have done so long ago. Seldom do they venture so far south, but there was one from my roost—Eíred his name is—that curiosity drew into these peaks. Upon the skyways was a messenger he had never encountered. A white hawk, he said it was, and thought it to be of your stock. He followed the messenger on its return flight, all the way to the white tower of Deavorás where it perched upon Melinta's very arm—"

"A mere pet, it seems—"

Amarog's scowling laughter filled the hall. "Denial does not become you, highlord. Eíred did not fly all those leagues to Deavorás to watch a pet and its master at play. He remained for a long while, and saw the white hawk shift into human form, and share many tidings with the king."

"What did it say, then? This white hawk."

"He delivered your whereabouts, mentioning the hall and the little valley below. Melinta now knows that men dwell here, but there is more! He knows also that the Keeper of Fates has come west and is among them."

At his words, whatever subtle sounds within the hall ceased completely. Not even the wind seemed to be wheezing any longer. Though he tried to downplay the weight of Amarog's tidings, the dismal look upon his face betrayed any attempt to conceal his despair.

"Ah, so you know of what I speak," said Amarog at length. "I thought so. So where is he, highlord? Where is this Keeper of Fates? We have traveled far to see him."

"And you will return without the pleasure."

"Come now, highlord. I have showed you mine, now you must show me yours! I want to see him; *we* want to see him. Where is he?"

But when Orion opened his mouth to retort, Lucian's voice answered from the corridor. "I'm right here," he called.

Every head jolted to the lone figure at the edge of the hall. Lucian was not entirely sure what had possessed him to go to the Great Hall; it just seemed right. Perhaps it was the dream that urged him to do so. Though his dreams had indeed been strange of late, this had proven strangest. It seemed so real, so vivid, so infinitesimally different from reality that he wondered if it had even been a dream at all. Aries had been there, and they had been talking. But suddenly Leo appeared, bearing tidings that caused Aries to flee. Then both vanished, and no matter how hard Lucian tried to follow, his passage was denied. An unprecedented fury filled him—an anger that propelled him to dismantle many objects in his chamber.

It was the chill of the floor that woke him. The hearth had housed only dying embers, and the room had largely become dark. He didn't even recall falling out of his bed. But rather than contemplate how he wound up on the ground, he took up Excebellus and left the room with the absent air of a sleepwalker. The corridor had been cold and empty, and a horrid smell was tarnishing the air. Something like fear was building up inside him, yet the stronger it became the more urgently he went on. A new strength seemed to fester within him. He no longer felt clumsy or weak. Excebellus no longer seemed an ambiguous accessory in his hand, but a golden extension of his arm that he strangely longed to wield.

When the opening of the corridor came into view he saw many shapes before the backdrop of night. The unmistakable figures of Orion's knights stood gathered before grotesquely shaped beings, some slouched, some settled on all fours. Seeing only their shadowy silhouettes, they appeared to Lucian as a pack of wolves—pointed ears, slender, angular limbs, and gleaming eyes reflecting the torchlight. Orion stood in the foreground conversing with one of them. This creature stood upright like a man, and because he was closer than the others Lucian could see his face. There was enough evidence upon it to suggest that he had once been human. His brow, however, had become bulged, beneath which were deep-set eyes that indeed bore wolfish qualities. His limbs, while similar to the others', were well-muscled. Hair sprouted from his entire person in coarse patches, though the sickly hue of his skin was discernible through their cover. Inside his lipless mouth were fangs.

Suddenly he remembered something Leo mentioned in his dream: *They have come,* he had said. *The Netherlings.* Sure enough he even glimpsed Leo near the high doors overlooking the night, clad in the same attire in which he had appeared in Lucian's sleep. Aries was with him also, his mighty hammer extended.

That wasn't a dream, he thought instantly, and felt as though he walked naked into a crowded room. At once he felt threatened. The pressing feeling that he was being sought welled up inside him. The anxious, heavy sensation that he was in a place he shouldn't have been tensed his limbs. They were there for him beyond any doubt.

So why wasn't he afraid? Perhaps for the first time since he left home, the nagging sense of fear was gone. Instead he felt only angered and annoyed. He was tired of being searched for; tired of being hunted; tired of wondering what new terrors would find him in the deep hours of the night. Wearing his anger like a shield, he went on cautiously.

Quietly he stood for many moments, listening. The creature asked for him once. Orion would not answer. Then the creature prodded insistently: "Come now, highlord. I have showed you mine, now you show me yours! I want to see him; *we* want to see him. Where is he?"

What happened next was as involuntary an action as breathing. "I'm right here," Lucian heard himself say. Then it was as though something else took hold of his body.

He watched himself step out of the shadows and raise Excebellus outward. Before him now the beastly creature stood blankly.

"Ask and you shall receive, I suppose," it answered, its eyes blaring hungrily as it skulked forward.

Orion moved faster than wind to block its way. "One more step and it will be the last you take," he warned.

This proved enough warning for the creature to recoil. "Now, now, highlord, we've talked about that temper of yours. There's no need to put your mean face on. I just want to get a good look at him, that's all. After all, if this is the one, I've as much a right to see him as you."

"You lost that right."

The creature slipped forward cautiously, but Orion would not move. "Bygones," it said. "Can't you allow me this small decency? He's not here after all, the—ahem— Great Sage."

"From here the only steps you take are towards the door," said Orion. "I have no qualms with slaying you where you stand."

"Let him come." The voice was Lucian's own, and even the creature itself looked on him bewilderedly. Suddenly fear presented itself again and gathered quickly. Sweat began to bead up on Lucian's forehead. Slowly he began to slip back into the shadows.

"Shall I follow you up the corridor?" asked the wolf over Orion's shoulder. His companions' gargled laughter rose up from behind the wall of knights.

It was not until then that Lucian realized he was pedaling backward steadily. From where Orion stood, he appeared as a shadowy figure distorted by Excebellus's blue-and-green lights.

"It is evident," began the creature, "that I will not be permitted to travel that far tonight." It shot a sidelong glance at Orion. "Thus if anyone must make themselves present it is you, Keeper. That is, if you *are* the Keeper. Come out, come out, Keeper. I won't bite, you know."

"Lucian, stay where you are," Orion ordered.

And that is exactly what Lucian did not do. Striding

forward now he appeared again. Warily he approached, afraid of the creature for its horridness and of Orion for having disobeyed him.

"That's it," said the creature. "Just a little farther. Oh, yes. Look at you. And you've got a little sword, too. How darling. Let me see you."

Lucian now stepped within reach of the monster. Orion stood as unmoving as a statue, his expression of grim incredulity. From the doorway his knights looked on nervously. Over their outdrawn weapons the Netherlings alertly watched to see what would happen. The creature then began circling. Orion's blade remained poised between its shoulders, ready to penetrate at the first sign of trouble.

"This is him, then," it said, snarling and winding its way slowly around Lucian. "*This* is what you've waited three thousand years to find? This schoolboy masquerading as a soldier in the knickknacks of his betters? I almost feel silly for coming so far." Then it stopped its slow coil, and stooping close to Lucian's ear, whispered, "Almost."

A searing shiver slid down Lucian's spine. Goosebumps poked up along his neck and down his back.

"Enough, Amarog," demanded Orion.

The hulking beast stood erect then and stepped back, as if reluctantly passing up a tempting meal.

"The business of Ren Talam is none of the Forsaken City's," Orion continued, coming to stand once more between Lucian and the beast.

There was a long moment when Amarog stood studying Lucian, and Lucian, afraid a sudden movement might spark a chase, remained poised and still.

"Keep him," said Amarog finally, with the absent air of one denying a free sample of some odd dish. "He will serve no purpose to us, the half-man he is." Amarog's cronies began chuckling. Lucian did not understand why, but somehow he took great offense to this.

Finally the beast proceeded toward the door. When he was further away he turned around and spoke again. "It was rash of me indeed to set my men upon this endeavor. The Forgotten Plains, as you have named them, are wide and unforgiving, and our trek will seem longer knowing it was in vain. But I'm surprised, Orion Highlord, to find this stranger welcomed among you as a king."

"May it fill you still, then, as you return to your ruins."

Amarog chuckled darkly, and Lucian shuddered at the sound. "It takes more than prophecies to make a king, highlord. In the end they are only absent words."

"Other things must suffice when blood fails," answered Orion.

At this gibe Amarog and many of his companions bared their fangs and hissed. "Come, gents," he barked. "Let us fly while the moon still lingers." With that his twelve followers backed away hesitantly and sped off into the night. Amarog was beyond the doors when he turned back for the last time.

"Oh, there is one more thing, Orion Highlord," he said. "Give my sister my best, if you would. It's a pity to have missed her."

Then he raced beyond the stairs and was gone. Knights followed in their wake to assure the only direction they took was homeward. Two remaining casks of ale were brought out for those who stayed behind. Leo suggested Lucian have a drink or two, as it would be a good way to "reset his nerves". But Lucian did not feel much like drinking, or lingering in the Great Hall any longer. It still reeked of Netherling. Amarog's breath still felt hot on his face. Retiring to his chambers, he took to lying in his bed. Though cold he did not bother with the hearth. Instead he lay beneath his furs, trying to blot out the horror of his recent experience—an attempt made all the more difficult as the howls of the Netherlings rose up over the northern plains.

16

Jadyn

For some reason, Lucian thought that when he opened his eyes he would feel something similar to a hangover. He was mistaken. In fact he felt more refreshed and invigorated than ever.

I might not be fully awake yet, he surmised. Thus he opened his eyes wider. The fervent gleam of morning fought to squeeze through the cracks of his balcony doors and the smell of something like fresh pine was distributed sweetly throughout the room. Sitting up and stretching, he moved to the bedside and dangled his legs above the floor.

I feel like I should feel worse than I do, he thought. *Much worse.* But he couldn't remember why. The lingering sense that he was forgetting something kept toying with his thoughts. His mind housed a blankness similar to that day in his former life when he had forgotten Jem's birthday. It was all too soon before he remembered, however. Suddenly a wash of realization came over him, much like it did before he had sped off to the creek. *The Netherlings,* he remembered.

In his waking moments his encounter with Amarog only hours ago seemed the vague fragment of a dream. He hardly remembered walking into Ehrehalle to confront him, and he was still having trouble understanding why he even bothered. Leo had told him to stay behind, and he should have listened. But, strange though it was to him, he was glad he refrained.

It wasn't so bad after all, he thought. *He was just a*

man. A man-wolf. A wolf-man. Whatever he could be called.

In the corner by the door he saw Excebellus leaning against the doorframe. The sapphire and emerald gems upon the pommel glowed brightly in the dim. "You would have protected me, wouldn't you have?" he said. It was the first time he ever spoke to his sword aloud.

Making as if to stand, he was brought to attention when he heard a whispering voice suddenly answer: *Yes.*

There was no muscle on his body that flinched for a long moment. Only his eyes darted left, right, up, and down for any sign of the voice. The doorway was empty, and the only other opening to his bedroom was sealed by solid oaken doors.

I'm losing my mind, he surmised, nodding with the expression of one who has acquired a long-sought answer.

Coming to his feet at long last he stretched, finding it hard to recall a time he felt more replenished. The bed had done him wonders. It perhaps rivaled the comfort Orion's had provided, and could not even compare to the one he slept in at home. He tried to guess what the hour was. *It's probably almost noon,* he guessed. *It was almost dawn by time I went to sleep, and I feel like I've slept for a full day.*

Turning to the chest in front of his bed, he rummaged through for clothes. Orion had seen it filled with numerous shirts and pairs of breeches, as well as thick socks that warmed his feet just by looking at them. He dressed quickly, throwing on a green tunic embroidered with Orion's usual sigil and a pair of brown breeches.

"Finally," he said to himself. "A shirt that actually fits."

Indeed this tunic was much more form-fitting. *Orion probably realized how ridiculous I looked in the other one he gave me.* Then he felt sickly. *And everyone else must have too! Why am I so hungry?*

After the feast the night prior, Lucian thought he might never eat again and still be full. Throwing open his door he took a peek outside. The corridor was empty, but the ends of a delicious scent reached him from the Great Hall. Breakfast. *Count me in.* So it was he trotted off, shutting the door in his wake and salivating.

As far as activity, Ehrehalle boasted little this morning. Only six out of the plethora of tables from the feast remained. Here and there a knight sat. Some were fully dressed in their plates and mail, others were lounging in casual attire similar to Lucian's. The great doors were open to the outside world. Beyond, the adjacent arm of the mountains glowed red, with flashing snows atop the higher summits that jolted blindingly if caught by the sun at the right angle. Gray arms of smoke reached up from Dwén Marnié, though of the village Lucian could see nothing from where he stood.

He glimpsed Orion first, sitting atop one of the tables with one leg crossed over the other and reading a sheet of parchment intently. When he saw Lucian his gaze became stern, and he set the parchment down and looked upon him quizzically.

"I would have a word, if you don't mind," he said gravely.

"Alright." Lucian phrased this as more of a question than a statement.

Orion led him by the cloth of his shoulder to the opening of the corridor from which he had just arrived. "Your actions last night were inexcusable," he said in a sharp whisper. "When I tell you to stand down, you stand down. If I give you an order, you follow it. If one of the *knights* gives you an order, you follow it. I will not have you waltz about with reckless abandon. You do not know what it was you were up against. Remorseless creatures. You think beasts frighten you? Try beasts with the minds of men."

Lucian matched the fierceness of Orion's stare. "Is that all?" he said lazily.

Orion straightened his posture and backed away a comfortable distance, a subtle, dubious expression on his face. He simply nodded in response.

Lucian walked away without a word, anger rising in his stomach. He could hear Mary's voice in his head. *What has gotten into you, Lucian Rolfe? How* dare *you speak that way to your elders?* Strangely he did not care. If his elders could speak to him that way, then he would speak that way to them. It was only fair. Perhaps an evening with the Netherlings changed his outlook on things. Perhaps he was at his wit's end. Perhaps he simply had enough of other people fighting his battles for him and telling him to hide in a corner like a child. Lucian didn't know. All he knew was that he felt different today, and not a very bad different at that. His mind felt free for the first time ever. Not even in Amar had it been so clear. His body felt strong and warm and raring. He liked this new feeling. He didn't want it to go away.

He filled two plates with eggs, potatoes, and thin slabs of beef no doubt left in stock from the feast. Stacking them atop each other, he took them to a table nearest the door to eat. The fresh breeze was cold and rejuvenating; a perfect complement to the heat from the fires within the hall.

Scold me like that, he kept saying in his head. *Like I'm six. Just because he was afraid doesn't mean that everybody else was.* That's when he stopped chewing and finally put his utensils down, remembering how rank Ehrehalle was with fear and how little of it belonged to him. He was frightened, sure, but not afraid. To him they had always been different things. Fright was fear of the present, thus the Netherlings and Amarog indeed *frightened* him; but to be afraid was something else entirely. To be afraid meant to be fearful not only of the present but of the present's effect on the future. He silently gaped at how he bore none of that in the wee hours of the morning in the face of such horrid beings. Not once did he take into account the likely reality that Amarog could have cloven him in two with one deft swipe of his claws. Not for one moment did he take time to think about the overarching picture and the true reason why he was in Ehrehalle to begin with. In that regard, he did act recklessly. It now angered him not that Orion scolded him, but that it was a much-warranted reprimand. Yet still the curiosity of his own courage is what perplexed him most. Then he thought of something he hadn't before. *The ale,* he thought. *Beer muscles.*

You fool yourself, someone whispered. Involuntarily he sat upright. It was the same voice he had heard in his bedroom—cold, sharp, and shrill.

"Who said that?" he said, turning around and beckoning everyone present with his eyes. The din of general breakfast conversations quieted as all eyes fell on him.

"Said what?" Lucian turned to see Aries, who had just mounted the stairs and walked into the hall from outside. The clatter of forks on plates and the humming of quiet conversations resumed.

Lucian was silent for a moment, then bent his head to his plate to continue breakfast himself. "Nothing," he said quietly.

"How did you sleep?" said Aries, putting his hammer to rest on the table and sitting across from him.

The initial quake the weapon sent through the table knocked some straying eggs off Lucian's plate, and he stared into the eyes of the moonstone ram before answering. "Well, thanks."

"Glad to hear it," said Aries. "No one thought you would manage it, what with meeting the Netherlings and all, and Amarog especially."

"I managed fine," replied Lucian through a mouth full of potatoes. "Why are you sweating?"

In fact Aries was perspiring profusely in his gray rag of a shirt. His golden locks were matted with sweat and clinging to his brow, and his hands and wrists glistened with moisture as well.

"Training," he said matter-of-factly. "Me and some of the others. We've a small training room down the right corridor where we go and whet our skills some. You should join us some time. Might learn some helpful tips."

"I'd like that!" Lucian exclaimed merrily. "And I can bring Excebellus."

"Absolutely," Aries smiled. "Though we usually spar with blunted or wooden weapons. You can accompany me tomorrow."

Excitement filled him. "I'll be there!"

Lucian could not help but remember the day he witnessed Aries and the others fighting in Ravelon. He never thought an act so destructive could be done with such grace and beauty. Though the weapons they wielded were heavy, they swung them like steel feathers. To Lucian it appeared more like a dance than a fight. There was nothing cumbersome about it. Every attack and parry seemed to have certain rhythmic qualities that flowed together seamlessly. *And I'm going to learn them,* he thought eagerly. *No more hiding. No more being told to cower in a corner. They'll see.*

Just then a slew of birds funneled through the doors. Most of them were ravens, though some brown hawks were among their number, along with many other small birds such as finches and warblers. Those breaking their fast became startled and ducked as they swooped in, and as soon as they touched down their figures sprouted into those of men. Eap was at the forefront of the gangly gathering. Like him the others were gaunt and very stringy. Lucian supposed that's what a lifetime of shifting between bird and man would to do someone.

The hall soon became filled with bustle. Apparently the folk of Ehrehalle still held their transformations spectacular also.

"Good morning, all!" shouted a brown-cloaked man with unkempt hair and golden-brown eyes. He entered as one of the hawks, and walked around with the swagger of one. "It is Thursday, of course. The thirty-first of August, to be exact. Plan your days accordingly and be sure to adhere to your schedules—"

Eap swatted him aside and came forward. "Orion Highlord," he was calling. "Orion Highlord?"

That was when Lucian stopped paying attention. Turning his eyes back to his plate, he played absently with his food.

"What's the matter?" said Aries.

"August 31st," answered Lucian. "Today's my birthday."

"Well Happy Birthday, then, of course! And what better place to spend it, eh?"

Lucian gave a wan chuckle. In fact he knew many better places to spend it. The thought that a year ago today he was in MaDungal's Pub having songs sung in his honor and drinks brought to him at will awoke in him a new moroseness.

"And how old are you today?" Aries continued.

"Eighteen."

"Ah, the splendor of youth," replied Aries wistfully. "I don't even *remember* when I was eighteen. But then I don't really recall when I was one thousand-and-eighteen."

"Well at least you don't look much older than twenty-five or thirty."

"Sometimes I'd rather look my age and *feel* twenty-five or thirty than have it the other way around."

Aries's attention, however, was now intent upon the meeting between Orion and his messengers. Around him and Eap they flocked, every ear bending upon Eap's words. Lucian too turned around after a moment and saw Eap speaking animatedly before the aptly-listening Orion. Though his expression gave no inkling to his inner thoughts, both Aries and Lucian guessed that he was hearing similar tidings to the ones Amarog delivered.

Now Orion was speaking, and his eyes gravely passed to every one of his listeners. Then after several moments the flock of shape-shifters darted out of the hall. Leaping off the high steps in groups, they were winged and airborne before Lucian realized they were leaving. Far beyond, their shapes grew small as they went their separate ways. Then Orion passed down the center aisle toward the door, his men broaching the subject of his meeting all the way. He did not speak until he reached the table where Aries and Lucian were sitting.

"Eap has confirmed Amarog's account," he said with a subtle sharpness. "If this is true we must begin to take precautions. I will not speak so openly of it here, however."

"Why not?" said Lucian disconcertedly, knowing well that Orion wished to be out of range of his hearing before he shared his account with Aries.

Orion shot him a swift look. "Not now, Lucian."

Aries passed a look to the two of them as if to silently inquire what spurred the obvious tension.

"In the Chamber of Councils, Aries," said Orion. "One hour. And tell Leonysus when you see him."

With that he walked off, passing to every table and spreading word to the rest of his knights.

"Don't think anything of that, Lucian," said Aries. "He means well."

"You seem to say that about everyone who doesn't mean well."

Aries smiled. "I really mean it, though. A lot on his mind, that's all. You scared him half to death last night when you came down. He thought he might lose you."

"Lose me?" said Lucian with a hint of incredulity. "Like I'm one of his possessions?"

"It's not like that, Lucian. He cares for you. I know he does. You see, he—well, I suppose now isn't the time."

"Go on ahead," Lucian said, not unkindly. He did not want to hold Aries up any longer, as he seemed to be growing anxious in his seat. "Don't worry about me. I've got something else in mind that I'd rather do anyway."

Not long after Lucian's third helping, Aries rounded up those nearest him and proceeded to wherever the Council of Chambers was located. Alone and full, Lucian retrieved his cloak from his bedroom and proceeded out of Ehrehalle and into Dwén Marnié. There was a certain someone to whom he wanted to introduce himself formally.

Enough time was afforded to him to turn back as he descended down the sloping roads into the foothills of the mountains. He contemplated retreating every twelfth step or so, but managed to muster his courage. It was strange to think that just last night he walked sure-footedly into the face of the most horrid creature he had ever seen, yet now he trembled seeking the most beautiful.

The little wooden cluster of Dwén Marnié was yet small in the valley below. Smoke rose from several chimneys, making the village seem somewhat busy. Folk walked about pushing wheelbarrows or leading small animals to their paddocks. Children ran about still playing with their stick-swords. And Lucian descended upon them like a prince who had been warming his father's throne. Immediately he felt overdressed for the occasion. Everyone he saw was dressed in rags and dirty from their day's work, and here he was in a sparkling green tunic with half a dozen white lilacs in his hands.

I'm going back, he decided, when suddenly a man's voice called out from behind.

"Hey you!"

Turning around slowly, Lucian looked down on a squat, burly man with a potbelly that threatened to burst out of his soiled white shirt. His hairy forearms were exposed as his sleeves had been rolled up past his elbows. Sweat glistened off the bristles of his black beard and atop the round peak of his bald head.

He pointed with a finger thicker than a link of sausage. "You're that chap from Ehrehalle, ain't you?" he asked. *"Lucas."*

"Lucian," corrected Lucian.

"Ah, that's right. *Lucian.* Not one for names."

There was an awkward moment when Lucian did not respond. Instead he stood staring blankly, not processing or seeing much of anything. From where the villager stood, however, it appeared as though he was frozen dumbly.

"Everything alright there, lad?" he asked. "You gonna stand there like a stone or come down and talk with me?"

Lucian shook off his state of idleness. "I'm sorry," he said, walking down the small hill and standing in front of the man. "Good to meet you." He extended his hand.

"Yinsed," the man answered, clasping his thick hand around Lucian's slender one and threatening to crunch it bone for bone. "You can call me Yinny if it pleases you. *Ah,* for me? You shouldn't have." Lucian was confused for a moment, then noticed with a spark of embarrassment that Yinsed was alluding to the flowers he carried. At once he hid them behind his back and blushed.

"Not for me, I take it?" exclaimed Yinsed. "Ah, I'm only having fun with you, kid. Some pretty lady, I'd imagine. Very nice of you, that." He smacked Lucian firmly on the shoulder. Any harder, it might have dislocated.

"Anyway, I was trying to find my *own* kid, but I guess you'll do," continued Yinsed. "These kinds of things can't wait, see. I've got the furnace as hot as it needs to be. Any hotter I might burn down the village! It's happened before. Not me, of course, but this feller I knew. Come, if you have the time. Need an extra set of eyes."

Why not, Lucian told himself. He thought maybe spending some time with Yinsed would ease his nerves a bit.

As it happened, Yinsed was the village blacksmith. Not only did he provide the folk of Dwén Marnié with fine pieces of sturdy weaponry, but filled many orders for Orion and his knights as well. "Great lads, they are," he said. "Respectful. Know a good blade when they see one. They've all got their own, sure. But they trust them to me when they need fixing."

His forge was in a long wooden cottage. It proved very spacious, with a thick floor of stone and a wide-bellied furnace at the far end of the room to which he hurried, beckoning Lucian to do the same. "Quickly!" he shouted. "Grinded it this morning, I did. This one was a bugger to get the point right. It's been hardening now for a good while. That's why it's so awfully hot in here. I just hope it hasn't been too long."

Throwing on a pair of thick gloves, Yinsed removed the blade from the fire. In his hand it seemed as though he held a lick of lively flame made iron. Embers leapt off of it as he brought it to the side to where something like a basin stood. "Now it's to the tank for this one," he said. "Gotta be quenched, it does."

A sound like a thousand sizzling strips of bacon penetrated the hall as the piping hot blade delved into the cold water. Instantly a thick plume of white steam rose up and filtered through the forge.

"What do you need me to do?" asked Lucian with fascination in his voice. It was the first time he had ever seen a sword being made. He thought with excitement that he would perhaps get to make one for himself, although he had just about as good a sword as anyone cooped up in his bedroom.

"Well, I reckon you've already done it," said Yinsed. "One

man job from here on out, really. I just needed an extra set of eyes in here to make sure I didn't, well, you know, off myself."

"I see," said Lucian glumly. "Well, if that's all, I think I'll—"

Suddenly a voice like soft music chimed from behind him. "Daddy?"

Lucian bowed his head and turned slowly, as if the very tramp of death had stopped at the door. It was her. At once he felt frozen in place, too frigid to move or speak. Shaking at the knees he stood trembling. *Why do I always get like this?* In the chasm of his chest his heart thumped at will. The fumes and stifling air of the forge seemed to become hotter and he sweat all the more.

"Jadyn!" exclaimed Yinsed with a twinge of anger in his voice. "Where've you been, dove? You always miss the good part."

Lucian heard Jadyn approaching cautiously, her steps light and soft like a stalking predator. *She's not that bad, you idiot. Well, she might as well be trying to kill you for the way your legs are quaking.*

"I'm sorry, Daddy," she answered sweetly. "I was helping Annabelle in her garden. She really is getting too old to keep up with her routine."

The blacksmith smiled. "Yes, well, lucky for you I had a keen set of eyes here. Sweetheart, this is—"

Lucian turned so abruptly that Jadyn jumped. He extended his hand as a statue might when brought to life, fingers clenched at the end of a stiff and unwavering arm. Suddenly he did not care if he looked ridiculous. There were weaponless battles that he would not have others fight for him either. He came all this way to tell her his name and he was going to do it if it killed him—which, he felt in this moment, it just might.

"Lucian Rolfe," he said quickly, as one trying to finish a sentence before a sneeze.

"Come again?" she said, raising a thin eyebrow and smiling.

He took a deep breath. "My name is Lucian," he said,

articulately this time. "Lucian Rolfe."

Jadyn took his hand into hers, and it was warm and soft and sweaty, or that might have been his. He neither knew nor cared. It was a touch different than when they had been dancing. In Ehrehalle it had been a matter of circumstance. The dance was the cog around which the wheel of their union spun. This touch was unprecedented, with nothing to spur the other into action but willingness. Lucian was unsure as to why he was now thinking like this. He used to make fun of girls for overanalyzing simplistic actions. But when their hands met it felt more than a mere handshake. It felt, to Lucian at least, like a token of Jadyn's acceptance of him—a reward for his bravery.

Inwardly he gaped at how lady-like she appeared even in her blacksmith's attire. Somehow she was more beautiful in her charred jerkin and tattered breeches than she had been in her gown. The gold of her hair, in many ways, seemed fairer now that it was pinned back, frizzled from the heat and damp with sweat. If anything the dimness of the room intensified the fire in her pale-blue eyes, the look in which suggested, if only to him, that she was glad he came. His tension began to subside at this realization, and relaxing his hand in hers their clasp became almost seamless.

Then Yinsed cleared his throat. "Ahem." Immediately their hands shot down to their sides, as if they had been caught in something forbidden.

Looking incredulously (and somewhat embarrassedly) into Lucian's eyes, Jadyn said, "My name's Jadyn." It was short and without the verve that Lucian had expected coming from a girl so beautiful. Anti-climactic though her introduction was, however, it was more than he would have received by giving up and returning to Ehrehalle like he was going to. Thus, mad as he was at Yinsed for nearly ordering their separation, part of him could only thank the smith for making him stay. After all, he did make finding Jadyn as easy as it could have been.

"Suppose I'll be going," said Lucian, breaking the long and tense silence that had taken hold of the room.

"Thanks for your eyes, Lucian," Yinsed mumbled.

"Any time." Retrieving his flowers by the quenching tank, a bolt of anger pursed through him. The heat of the forge had caused them to shrivel. The white petals, which had once reflected the sunlight, were charred and flimsy, and the stems they crowned were now brown with decay.

Stuffing them under the crook of his arm he bid them all farewell. "Good to meet you," he mumbled to Jadyn as he passed.

"Same," she said shortly.

He was in just about the same spot where he met Yinsed when he heard Jadyn's voice call to him. Turning hesitantly, he was surprised to see that she was already coming up the hill.

"Sorry about my dad," she said as she came to stand in front of him. "He doesn't like boys much."

"He seemed to like me just fine until you came in."

They both laughed.

"He didn't come to the feast last night," she said, "so I don't think he knew we knew each other—though we only know each other's names."

"That's not entirely true," said Lucian. "You know I'm not much of a dancer."

Jadyn's face flushed as she tried to conceal her laughter. It was not to be subdued, however, and when she laughed it seemed to Lucian the most wonderful sound he ever heard. Even when she snorted at the end it seemed like music. At that she shot her hand up to her mouth and looked at Lucian embarrassedly. "Sorry," she said, nervously. "Sometimes I can't help it when something's really funny. You weren't all *that* bad, though I did have to ice my toes last night and this morning, and I think you might have broken one or two."

Lucian grimaced. "I'm sorry, I really never—"

"Relax, I'm joking." She whacked him playfully on the shoulder with a strike dangerously close to the strength of her father's.

"You know," continued Jadyn, "when I met you in Ehrehalle I didn't think you knew how to talk. I thought you were a mute or something."

Lucian could not help but laugh in spite of himself. "So did I for a minute."

"You shouldn't be so tense. It makes people do silly things."

I'd like to see that dainty frame go on the quest I'm on and not be tense, he thought to himself. That thought, however, backfired, for now he indeed took in her "dainty frame": the curve of her hips in her tight brown breeches; her slender waist complemented by her well-fitting jerkin; the way the little muscles in her neck flared as she spoke.

"You're right," he answered eventually, looking as far beyond Jadyn now as he possibly could. He somehow felt like he had violated her, and wondered if Jadyn knew he had been studying the makeup of her body. "Sorry."

"Don't be," she chimed. "It happens. Hey, what do you have there?"

She alluded to the dreary stems sticking out from under Lucian's arm, and asked the question as though she already knew the answer.

"Oh," said Lucian. "Nothing. Just something I found."

"Honestly?" she said with a curt smile. "That's the best lie you could come up with? You're not one for thinking on your feet, are you?"

Embarrassed, and seeing no reason to drag the lie out further, Lucian held out the lilacs and looked away. "These were for you," he said.

He couldn't watch her accept her dying gift with feigned alacrity. She gasped, however, perhaps pitying his pathetic attempt at a present.

"They're beautiful!" she exclaimed.

"You don't have to do that," said Lucian morosely. "I know they're—"

But when he looked Jadyn's nose was buried in a white, snowy field of lilacs. The flowers she held were not the ones he had left with from the forge, but a set that was fresh and green. Confusion drew him to attention like a bucket of cold water.

"How?" he stammered inaudibly. *I saw them wilted and*

dead.

"They're my favorite!" she exclaimed. "How did you know?"

"Lucky guess," he said, scratching his head.

Just then Yinsed's gruff voice was heard from the forge down the way. "Jadyn? Where are you?"

She spun her golden head around. "I have to go," she said, turning back quickly.

"I figured."

"He means well."

Lucian released a short chuckle that Jadyn seemed to be confused by.

"Tonight, maybe?" she asked. Her brow furrowed, and her expression suggested that she was afraid of overstepping boundaries that Lucian had no intention of setting.

"Tonight what?"

Jadyn smiled. "Tonight then," she said. "I'll see you up there." With her eyes she alluded to the Great Hall high above them over the hills. "I have to do something anyway."

"What do you mean?" asked Lucian curiously.

"You'll see," she replied in a suspicious tone. "If you're brave enough."

She made as if to scamper off when she turned and came back. "How rude of me," she said, and kissed him on the cheek. Then with a bright smile she fluttered away and was soon out of sight. He felt the warmth of her lips on his cheek all the way to the Great Hall.

17

The Riddle of the Ruby

"We can do better than this, men," said Orion, slouching back in his seat and rubbing his temples wearily. It had been over an hour since the Knights Eternal entered the Chamber of Councils, and in that time the only thing agreed upon was that they were in trouble.

Around their stone, ovular table, twenty-five knights sat perplexed beyond measure. Amidst their number were Orion's twelve shape-shifting messengers, clad in their old and tattered robes. Outspread across the table's wide girth was a large and weathered map of the west. Small chess pieces representing Melinta's forces and Ehrehalle's own had once been in place upon it. They were now shattered, their fragments distributed wherever Leo had flung them.

The room was largely silent but for an errant cough or other bodily noise here and there. Once in a while someone would chime in with a suggestion or a plan, but the truth of it was that such moments of need had become foreign to them. During their meeting it had become all too evident that three thousand warless years could make even the greatest warriors rusty. However tuned their skills might have been, their strategic minds needed a bit of sharpening.

When it became clear that every mind had escaped its owner, Orion spoke again. "It is imperative," he began, "that we maintain the higher ground. This we know. And so far we have it. Melinta must come up to us, and thus we have a distinct advantage."

But these had become empty words, repeated

consistently throughout the duration of the meeting so that the weight they might once have held was gone.

"Again, Orion," began Leo gruffly. "You're speaking too generally. Higher ground is indeed advantageous, but Ehrehalle is not a fortress. The battlements can hold three archers at best. That means six archers altogether. Assuming they all hit, six arrows per volley won't even put a dent in the force he is bringing. *If* what Eap says is true, of course."

Eap's beady eyes peered hard upon Leo. "Must we bicker like children, Lionsbane?" he said lazily. "A hundred men. I heard it from his own mouth and later saw them mustered. There will be no Morgues in their number, either. No cumbersome beasts who are easy to kill from a distance. One hundred of his best, and that means one hundred Fairies—one hundred trained assassins who can move as silently as a tendril of wind in the grass, if not softer."

"One hundred against twenty-five," said Leo. "Four to one odds. I like our chances, but there's too much at stake here. We've got the villagers to worry about, and of course there's Lucian—"

"And six is too large a number to subtract from our force as it is," added Aries. "If we put six archers in the battlements we'll be left with nineteen men on the ground."

"We will set up shelter for the villagers within the mountain," said Orion at length. His voice had become dry and heavy with strain. Never before had the pangs of such business hampered him so. To his knights he now seemed aged and worn, stooped at the shoulders with heavy-lidded eyes. Suddenly he felt old, inadequate, and disheveled, like a withered branch upon a once mighty tree that the slightest weight could break. He continued gruffly, his voice grave. "Tomorrow I want knights going into Dwén Marnié ordering evacuation. Tell them to bring only what cannot be spared. By nightfall the village must be cleared. If Melinta's force marches in through that valley, they will no doubt set it to the torch. And when the fight comes, Leo, Lucian won't even be close enough to hear it."

All fell silent once again. The air about the room

had grown dismal, and every face within was sullen. Orion felt as though he looked separately into thirty-six mirrors. Thinking back to the feast just one night ago, he remembered sadly how joyous and carefree all his men had appeared. To look at them now, melancholy and weary, was almost too much to bear. What dampened his heart even more was that they still trusted him to lead them like they once had long ago, and for the first time he was not sure if he was capable.

"I never thought it would come to this," he heard himself say. The eyes of all his knights and messengers rose up to meet his. "I should have foreseen this, my friends. I fear my blindness has failed you all. News travels now in many ways. How could I not have known our location would be discovered?"

"No," said a rumbling, bear-like voice. Streph the Summit stood from his seat, his figure doubly daunting to those seated nearest. "You haven't failed us unless we say you've failed us. And I say I would fight with you against a hundred if it were the two of us alone."

Then Bravos, who had been seated to Streph's right, stood beside the towering giant with a hand on his breastplate. "Our minds may have strayed from war," he said, "but never our hearts from yours. You have mine, until the end."

Soon twenty-four knights and twelve messengers were on their feet speaking in fervent accord, every set of eyes wide upon their captain. A new courage festered in Orion's heart, or perhaps it was a courage long dormant that had woken. Vaguely now he could recall what it was like to have men at his call—to be plotting battle strategies and maneuvers like he had many ages ago. Then he too stood, the twenty-fifth knight, the chamber's thirty-seventh man, and returned every stare with a look of fire.

"It will be trying," he said. "Twenty-five against one hundred, as it stands—"

Then Eap's voice interjected from between two towers of knights. "Make that twenty-six, Orion Highlord," he said eagerly.

"Twenty-seven," the messenger beside him said a fraction of a second after Eap had spoken.

"Twenty-eight," said another.

One by one every messenger pledged their service. Leo quaked with a quiet laugh. "That was easy enough," he said. "Our force just increased by twelve, and you didn't even have to leave the room."

A mad thought crept into the deepest chasms of Orion's mind: maybe victory could be achieved after all. While Melinta's men would be driven only by ambiguous motivation, his would be fighting for their home and the protection of all within. Such need at times could even any odds.

Every set of eyes was ablaze. Even the messengers, most of whom had never held a sword before, seemed to be brimming with excitement at the thought of doing so. Hunger enveloped the room like a physical entity. Orion could feel it even as he sat and helmed the plot. Every pair of ears was bent upon his words, words Orion now spoke with a blatant confidence. The swagger and poise of his former days were slowly returning. His men were starting to believe.

"Double training sessions," he ordered. Suddenly he could hear his voice renewed. The vigor it had once possessed flooded out the weary, battered air with which he entered the chamber. "We will utilize all three training rooms inside this rock. Leo and Aries, you will lead the sessions in Room I; Camien, Bravos, Room II; Streph and I will lead the sessions in Room III. Training will be before breakfast and after dinner. All those expecting to fight are expected to attend. A list of names and where to report for training will be posted at dawn in the Great Hall. They want to take our home, men. What are you willing to do about it?"

Lucian floated all the way up the corridor. A tumult of excitement that could not be stifled was overwhelming his spirits. Singing fragments of old songs that he thought he had forgotten, he all but skipped into his room—

—and stopped cold suddenly, for there stood Ursa, folding blankets and straightening the sheets of his bed with a glacial scowl on her face.

"Good afternoon," Lucian said, trying to sound proper. For some reason he felt as though Ursa would demand nothing less.

"Certainly seems so," she said shortly, alluding to his cheerfulness and whipping a blanket out in front of her.

Lucian went to the balcony doors, which Ursa had opened at some point. Far away the plains of Reznarion stretched northward, and the Silverthread twinkled here and there as it flowed east. Outside, its tributaries sighed as they sloped down the stalks of the mountain. Lucian stood for a long while taking in the scenery. The plain in itself was dismal indeed. As much as Enormeteren had proved golden and bright, Reznarion proved just as dull and dreary. Yet there was something about it that suggested it had once been beautiful. Somehow, if Lucian looked close enough, he could almost see it in its former glory. Vast farms and meadows, large and busy towns by the river, a high gray-stone city in the distance, and all the while the shimmering golden folds of Reznarion beneath.

"You are looking rather handsome this morning," said Ursa's voice from behind him.

Pulling himself away from the balcony he turned to the woman. "Thanks," he replied. He would have expected a poetry lesson from a dragon before a complement from her. "Orion's," he continued, alluding to his attire.

"Indeed," she said shortly, setting the last of his blankets down in a fur stack on the end of his bed. Then she turned and looked at him with eyes like ice, standing frigid as an age-worn statue. She had this way of speaking so that only her lips moved. Meanwhile her eyes peered hard and unblinking, and every muscle of her body remained still.

"I trust your stay has thus far been accommodating?" she asked, though to Lucian it didn't seem like she would care even if he said it hadn't been.

"It has."

Ursa issued the subtlest nod. If she hadn't blinked

Lucian might not have realized she moved her head at all.

"There was that whole thing with the Netherlings last night that was a little unnerving," he said, "but in any case—"

"Netherlings?" she said sharply. Suddenly her eyes widened. Her posture slackened as a look of fear came over her pallid face. "The Netherlings were here? When?"

Lucian looked at her blankly, confused not at her question but the urgency with which she spoke.

"Speak, boy!" she screeched.

"Last night," said Lucian, stepping back toward the doors of his balcony. "Or this morning, I guess. Before dawn. After the feast."

"And you saw them?" She said this in such a whisper that, had she been further away, Lucian would not have heard her at all. It was strange to him that the first emotion he experienced her display was fear.

Lucian's brow furrowed as suspicion filled him. What he had mistaken for Ursa's fear he knew now to be her incredulity. It was as though she envied him for marveling in a sight which she was denied. "I did," he answered curiously.

Ursa looked away. Nothing about her demeanor betrayed any inner emotion she might have been feeling in this moment, yet Lucian could not help but wonder if she knew something he didn't. Something, perhaps, that had even escaped Orion.

"Ursa?" Lucian said softly. With a subtle jerk her eyes were on him again, and they seemed to house a weariness that filled her face with age. "What are they? Do you know?"

It was all too evident that she did. Now that the subject was broached Lucian decided to take advantage and learn all about them that he could.

Sullenly Ursa looked away again and spoke to the ground. "I do," she answered in a broken, quiet voice. "Perhaps better than anyone, I do." Then she sniveled as if in tears, and Lucian, as if by instinct, came to her side and took her hand. It was cold, as he expected, but soon warmed in his. Somehow he felt that her grief revealed a hidden beauty about her that she longed to conceal. It was the only human emotion she proved she was capable of.

"Do you want to sit down?" Lucian asked.

Though he spoke softly, Ursa's head shot toward him as if she had been startled. Her red-brimmed eyes housed the moist gleam of despair. Tears began to run in glimmering channels down the gaunt slopes of her cheeks. She sat, but never released Lucian's hand, and thus he stooped with her to the bedside. Instantly feeling awkward, he made as if to relinquish his grip when she clasped her fingers tightly around his. "No," she said, demandingly. For a moment the sharpness of her voice returned, and he cowered briefly. Then she recoiled, and her grip subsided, but did not let go. "Forgive me," she said softly. "I don't want to be alone. It pains me that I have been so cold towards you. You did not deserve that, innocent traveler as you are. That was why I came here to begin with, though I planned on being gone before you arrived."

"Don't worry about it," said Lucian plainly.

Then Lucian saw Ursa smile for the first time, and though small, her expression filled her face with a new vigor and beauty. It was as if a sunken world of night was experiencing dawn for the first time before his eyes.

"You're like him, you know," she said. "Orion. There is much you share in common. He was once ignorant, as you can imagine, however short-lived his ignorance was. Always pestering, always prodding, always pondering. At your age he probably carried the woes and burdens of men thrice his years. Self-inflicted, of course. Always putting more pressure on himself than was needed, but never enough to break him."

"He's angry with me," said Lucian after a while. "I went into the Great Hall last night while the Netherlings were there. Leo told me to stay behind but, I don't know, I guess I was just curious. So I went. I wasn't afraid or anything like that, which is surprising if you knew me. Orion was furious this morning."

Whatever glee apparent on Ursa's face subsided at the mentioning of the Netherlings. "He had every right to be," she said. "They are not a force to be meddled with."

"I don't even know what they are," said Lucian. "That's why I was hoping you could tell me. I saw them just fine. They looked like werewolves, only bigger if that's possible. The biggest one came right up and spoke to me. Said he came looking for me. His name was Amarog, and he—"

At the mentioning of Amarog, Ursa's face turned two shades paler. Her grip tightened once more and fear raced to the forefront of her eyes. "Amarog?" she said nervously. "He yet lives?"

"Looked pretty alive to me last night."

Then she turned her face away, her eyes darting absently to and fro as if in urgent thought.

"Who is he?" asked Lucian at length.

"As vile a creature as has ever walked this earth," she answered sharply. "Just like the rest of them. I am sure Orion has shared with you the tale of the Mortal Damnation? The Day of the Wizard? The day the Great Sage wiped mortals from the face of the world?" Lucian nodded. "He issued rewards that day, certainly. Orion and his knights, along with some of their spouses and children, received the gift of immortality for their valiant acts on earth, and were thus given Ehrehalle in which to live in peace.

"But there were those among men too evil even for death, and so Ation cursed them with the same gift he gave to us: immortality, yet of the poorest means—to live out the remaining ages of the world as the decrepit beasts they so long emulated. It is amidst the ruins of their fallen city where they are doomed to dwell; in Dredoway across Reznarion. That is their tale in summation, or as much of it as I care to speak."

"So they were men once?" asked Lucian incredulously, as if to himself.

"If one can call them men, yes. Though I would refer to them otherwise, being too dishonorable even for death. Scoundrels, they are. Devils with as much moral as a lick of dragon-flame. And Amarog is vilest of all." Then her gaze grew sullen, and the verve with which she spoke began to subside. When she spoke again her voice was quiet, as if

240

she were trying to hide the words even from herself. "He was my brother," she admitted dismally. "The last king of Dredoway. It was only the second month of his reign when Ation came down from Zynys. The mortal throne has remained empty since."

Lucian sighed inwardly. "Great," he said under his breath.

"I beg your pardon?" said Ursa.

"It's just, well—" Just then he took the Key from under his pillow and held it out to her. Receiving it from him she held it up to her face and eyed it studiously.

"It *is* beautiful," she said. "Well-shaped and wrought as Zynian crafts often are. But you had best keep it hidden, as you had it. You would not want this to fall into the wrong hands."

"That's just it," Lucian replied. "It doesn't really matter *whose* hands it falls into. It won't work unless that ruby lights up. And the only way that ruby will light up is if all three thrones are claimed. That's why the emerald and sapphire are glowing right now. That's why the ruby is dim:

> *"Blue for the Moroks, strongest of all;*
> *Green for the Fairies of Light;*
> *Red for the Men whose will shall not fall*
> *In the hour of the final fight.*

"That's what I was told, anyway. And seeing as how I don't know up from down about this thing, that's what I'm going to trust."

"It is a wonder to me that the old rhyme is still sung," said Ursa. "It was written long ago and forgotten, at least to my knowledge. The hour of the final fight is long past; the will of Men has fallen indeed. No descendant of my father's exists. Amarog has already been stripped irrevocably of his right to rule. The throne cannot be claimed."

Lucian rose from the bed, frustrated and tired. For a long while he stared absently across the faraway plain, then bowed his head sullenly. "I can't go on that," he said. "I can't believe that. The second I believe that, it's over. The second I believe that, this will all have been for nothing. I didn't leave my home for nothing. I didn't leave Mary, Jem and Mac for nothing. I left them for this." He held up the Key by its teeth. Even in the light of day its shining gems were not subdued. "I have to believe there's a way it can work."

Ursa was silent for a while, a blank expression on her face now radiant in the shining light of day. "I stand by my original claim," she said at last. "You are more like him than ever. But the news you have shared with me fails to raise my spirits. The Key was made to respond to bloodlines, it seems. Otherwise how else would the gems know when to blaze and when to falter? If that were not so, any one of Ehrehalle's knights could march into Dredoway and claim the throne for himself.

"Orion tried once, long ago. Though given a new hall and a fresh land to govern, much of his heart remained in Dredoway. Surely his claim to the throne was better than anyone's, having married into my bloodline and later being rewarded for his honor and valor by Ation himself. Yes," she said with a twinge of a smile, adhering to Lucian's dubious expression, "we were indeed married once. The throne, however, would not accept him. You see, Lucian: the Three Thrones are each crested with their respective jewel, much like the Key. A great ruby is embedded in the crest of Dredoway's throne that once blazed when the rightful king was seated upon it. Yet when Orion took the seat it remained dim, and has ever since its light went out."

Ursa's account made horrific sense to Lucian. The more he fought against believing it, the deeper the inevitable truth sunk in. If anything he was glad he broached the subject with her. Never in a million years would he have thought she was as knowledgeable in such matters as she had proved. Yet he supposed she perhaps knew more than any, having been the daughter and sister of two kings and the wife of a highlord.

But there was still a part of him that refused acceptance. Still there was something that made him believe. He could not have been given a hopeless errand. Or could he?

Gamaréa could not have been sent across the sea to lead him on a fruitless quest. Or was he?

"I have to believe," said Lucian heavily, though even as he said this whatever belief he clung to was seeping out of his heart.

"Believe then," said Ursa. "At times faith can protect us where swords are of no use." Then she came to him and lay a hand gently on his shoulder. Before long she turned and made to leave. Turning back in the doorway she said, "Such hope has perhaps never been given to a single cause before. It will take all of yours to see it done, and undoubtedly more than that, I fear. The riddle of the ruby was never in your hands."

Then she left, sweeping down the corridor. Lucian stared blankly at the empty doorway until the echoes of her steps passed beyond the edge of hearing.

18

The Arena

Dark thoughts riddled Gamaréa's mind that night, and rest came with difficulty, if at all. At the forefront of his mind were Lucian and the Key. Where was he now? Was the Sage wise to instruct Didrebelle to pursue him instead of the boy? What would Didrebelle's fate be when the day was done, and what would become of Medric should he not return with Lucian? Such questions left him comfortless, and it seemed as though the night was endless in which he sat in the darkness dangling his feet over the slate.

The two slaves whom Didrebelle had drugged did not begin to stir until hours after. One of them was plump, everything about him round and hairy; the other was without much flesh at all. It was certainly the oddest possible pairing in that dreary, forsaken place.

The skinny man nudged the other. "Oi," he said, his voice screechy. "Would yeh look at that! He's awake." The prisoner's face was long, from his forehead to his chin, with the most sunken cheeks Gamaréa had ever seen.

The fat one's attention was on Gamaréa now as well. "Say now!" he cried. "Reckon 'e is. Out fer a while, you were; figger'd you was dead. Nearly waged on it, we did."

Gamaréa could not help but issue a small smile. *It would have been a decent bet.* "You were wise to decide otherwise then," he replied. He could tell by their accents that they were Moroks, perhaps even from Titingale or Dwén Alíl. He thought briefly of Podrick Worthwent.

"Good to have a new face 'round here," said the skinny

one. "Jus' been me an' Pubs fer a lofty while."

"Pubs, eh?" said Gamaréa. "Surely a nickname?"

"Indeed, indeed, fer me preference of ales. Use' teh frequent the bars in me past life. Real name's . . . wait now . . . damned if I even remember me real name. Been so long since someone called me by it."

"That is truly sad to hear," replied Gamaréa.

"Say now," said the skinny one, "you talk funnier than folk I'm friendly with round these parts. All . . . damned if I even know the right word for it . . . "

"Handsome," suggested Pubs.

The skinny Morok's face brimmed excitedly. "Now that's a good one, I reckon! I was thinkin' somethin' different, though."

Pubs scratched the dirty bald spot atop his round head. "Proper! I'll warrant 'proper' is the word yer lookin' for, Timms."

Timms's eyes widened. "Proper! There it is! You speak proper-er than anyone I've come by here."

Gamaréa smiled. "You must not have come by many, then."

"No, no," assured Timms, "I've come by me share. Rather dull lot round here, if my opinion's worth anythin'."

Even as Timms innocently prodded, Pubs took note of Gamaréa's distraught expression.

"Say now," he said quietly to Timms. "Don't really think the lad is up fer much talkin'. *He's* here in front of us, see, but his mind ain't nowhere near here, if yeh follow me."

"You, on the other hand, Pubs, are a clumsy talker. 'Ow could 'is mind be somewheres else? 'Is body wouldn't be workin' . . . Unless . . . " Then Timms turned his attention to Gamaréa. "Say now, you wouldn't 'appen to be one o' them magical peoples, would yeh?"

"Timms!" scolded Pubs.

"Alright, you! I mean no offense to him. Just chatting with the lad. 'Sides, I've a right to know if I'm sharing a quarter with someone of 'igher standing."

"I am of no high standing," said Gamaréa calmly, as if to himself. "I am a prisoner same as you; but one whose time is nearing."

"Time nearing?" asked Pubs.

"To what?" said Timms concernedly.

"Death, I suppose," answered Gamaréa.

"*Death?*" prodded Timms. "What yeh do to deserve that? Kill someone? Poison the muck at muck hour?"

"I attacked a guard."

Pubs gave a sound of acknowledgement. "I didn't know they could get yeh fer somethin' like that," he mused. "How they killin' yeh? Heard they been hangin' folk fer misbehavin'."

"Shh!" hissed Timms. "Why yeh got teh go feedin' 'im thoughts like that!"

"Jus' sayin', is all!" Pubs said defensively.

But Gamaréa interrupted their bickering. "I am afraid they have chosen a different path for me," he said. "I am sentenced to fight in the arena."

The two prisoners gasped simultaneously. Then Timms struck Pubs on the shoulder. "I told yeh it was real!"

"Alright! Yeh didn' have teh do all that with yer hand!"

"It is real," said Gamaréa. "I am to be summoned there at noon."

"That is a downright shame, I'm afraid," said Timms sadly, placing a hand over his heart as though already lamenting.

Pubs shot him a stern glance.

"What?" defended Timms. "He's more a right to know as any."

"A right to know what?" asked Gamaréa.

"Don't start, Timmsy," implored Pubs.

"Fear I've got to, Pubs," said Timms. "It's just . . . well . . . damned if I know how to say it without sounding all . . . *cruel* and what not."

Gamaréa's hard stare urged Timms to continue. "It's just that they say no one 'as survived, is all," he said disconcertedly.

"There yeh go, Timms," said Pubs angrily. "Whip off yer trousers and piss on whatever hope he's got left, why don't yeh?"

"I have heard the rumors," said Gamaréa plainly. "There are none to survive the arena. But I know those rumors to be false."

"As do I," Pubs seconded. Timms shot him an incredulous stare. "What?" continued Pubs. "You had yer turn, now I'll take mine."

"But you *never* believed in the arena," Timms protested.

"Never believed meself, yeah, but that don't mean I never heard the stories."

"What stories have you heard?" asked Gamaréa, his interest piqued.

"That there is one said to have survived it," continued Pubs. "A man, they say—biggest anyone's ever seen. Ferget the fella's name, sadly."

"It's not *Daxau* by any chance, is it?"

"Well there's a mind-tangler," said Pubs. "That's it; I'm sure of it. I'll be—someone who knows him personally. Come to think of it, you don't look so small yerself. I'd even bet you equal him in size."

"In stature we are nearly equal," Gamaréa confirmed. "But in heart mine cannot rival his."

Timms waved his frail, skeletal arms. "All sappiness aside," he said, "yeh've got teh consider a thing-er-two about the one they call *Daxau*." The way Timms spoke his name suggested he did not entirely believe in his existence.

"Like what?" said Pubs defensively.

"He fought a while back is all I'm sayin'—back when the arena was new and all, and the king's champions were limited. Once 'e killed the first couple the king decided not to risk more. They're useful warriors, after all, the champions. And after 'is showing and the profit 'e helped the king make, 'e wouldn't dare sentence 'im to *death*. Kept 'im 'round 'case 'e needed 'im again. Only smart."

Pubs stroked his chubby chin. "It is quite the business, if you ask me," he mused. "And it does make sense not to hang him after."

"Yeh don' 'ang a warrior like Daxau," replied Timms. "Not 'less his skills ain't what they used to be."

"Well," said Gamaréa, who had heard enough, "for all

my skill with a blade, I fear that its limit will be met. My presence sits ill with the king; he would have me dead, profit or no."

"That's too bad then, lad," said Pubs sadly. "Too bad indeed."

The door slid open just then. Pubs and Timms watched in disbelief as two guards seized Gamaréa from his mount and walked with him to the door. Neither Pubs nor Timms saw or heard from the Morok that day or ever after.

Shortly after being led through the doors, Gamaréa was blindfolded and loaded into a carriage waiting outside. It was a long while before the churning of the wheels ceased, and even longer until the cloth was removed. When he could see again, he found himself in an armory of sorts. Meager swords were mantled upon the wall, every blade chipped and weathered. There were shields there also, along with other random pieces of equipment, but he was instructed to choose only a sword.

Just then he thought of Dawnbringer, and what ill fate must have befallen it. He would have given anything to wield it on the sands. This lottery before him was without an obvious choice; all were equally tarnished, and there was not a selection that was likely to give him any sort of advantage. So it was he took hold of the nearest blade within reach and was done with it. He was then ordered to remove his garb, which was replaced by a modest cloth that wrapped him at the waist. A leather strap was given to him to assure the cloth would remain fastened lest his smallclothes be exposed to the crowd.

Other than issuing their commands, the guards were silent. Gamaréa was hoping they would speak to each other about the upcoming events so that he might come to understand exactly what he would be dealing with. But after they clothed him they led him away down the long, dusty corridor of old, moldy stone to where he could hear the rumbling crowd that had gathered above.

Soon Melinta's oration quieted the audience, and Gamaréa heard the edges of his powerful voice seep through the dense ceiling of stone. He could not make out the words of his speech, but in time they sent the voices in the crowd into a clamor. With excitement, perhaps, or with thoughts of vengeance.

"Stand here," said one of the guards, who nudged Gamaréa onto a wooden platform that was supported by two heavy chains.

"Wait—" Gamaréa began.

But it was too late. From above came a sound like a great horn, and the guard who had instructed him to stand upon the lift was now yanking a lever beside him. Suddenly the ceiling opened, and the blinding light of day flushed through. A sound swift and terrible, like a sudden tumult of roaring waves, overtook his senses. As his rugged figure came into sight, cowering for the powerful onslaught of the afternoon sun, the crowd voiced their displeasure vehemently.

Then Melinta's voice rose up again, speaking foul words of Gamaréa as if to spur the crowd's hostility further. Though he had most certainly revealed his name and heritage already, Melinta continued his oration by explaining the laws of Cauldarím that Gamaréa had defiled. Yet above their boisterous voices, Gamaréa was only able to hear "breach of peace."

Gamaréa saw that smug little slit of a smile cross Melinta's face as he waved his hands to quiet the spectators.

"Yes, yes I know!" he exclaimed loudly. "Such penalties warrant death, of course! Yet it would be a shame for the hangman to ensure the end of such talent." More jeers; it was a while before Melinta was able to continue. "This Morok's craft is war, and so his skills will be tested today before your watchful eyes in honor of our new warden! Though, regrettably, he cannot partake in the festivities on account of important obligations, I trust the day will see him honored."

Important obligations? Gamaréa wondered.

An impartial applause followed. Wasting no further time, Melinta signaled the guards below to escort the first champion to the ring, and once again the bellowing of the horn rose up over the lofting stands. In response to the blast, the gate that had long remained closed was opened, and two Morgue footmen emerged from the shadows with a beast, bound and convulsing with rage, that bore a striking resemblance to their own make. And, in fact, as Gamaréa could see when they unmasked the creature, it was indeed a father specimen of that ancient race of Morgues.

So there's that . . .

Even the hulking Morgues, armored as they were, fled back into the gateway when the Minotaur was unbound, though the beast had not issued a sudden movement. Instead it stood there, as if confused, breathing heavily, its muscled back heaving up and down as though it had been without oxygen for an extended period of time. It wheezed as it panted, and issued other bull-like sounds, only much more menacing. For a small moment it seemed to be unfocused, its black eyes lazily scanning its surroundings, its coiling horns winding on either side of its head like giant tree roots.

But then its eyes became fixed and intent, as though a light that had been dormant within them was rekindled, and they locked on Gamaréa standing feebly with his sword several yards away. He had knowledge of this creature, both through old tales Tartalion shared with him and historical documents he read in passing—but even still, he believed their existence to be no more than myth until now—now that its muscular body pulsated with fury before him, its eyes aglow with unprecedented barbarity, beaming wildly at the only thing in its path.

Though it was meant to be a test of brawn, Gamaréa realized he could not treat it as such. Perhaps that was how Melinta supposed he would fall. But it was impractical for one to think they could match blows with a creature of this magnitude. There were none among the Three Races who could possibly contend with the strength of a Minotaur. Casting any thought of overpowering it aside, he merely began walking a steady circle around the ring under the creature's scrutiny.

That which cannot be overpowered must be outwit, he

thought to himself, when suddenly the beast, which might have become uncomfortable when Gamaréa set himself in motion, charged frantically. Sliding away quicker than he thought himself capable, Gamaréa evaded what would have been a demoralizing strike. Above, the crowd roared with excitement.

Now, with the Minotaur's momentum sending it off in the direction it had charged, it took a moment for the brute to come to a complete stop. Having come up empty, the beast took to looking around, seemingly confused and baffled.

So it is dumb . . . Gamaréa calculated.

As though it had taken offense to his very thoughts, the Minotaur spun around. Seeing Gamaréa unscathed and in a different spot apparently infuriated it, for it charged again with a bellowing wail. In its vengeful pursuit, however, it managed to trip over its own two mammoth-like feet.

. . . and clumsy.

Crucial components were at hand now. There must have been a way for Gamaréa to use the Minotaur's aggression, stupidity, and clumsiness against it. *I will remain still,* he formulated. *I need to let it charge at me.* The very thought set his heart to pounding, but it was what needed to be done—the only way to use the beast's power against it.

For his plan to be executed successfully, however, he needed to understand the Minotaur's striking pattern, if it had one. Did it thrust headlong, throwing itself at its victim with a somewhat linear trajectory? This would certainly allow for each point of its horns to pierce its enemy simultaneously, no doubt issuing instant death; or did it prefer plowing over its victims and inflict death by means of trampling? Both seemed possible. After all, it had practically tried both methods on him already.

I need to test it. Gamaréa gulped at the thought. *I must insert a test within the test.*

Steadying himself, he waited nervously for the beast's advance. Seizing its moment to strike, the Minotaur sped toward him, quaking the earth as it charged, and launched itself headlong like an arrow. Flipping backward, Gamaréa dodged the blow by inches, the hair on the beast's stomach tickling his nose as its huge mass leapt over him. A heavy THUD shook the ground behind him, and the sands hissed as the Minotaur slid away on its stomach.

Headlong then, Gamaréa determined. *Right.*

Grimacing as he rose to his feet, Gamaréa could feel the wounds across his back opening again, the warm blood rising to the surface of some of his fresh scabs. But he could pay no attention to past wounds. Before him the Minotaur was rising again in a new kind of frenzy, beating its chest and wailing in madness.

Rampantly it accelerated forward. Gamaréa planted his feet loosely into the earth. The Minotaur lunged—

The next moment happened quickly, like a lightning flash. At that exact second, Gamaréa spun, evading the Minotaur's would-be hit in one fluent motion, slicing its left leg from its frame as it dove past in one clean swipe. Crying aloud in agony, the Minotaur lay atop the copper earth, bobbing its destroyed body up and down as though trying to create a crevice in the ground. Soon black blood pooled around it, steam beginning to rise from the thick, dark puddle that collected. It seemed much smaller now than when it had been led through the gates. There was a moment when Gamaréa pitied the creature. Wild things were best left in the wild, he always thought, especially beasts as untamable as this.

Placing a sandaled foot atop its heaving chest, Gamaréa drove his sword mercifully through the Minotaur's heart. The frantic movements ceased instantly. Silence fell over the crowd. Had the murmuring not ceased so abruptly, Gamaréa might have forgotten the crowd was even present. Yet there they sat, wide-eyed and perplexed, with horrified stares of incredulity at the scene before them. Many turned to Melinta's balcony imploringly. Could this really have just happened? It was not supposed to . . .

Reality setting in, a fiery rage enveloped Gamaréa's heart. Whatever remorse he harbored for the creature was gone. It was not a Minotaur he had killed, but a piece of Melinta's plan. Grabbing its head by one of its massive horns, he began hacking away at its neck. Cries lifted from the crowd, many saying to turn and watch the scene that was unfolding.

Only the strength of a Morok could have hacked that weak sword through the thick skin, sinews, muscle and bone of the Minotaur completely. With a deft yank, Gamaréa parted the beast's head from its shoulders and held it aloft so that Melinta could see. It was heavy, like holding up a boulder. He could hear the blood dripping off the torn flesh. Some of it splattered warmly onto his toes. When he was sure Melinta had seen, he flung the head away with a mighty heave, sending it rolling awkwardly beside the motionless corpse.

* * *

The king's lips quivered with rage, flames of vengeance burned within his eyes. This was the method by which the Morok would be undone. It was guaranteed! Yet it was not so. Melinta turned to Thaldrid, who was sitting beside him, struck dumb by awe and fear. "Go down there," he said, clenching his teeth so tightly it was a wonder they did not shatter, "and tell them to release the wolf."

"But, Your Gr—"

"NOW!"

Against his better judgment, Thaldrid continued. "Your Grace, you would risk another to the task of killing the Morok? What about the—"

"I will risk them all if I have to!" Melinta was beyond outraged now. "He must fall here. Now. Before the eyes of Dridion!"

And so Thaldrid swept off hurriedly, a swell of regret in his heart.

It took twelve servants to completely dispose of the Minotaur's corpse: two to carry its leg, three to hoist its head, and the rest to load everything else onto the retrieval cart. Gamaréa reveled as he watched, waving smugly at the only one who dared look his way.

Soon the cart passed beyond the shadows of the gate. Standing motionless beneath the bold, unveiled sun, Gamaréa began to sweat and grow weary from his efforts against the Minotaur. The crowd hummed with anxious chatter. What was to happen next? Anything?

As if in answer to his silent questions, the horn blew a second time, and out of the gate, led by a leash of coiled steel, came four Morgues with a magnificent—yet defiantly odd—creature in tow.

That's not a—

But it was Melinta's voice who bellowed above all other audible sounds. "BEHOLD!" he exclaimed, gesticulating excitedly from his balcony. "I give you the nine-tailed wolf!"

I guess it is then.

It was much larger than a common wolf, its stature comparable to that of a lion's, even. Gamaréa knew their kind to inhabit only the farthest reaches of the eastern mountains, where harsh winters were said to have taken complete hold. But he cared little about where it came from, and much more about where it was now. He had learned of its defenses long ago in his studies with Tartalion. The nine tails swinging behind it were certainly exotic features, but when called to action were some of the deadliest weapons in the world. Each tail was covered in sharp sickles, and they jingled shrilly as it walked, as though comprised of fine wind chimes. Beneath the sickles, its skin was thick and leathery, allowing it to whip its sickle-riddled tails in lashing motions. One tail alone had the capability of cleaving a man in two with one swipe, or so it was lored.

But nine?

The volume of the crowd mounted again as Melinta called for the horn. It rang long and voluminously through the depths of the arena and out into the vast beyond. Upon its call the wolf of nine tails bounded swiftly toward Gamaréa with the grace of a steed. For a fraction of a moment, he wondered how he could bring himself to smite a thing so beautiful, its coat of gold flickering beneath the high noon sun, giving it the appearance of a statue that had been brought to life. Reality, however, fell over him quickly as the wolf sped within striking range.

Gamaréa peddled backwards. He could hear the wolf snarling as it exhibited its fierce cunning. Now within close range Gamaréa could see its true grandeur. It was not much smaller than a bear, but as sleek and limber as a lion, with a body that had to be nearly ten feet in length, if not more.

He quickened his pace, for the wolf remained an uncomfortably close distance behind him.

You're big, he thought, *but let's see if I can't tire you out a bit.*

In a quick, fleeing motion Gamaréa darted leftward, quite literally running for his life. Feeling the hot breath of the approaching wolf at his exposed back (whether it was bleeding or sweating he could not tell anymore), he managed to stop himself short by sliding. Jerking upward quickly, his momentum having stopped abruptly, he sped off to the right.

Not a soul in the arena had ever seen a display of speed such as this. Gamaréa managed to cover so much ground in such a small interval of time—cutting, crisscrossing, diving, and sprinting—that the wolf, though for a good while it remained at his heels, was becoming noticeably fatigued.

Alright, he told himself, *you are tiring it out just fine, but you have to kill the damn thing.* To do so, he would have to start paying heed to its tails, which were no doubt going to be thick and tough to cut through.

You cannot yank them off, he contemplated. *That will rip the skin right off your hands. You need to cut them. If that thing can hack off a Minotaur's leg, it can damn well cut off these tails . . .*

With the wolf's speed beginning to falter, Gamaréa risked running within striking range. Seeing its chance to grab hold of him, the wolf lunged forward, lashing its tails with vengeance. Gamaréa failed to prove the quicker. A sharp jolt of stinging pain seared through his left thigh, and looking down he saw a fine gash, as from that of an adept knife, beginning to spew blood down his leg.

The wolf spun to face him as he hobbled away grimacing. As he fought to quicken his pace, he staggered and fell. Already the wolf was in hot pursuit, and nimbly it leapt through the air as if to finish him. Adrenaline caused Gamaréa to shift his position in the sand, and as a result the wolf jumped over him. Its enraged pursuit was not without consequence.

As the wolf sailed over him, Gamaréa's blade swept through the air so unhampered that he thought he had missed. Yet now he heard the wolf cry out, and looking to the ground in front of him saw that two of its nine tails lay tattered and limp on the sand. Jerking its head upward in apparent pain, the wolf focused its attention on him again.

By this time Gamaréa had managed to rise, his leg throbbing and the arena's sand stinging in his open wound. For a moment he and the wolf locked eyes before it came charging, relentlessly and tactlessly. With what strength was left to him, Gamaréa again proved the swifter. With another deft swipe of his tarnished blade, he sidestepped and hewed three more tails from the wolf's hide.

Five down . . .

Gamaréa fell upon one knee in weariness and pain, employing all of his effort to rise. With dread in his eyes he looked upon his weakened adversary. Having lost five of its tails, the wolf's golden coat, once magnificently glinting beneath the afternoon sky, began to fade. The sun did not seem to reflect off of it nearly as much as it had when the animal was first led onto the sands. In the light of the unveiled sun, it seemed as though an abnormal creature, old and hideously grotesque. Its senses were noticeably fading. There was no poise left in its movements; it carried itself toward Gamaréa as a drunk carries himself to bed, stumbling, croaking, and glossy-eyed. The four remaining tails at its back wilted like malnourished plants.

Its jaw parted feebly, and its tongue hung loosely as it panted with fatigue and agony. A trail of bright red blood followed in its wake. Lunging again clumsily, as though it could not think of anything else do to, it nipped at thin air. The attack was horribly simple to evade, and having done so Gamaréa found himself at the wolf's back and cut its remaining tails without trouble.

Undone, the wolf quivered on its long, slender legs. Before Gamaréa's eyes, the hue of the wolf's coat dissolved into a sickly, pallid gray. Whimpering as an injured dog would, its front legs gave out from under it before the wolf toppled completely. Having rendered it powerless, its weapons scattered and bloodied across the sands, Gamaréa, with a proficient poke of his blade, finished it instantly and with mercy. The nine-tailed wolf became limp, and when Gamaréa peeled his eyes away, he looked once more to Melinta's seat, where he was sitting on edge.

Within his suite, in the midst of the excited crowd, Melinta's stomach churned. *This cannot be,* he thought wildly. *Only one other has survived my trials here . . . Only one!*

He stood, fury quaking his knees. "RELEASE THE CRIOSPHINX!" he cried, his call ringing nearly as loudly as the horn's third blast.

Again the weary gate opened, and into the ring entered the criosphinx, its eagle-like wings spread, boasting their reddish-gold plumage and a wingspan easily over twenty feet long. When they flapped, dust and sand clouded it in a brownish mist, and hideous noises issued from its ram-like head as it trotted forward with its lionesque frame.

Gamaréa wondered for a moment how many beasts Melinta truly had at his call before rolling his eyes, shaking off as much weariness as he could, and preparing for another bout.

19

The Eyrie of the Bólgs

Lucian was reclusive for the remainder of the day, only coming out of his room to eat when it was time for dinner. In the hall he held an empty conversation with Aries about general things. Leo joined them moments before he left, but Orion was nowhere to be found. He was "taking care of things," Leo mentioned, and that was the end of the subject.

He did not tarry after he ate. Instead he returned to his bedroom seeking solitude yet again. Many things were plaguing his mind. Thoughts of the Key festered at the forefront. What was going to happen if the ruby was never lit? *You can't think that way,* he scolded himself. *You can't afford to think like that.* It was not the first time since his conversation with Ursa that he told himself this. Every once in a while he would lift his pillow hoping to find that a red light had joined the rays of blue and green. Nothing. *Worth a look,* he thought. *Not a big deal, I guess. It's only the end of the world.*

A smaller thought that kept peeking out from behind the bigger ones was the episode with the lilacs. *I saw those flowers dead. To the last petal!* Yet when Jadyn held them in her hands they were as fresh and white as when he first picked them. *What was all that about?* A farfetched thought came into his mind that Jadyn might have had some hidden healing power, like a witchdoctor or something. There had been folk in Amar who made such claims, after all, though they mostly brewed herbs in pots and called them potions.

She doesn't strike me as that sort, though. Besides, if she knew she was going to revive the flowers, she wouldn't have acted as surprised as she was.

Lastly, he was constantly reminded that she was coming to see him this evening. After his meeting with Ursa, the earlier events of that day seemed to have occurred a week prior. *And I look like this,* he told himself. *Fantastic.*

Wrapping himself in his cloak, he proceeded down the corridor until he came upon the opening to the Great Hall. There a knight or two were loitering absently, but Orion was nowhere to be found. This had been Lucian's main concern. He was almost certain that Orion would not condone his sneaking out so late at night, what with Netherlings proving they could wander freely into and out of Ren Talam. Nor did he wish to confront Aries or Leo. Though they would be less likely to reprimand him than Orion, he did not want to put them in the position to hide anything from him.

Hooding himself, he slipped away silently. The knights who had been conversing never bothered to look up. Outside the night was cold, and a brisk wind flitted strongly by at times. Torches lined the high stairwell leading down from Ehrehalle, and in their gleam he could see neither Jadyn nor evidence of her coming. Once down the stairs and on to the road he bore right, into a shadowy crevice between the stair and the mountain wall. It was dark here, so dark that not even a keen eye would have seen him.

There he stood waiting nervously. *What am I doing?* he thought. Dancing with Jadyn was fine. The room had been crowded and nothing outside of a clumsy dance was expected of him. Seeing her in the village was innocent enough. The lanes were busy and the daylight was broad. But now it would be just the two of them. At night. In the dark. Doing something for which bravery was a prerequisite. He could only imagine what she had in store. He almost didn't want to subject his mind to such open contemplation, yet contemplate it did. Suddenly he wondered if his breath smelled.

Several empty minutes passed, and he felt sillier with

each one that went by. *This is stupid,* he told himself after a while. *I'm out here waiting in the dark, in a hood, in the cold, not even knowing what I'm waiting for.* Thus he waited until he could simply wait no more, but just as he made to step away and head back inside, firm arms clasped him across his chest from behind. Startled and afraid, he spun wildly, and before he knew it he held the golden-haired perpetrator in submission. What startled him now was not the fact that Jadyn managed to spring up from behind him, but how he managed to subdue her immediately and without thought.

Releasing her quickly and embarrassedly, he apologized until he was blue in the face. "I didn't know you were you," he kept saying. "I didn't mean—are you alright?"

"I'm fine," she said, though her voice was a bit shaken. "You startled me as much as I tried to startle you. I didn't know you could do that."

"Neither did I," he said under his breath.

"I guess it must rub off on you, being with the knights and all. I'm sure they must be teaching you a thing or two."

Actually they coop me up in the highest bedroom like I'm some innocent damsel, he thought. "I guess so," he said.

Even in the darkness her eyes seemed to glitter, like pale blue stars fallen to earth and fighting to stay alight. A heavy silence fell between them. Lucian could not help but feel tense. His feet seemed welded to the ground, and everything about him felt cumbersome and imperfect.

Then Jadyn said, "Are you ready?"

"For what?" Lucian asked.

She picked up a large wicker basket that she had set down beside her. "Follow me."

It would have been easier reaching the summit of Shír Azgoth had they just walked to Lucian's room and climbed up over the balcony. Risky though the climb would have been, they would not have been as weary had they survived it. The ascent took the better part of an hour at a brisk pace, finishing at the end of a steep, spiraling road that had no doubt been made for such purposes.

On the way up Lucian and Jadyn talked of simple things. In his typical suave manner Lucian began with the topic of weather, but Jadyn had this way of making even general subjects interesting and fun. Cheerily she talked about her interests. Listening to her voice was so soothing to him that he could have listened to her go on about why she preferred strawberries over raspberries all the way up the mountain. He seemed to get so lost in her words that they failed to sound like words at all, becoming just a sweet-sounding wind bearing the pleasant tones of her voice. She looked remarkably beautiful in her simple attire. An old, worn cloak of gray concealed her garb, but through the loose gap of folds Lucian saw she wore a different jerkin than earlier, evergreen and of a velvety fabric. The breeches she wore were different also—a darker brown than the pair she had donned that afternoon, and much more kempt. They were her father's when he was a boy, she said. The absence of a mother prevented her from acquiring hand-me-downs fit for women.

"It's no matter," she mentioned. "I prefer these to those uncomfortable gowns and corsets. The last time I wore one it only made me feel fat, like one large inhale would burst it at the seams. Besides, my father's old things are great for traveling. Warm and comfortable and able to take on some wear."

Apparently Jadyn and her father were very close. She had a secret love for his profession and had often tried her hand at weapon-forging. "I've got a knack for it too," she added. "Made a couple fancy daggers in his forge, and one sword that I've named Rosie."

At this Lucian laughed. "Rosie?" he said. "Swords are supposed to have daunting names, aren't they? Leo's is called Lionsbane, and I had an old friend who named his Dawnbringer."

"Let me ask you something," she replied. "When you're skewered on thirty inches of steel, are you really going to care what the swordsman's named the skewer?"

This made strange and horrific sense to him.

"Besides," she continued, "I kind of had *something*

daunting in mind. Rosie, as in a rose, as in thorns. It was the first thing I thought of. She's kind of shaped like a thorn too. Curved, slender, sharp—really nice blade. My dad even taught me how to engrave the steel; I drew a rose curling around the fuller."

Lucian would not have expected this coming from a girl like her. The further up they progressed, the more his perspective of Jadyn changed. Not all girls, apparently, were dainty and yearning to be protected like stories often depicted them to be. Many girls—Jadyn included—could fend for themselves just fine.

When the conversation turned to the topic of Lucian, he kept things as general as he could, choosing to omit the Key and his quest from as much of his account as possible. Jadyn was a girl who was enveloped in the tradition and customs of her home. These topics livened her spirits, and when she spoke of them it was with passion and mirth. So it was that Lucian wanted to share with her the parts of him that he was most passionate about. The parts of him that were buried in the ashes of Amar.

All talk ceased, however, when they reached Shír Azgoth's summit. The display before them was too breathtaking to comprehend. Even under the cover of night Lucian felt like he could see every reach of the world, all the way to the sea. The entire breadth of Reznarion was deposited below in a vast expanse of pale silvers, dark blues, and blacks. Far across the northern folds he even glimpsed the ancient ruins of Dredoway where the Netherlings called home, tucked within the foremost arms of the Morin Mountains, and gaped at how dreary and beautiful something could seem all at once. High above the stars were able to shine freely in their blazing multitudes. In a ball of cold fire the waxing gibbous of the moon felt close enough to touch.

"Do you come up here often?" asked Lucian, with the air of one on the threshold of a dream.

"Only sometimes," answered Jadyn, her voice similarly stolen. "I used to come up here to think. It's as good a place as any, if you can imagine."

He had no trouble at all believing that. Though the

altitude was extreme and made breathing subtly toilsome, it was as efficient a sanctum as he had ever seen.

The crown of Azgoth was wide and surprisingly flat, until the plateau jolted upward into a towering knife of rock to their right. A large ring of sharp stones emerged from the center of the plateau, and in the narrow gaps between them Lucian thought to see movement. Jadyn put a finger over her lips as if to quiet him, though he really didn't need a warning. She approached cautiously with Lucian warily following in her wake.

"Where are we going?" he asked as quietly as possible, though his whisper was shrill with fright.

In answer Jadyn wove a dismissive hand behind her back as she crept along with her basket. When they drew closer Lucian thought to hear low voices grumbling. Jadyn yanked him close. "Listen to me carefully," she said with a chiseled, authoritative tone. "You need to approach this with caution."

Their faces now were mere inches apart. Though Lucian heard her voice speaking, he could only think of how delightfully nervous and excited he was becoming.

"Do you hear me?" she asked. "Lucian?"

As if coming out of a trance Lucian answered, "What? Yeah . . . *yeah*—I hear you."

Without preamble she stepped forward between a gap in the stones. "Careful," she said, holding out her hand and helping Lucian through.

Immediately the land delved downward into a large crevice. The perimeter of stones wound around them in a circumference of about a hundred feet, and in the very center were three of the most grotesque creatures that Lucian had ever seen.

"It's important," began Jadyn, "that I hold the basket out like this." Opening its lid, she proceeded to hold the basket out in front of her with one hand.

"What's in it?" asked Lucian. "And *what* are those . . . *things?*"

"Bólgs," Jadyn answered. She might have been telling Lucian the time for the matter-of-factness of her tone.

"They like meat when they can get it." She displayed a flimsy flank of meat as evidence. "I'm afraid they've only been able to pick off straying birds that happen to rise up to these climes; and they're not a big enough meal are they, my sweeties?"

"Noooo," bellowed one of the bólgs in answer, with a voice like a low-toned war horn. The creature who greeted Jadyn was the largest of the three. It had been stooped over with its spike-spined back turned, and when it came toward them Lucian saw that it was round-faced and lanky for its height, which may have been well over nine feet. On two legs it towered, its figure close to humanoid and the hue of its skin a pale shade of blotchy blue.

"All elbows and knees these guys," said Jadyn. The creature gave a deep throated moan as it approached on all fours, dragging its knuckles in an ape-like manner. When it came close enough it plopped down to sit and was wreathed by a cloud of dust. Here beneath the unhindered moon Lucian perceived the bólg for the better. The vertical disks of its reptilian eyes stared back at them questioningly, its inner set of eyelids closing vertically before its outer pair closed horizontally. Its slit-like mouth, much like a lizard's, was gaped slightly to reveal bluntly pointed teeth. Horizontal streaks of dark blue lined its face here and there, and wisps of gray hair sprouted sporadically from atop its largely bald skull. At the sound of their approach, its pointed ears perked up.

"Ja-dyn," said the creature. "Trou-ble." It gave a look to the place it had been sitting. Only now could Lucian see that the third bólg was lying almost lifelessly. Every now and then its frail diaphragm would rise infinitesimally. The other creature hunching over it seemed to be stroking its head and moaning sorrowfully.

Jadyn did not respond. Instead she groped through her basket for the biggest flank she could find. "There you go, Pike," she said cheerfully, tossing the meat to the bólg. Pike let the steak fall onto his lap before bringing it to his mouth and swallowing it whole.

"Now let's see if we can get the others over here," she

continued. "Nod, Marcie, come get supper!"

"You've named them?" Lucian asked. He had managed to keep a safe distance as Jadyn fed Pike, but had approached cautiously as the bólg was feeding.

"Of course!" she said. "They're like people, you know. Like a little family. And people should have names."

"Ja-dyn," muttered Pike in his grumbling, almost inarticulate voice. "Nod hurt. Nod not good."

"Hey! Marcie! Nod! Come and get it!" Jadyn called genially. "Sometimes they can be stubborn, you have to understand," she said, turning to Lucian. "But once they've got a full belly they're just precious." Fumbling through her basket she began walking toward Marcie and Nod.

"Jadyn," said Lucian. "Can't you hear what he's telling you? What—Pike (?)—is telling you? The one you're calling Nod is sick, I think."

Jadyn continued to approach the others cautiously, fumbling through her basket as she went. "Is that it, Lucian?" she said mockingly with a flirtatious smile. "Is that what Pike is *telling* me?"

"That's what I heard."

"*Lu*-cian," said Pike curiously, then repeated it confidently as though reaching a sudden realization as to what he was saying. "Lu-cian."

Feeling awkward, and somewhat frightened now that Pike's attention had been drawn to him, Lucian raised a feeble hand. "That's me," he said.

"Help . . . us . . . " said Pike slowly. To Lucian, the furrowing of his brow suggested that he might have been confused. "Lu-cian. Help—us."

"Jadyn, it sounds like Pike needs help," Lucian repeated firmly, afraid now that if help was not given, he might end up as Pike's next meal.

"What's the matter with him?" she said, dangling a piece of meat out for the one she called Marcie. "Marcie! Come on, girl. I came all this way to bring you dinner and you're not even going to say hello?"

Suddenly Marcie jerked her rotund blue head at Jadyn and shrieked. If an eagle could roar, Lucian imagined that was what it would have sounded like. Too quick for himself to comprehend, he was in front of her, shielding her with his arms outstretched. When he registered what had happened, fear gripped him so tightly he felt nauseous.

"Marcie," he said, surprised to hear the resolve in his own voice. "Marcie, listen to me. We are here to help. We're not here to hurt you. Trust me."

Why did I say that? Why? You've done it this time . . .

Marcie stood now. Lucian saw that she was perhaps a head smaller than Pike, though her lower half was a bit broader. Scraping the gravelly floor of her eyrie with her three-clawed feet, she bobbed up and down atop her knuckles. Her eyes were wide upon them, upon Lucian, big and bulging and largely reptilian.

"Help—us—then," she said. "Boast—ful man. Stu—pid man. Like—the—rest. 'No—ther—knight."

"Lu-cian," said the voice of Pike. Soon the towering bólg's shadow eclipsed him and Jadyn. Lucian's eyes did not even align with the bólg's blue pelvis. With a finger perhaps a foot long Pike pointed to Nod struggling upon the ground, wrapped in his own lanky arms.

Jadyn whimpered behind him. "They've never acted like this before. I'm scared, Lucian. What are we going to do?"

But all fell silent, a silence broken only by Marcie's and Pike's deep-throated grunts and Nod's struggling breaths.

Then Marcie bellowed suddenly. "HELP—HIM!" Her shriek echoed far across the night.

Jadyn fell back in tears. "Bad girl!" she mewled sheepishly.

"Stay back, Jadyn," said Lucian. "I—I'm going to help him."

"You're what?" she said incredulously. "You don't know what you're doing."

"I'm going to try," he whispered, passing subtle sidelong glances at the bólgs surrounding him. "Doesn't look like we have much of an alternative." Gulping under the fierce scrutiny of Marcie's unwavering gaze, Lucian reached over his shoulder. "Give me some meat."

Sidestepping cautiously, Lucian proceeded toward Nod.

The low bellowing of the ailing bólg was devastating to hear, even for someone who had never known what a bólg was or could have possibly been. Nod's back was turned when Lucian knelt behind him. Taking hold of one of the bólg's elbows, he rolled him over with ease. Struggle was wrought across the creature's face. Jadyn was right. They did seem all too human. Nod's brow was furrowed and his expression was a concoction of sorrow, fear, and pain. Though his eyes had been closed, he opened them upon being rolled over, and stared half-lidded at Lucian. Every now and then his pale, lizard-like eyes would roll back under his slightly-ajar lids before returning even blanker.

"Nod," whispered Lucian. "My name is Lucian Rolfe. I'm here to help you. Stay with me. Have something to eat." Gently Lucian moved the slab of meat toward Nod's mouth, the gap of which was narrowly opened to expel toiled breaths.

"Not—strong," Nod struggled to say. "Won't . . . rip . . . flesh . . . "

Lucian considered for a moment. "He says he can't rip the meat. He doesn't have enough strength."

At once Marcie reached out and took the meat gently from Lucian's grasp, returning it to his hand when she ripped off a chewable-enough chunk. Nod received it slowly and carefully, though Lucian nearly had to stick his fingers completely in his mouth. Laboring in chewing and grimacing in swallowing, Nod ate.

"Bet-ter?" asked Pike, passing nervously back and forth on his knuckles and exhausting grunted breaths in desperation. "Nod bet-ter?"

He's dying, Lucian wanted to say. *I can't save him. I don't know why I'm even trying.* Without plan or alternative Lucian rested his hand atop Nod's, who was hugging himself as though cold with clawed hands thrice the size of Lucian's own. *Poor Nod,* Lucian thought. *Poor Pike and Marcie. Maybe he's their son or brother . . .*

Just then Jadyn knelt beside him and looked sorrowfully at the dying creature. Wrapping her arms around Lucian's shoulders, she cradled her golden head beside his and wept. "Poor Noddy," she whimpered. "He was such a good boy."

Jadyn's sniffling soon became the only sound atop Shír Azgoth, there in the Eyrie of the Bólgs. Under the stars and fading moon Nod drew his final breath. Lucian felt the bólg's sporadic breathing cease several moments after he laid his hand atop Nod's hard and icy claws. When he saw that Nod was dead, Pike shifted from behind Lucian, and his great shadow lifted. Stooping her head low and walking sadly away, Marcie followed in his wake.

20

The Flame of Parthaleon

Gamaréa's knowledge of the criosphinx was minimal, though he knew his odds against it were better than they had been in his bouts with the Minotaur and wolf. It did, however, seem young and athletic, and the fact that it was largely herbivorous did not serve to blunt the ram-like horns atop its head or make its wings stop flapping wildly.

Suddenly it leapt upon its hind legs, and with its forelegs began beating the ground. No doubt, this method was meant to intimidate Gamaréa—a tactic soldier's often used in war by beating their shields or chanting. Granted, it was somewhat effective. If they had been alone on a hillside somewhere, Gamaréa would have retreated no questions asked.

Perusing about on its strong legs, its height nearly matching that of a horse, the defiantly odd creature prepared for its move, clawing and screeching, issuing sounds comparable to an enormous bird of prey. Wary of the horns, Gamaréa focused most of his attention on the criosphinx's head. Stooping its neck low, like a bull ready to fling itself, it kicked up dust with its right foreleg, screeched again, and immediately stampeded toward the Morok. It was an easy strike to evade, even in his weariness.

Average speed, at best, Gamaréa recounted to himself. A cold numbness began to filter down his wounded leg, which he had bandaged tightly with a slice of a nearby banner waving upon the lower stands of the arena. But the idle time that passed between the clearing of the wolf's corpse and the entrance of the criosphinx undoubtedly caused his already-weakened body to grow tense. Now he was wary of his aching muscles, and his sore and stinging back. Standing there with just a modest cloth fastened around his waist by a thick belt of sorts, he noticed his body for the first time. His hands, arms, and chest were covered in blood of various hues—his own purplish-crimson, the Minotaur's black, and the wolf's ruby. Would the criosphinx's join them? Or would this be the champion to best him?

Again the beast bellowed, its wail long and deep and unlike any he had ever heard. Beating its wings resoundingly, it came charging through a cloud of dust. Gamaréa prepared his sword to strike, but to his surprise the beast took flight, launching itself over him at a height he did not think it would be able to reach. Upon touching down behind him, the criosphinx charged again, this time with a surge greater than its last advance. The speed at which it accelerated this time caught Gamaréa off guard enough that he barely had time to react, and when he did the attempt was feeble.

As he leapt to escape the brunt of its sharp horns, the beast managed to flip him backward on to its back. In a frenzy it raced around the ring for several yards before it threw Gamaréa off, sending him rolling chaotically upon the hard earth. Coming to an abrupt stop against the ring's outer wall, he felt as though his body was broken.

At that moment, all he knew was pain. At best, he could see foggily, and the sounds of his surroundings were muffled. Pain, horror, and sadness filled him. Defeating the Minotaur was encouraging; besting the wolf instilled hope. But now that hope faded into darkness. Unable to rise, he managed to roll upon his side, and saw only blurred images except for the beast. It seemed to be waiting for him to stand, to retort, to do anything, but Gamaréa could not make a move to do so. All his senses faded; he felt his back throbbing, but did not feel the sting.

Lucian ... It was the only thing he could think of at that moment. *Lucian* ... He wished he could rid the thought from his mind so that he might take his final breaths in peace, but the image of the boy and the Key were unfaltering.

Lucian . . .

Vaguely, he heard the criosphinx lift its head aloft and howl. Everything about its movements seemed slow and dreamlike—its paws beating the earth as it charged, its wings flapping heavily in the wind. He closed his eyes. When he opened them he was on a distant shore where a marble estate rose up out of a golden field of wheat. Soft upon the wind he heard the subtle ringing of swords. Then, as though the scenery wheeled before him, a child sparring with his elder came suddenly into view.

He recognized both. Tartalion Ignómiel stood in the wonder of his youth, and the child was Gamaréa, not long after Tartalion had taken him in. He heard the swords ringing lightly as they touched and the wafting of their drapes as they sparred, but for a long while no words were audible, until he heard Tartalion: "Step lively. That's it! Back straight, we cannot have you slouching. Straighter. There it is! Arms out; both hands on the hilt. Chin higher. Higher! Swing with your body, not just with your arms. Rise when you have fallen. Rise! Rise! Your pain is the kindling by which your fire shall rage. Rise!"

And suddenly he was in a different place altogether, and there was a sound like heavy waves crashing, and as his senses returned he saw the criosphinx's head directly over him, heavy and grotesque, its tongue hanging from its square jaw, its neck wilting for the heavy horns on its head. It was several moments before he noticed that his arms were outstretched, holding firm to his blade—the blade that was embedded nearly up to the cross-guard in the creature's chest. With great effort, Gamaréa brought himself to one knee before standing entirely, doing his best to will the dying creature off of him. Patches of weariness overtook his sight for a moment before things became clear again. In the distance, just underneath an archway used as an exit, he thought to even see the image of Tartalion watching him. But as quickly as he imagined it, the image was gone. Another trick of his mind, it seemed, but he interpreted the vision as an omen of good fortune. *Perhaps I won't meet my end today after all . . .*

"NOOOOOO!" Melinta bellowed, drawing the attention of the nearest spectators. Thaldrid had only returned moments prior from delivering the king's first message to the gamekeepers when he grabbed hold of the frail Fairy's robes and shouted, "You tell those ingrates to release everything! I don't care how many beasts we have to use, he will die in this arena, in front of everyone!"

Thaldrid, tears welling up in his eyes, ran off to do Melinta's bidding yet again.

When the horn bellowed a fourth time, the doors remained closed. Instead, the fourth champion rose up out of the ground on an elevating platform similar to the one on which Gamaréa had entered. It was a beast more terrifying than any he had seen in his long span of life, tethered though it was to an iron rod planted into the slate on which it was delivered.

Parthaleon take my soul. What devilry is this?

But as the two combatants locked eyes, Gamaréa recognized the beast as one that had always fascinated him in his studies. Yet the etchings from his texts did the actual creature no justice. It was a kórog, bigger than a lion and more savage than three.

The beast utilizes four killing mechanisms, Gamaréa remembered Tartalion to have said. *It will grab smaller prey, such as rabbits, in its paws and crush them to death.* Gamaréa clearly saw those; flattened from supporting its sheer weight, each the size of a man's head.

Larger prey, such as deer, sheep, or even horses, it will pierce with its claws, each roughly nine inches long, and sharp enough to cut through flesh, muscle, tissue, and bone in one strike. Gamaréa did not have to get any closer to see how that would be possible. Black as ash, the Kórog's claws seemed to puncture even the stone tablet upon which it stood.

There are two incisors in its mouth that can grow to

eleven inches in length, capable of puncturing wounds in the victim's flesh nearly the circumference of a child's fist. And there they were, flanking the mouth of the beast, sharpened to an even sheerer point perhaps when it was sleeping.

These are all satisfactory, of course, yet its deadliest weapon is its tail. It is built like an axe, and can sometimes be more effective. Gamaréa could see its axe-like tail plainly now, as the kórog took to swinging it almost absentmindedly behind itself. What was more, someone had taken it upon themselves to weld iron to the bone protrusions, making the tail resemble an official axe even more so.

Superb. Right. Crushing, clawing, biting, axing. Which way do you want to die?

He could picture himself sitting in the firelight of Tartalion's study, sifting through page after page of yellowed parchment looking at sketches of the kórog, and reading accounts from various explorers. It was such a fascinating and benign subject that Gamaréa used to feel as though he was listening to a ghost story—accounts of a fictitious creature made up to scare children into obedience. But there it was before him now, made flesh and bone, trying to free itself of its bond so that it could rip him to pieces.

But a quick memory came to him just then, a newfound recollection presented by the voice of Tartalion yet again. *For all its cunning, the craft of its very making is in fact the thing that dooms it.*

What do you mean?

He recalled Tartalion having shown him a diagram of the Kórog's anatomical structure. *Do you remember the image of the spinal cord from your anatomy lessons?* The young version of himself nodded. *Then tell me where the beast's spine should end.*

Gamaréa saw himself point to the base of the Kórog's back, just before the beginning of its tail. Tartalion shook his head. *A safe guess, though incorrect. Look harder.*

It was then that Gamaréa noticed that the kórog's spinal cord continued on to the end of its tail, instead of stopping before it like most four-legged mammals. The image burned like a flame in his mind.

Severing the tail, Tartalion explained, *in turn severs the spinal cord, causing instant paralysis, if not death. Good luck getting to the tail, mind you.*

Gamaréa laughed subtly in spite of the situation. *I don't think I have much of a choice.*

It was the strategy by which the battle would have to be won. There was not much of an alternative. His plan affirmed, all Gamaréa could do now was wait. Not long after the Kórog completely emerged from underground, a Morgue soldier fired an arrow from his post above, sending it ringing against the iron rod and severing the bond that kept the beast at bay.

Now the relentless trial continued as the Kórog came loose and charged, but Gamaréa focused only on the voice of his mentor. *The speed and endurance of the Kórog is unparalleled; trying to outlast it is folly.* But he had to keep moving. It constantly leapt at him, causing him to jump left and right if only to avoid being bitten or sliced by a claw. An eternity seemed to have gone by since the Kórog was unleashed, their quick and dangerous dance seemingly never-ending. Gamaréa was sweating and panting, fatigued and in pain, but he had to press on. He knew, however, that if he did not reach the tail quickly, he would falter. But the Kórog proved too elusive and strong, and it was nearly impossible to find an effective angle from which he could strike.

Darting away from the beast in response to one of its lunges, Gamaréa was tripped by one of its thick paws and sent rolling to the ground near the center of the arena. Something in his lower back had been injured, and, though he fought against everything he had to rise again, he could only crawl to the iron rod that had once prevented the beast from attacking. There in throbbing pain he tried to prop himself up. Using the rod for support, Gamaréa painfully brought himself to his knees. The fall had inflicted a bloody, burning gash along the left side of his face, and it was several moments before his vision returned to focus, but when it did he saw the Kórog closing in. Cackling and salivating, it bellowed a menacing roar before lunging for what would be its killing strike. Gamaréa closed his eyes, putting a hand over his face as if that alone would shield him.

The shadow of the leaping beast was over him, becoming darker and darker, until he could almost feel its weight—

When suddenly there was nothing. Gamaréa, who had clenched his eyes, found himself in darkness. His vice-like grip upon the iron rod slackened; his palms were sweating. What had happened? But then he realized . . .

The only darkness that had fallen was the shadow of the beast looming over him, impaled by the iron rod, and the moisture that had caused his grip to slacken was its dark blood oozing down the shaft. It took a moment for Gamaréa to register what had occurred, but when he did he was quick to slide out from underneath. Limping and grasping the small of his back, he felt more disgusting than he ever had in his life. His skin was warm and smelly and sticky from all the blood that had collected. His beard and hair were damp and matted, and the gash down the left side of his face was stinging from dirt that had amassed. He could feel a cold tingle as it began to swell. A similar sensation ran down his left leg. His bandage was tightly fastened indeed, and the numbness was now running into his toes.

The disapproving groans of the crowd suggested to Gamaréa that they were not thrilled by the fact that he was still alive. Looking up to the king's balcony, he saw only wide-eyed faces, but they were not looking at him. Following their gaze back to the Kórog, Gamaréa saw, to his dubious horror, that the beast was attempting to propel itself from the rod's grasp. Suddenly, with a maddening shriek, the Kórog yanked the rod from the ground and proceeded despite the fact that it had been impaled entirely through its midsection.

Wonderful.

This, however, was not the beast that had nearly handed Gamaréa his death. Its motions were lazy and clumsy. Blood was beginning to issue around where the rod had penetrated. It must have missed its heart by centimeters.

Gamaréa stumbled away, his back still throbbing, his leg still heavy and cold, unable to maintain any sort of straightened posture. With great effort the beast lunged one last time, and in an effort just as trying, Gamaréa evaded, and hacked off its tail.

The Kórog fell instantly, twitching somewhat upon the ground until it moved no more. Then Gamaréa too dropped to his knees. A tumult of weariness fell over him like a heavy shroud. His vision was faltering, his hearing nearly gone, his body worked beyond its limits. The taste of bloody sand filled his mouth before he realized he had toppled. Melinta, anxiously anticipating his fall at last, stood in his balcony with excitement—

And was infuriated to see Gamaréa's shoulders begin to move as he slowly struggled in pushing himself up again, until at length he stood upon his feet impossibly, wobbling, weary-eyed and pale. Across his filth-riddled face his long brown shanks hung matted and wet with sweat and blood and sand. Within his throat kindled a flame he longed to spurn forth, but hadn't the strength to muster a call that would be heard over the bustling crowd. Instead he merely pointed, raising his sword-hand slowly as though a great weight tried it down, and Melinta stood exposed at the end of its reach, fear brimming in his beady eyes, even with the knowledge of the final champion he kept in waiting.

So it was without haughty speeches or angered cries that Melinta signaled the gatekeeper one last time, and the door swung open, and all who stood before it were sure to flee in utter haste. Thrusting unbound into the ring was the oldest form of evil known to any corner of the modern world: a Fire Drake from the land known throughout every kingdom as Parthaleon, the underworld realm beneath the sweltering, ashen grounds of Nundric, Domain of Demons, where only the blackest souls festered.

There before him now stood the last of an ancient breed—the last of all that remained of the Drakes that once roamed the world. Drakes of both Water and Earth had been extinct for thousands of years, and, since a Fire Drake sighting had not been reported since the middle of the Dark Ages, Gamaréa believed their kind to be extinct as well. But this was no mere Fire Drake. It was the infamous beast who heralded all the races of the damned, leader of all that spat fire, guardian of all that was black: Ignis, Lord of Parthaleon itself, who guards (or guarded) the very gates of the underworld.

Though Ignis remained at the mouth of the gate, Gamaréa felt the flame rising off of him, humid and sweltering, the stifling smell of brimstone and rotten flesh strangling the air. Ignis approached on four colossal three-clawed feet, Flame engulfed him. Sharp horns sprouted from the tip of his huge head and at the bottom of his jaws. When he lifted his head to release his ghastly, shrieking cry, his dagger-like teeth were revealed. Then, when he inched close enough, Ignis peered down at Gamaréa with eyes as yellow perhaps as the embers in which he was conceived.

You should have known a moment like this would come, Gamaréa thought dismally. *When sword and arrow and armor would count for nothing.*

But all thought now fled from him as Ignis swooped forward, eyes like small yellow globes glowering through the burning embers and fumes emitting from his scales. His sword meekly in hand, Gamaréa turned and cantered off as best he could. A sound like a mighty gale rose up behind him; Ignis had taken flight, belching fire and shrieking. His cries were horrible, ringing long and loud throughout the great expanse of the venue. It was a sound that in itself nearly knocked Gamaréa off balance, and he even noticed that many of the spectators had fallen out of their seats, grasping their ears and crying.

This was the end—an insurmountable challenge. Everything around him slowed. He was no longer in the arena. The crowd's excitement was no longer audible. The gleam of Melinta's white robe no longer glowed in the corner of his eye. All went quiet. Wheeling past him came moments from his past like a vivid dream, and in the background were stars and misty shapes that he could not discern. *The end,* he realized, uncomfortable with the way he was accepting it. Ignis prepared to finish him—

And was thrown back. A sudden beam of vivid white light, more terrible than the sun, burst across the sands. Now behind him, as though a whisper, Gamaréa heard a sound like breaking glass, but he could not turn. The light before him was too bright and wondrous for his senses to perceive anything else. It seemed like an eternity that the beam had been shining when another beam, just as relentless, rode parallel alongside the first, and the sound like glass rang shriller, until at last Gamaréa's senses returned, and the lights were gone, and he was able to turn once more to see that Ignis's flames had been extinguished, his defenses taken down.

It was not until this moment that Gamaréa realized he had fallen upon his back in the cacophony of light, but Ignis noticed indeed and strode forward to loom over him, his shadow devouring the remaining daylight and casting all around them into darkness. With what strength he had left, Gamaréa struggled out of the beast's shadow, his back burning with a sudden fire. Sand and dust littered the reopened wounds across his back now, and every sudden movement proved excruciating.

Even without his fiery cloak, Ignis remained most lethal. But Gamaréa could not rise, and what was worse, when he made any attempt to, he was kicked back down by the beast's large claws or swatted away by his tail. The more Gamaréa crept away, spider-like upon the singed earth, the faster Ignis pursued, until finally, in one heavy jab of its head, the Drake tried to seize him in his mouth. Gamaréa managed, somehow, to roll over and evade the blow, and in turn stuck his blade into Ignis's neck. But the weak sword was no match for Ignis's scales, hard as they were, and merely became lodged within their rock-like composition. It did, however, infuriate the beast, who now reared his ghastly head and cried aloud, beating its fireless wings and taking flight over the arena.

Gamaréa, holding firmly to the hilt of his sword, clung desperately as Ignis launched himself skyward, shaking and bellowing, seeking freedom from the nuisance hanging from his neck. In the air he twisted, turned, zigzagged, and dove, until his rampant climb brought them to the clouds, the arena rendered to a mere pebble beneath them.

Finally Ignis felt the sword come free, but was dismayed to feel an odd sensation upon his back; for there, mounting him as though he were a steed, was his little inexhaustible foe. Wildly, Gamaréa hacked at Ignis's back and shoulders, but even employing all his strength to the cause could barely lacerate the Drake's tough skin. He turned his attention to the wings, now beating fiercely, and noticed that they were comprised of something softer, and with all the might he could muster, Gamaréa set his sword to work on Ignis's right wing, and was pleased to see that it began to rip. One more stroke would amputate it entirely . . .

But the beast would not be undone so easily. Turning itself away, he flipped upside-down so that Gamaréa clung to the very wing he had broken. Ignis in turn began snapping at Gamaréa's dangling legs, which constantly tried to kick away his advances. All around them the world howled.

Ignis, however, could only fly in such a manner for a short period of time, and came upright once more after Gamaréa's weight had nearly ripped his wing off completely. It took one more modest lash to sever it entirely, sending the crimson piece of useless flesh down through the clouds beneath them. Suddenly their swift descent began.

Yet Gamaréa persisted. The Drake bellowed, trying with all the strength he could summon to shake the pest from his back. Gamaréa fought with all his might to hold firm, but it was a difficult task. Trying to maintain footing was nearly impossible; trying to make effective use of a sword an insurmountable challenge.

It became apparent that there was only one way to escape. Gamaréa could destroy the beast, but not without destroying himself. It was a task he would rise to—not because he wished to end his own life, but because he understood now that Ignis's death would mean a great advantage for Lucian. With the gates of Parthaleon forever unguarded, gaining entrance to the underworld realm would not be nearly as impossible.

With this mad hope filling his spirits, Gamaréa shifted his focus to Ignis's remaining wing, and he slashed madly, paying no attention to his wounds which were now fully open and bleeding and more agonizing than fire. In a cloudy blur he struck even as the world rose up to meet them, summoning all the anger he had ever known, all the love he ever held for the few who were dear to him, and the one solitary hope he kept for Lucian. These he wrapped into one surge of emotion so that he struck with something wilder than rage.

The final tendons separating, the wing came free, falling to whatever abyss would claim it. Their descent enlivened vigorously. No longer could his one remaining wing parachute them to the ground. Ignis cried out, shrill and ear-splitting, but the fire in his eyes soon dimmed. Dropping his head in defeat, Ignis fell into a headlong plummet. Wind roared like a thousand hurricanes compounded into one. Gamaréa gripped with all the strength left in him so as not to be swept off of Ignis's back. The arena was in sight below—a microscopic circle beneath them. In a moment it was upon them. Ignis was dead. Gamaréa felt whatever life left within the drake expel itself and render the beast rigid. No evasive maneuver could be achieved. Gamaréa closed his eyes and braced for impact.

Then all went dark.

21

Bólg Friend

"Lu-cian," Lucian heard Pike say. "Nod—not—come—back?"

Now sorrow began to grip Lucian as well, and he breathed heavily as tears came. "No, Pike," he said. "Nod not come back."

Then a horrible sound lifted from Pike's throat, a terrible, sorrow-filled, rumbling wail that seemed to shake the stone ring in which Nod perished. In furious grief Pike beat his fists upon the ground. "No!" he bellowed. "No, Nod. No, Nod. No."

"Look at him," said Jadyn, helping Lucian to his feet. She wiped a tear away from her glowing eyes and stared studiously at the two bólg's near the edge of the ring of stones. "They really *are* like people."

By this time Marcie had made her way over to Pike and seemed to be trying to console him. It looked more like wrestlers seeking purchase in the other's stance, but it was affection and compassion nonetheless.

Then came a sound that made even Pike, now blind with sorrow, stop cold. It had been a voice, low and whispering, in the same, strange tone that only a bólg could employ. "Pike, Nod—good," said Nod.

As if refreshed from a deep slumber Nod rose to his feet. The smallest of the three, he stood maybe six inches shorter than Marcie, who (Lucian could only assume) was now overwhelmed with mirth. When Nod came to his senses, Pike greeted him enthusiastically, and many strange sounds were issued during their reunion, sounds that Lucian determined were those of joy.

Now that the bólgs were distracted Lucian leaned in to Jadyn. "I think now's a good time to leave," he whispered.

"Why?" she asked. "Look at them! Look how happy you've made them. I don't know what you did, but Nod was dead, or close to it at least. Now it looks like he's never ailed a day in his life."

"I didn't do anything." The words came out quickly, as if he was defending himself against an allegation. "I just kind of put my hand on his. It was cold, and I could tell by his breathing that he wasn't going to make it. I guess I was wrong."

Just then Pike detached himself from the others and hobbled toward them. When towering at his full height, it was a strain to look into his eyes. "Bólg—friend," he murmured in his low, grumbling manner, reaching down with a saucer-sized hand and patting Lucian's head. It was a surprisingly gentle tap for a bólg, though Lucian nearly soiled himself being subjected to it. "Bólg—friend al—ways."

There was a long silence that Lucian felt he was expected to break. "You're my friend too," he said finally. Pike, as if he understood, grunted and nodded sharply.

Then Marcie and Nod came to stand abreast of him. They looked joyful, if the expression of bólgs can be read. Stepping forward, Nod knelt before Lucian. "Nod—in—debt," he said. "Need—of—Lu—cian, deed—of—bólgs."

Lucian smiled. Jadyn was right after all. They really were like people.

"I think he likes you," Jadyn whispered in Lucian's ear.

Touched though he was, Lucian had had just about enough of being within swatting-reach of creatures nine feet tall. "Er—uh—thank you all," he said in his best attempt to sound lordly. "It was really a great privilege meeting you. The lady and I must be going now. The hour is late and our limbs are weary from the climb."

Cautiously, but with no lack of alacrity, Lucian and Jadyn sidestepped toward the gaps in the stones, smiling and waving like guests feigning hesitance to leave an uncomfortable lodging.

All the while the bólgs called behind them.

"Go," said Pike, "Lu—cian bólg—friend. Ja—dyn bólg—friend."

"Bólg—friend," repeated Marcie.

"Bólg—friend al—ways," said Nod.

22

The Slayer of Ignis

Through his waking eyes, Gamaréa could tell that he was on his back. The crater in which he lay was deep, and he found himself upon something hard. Was he buried? Was he now a spirit watching his own burial? Holding his hands out in front of his face, he moved his fingers as if to test the limits of his consciousness. To his surprise, they wiggled. When his senses returned, he realized he was lying upon the huge, sickly-orange corpse of Ignis, who looked more horrible in death than he had in life. His skull was crushed, and the position in which he lay seemed awkward and unnatural.

How am I alive? How long have I been in here? Gamaréa asked himself. Vaguely he heard the crowd above. *It must have been a moment ago, at most,* he determined. Sitting up, he shook the weariness from his head, then, cumbersomely, climbed up Ignis's spine and along his tail, which coiled out of the hole like a makeshift ladder.

He imagined Melinta would never forget the moment he saw the two hands emerge from the crater. *How can this be?* he seemed to be pondering frantically, the sheer unfeasibility of his survival bringing him nearly to furious tears.

But there he was now, fully emerged from below. Gamaréa planted his feet as best he could, for his knees were indeed wobbly. The cloth he wore was tattered and all but destroyed, the blade he had wielded severed in two. Various parts of his body were lacerated and bloody, with his own blood and that of all his victims. Across his face his matted hair fell, sweaty and dark. But the thing the crowd would remember above all else they witnessed that day were his eyes. He whom death excused five times peered up at Melinta as though he wished to look at nothing else, with more ferocity than any combatant that had been led onto the sands that day.

He wanted to shout up to him, yell something that would surely chill whatever blood remained warm within his heart, but he refrained. There was no strength left within him to muster anything but a whisper, and thus he chose only to hold his silent, menacing stare. And, though he could not know it, it was stronger than any words his voice could have produced.

Gamaréa watched as Melinta's guards entered the king's balcony and escorted him away, aiding him to his feet like a helpless child who had been denied sweets. Even from below, Gamaréa saw little discrepancy between the king's white robes and the pallid hue his skin took on.

Then he too was retrieved from the arena. It was somewhat amusing how much caution the guards were exercising as they led him away. Timidly they escorted him down the darkened tunnel, through the same passage where five beasts from the world's most shadowed corners had been led to their doom. From the stands the crowd began to file away out beyond the venue where their carriages were waiting. Had any sort of sound been issued, Gamaréa did not hear it.

23

A Thousand Years

Gamaréa spent the next two days in the medicine hall, surprised to learn that it was by Melinta's order. He heard something about "precautionary reasons". Timms and Pubs were absent, perhaps having fully recovered from whatever ailments they had sustained, and Gamaréa was strangely disappointed despite scarcely knowing them. His return, no doubt, would have rendered them spellbound, and they would most certainly have been eager to learn about his fairings in the arena, and he just as eager to share them. There was a sudden, warm burst of worth now coursing through his veins. *Did that really just happen?*

His body ached dreadfully, and since his departure from the arena, he began to grow more conscious of where his own blood mingled in the splatter of death covering his skin. But somehow, the pain did not faze him. A swell of adrenaline rose up within him like a tumultuous storm, and when the reality of his fairings on the sands sunk in, he even felt as though he could go a couple more rounds.

The silence was disquieting in the lonely chamber, and even more so when Gamaréa recounted the volume of the boisterous crowd during the fighting. Even more disquieting was the realization that he had, for now, escaped his execution. He wondered what Melinta was up to at that moment, after witnessing not one, but five of his prized champions squandered. It was all but obvious to Gamaréa that Melinta had not secured such brutish creatures to merely entertain a crowd. Surely he had not subjected his men to the dangers of the wild to capture such creatures for the purpose of sport. They were meant for bigger things, no doubt. Bent to the king's will, the five champions Gamaréa faced would have certainly turned the tide of the coming war.

And Ignis . . .

What strings did he pull to secure him?

Regardless of the fate waiting for him, a feeling of completion came over Gamaréa, dangling his feet over the edge of his slate. The defeat of Melinta's champions meant a small victory for the free world. Even if he was put to death, which he felt was likely, a large portion of Melinta's firepower was now undone.

The smile which he was unable to suppress quickly faded as he heard the cell door begin to open, but returned tenfold when he looked upon the face of Didrebelle, bearing a tray on which was balanced a steaming bowl, a cup, and a pewter pitcher.

The Fairy smiled wide. "You should be dead," he said, feigning curtness.

Gamaréa laughed. "There was not a moment when I wasn't at death's brink."

"Eat this." Didrebelle handed Gamaréa the bowl. It was filled with hot soup, which, for once, did not bear that sickly greenish hue. "It is from Deavorás. I have prepared it myself; I would not be too trusting of your food or drink supply now that you remain alive."

It was undeniably the greatest thing Gamaréa had tasted in a long while. The soup was the perfect temperature, and the meat within it absorbed the broth and was soft and tender. Cold water filled the cup to its brim and was painfully refreshing. He ate and drank like a man possessed, Didrebelle refilling his cup every other minute or so.

"The show was in your honor,'" said Gamaréa after taking a lengthy drink and releasing a sigh of satisfaction. "Nice of you to stop by."

"Indeed it was," said Didrebelle plainly. "The events in the arena have always been in honor of someone or something. How else would he be able to rationalize them?

My presence, however, was not actually required."

Didrebelle acknowledged the expression of disappointment that crossed Gamaréa's face. "My absence was not by choice," Didrebelle assured. "Important business required my attention—business that may set our plans from here in motion."

Just then the sound of guards patrolling the corridor was heard plainly, and Didrebelle spun his head around alertly.

"I have to go," he said shortly, hooding himself and advancing quickly toward the door. "Perilous roads open to safe passages. But you've yet to travel all."

"Wait—" demanded Gamaréa, surprised at how desperate his voice sounded.

But Didrebelle had crept into the shadows, recognizable only as a humanoid shape in the darkness. "The dawn draws near," he whispered, "but now the night is blackest."

As he swept away, only a glimmer of his crystalline eyes flickered in the torchlight. Not even his fleeting footsteps were heard carrying down the passage.

"You speak in riddles!" Gamaréa shouted to the spot where his friend had been. *Damn him.* Only now was Gamaréa conscious of the fact that his hand was pleadingly outstretched, as though trying to catch the tail-end of the fading wind. He paid no attention to the two guards entering.

The foremost of them yanked him by his reaching arm to pull him off the table. "He seems well," he said, a twinge of surprise in his voice as he locked arms with Gamaréa as if to help him away.

"Up with you," said the second, taking out a rag and blindfolding him.

Before long, fresh air captured his senses—or, *fresher* air, at least, as the smell of decay and horse dung still loomed large on the wind. He felt new arms grabbing at him from above, and found himself being loaded on to a carriage which before long set away upon a rough road. It might have been a quarter of an hour later when it stopped. Soon he was escorted down and could see again.

The barracks at which the cart had stopped was his own, though he felt years removed. Just a hint of the daylight was allowed to filter through as he was led down the old, dank corridors to his cell. When its doors opened, he was left to walk in on his own without the slightest hint of a shove. There he stood, looking around as though the loneliness and silence were old belongings he wished never to gaze upon again.

The inmates were in the fields tending to their usual duties, and so with nothing to do but sleep he curled up in the shadows of his cell and found what rest he could. A chill ran through the concrete floor, and the itch of the dirt particles, which he had once become used to, distracted him again. But sleep did manage to find him, however difficult he thought it would be to achieve, and he did not wake until a guard came rapping on his cell door.

Gamaréa's eccentricity as he woke must have startled him, for the guard jumped back with wide eyes; he might have woken a sleeping bear. "Sorry to have disturbed you," he said, humbly. "Dinner will be held shortly."

Gamaréa nodded, as if allowing the guard permission to enter. Walking through the fields now showed him many things. There was a very awkward vibe issuing from the captives around him, all of them having taken the shape of incredulous gawkers. Furthermore, the constant courtesy being displayed by the guards was more disquieting than when they had been aggressive. Though he very well may have been concussed, it seemed to him that they were treating him with something like respect. Respect! He welcomed the awkward hospitality, and even more so when he was escorted to the front of the muck line and given a thick slice of bread from a fresh, warm loaf. It was a welcomed alternative to the main course, which resembled regurgitated carrots all too closely.

If he thought he could not be more pleased with the way things were carrying on, seeing Daxau with an empty seat beside him doubled his merriment. Upon seeing Gamaréa, the powerful man stood in disbelief, a wild smile splitting his bearded face genially in two as he extended his muscle-roped arms and locked Gamaréa in a firm embrace.

"Of all black-magic spells, damn you!" exclaimed Daxau joyously. "Forty lashes yet still you continue to defy practicality. It was a miracle in itself you survived *that*."

Locking eyes jovially, they laughed like children. Only then did Gamaréa notice the bruise running along the left side of Daxau's face from when he had fought to keep the whip from his back. His eye was swollen also, but the bruise was beginning to fade.

"Come and sit!" said Daxau, as though welcoming Gamaréa to his own table. "I see you are already beginning to get the royal treatment."

Gamaréa did not know what that meant at first, but he saw Daxau's eyes on his tray and the fresh loaf of bread that lay there. The Morok smiled. "Here," he said, ripping the bread in two. "Please, take it."

Daxau's eyes moved from the bread to Gamaréa dubiously. "I couldn't," he said. "I can't impose on your earnings."

"I insist," said Gamaréa earnestly. "I would share this with no other."

Daxau smiled and reached out reluctantly. Gamaréa, as if in fear Daxau would recoil, pressed the piece of bread into his hand. Looking at the bread as though he beheld a kingly heirloom, Daxau said, "It's been quite some time since I felt the touch of bread." He took a bite and chewed slowly. "Un een lungr sin I tust it." His eyes closed with pleasure; when they opened they were wide and bright, and a smile came to his face. "I will repay you," he said gratefully. "In this life or the next."

"There are no debts between friends," answered Gamaréa. "Now eat, will you? I don't expect these rewards to last."

Daxau took another small bite, this time waiting until he swallowed to speak. "I heard rumors of your fairings in the arena throughout the grounds, though I'm ashamed to admit that I didn't believe them."

Gamaréa swallowed a bit of his bread. "I am still working on believing it myself."

"We saw his champions gathering in the courtyards of Deavorás." Daxau's eyes gazed both in wonder and perplexity as he recalled what he had seen. "Such a collection of beasts, I think, have never been assembled."

"And there won't be again."

Daxau released a slight chuckle. "I never thought such a fair city could host the blackness that came out from under that tower. Beasts of horn and claw, beasts of axe-like and sickle tails—beasts of fire. I simply thought he was adding pieces to his army for the war that is abroad, but not once did I imagine them to be his champions."

"It was a most uncommon event."

"And you slew them all, yet remain humble." Daxau was smiling, though he may not have realized it. Taking another bite of bread, he shook his head as though perplexed. "Two, three, even four men I can fathom—but beasts from the mountains and forsaken lands across the world . . . It's a marvel. And the Black Guardian! The very dog of the sorcerer himself . . . "

The slight curve of a smile came to Gamaréa's face, though speaking the name of Ignis, even in death, made his bones shudder. "The plains of Parthaleon will remain unguarded for some time now; but guard or no that realm is nearly unreachable."

Daxau laughed as though having heard some joke. "The Slayer of Ignis already seeks passage across the Black Plains."

But Gamaréa thought better than to discuss the matter further. "And how have you been faring?" he said. It was a feeble attempt at a subject change, but he believed Daxau got the point.

"More of the same," he replied. He might have been drudging on about the unchanging routine of a common job. "Nothing changes around these parts. The king's monument is nearly finished. A week's time will see it done."

Gamaréa strained to not allow this information to appear as though it troubled him. "And what would become of us when there is nothing left to build?"

"Your guess is as good as mine," answered Daxau. "He'll find something else for us to build, I guess. Another monument condemned to age and ruin."

Gamaréa lifted his cup and feigned a smile. "As are we all, my friend," he said, taking a drink.

Daxau's gaze became fixed. "Us, maybe, but not you," he said softly, as if to himself.

Gamaréa returned a perplexed stare. "I am not sure I follow you," he replied.

"We will come and go. Our bodies will be replaced with others once we've gone. But you—tongues will host your name for a thousand years. 'I lived in the age of the Slayer of Ignis,' they'll say, or something to that tune. You wrote your name down in the histories when you overcame that beast, immortalizing it. It can't be tarnished now—no way."

Daxau then lifted his cup, as though in belated response to Gamaréa, and took a drink of his own. "Cheers to you then, my friend. I count myself lucky to say that I've shared words with you."

Gamaréa smiled. "You offer me more credit than I deserve, and speak as though I am of the Wizardrim itself—but no Fairy scribe will see my story into tales or songs. Such an act would be blasphemous and punishable by death. I fear the happenings here will die with you and me, to be buried in the earth or burned on whatever pyre our bodies may lie."

Daxau finished his final portion of bread.

"I like my version better," he said.

24

The Sloping Road

The rejoicing of the bólgs echoed long into the night. Even when the summit of Azgoth was lost again above the clouds they heard the low rumbling groans of Pike, Marcie, and Nod, like moaning winds over far hills. Jadyn and Lucian allowed for those to be the only sounds of their return trip, at least for a long while. Wrapping herself tightly in her cloak Jadyn cantered on with the gait of one unable to bend entirely at the knees. Her face had become ghostly and her cheeks tear-stained. Red rims circled her glossy eyes, the blue of which appeared to have grown paler still.

It seemed an age since they had climbed to Azgoth's crown. Lucian tottered on confused and sullen, remembering suddenly how happy he felt walking beside Jadyn, being in her company—hearing her talk of the things that made her smile. It had been all he could do to stand close to her, but not too close. He never thought the journey home would be as different as it was proving. Now she would barely look at him, and he did not know how to make her. Was it him? Did the experience with the bólgs affect her as deeply as it had himself? Was it something he said? *I didn't say anything,* he recounted nervously. *Girls . . .*

It was colder now than it had been on the way up. The night had failed to wait for them, and he only hoped that it was not too much past midnight. Constantly the recurring daydream of seeing Orion waiting for him at the doors of Ehrehalle plagued his mind. *I wouldn't be surprised,* he thought to himself. *And with Jadyn here . . . What would he think?*

Lucian was not sure how far into their descent it was, but there was a very specific point when the silence between them became discomforting. Mustering his courage and subduing his blood-flow as much as he could, he trotted up beside his briskly walking companion. "Hey," he said sheepishly, then swallowed before summoning more of his nerve. "Is everything—er—alright?"

"Fine," said the voice from under the gray hood. "Just a little shaken is all."

"Did I do anything to—you know—hurt you?"

At this Jadyn's shoulders bobbed with inaudible laughter. "No," she said. "In fact, I guess what bothers me is what would have happened if you *didn't* do anything." She tightened her hold upon herself. "Marcie—I've *never* seen her like that. She's always been the sweetest thing. Tonight I thought she might kill me." She sniffled again, and let an errant tear splatter on the folds near her neck.

Lucian nodded, unsure of what to say at first. "She was scared, I guess," he said at length. "And sad. Haven't you ever been sad and just wanted to be alone?"

Jadyn's silence was affirmation enough.

"I think Nod was her son," Lucian continued. "*Is*, I should say. I guess some mothers really care about their children."

Suddenly his heart delved ever so slightly. Never before had the pangs of a motherless childhood weighed on him until now. Mary had indeed proved an invaluable maternal figure, and he was grateful for having been in her care, but there were subtle things that only a mother could give her son. Things that only now he began to miss.

"What do you mean by *that?*" said Jadyn, somewhat sharply. "I told you about my past in good faith—"

"I'm not talking about *your* past," Lucian retorted, as sharply if not sharper. Then he recoiled, for not only did he realize the affect his tone had on Jadyn, but that he inadvertently broached a subject he never meant to discuss.

"I'm sorry," he said feebly. "I didn't mean to snap at you, it's just . . . I don't know . . . I never had a mom—a *real* mom, I should say. Seeing Marcie tonight made me realize how—I don't know—*universal*, I guess, motherhood is. The truth is I was abandoned, Jay. Mary told me my real mother left me on her doorstep when I was barely a week old. I don't know. It kind of played with my mind growing up, you know? Made me think I had some kind of deficiency or a problem that I just couldn't put a finger on. Even in her rage Marcie showed me the beauty of a mother's love for her child. She would have stayed with him to his death. Her *and* Pike. They would have stayed there stroking his head and comforting him until there was nothing left to comfort. And then there are others too weak to face the responsibilities of parenthood, who at the slightest hint of adversity abandon those it's their duty to protect."

He had never spoken like this before. When he finished he closed his mouth, surprised those words had filtered out of it. The voice seeping through his lips had been his, but the words were certainly not his own. Maybe he was growing up after all.

"Wow," said Jadyn, short of breath. "You haven't been holding *that* in at all, *have* you?"

"I'm sorry," said Lucian. "I don't know why I'm feeling this way. I didn't want to mention that—I've actually *never* mentioned that. It just kind of came into my mind."

"You don't have to apologize," Jadyn reassured. "I've had thoughts like that sometimes. Only mine aren't as warranted as yours, sorry to say. My mother died having me. Whenever I see or hear something and wish I had a mother to share it with, I start to feel vengeful against myself. If it wasn't for me, she'd still be here. Sometimes I wonder if my dad thinks the same thing."

"That's not fair to him," said Lucian quickly. The words had barely come out of Jadyn's mouth. "I saw him today. Trust me, that forge was filled with the air of a man who loves his daughter. I sensed it once you came in."

"So *that's* why you left so fast," she said smiling. Her face seemed like a jewel encased within the shadows of her hood.

"There was scalding hot metal around. I wouldn't have

been caught dead in there a minute longer."

The weariness and despair that had been wrought across her face was slowly vanishing, and just as the dawn brings light to reaches long bathed in shadow, her features were ablaze once more in their former splendor.

"You're funny," she said. "And you have a way with words."

Lucian was laughing inwardly. *You obviously don't hear many words.*

"Maybe that's why they responded to you so well," she continued. "The bólgs. At times I could have sworn you had an understanding with them, as if you could—I don't know—understand what they were *saying*, for crying out loud. It was cute, though, the way you were talking to them. They're like people, yeah—characteristically, at least. I think they liked the conversations you were staging."

Lucian could not help the look of confusion that crossed over his face. "*Staging?*" he said. "I wasn't staging anything. They *were* talking to me, and I to them. I actually started to get nervous when you were ignoring Pike. He was all but pleading with you to help Nod. I thought that if something wasn't done soon, their next meal would have been us."

Jadyn laughed. "You *are* cute."

But Lucian kept his heart in reserve, too confused and presently agitated that Jadyn was belittling the experience he unwillingly had on the mountaintop. "You mean to say you didn't hear them . . . *speaking?*" he said bewilderedly.

Jadyn stopped in her tracks and turned around. "Look," she said, "it's getting old, alright?"

"What's getting old?" His voice had become suddenly demanding. He heard what he heard, and almost paid the price. "Those bólgs were talking. You really didn't *hear* them? Pike was speaking right *to* you at one point!"

"Lucian, that's enough. You're starting to scare me."

"*Jadyn, help us*, he said. *Nod not good.* Pike said those things."

"Lucian, stop."

"Stop what? That was what I heard. And a great deal more."

"You're *scaring* me. *Stop* it!"

She was whimpering again, in the same desperate tones as when the bólgs were threatening them. With a deft thrust she shoved him, and Lucian stumbled forward. He stopped himself after tottering a few paces away, and when he looked on her again he saw her lower lip dancing and tears beginning to form.

She's really not lying, he thought. Suddenly an odd feeling took hold of his stomach. "You really *didn't* hear them, did you?"

A loose arm of wind rustled by them, dragging small particles of dust with it past their feet. These were the only sounds for several moments. In that time of unwavering stares, Lucian finally realized that he alone had heard the bólgs. Jadyn could not have. It all began to make sense: her obliviousness to Pike's pleas; her ignorance of Nod's predicament; her careless approach to feeding Marcie. To her they were just creatures she had been accepted by. To them she was just an innocent daughter of humans, harmless and generous with food. But what was *he* to them? He who was unknown to their culture and had nothing to offer but frightened glances. When Pike said his name it seemed as though he was hit with a moment of clarification, as if, strangely enough, he knew that he would come. Expected that he would.

And Nod. Though Lucian was as practiced in medicine as one of Mary's pies, he knew for certain that a small morsel of meat could not yank a creature the size of a bólg from imminent death. Something happened there on that summit, in that lofty Eyrie of the Bólgs. Something that Lucian had an inkling of but was not quite prepared to admit.

Jadyn shook her head, confirming that Lucian alone had engaged the bólgs in conversation. "I didn't," she said as though winded. "I didn't, Lucian."

Lucian looked away into the deepening night and was silent. Neither had moved from the positions in which they stood since the time Jadyn shoved him away. "You probably think I'm crazy," he said at length, somehow embarrassed to even look her in the eye.

Just then she swept up to him with much of her graceful gait. "No," she said reassuringly. "I don't think you're crazy, Lucian. I think you're special, that's all. I could kind of tell since the day I saw you arriving at Ehrehalle with the others. And being with you today confirmed it. You'll have to forgive me, I'm not very good at putting things into words so that they make much sense."

Lucian arched an eyebrow. "What do you mean 'being with me today'?"

Jadyn grimaced as if she had accidentally offended him. "Nothing bad, of course," she clarified. "It's just . . . I don't really know how to put it. The lilacs—"

"Too fast?" asked Lucian nervously. *Stupid. I knew it, too. There isn't a slow enough gear for these girls sometimes.*

"No! Not at all. I loved them. And they're my favorite, too." She added this last part as though an afterthought, and batted her eyelashes almost involuntarily. Lucian's heart rate went soaring. "It's just, well, I saw them in my dad's forge," she continued. "Dead. I thought it was unfortunate. They really looked like they had been pretty. And I knew you had brought them for me. It made me sad to see the way you left—dejected and disappointed. So I followed you, and asked for the flowers even though I knew the condition they were in. But then you pulled out a batch as fresh as I've seen in any garden, even Annabelle's. It would be a lie to say I wasn't scared at first, or that I didn't think it strange. I knew it couldn't have been a new bouquet because I saw you walking the entire way. And unless you moonlight as a magician, well . . . "

Lucian's shoulders shook somewhat as he laughed silently. "You're telling me you think *I* did that?" he said skeptically. "Replenished the flowers? I didn't do anything but stick them under my arm. All this time I thought it was something *you* did."

Jadyn's eyes hardened, and in them a faint sadness was housed. "I wish I had the power to heal ailing things," she said in a soft tone crowned by bitterness. "I've proven only to be able to destroy them."

"You weren't responsible for that, Jay, and you know it. You couldn't control what happened to your mother."

Jadyn's eyes were now completely frozen over. "Then we're not so different, are we?" Her tone was sharp as shards of glass. "Your gift and my curse. I couldn't control what happened to her just like you couldn't control what happened to the flowers, or to Nod. I killed my mother. The responsibility is mine. And the sooner you admit it, the sooner you can take responsibility for your gift. And the sooner you take responsibility, the sooner you'll realize what you are." With that she brushed past him, clutching herself within her cloak and walking wearily away.

Again! Girls! Don't say it. Don't you dare. Don't say anything. Nothing good will come of you opening your mouth.

"And how would *you* know what I am?" he suddenly heard himself retort. *You had to say something, didn't you? Why do you always have to say something?* "You don't know me enough to tell me who I am."

Jadyn's mouth opened sporadically before closing for good. There was a brief moment when her lips twitched and her brow furrowed, but whatever anguish or sorrow she may have been feeling noticeably subsided. Her stare again became stern and grave, her eyes like hardened nodules of ice embedded in her skull.

"You're right," she said sharply. "I guess I don't. I don't even know you at all."

Lucian immediately regretted speaking so rashly, and groped sheepishly at the air as if to retrieve the very words he had spoken. "Jay—"

"It's Jadyn," she nipped. "Whatever little nicknames you have for me you can cast aside."

"I'm *sorry* . . . " he muttered feebly. Somehow he did not suspect the night would end with him making an apology for a situation he wasn't sure required one.

Jadyn threw up a hand. "No, *I'm* sorry," she said sternly. "I'm sorry that I stood here and listened to your mother-issues and identity-crisis. Sorry that I saw more in you than you see in yourself. It must have sounded silly to you, me blathering on like a little girl about how great I thought you were. At least you have something to go back and tell your knight-friends. I'm sure they're yearning for a good story. They don't seem to get out much."

Don't get angry. Don't get angry. Even though she's starting to sound like Mary, keep calm . . . "It's not like that, Jay—den," he said as calmly as he could. The look she shot him caused him to correct himself immediately. "I'm just confused, I guess. I didn't mean to offend you. I *never* meant to. I'm sorry if I did."

A silent moment passed before Jadyn responded, though to Lucian it felt like an eternity. "I think you need to realize who your friends are," she said finally, her voice wavering once again. He could tell that she was hurt, and what frustrated him was that he did not know how to heal her. *No, but you can rejuvenate flower bouquets and creatures nine feet tall, apparently.* "And stop pushing away the ones who are only trying to care about you."

With that she turned in a twirl of gray folds and stamped off down the sloping road. There were countless things he longed to say, a slew of pleas to call her back, but despite the maelstrom in his mind and heart he remained silent, his hand absently hanging in the air as if imploring a fleeting dream to stay with him.

Resolute and prepared for another bout, if it came to it, Lucian started after her, when suddenly a familiar voice froze his bones and stood him upright.

"Let her go," Orion said.

He had been standing on a slight ledge nearly fifteen feet above that portion of the mountain road when he called to Lucian. Hooded with his dark cloak wrapped about him, he would have seemed a piece of the mountain itself had it not been for the gleam of his eyes reflecting the moonlight. In his left hand he gripped his long bow, to which an arrow was notched idly. Leaping down to the road, he landed nimbly, with the ease of one who hops from the last stair to the floor.

Throwing back his hood, his auburn hair was revealed, pale like the tendrils of a fading dawn, and his blue eyes burned with flames of condemnation.

Though he opened his mouth to speak, Lucian jumped at the chance for the first word. "What are *you* doing out here?" he asked coldly. "Were you spying on me?"

"Hardly," answered Orion grimly. "I have found no sleep since the Netherlings so freely crossed our border. I am scouting this road for activity. Yet I must ask you the same question. What are you doing out here, at such unearthly an hour?" Then he peered down the road to where the figure of Jadyn had been. "Though I think my answer is now en route to her own dwelling—"

"That's none of your—"

"Where she belongs." His eyes became graver still, and his words concealed a hardness that could have dented Leo's shield. "And you will do well to watch your tone, Mr. Rolfe. Your actions of late, while no doubt carelessly courageous, have been ill advised."

"You can't keep me locked up in that room," Lucian retorted angrily. "I'm not your property—"

"You are my responsibility." Orion's voice now flashed with an anger Lucian never knew he could express. "Three thousand years I have waited to find you, if only to keep you safe. I will not fail. I refuse to fail. If I have to chain you to your bedpost in order to keep you from harm, I will. Do not make it come to that, Lucian."

Anger now joined the sadness and disappointment left to him by Jadyn's departure. Now the very man he hoped to avoid was coming down on him, scolding him like some helpless child. He wanted to scream, rant, rage, anything to release the threads of emotion converging in his soul. Biting his lip and fighting to maintain some form of poise, he skulked backward. A fury dangerously similar to what he felt when Leo ordered him to stay behind while the others confronted the Netherlings manifested within him, but he harnessed and subdued it as best he could. Turning away from Orion now he too followed Jadyn's trail down the final stretch of the road.

When he reached the stair of Ehrehalle a pale light was festering on the northeastward horizon. Dawn was once again upon the world. Looking far below into Dwén Marnié, he saw small wisps of smoke beginning to rise from scattered chimneys. The village was waking. Jadyn, too, was down there, as angry if not angrier about the way their night transpired. *Chain me to a bedpost,* Lucian thought. *I'd like to see him try.*

25

The Luminos

Ehrehalle was already beginning to stir when Lucian climbed the high stair. The crisp air of morning hung coldly in the lofts, and the smell of newly kindled wood was diffusing its way throughout the hall. Several members of Eap's ragged order were present, along with a handful of knights all dressed down in silken tunics and light cloth breeches, stretching off their lingering weariness. All were huddled around a nearby post to the left of the doorway. There was grumbling and muttering, though Lucian could not determine with any certainty what it was they were grumbling and muttering about.

"Room *three?*" he heard one of the knights say when he managed to shuffle to the front of the bunch. "That's all the way up the mountain."

"You won't be making that trek alone, it seems," said another. "Eleven of us are going up there—thirteen if you count Streph and Orion."

There was much talk like this regarding whatever it was they were looking at. When the crowd dispersed to the breakfast tables Lucian saw that it was indeed a notice written in Orion's spidery hand. It seemed to be a regimen of some kind—a list of rooms and who was to report to each one, with a postscript signed by Orion himself:

Here follows the Schedule of Training, to begin this day after the breaking of fasts:

Room I - Aries, Leonysus Instructors:

To Attend:
Messengers: Eap, Conn, Néjer, Yewn
Knights: Reever, Marcus, Herald, Antlus, Damien, Rhaenór
Total: X

Room II - Camien, Bravos Instructors:

To Attend:
Messengers: Bons, Falm, Forcol, Tán
Knights: Evandrus, Frékis, Conri, Gavin, Keatson, Fabian
Total: X

Room III - Orion, Streph Instructors:

To Attend:
Messengers: Radcól, Áine, Balma, Spog
Knights: Antonus, Gerard, Lane, Byron, Cameron, Declan, Griff
Total: XI

As a reminder to all participating:

Training will begin this night following dinner festivities, and held henceforth before the breaking of fasts and after dinner until further notice. Be sure to consult the captains assigned to your station prior to commencing your service to Ehrehalle's cause. Oaths will be sworn during your inaugural session. As was Dredowan custom, once your oath is sworn it cannot be revoked. Until then, no bond is lain upon you to endure the coming storm.

Orion

"Training?" Lucian said to himself. He passed a sidelong glance at the knights and messengers sitting together across the long tables, being brought plates of eggs and meats. "Oaths? *The coming storm?*"

Just then more men began filing in through the doorway, and he was delighted to see that Aries and Leo were among them.

"Early to rise this morning, I see," said Aries jovially when he saw Lucian standing by the post.

Never to bed is more like it, Lucian thought curtly to himself. "What's all this?" he said, alluding to Orion's notice with a straying finger.

"Ah," said Aries. "I see he's posted the training schedule."

"He's posted it alright," said Lucian, perhaps with more fire than he meant to employ. "Any reason why I'm not on it?"

A startled look crossed Aries's face, and he moved a loose tendril of golden hair out of his eyes. "It's nothing personal, I'm sure," he said defensively. "It's for the knights, mostly. A little touchup for timing purposes and things of that nature."

"The messengers are even on here," retorted Lucian, looking abashedly at Orion's dozen shape-shifting fliers, most of whom had probably never held a sword in their lives.

Aries was spared further interrogation when Orion strode in and came to stand between them. "My good Aries," he said. "Any movement on the eastward slopes?"

"Nothing," Aries answered. "No sign of Netherling or any other creatures for that matter. Leo's search did not yield a find either."

"That is good to hear indeed. My road was empty as well—mostly, at least." He dropped an unnoticeable sidelong glance at Lucian. "But that is of no concern now. Are you prepared for your first session? It is a matter of import that these knights are fine-tuned and ready. As close to their former skill as possible. I have no doubt the adjustment will be made seamlessly. The messengers, however, will require most of your attention. There will only be four in your group. Perhaps some of the others will help share the load of teaching them rudimentary tactics as well."

"My worries are few," said Aries, nodding thoughtfully.

Orion gave a look to the hammer upon which Aries's hands were folded. "As they should be," he said, and walked away.

Lucian scowled at his back as he went to dress his plate with eggs and potatoes. "He barely looked at me," he said, forgetting Aries was beside him.

"Like I said before," Aries began, "he's just—"

"Trying to protect me, I know," Lucian answered with frustrated exasperation. "But he means well." *I'm tired of everyone trying to protect me. Don't they think I can protect myself?*

Bowing his head, he leaned against the post as though weary. In many ways he was. The journey up and down Shír Azgoth was beginning to take its toll on his limbs, and his sleepless night only made it worse. To compound matters, the thought of Jadyn and how terribly they had left things kept recurring in his mind. He wondered what she was thinking this very moment, if in fact she was thinking of him at all. *She probably doesn't want to see me again,* he thought sadly. Bitterness was present also. Bitterness toward Orion and his knights; bitterness toward the messengers; bitterness toward everyone participating in the training sessions while he was elsewhere.

"Are you going to have breakfast?" Aries asked at length.

Shaking himself out of his whirling daydream, Lucian stood upright. "No," he said. "I'm not hungry." It was mostly true. There were too many troubling thoughts going through his mind for him to eat anything just yet. "I think I'm just going to go up to my room. Probably grab a hot bath while I'm up there."

That sounded good to him. A hot bath would certainly ease the aches in his legs, and might even prove a slight remedy for his afflictions. He wondered if it would also answer some of his questions.

The boundless room of pools seemed to stretch deeper

into shadow than Lucian remembered. In his robe he stood peering fiercely at the Luminos in which he previously bathed, his eyes orbs of green flame intent and eager to perceive. The marble fountain sprouting from the bath was formless again, fashioned only in the generic shape of a tall, blue-veined vase from which thin streams of water delved into the basin. He knew it would change had he stepped in, reclaiming the likeness of the monumental warrior he once saw it boast.

But it was not in his interest to bathe just yet. Hesitantly he stood back, recounting everything Aries had told him about this device. *It can see into the future, and show you things that will come to fruition should the viewer choose one course of action over another,* he had said. *It can look into the past and show you what might have been had you chosen a different road. The most apt minds can even view loved ones from afar in the state they are currently in.*

Suddenly Lucian became all the more hesitant, unsure if he truly desired to see into the future at all. *What if it shows me something terrible?* he wondered, a great fear suddenly welling up within him. *What if every road leads to destruction?* He took a step back, staring warily at the bubbling basin as though it were a sleeping predator. *You have to look,* he told himself. *It might show you which course of action to take. It could save you.*

So it was he took two reluctant steps forward before stopping, for suddenly a new fright weighed upon him. *Do you really want to look into the past, either?* he asked himself. *Do you really want it to tease you with what might have been if you had forgotten Jem's birthday altogether and never went to the creek at all? Will it be worth it to see yourself loafing around the inn, or celebrating your eighteenth birthday at the pub while everyone is singing? Could you handle the sight of Amar still standing?*

The answer to all his inward questions was a resounding "No." He was not sure if he could handle seeing into the future, to risk glimpsing his own death or those of his companions. His heart would not be able to bear seeing Mary or Jem lying dead, or Medric in ruins, or Jadyn crying and hating him, or the world's end. What if one road led to the prevention of one evil over another? What if the world could be spared for the price of Mary's life? Jem's life? It was too horrible a thought to bear.

A glimpse into the past was nearly as daunting. Though he tried as best he could to refrain from thoughts of the east, he was so homesick that at times it manifested into a physical sickness. His stomach would wrench and his throat would tense and he would want to vomit or cry. What if the Luminos showed him that Amar could have been saved, alive with its cheerful townsfolk, had it not been for the evil he fished out of the creek? What if he saw himself among them, laughing and living the life an eighteen year-old boy should be living?

Yet there he stood waiting, having somehow fought off every urge to turn back. It was not long before he knew why. *The most apt minds can even view loved ones from afar in the state they are currently in.* Before he realized he had made them, he took three steps forward. The pale blue vapors rising in spidery tendrils over the water now warmed his face. He let the moisture from their touch bead up upon his cheeks and forehead before gathering his nerve, clutching the basin's thick rim, and peering in.

A young man, tall and wrought like a slender slate of stone, stood peering off a lofting balcony high upon his mountain hall. His mane of white-gold locks, draping thickly down to his broad shoulders, wafted gently in the breeze, along with his flowing robe of white in which he was clad. He had a beard to match, well-groomed and tidy, with arched eyebrows beneath which his eagle-like gaze glimmered fierce and blue. A thick belt of gold was bound about his thin waist, and the sword that must have hung there was now leaning beside him—a golden, gem-studded blade that looked all too familiar to Lucian. Only, in his vision, the three gems wrought along the curve of this sword's pommel were alight.

Clenching his hands upon the outer wall, the man looked out contemplatively. Beneath him was a white-and-blue sea of clouds. Here and there the traffic of crimson eagles passed below. Under the gaps of the clouds Lucian saw a vast city of silver and gold sparkling, its towers alight with the reflection of morning, its bridges busy with the passage of fair folk, and even a smell as sweet as pine rising up on the gentle wind.

It was indeed a breathtaking sight, quite literally. Lucian somehow felt as though he stood on the very top of the world. His blood seemed to run thinner, and the chill of the excessively high climes began to affect him directly. The bearded man's eyes kept coming into view, vexed and racked with thought. He wondered why, until he heard the cooing voice of another lurking behind him.

"Yours is a fair city, dear brother," he said. "Ours is a realm most sacred. This world could be ours in which to prosper. Together we can sew the seeds of our glory across its vast expanse. We will have children, and they too will have gifts, and in our multitudes we can make this world a thing of unimaginable beauty."

But the other did not seem satisfied by the speaker's suggestions, and stood staring blankly as if he had not heard him at all. "My good Sceleris," he said at length. *Sceleris,* Lucian thought as his heart gave a jolt. He knew of someone who once went by that name. "You speak of gifts when yours has yet made itself known to you. In due time, I have no doubt that it will. And for all we know it may prove the greatest of all. But the seed of my own has blossomed, for the dawn of my eighteenth year has come. My heart is resolute." Then he turned and glared hard upon his brother with eyes like cold steel. "If it is in my power to create, I will. It is my responsibility to do so. I will not hoard my gift within my tower, creating flora for sport, any longer."

Now Sceleris came into view, white-robed and not much smaller in stature than his brother. Younger in appearance than the other, but by no means slight, Lucian determined he was perhaps a year or two his junior. His black hair fell in soft strands down to his shoulders. His face was fair, soft, and angular, from which he stared with weatherworn eyes that seemed perplexed and worried. It was the first time Lucian had ever seen Sorcerian in his true form, the form in which he came into being in the high reaches of Mount Zynys above the clouds.

"Ation, they will destroy all that we hold dear," said Sceleris at length, sadness and despair meshed within his soft and rasping voice. "They will grow fond of war. There will be long feuds for supremacy. Some will relish in the servility of others. In time, it will shame you to claim responsibility for the evil you have created—"

"You cannot know of what you speak," shouted Ation hotly, turning to his brother and towering over him, an angry golden-maned lion reprimanding his overstepping cub. Then he recoiled, perhaps seeing the way his brother cowered.

Once out of his shadow, Sceleris gathered himself. "I daresay I have seen it," he said meekly.

"Then the gift of foresight is yours, you tell me?"

"Hardly. There are devices in this Mountain of Magic that even you are yet to find. But I have found them, and I have dabbled, and I have seen."

"And you have seen all you have told me?"

"And more."

Ation stood for a moment in contemplative silence. For a second it seemed to Lucian that he might be reconsidering his original plans, but then he turned to Sceleris with a stern gaze. "I am the *Great Sage*," he said at last. "If I say it will be, it will be. That is my power, and I will employ it. And if your foresight holds any validity, then I will see to reprimanding them myself should it come to it. Your devices cannot allude to every end."

"Can they not?" But Ation had already swept past his brother to leave, picking up his sword as he went. "Where are you going?" asked Sceleris nervously.

"To my forge," Ation answered.

Suddenly the scene changed. Lucian was unsure of the setting upon which he now looked. The world was dark and quaking. Great fires rose up from all sides. The sky above was grim and festering with gathering storms, and arms of lightning lashed out and slew mountain stones from their foundations. Two figures stood amidst the fury, one clad in dazzling white and gold that seemed to blaze within the gloom, the other kneeling in tethered, ashen rags.

"Sceleris!" called Ation over the maelstrom. "What have you done?"

Sceleris did not answer. Instead he stayed upon his knees with his head wrapped in his hands, his shoulders bobbing as he wept.

"Brother!" he cried at last. "The dawn of my eighteenth year has come. What is happening to me?" His voice bore the desperate tones of pleading.

"Is it you who seeks to rent the very world asunder?" Ation cried.

"I seek only the end of this torture!"

At once a new scene flashed. Ation and Sceleris stood across from each other in a great white forum. Square gardens bloomed in marble pens. Along the perimeter of the room were scattered fountains. Behind each brother was a mass gathering, an assembly of men and women all fair and ageless in glamorous raiment. The gleam of weapons glittered. They were older now, though how much older Lucian did not know. Ation's mane had become snowy white, and his beard, still well kempt, was graying. The same blue fire burned within his eyes, but there was despair in them also, blending with fear or sadness or both.

"I told you once that your creations would wreak havoc upon the world, Brother," said Sceleris curtly. "Yet for all your enhanced senses you failed to listen." He too had become great in stature. His black hair, once thin, had thickened greatly, with streaks of gray lining his temples. A black, gray-blotched beard sprouted now over the subtly-drawn contours of his face.

"Sceleris," Ation began. "Stand down. This is foolish. Surely your frustrations can be dealt with civilly—"

"I tried to warn you," Sceleris retorted angrily, approaching Ation and his gathering slowly but steadily.

315

"But my brother, the Great Sage, would not be subjected to adhering to the words of his adolescent brother. My brother, whose gift was newly upon him, would not admit the wisdom in the words of one younger. Arrogance blinded you as much then as it does now. We could have multiplied across this earth and made it a vast world of Sages far beyond imagining—"

"I will not suffer you to spread your seed any further," retorted Ation. Sceleris was now inches away, his golden mace jingling as it hung from his hand. "Yours is a tainted gift, yielding only the power to destroy."

Sceleris guffawed, and those at his back laughed with him. "Perhaps my gift *is* to destroy," he said contemplatively. "Though you might call it a curse. But our gifts are not so different, are they? For what have you created if not destruction, dear brother? Look into your all-seeing basin and tell me what you have forged. A segregated community of lesser beings who fancy themselves supreme above all others; a yellowing land that once was green, tarnished by useless deluges of blood. Take pride, Great Sage, but do not avoid the looking glass, for in it you will see my face."

"I will not," said Ation coolly, "for it will indeed be the only means of seeing you. I hereby banish you and your gathering from Zynys forevermore."

White-hot fury blazed in Sceleris's eyes. Screaming wildly, he raised his mace to strike when Ation sent his great staff skyward. The forum suddenly throbbed with pulsating lights of white and gold, and when the confusion cleared all that remained was Ation and those at his back, and a great, rigid hole by the door where Sceleris and his followers had been cast out into the far and unknown reaches of their nightly realm.

* * *

Lucian was unsure where the next scene brought him. The room was unnaturally white, and he immediately felt as though he had wandered into a dream. He heard the sound of a child crying, and soon saw four shapes huddled together. When the setting came into view he looked inside a large room with golden furnishings and many decorative hangings and linens. A woman lay asleep in a bed, sweating and sickly pale. A slew of women were tending her. Some brought cold towels and applied them to her forehead; others were running fresh blankets in to replace those that had been soiled and bloodied. He felt something almost instantly as he looked upon her worn face, though he could not tell what it was.

At the foot of the bed stood four people: two men clad in shining steel plates and blue capes, and two women, one in a velvety robe with a purple shawl, the other dressed plainer, in the same raiment as the maids. The second woman held a mewling child. The three crowded around her looked on anxiously.

"It was your father's wish to get the child off of Zynys as soon as he is born," she said, nestling the baby against her breast.

"You are certain that is the best idea, given the circumstances?" the other woman inquired.

"I cannot say, Nephromera, for the gift of foresight has never been mine," the woman answered. "Yet with alacrity I will say that his future has long been studied, and his gift, as has been seen in the All-Seeing Basins, will be the power to heal anything that lives and breathes under the sun, including himself. He will never know a mortal wound, nor suffer his companions to feel the sting of death. The Sage of Replenishment, some are calling him. The Sage of Healing. The Undying One. In these dark times, perhaps it is neither wise nor fair to hoard a Sage so powerful upon the Mountain when the world below will need him most. Your mother has deemed it time."

The smaller of the two men spoke then. As the group came clearer into focus, Lucian saw that his hair—like the others—was of polished white gold, and in his hand it seemed he held a spear whose head was shaped in the likeness of a golden swordfish. "Were it not for your expertise, Hilda, the plights of pregnant Sagesses would be frightening indeed," he began. "Yet I wonder if we should not hold council before casting ourselves earthbound with a babe in tow. His will be the power of replenishment, you say—to heal all those that have the means to live. Would our father not benefit from his gift as much as those below?"

Then Nephromera spoke. "A Sage's gift does not claim its host until his or her eighteenth year, Nepsus," she said sharply. "You know this. Until then he cannot help Father."

"Precisely," said Hilda, rocking the child in her arms a little more fervently, for it was becoming restless. "Nephromera is right. It would do nothing for your father to keep the child cradled on Zynys for eighteen years. He once said that if the day ever came when his creations needed him most, he would make himself present below to guide them. Since that won't be happening, I daresay his youngest son will be his delegate. It was his wish. It was his promise. It is his responsibility."

"Surely there must be another way, Hilda," retorted Charon at length. "We can't simply leave him alone down there. He'll grow up never knowing who or what he is. It may turn out that his purpose will be lost to him, and all this would have been for nothing."

Hilda, still rocking, tensed her brow contemplatively. "It will be your charge as his siblings to guide him then, when you can."

A troubled expression claimed the fair face of Nephromera. "That will be unwise. The Causeways of Apparition are heavily guarded now by Sceleris's forces. Travelers may be ambushed, and our brother is too precious a cargo to risk."

"And yet risked it must be," answered Hilda firmly. "The child must be earthbound within the hour."

A twirling, yanking sensation came over Lucian next, and when the next scene leveled out, his true body felt the slight pangs of vertigo. Suddenly he was surprised to see that the next vision was not new to him. *I dreamed this once,* he recalled silently. *On the way to Ehrehalle. I dreamed this!* At once he felt as though he was being carried, gazing up from the nook of someone's arms. The world was dark. Stars were strewn above. *Why subject his youngest child to walk among the damned?* he heard a voice whisper.

Having heard his voice a moment ago, he recognized it as Charon's. *Because it will one day be his responsibility to rid them of their plight,* a second voice responded. To Lucian it sounded like the woman—Nephromera, he thought her name was. *You know he will be the only one over whom Parthaleon will have no power.*

With that he felt himself being placed down on a hard surface, and looking up he saw something like a wooden house that seemed vastly foreign yet strangely familiar to him. *The inn?* he thought to himself. *Wait—how?* The three clouded figures loomed over him, staring studiously. *Lucian.* Nephromera's voice came as a faint whisper, yet he heard it plain as day. *Lucian.* His name seemed to echo now, and the more his true body fought to detach itself from the Luminos it would not let him go. *Lucian . . . Lucian . . . Farewell, little brother.*

What came next was a rapid whirlwind of images. Lucian saw himself as a child, running, playing, and laughing. The finding of the Key flashed before his eyes momentarily. Suddenly a montage of his flight from Amar with Gamaréa sifted along like the pages of a book beneath a deft thumb. In milliseconds he was out of the Black Forest and into Elderland. Didrebelle was there, and Mary, Jem, and MaDungal. Then all too suddenly Tantus was at their backs and they were running. The eternity it took them to weather the Mountain of Dreams was reduced to fractions of a moment. Beelcibur's ire was hampered by the swift current in which the visions moved. Ravelon was merely a flash of activity. Gamaréa's capture and his own retreat from the Matarhim were hammered down to infinitesimal shards of a much more devastating scene.

Then a sound like thunder bellowed and shook the world around him, and he stood in the darkness looking up to Ehrehalle, black with night and glossy with rain. In the howling wind the torches danced before the storm snuffed them out entirely. When the lightning flashed he saw before him shapes of men, armored and in an ordered rank with weapons at the ready. Their eyes latched unwaveringly to a sight over Lucian's shoulder. Another lightning strike afforded him a look at what was there. A golden sea of Fairy soldiers stood lined and glaring, their numbers folding over the foothills and nearly down into the valley by the hundreds. *Storm that is to come,* a voice whispered. Suddenly he remembered Orion's postscript from the notice, and realized he alone now stood between Orion's knights and that very storm.

With great cries that lifted even over the thunder, the forces converged, but before Lucian could even react he was in his bedroom high up within the mountain. His balcony doors were cast open to reveal the night of gloom. Wind roared fiercely by, yanking with it thick diagonal walls of rain. They slammed off his balcony and the wall enclosing it, splashing off the stone in hundreds of white explosions. Again he was only able to see by the light the rigid strands of lightning afforded him. The plains of Reznarion beyond were black like a frothy, storm-tossed sea frozen in time. Suddenly a voice whispered: *More men.* Lucian looked around anxiously. He had heard this voice before. *More men,* it repeated. It seemed all around him, its source undetectable. *More men,* it said a third time.

"More men," Lucian repeated, whether in this lucid dream or in reality, he did not know. "I don't understand."

More men, the voice repeated. *The storm has come.*

"Where am I going to find more men?" he heard himself say. "The only men who can help us are here already, and in the valley. Other than them, there aren't any." He was all but pleading now.

The city, the voice answered. As if to clarify, a lightning flash illuminated the stark ruins of Dredoway beyond.

"The *city?*" Lucian asked, but before the words were even out of his mouth a new scene was on him. A high gray wall, weatherworn and dented from years of wear, loomed over him. Before him was an unnatural entranceway—a great gaping hole, rigid from having been blown through. Debris and bones lay scattered everywhere within. The lofting fragments of once mighty towers rose up along roads that had perhaps been busy once. With every flash of lightning he saw shadowy shapes hunched upon them, staring down as he alone braved their domain. Even when the lights went out their gleaming eyes still held him.

I won't go, he heard himself say.

Flash.

He was in front of Ehrehalle again, the storm raging as fierce as ever. Hundreds of white-clad Dridion soldiers stooped over the bodies of the dead, pillaging. To his horror he saw his companions among the corpses. Aries lay dead with his hammer splintered beside him; Orion was strewn upon a stair with a spear through his belly; Leo had been penetrated several times by arrows, still clutching his shield that had suffered several dents. Then Lucian's heart lurched and threatened to shatter in his chest, for there amidst the bodies he saw Jadyn. She lay beside her father. Even in death her eyes fought to hold their blue fire as long as they could, yet when Lucian knelt beside her that fire noticeably faded. Screaming, he took hold of her hand when suddenly he was taken away from the battleground. The touch of Jadyn's hand was still upon his, but he soon saw to his dismay that the thing he was clasping was now the hilt of Excebellus. The raging din of the storm faded as he looked upon the golden sword and gleaming gems, until there was no sound at all.

Then out of the eerie hush that had enveloped the room, he heard a shrill whisper. *The city,* it said.

Suddenly, as if an entity within the basin heaved him away, Lucian was thrown onto his back. On the floor he lay gasping in a slowly developing puddle. Aside from his largely fruitless bid for air, the only sounds in that strange, cavernous room were the slowly draining fountains.

My head must have been completely under, he thought, sitting up and sucking in painful chunks of air. Soon his struggle to breathe subsided, and he sat bewildered upon the damp floor recounting all the images the Luminos had shown him. As if beneath a dim spotlight, the basin glowed amidst the deepening shadows, imploring him to remember. "The Sage of Healing," he muttered to himself. He remembered that much. "*Earth*bound?"

The earliest fragments of his visions were almost

completely lost to memory, fading from his waking mind as dreams are wont to do. Yet the latter visions remained plain for him to recall. If he closed his eyes he could almost picture that gold-furnished nursery to the last detail, as well as the four people huddled around the mewling child. "The Sage of Replenishment," he recounted confusedly. "Earthbound?"

All his thoughts seemed to lead to the dream-like representation of Mary's inn. When seen in the Luminos it had initially appeared as a place as foreign as the far seas, but he knew it was the inn—down to the last smudge on the old golden knob and the smallest chip in the stained-wood siding. He would have sworn on it. It had come to him before, that vision. In the deep night within the narrow mountain passes of the Red Peaks it had shown itself to him. He felt as though he was being carried then as well, with the same three figures gathering over him studiously. Only in his dream their figures had been distorted, blurry white human shapes with indistinguishable features. In the basin they appeared real enough to touch. He could see their faces as plainly as if they stood before him in that lonely room lost within the midst of Azgoth. A beautiful woman, gowned in a robe of velvet, had set him down. Draped over her shoulders was a sparkling blue shawl. Upon her head flowed cold starlight made hair. Behind her stood two men, both fair and radiant. One was taller than the other, his face hard and his hair like a lion's mane woven by stray licks of sun-flame. The other was smaller by no less than a head, his hair the same hue as the other's yet more kempt, his eyes cool like bulbs of ice from a winter sea.

What was most perplexing of all to Lucian, more vexing even than the maelstrom of visions to which he had been subjected, was the sudden realization that these people were not strangers at all. Indescribably he felt as though he knew them, as if he had seen them long ago and subconsciously awaited their return. The basin acted only as the mechanism by which their memory was pulled, and as it claimed supremacy over his other thoughts, Lucian recalled the last words he heard them speak. *Lucian . . .*

Lucian . . . Farewell, little brother . . .

It would have been a feat for him to peel his eyes open any wider. "It can't be," he muttered to himself, his eyes darting left to right as though watching a swift match of table tennis. "*I* can't be . . . " But it was all making sense to him now. The more he whittled down the different meanings of his visions, the narrower the possibilities became.

"Nor should you be," cooed a soft voice from behind him. Giving a start, Lucian spun to see Ursa leaning in the shadows of the doorway. The light from the basin seemed to pulsate, her figure coming into and out of view with it. "This is certainly no place to be wandering," she said. "And the Luminai no devices to be toyed with. They are the bane of men's minds, some say. Trouble awaits the viewer who views too long."

Lucian stood and wrung the dampness out of the lower flaps of his tunic. "Trouble?" he said, trying his best to feign disinterest. "Like what?"

"Like the yielding of said mind to the power of the basins," answered Ursa evenly. She might have been explaining why water was wet. "Men have wasted their lives peering through its clouds of vapor, trying for all their worth to claim the gift of foresight for their own. Gifts that were never meant for them to have."

"It sees into the future?" asked Lucian, with his best attempt at obliviousness.

"So it is said," she answered. "Yet my account is bred on rumor only. As for myself, I have never risked a look into one of these basins."

"Not even when you've taken a bath?" prodded Lucian innocently. "Do you close your eyes, then?"

"If I desired a bath, Mr. Rolfe, I would take one in the privacy of my own chambers." Her voice had grown sharp, suggesting to Lucian that even alluding to her nakedness had offended her somewhat.

He paid no mind to that, however, for a new vexation was on him. "Your own chamber?" he asked, not bothering to mask the incredulity in his voice. "I was under the impression that this was the only bath chamber."

"You were under the *wrong* impression, I'm afraid. I do not doubt you mean to say this is the only bath chamber you *knew* about. Did you not once find it strange that in a room so boundless you were always alone? There are other chambers in which to bathe, Lucian—"

"Orion wanted me to come here," he reasoned sternly, turning and speaking into the darkness as if reprimanding himself. "He wanted me to see."

"Only too true," said Ursa, sweeping two modest paces into the room. "Very deft in his ways is the highlord. Though I must say it was not always so—"

"But why?" Aggravation resonated in Lucian's voice like moss on stone. "Why is it so important to *him?* It's my future, anyway. Not his."

"When you know someone for as long as I have, Lucian, the boundaries of simply *knowing* them are entirely severed. In many ways part of me has become Orion, and part of him has become me, though we fight with our own minds to deny it. He was set on a mission much like you in ages past. To find you. To bring you here. To keep you safe. It was a duty given him, he says, by the Great Sage himself. Thus he has claimed a sense of entitlement, to know at least that he has not been led astray. That you are the one he was meant to find—"

"Well nothing I saw answers that question; that's for sure. And like I said: whatever it *did* show me is part of *my* future—*if* the visions were even real. They wouldn't affect him in the—" But then his mouth clamped shut as images of the massacre of Ehrehalle replayed through his mind.

At once he turned to leave, his eyes brimming with a sudden fear. "I have to go," he muttered as he breezed past Ursa.

"Not to the city, I hope," she said as he was three paces out the door. Despite the soft indifference in her voice, her every syllable seemed sharpened. Lucian made as if to turn, but thought better of it. Bounding down the corridor, he was soon out of sight.

Ursa shook her head, cast her eyes to the floor, and followed slowly in his wake.

26

Negotiations and Bribes

Gamaréa's night was sleepless. He lay on his back in the corner of his cell bathed in the little light of the pale moon that seeped in. Many things passed through his mind. Daxau's words were a mainstay—four words hastily spoken yet everlasting in memory. *For a thousand years. For a thousand years. Tongues will host your name for a thousand years.* Only now was the realization beginning to settle in. He seemed to be able to recall all the tales he had read of old heroes—men long dead, immortalized by the written word. It was a desire, he thought, that was too bold; but it was a desire nonetheless. Why should his feats not be storied throughout legend? Why should his tale not live on for a thousand years?

The memory of the arena's sounds soothed him—an imagined ambience of thunderous cheers and ringing swords as though the wind itself was reliving the moment outside his cell. Not a week earlier he reached the peak of the heavens on the back of the Lord of Parthaleon, only to smite him there and return to earth on his mangled corpse. Such a rush of adrenaline and fear would never again be replicated. Some part of him now desired the arena like a lost lover, and his muscles yearned for the thrill of battle.

But he remembered the words of Didrebelle also. It was not often that the Fairy spoke in riddles, and only then in times of need and secrecy. *Perilous roads open to safe passages, but you've yet to travel all.* Perhaps the main reason that these words plagued him was because he found it difficult to imagine a road more perilous than the one he had just weathered.

The dawn draws near, but now the night is blackest. Surely this could have meant a handful of things. Was the dawn the promise of a brighter day? Was Didrebelle's plan to escape taking form? A surge of doubt, fear, and the cold, incomplete sensation of unknowingness took hold of him. *How* was the night blackest now? *What* perilous road was he yet to travel? It was beyond unnerving to think there was something more perilous than a confrontation with Ignis.

Didrebelle knew something. The approaching guards that day had thwarted his opportunity to tell Gamaréa exactly *what* he knew, and the possibilities vexed him until dawn.

The next morning, Gamaréa was shepherded into the fields routinely with the rest of the captives, but was approached by a small party of guards before he was ten paces from the door. The Fairy leading the assembly mentioned briefly that Melinta requested his presence in Deavorás. Loading him swiftly into their carriage—not bothering with a blindfold—they led him there with haste.

By now the sun had almost fully risen. Melinta's white courtyard was empty and glinting with dew. Near the great doors of the king's hall he saw Didrebelle standing casually with a host of Melinta's servants, though he purposely paid Gamaréa little attention. Gamaréa's party brushed by them and into the hall, and there was Melinta, sitting at his long, marble table with three other guests whom Gamaréa did not recognize.

The doors closed shortly after his company entered. Their numbers had strengthened in the little time it took to file into Melinta's hall. Didrebelle came into view alongside them, wearing a stone-like expression. The king was sitting at the head of his long marble table, accompanied by three other well-dressed Fairies whom Gamaréa did not recognize. Clad entirely in robes of gold-embroidered emerald, they sat with stern, studious looks on their long and ageless faces, such as Gamaréa felt the familiar sensation of being thoroughly scrutinized.

Melinta, who had been in the middle of a conversation, ceased speaking immediately when the group strolled in, devoting the entirety of his attention to Gamaréa. To his surprise—or was it dismay?—Melinta wore the brightest of smiles. Standing to greet him as though he were his own son, he exclaimed, "There he is! The champion in the flesh!" Laying two firm hands upon Gamaréa's broad shoulders, Melinta locked eyes with him genially, as though Gamaréa had done him a great service by slaughtering five of his rare champions.

"The rest of you may go," Melinta urged, not unkindly. The guards flanking Gamaréa bowed and dispersed, their mail jingling as they strode away. Somehow the air seemed lighter now that he was out of their shadow.

"Not you, Diddy," said Melinta quickly to Didrebelle's back. Gamaréa was relieved when Didrebelle came to stand beside him, and shot him a quick, undetectable glance that asked *Diddy? Really?* To which Didrebelle's eyes responded, *Don't ask.*

Melinta swept away from them and strode back to his table, clasping his hands so that their clap reverberated off the walls of the cavernous room. "Please eat, Morok!" he insisted when he resumed his seat. There was a large bowl of shining red apples that he nudged in Gamaréa's direction.

Didrebelle and Gamaréa took up an empty seat beside each other. It was Didrebelle who reached in for an apple first, hoping to catch even the slightest look of urgency in his father's expression to betray his attempt at poisoning. But the king remained collected and unbothered, and the only look he gave his son was one that urged him to help himself.

So it was Gamaréa took up an apple and crunched just deep enough so that he missed the core. The fresh, sweet juice was indeed pleasant and cold. "You have summoned me?" Gamaréa said through a mouthful.

One of Melinta's guests turned his attention to the

king with surprise in his voice. "The slave speaks when unbidden?"

Melinta put his hand up in gentle reproach. "Fret not, Hálda," he assured softly. "Our champion knows little of the ways of Dridion, his stay in Cauldarím having been so brief." Then he turned his devilish, smiling face to Gamaréa again. "Indeed I have summoned you, Morok."

The king heeded Gamaréa's expectant look. "It seems your name is popular among the tongues of Deavorás citizens now. *And,* they say word has traveled east for nearly thirty leagues. Such hysteria does not surprise me, however. Your victories were more than impressive. You are no longer regarded for who you are, but for the capabilities of your blade and strength."

Such fickle hearts. "Is that all?" He bit into his apple once more.

Another of Melinta's guests stirred in his large seat, his dark, beady eyes peering ceaselessly upon Gamaréa with loathing. "You are too lenient with your slaves, my lord," he said. The tone of his voice had started off confident, but trailed into a whisper when Gamaréa's eyes bore into him.

But again Melinta turned the statement away. "You are a Morok of business," said the king to Gamaréa. "And business propositions are always welcome in my hall." He laughed darkly. "I will get to it, then. It is no secret now that folk will travel long distances to watch you fight again—and pay well. Are you aware that the feats you have accomplished have never before been achieved? Thus it is my rare privilege to offer you the opportunity to reap some spoils worthy of the champion you have become."

Gamaréa became perplexed, and, though he could not see Didrebelle's expression, he noted the new stiffness of his companion's posture.

"Spoils, you say," said Gamaréa, not bothering to subdue the curiosity in his voice. "And what spoils may a slave reap?"

"Please, please," said Melinta grimacing and waving his hands about, "let us not use that word here. You are a captive, yes, but not a slave. Had you been a slave, you would be in the fields of Cauldarím as we speak, and I would be having lunch."

The look in Gamaréa's eyes suggested to Melinta that he had his full attention. "As you know," he continued, "I am in the grueling process of organizing a war. War means funding, and funding means coin. Dridion, rich as she is, hasn't nearly enough sustained to fund this war. Feeding my army alone will empty the vaults. Morgues are valuable in a tight spot, but they eat three times the amount of my men, and I have secured thousands of them—but listen to me, I am rambling. Anyway, the very fact of the matter is with the times as pressing as they have become, it is now evident that I need a separate means of income. That is where you come in."

As if in response, Gamaréa stroked his beard and looked upon Melinta quizzically. The king went on. "The arena outside of Cauldarím holds fifteen thousand spectators. Dridion's nobility comprises the vast majority of that sum. As you may or may not already know, theirs is quite the insatiable appetite for sport and bloodshed. Just look how many turned up to witness your ex—excuse me . . . your trials. With your name on every tongue, all that needs to be done is promoting. Errand runners will be sent to every corner of the realm with advertisements, and your name will fill the arena once again."

Gamaréa was indeed listening intently, but by no means was he prepared to aid Melinta economically. Now it was only a question of choice. Whether Melinta considered him a prisoner, captive, slave, or belly dancer did not really matter. He was still subject to his wishes. Whatever the king had in mind for him would come to fruition regardless of his own desires. There was no version of this meeting where Gamaréa would have his way.

"You want me to fight again?" said Gamaréa, his voice so expressionless it was difficult even for Didrebelle to know how he was feeling about Melinta's words.

"Of course!" said Melinta, as though surprised Gamaréa even posed the question. "Such talent should not wither away inside a cell. Look at you! You are a flesh-covered weapon, a paragon of warriors, and you know it too. You cannot sit here and claim that part of you does not lust for the arena. The spectacle, the fervor, the roars of the crowd—you cannot convince me that it all fails to resonate within your loins and cause your roiling blood to keep you from sleep."

As much as he hated himself for admitting it, it was impossible for Melinta's claims to hold another ounce of truth.

"So what do you say?" said Melinta, after a long and heavy silence. "Make Dridion rich, and in exchange earn yourself some coin as well."

A throaty laugh seeped out of Gamaréa. "And what would I do with coin? What worth would it have to me locked away in Cauldarím?"

Melinta smiled impishly. "There is nothing in this world that cannot be bought," he said quietly. "Even a price for your freedom can be negotiated. And thus we come to it: my proposition. Use your growing popularity to your advantage. Put hinds in the seats and coins in my purse. Make Dridion rich beyond comparison, and you have my word that when you have enough coin to buy your freedom, you may leave this place, and consider your safe passage across the breadth of this country granted."

It was a tempting offer, though his blood boiled strangely at the fact that he was even considering it. Whether it was hatred toward himself or the white-robed snake before him, he did not know. It might have been a mixture of both. But a freedom that was granted meant many things. Firstly, it meant the end of sneaking around and plotting. If Gamaréa was guaranteed safe passage out of Cauldarím and across the breadth of Dridion, it would certainly make it easier to find sleep. Being on the run for so long came with its price. Weariness was one thing; the psychological wear and tear was another. Without a battalion of Dridion guards on his trail, his search for Lucian could resume without hindrance.

Rid these thoughts from your mind, you fool, he scolded himself. *You cannot trust the words of a serpent. He would never openly release you from his nest, knowing you alone have thwarted him for so long. You've yet to even ask the cost of your freedom . . .*

He shifted in his chair. "And how much coin must I earn to gain my freedom?" asked Gamaréa boldly and at long length. "What cost am I to you?"

Melinta tapped his long and bony fingers on the table in front of him, a studious look upon his face as he gazed unblinkingly upon the grisly face of the Morok in his dirty rags. "As I see it," answered Melinta cordially, "you have denied me a great service by rejecting my original offer to fight for me. Thus, I will hold your debt repaid when enough coin is raised to at least feed and arm my army. When you have earned me that amount, I will consider your freedom granted. Until then, you must fight whenever I call."

Hatred welled up in the pit of Gamaréa's stomach as his eyes, seeming as though of fire, glared hard upon the king. "So be it then. When will I fight?"

The king laughed and looked to his guests. "You see, my friends! A true champion. Not a week removed from defeating such grueling competition and he already seeks his return to the sands." The Fairies at Melinta's table chuckled lightly, if only to humor him.

For the first time, Melinta took a swig of his wine that had been sitting idly beside him. When he lowered it to the table he said, "Three days from now. Noon. That will be a fitting time, I trust. Enough time to ready the errand runners and send them to every corner of the country with news of the event. Most will leave upon first notice, I am sure."

"As you wish," said Gamaréa impassively. "Summon me and I will be ready."

Melinta smiled. "Good," he replied softly. Then his eyes brightened, and only then did Gamaréa realize that some form of darkness had briefly taken hold of them. "So be it."

Melinta rose from his table then, and the others were soon to follow. He signaled two guards to escort Gamaréa out, and when they left the room Melinta sat again and addressed the others.

The first who had spoken, Hálda, said, "I stand by my earlier claim, Your Grace. You show much lenience with these slaves. Even Aromé says so."

"And if I may say so, Your Grace," said the third guest, "your negotiation was much too bold. Never before has a king negotiated with a slave, let alone summon one to his own table."

"And he never will again, Darondill, son of Drastin. Fret not, my counselors—for all my madness there are methods that may yet be apparent to you."

Didrebelle fought not to openly guffaw.

"So you mean not to grant his freedom?" asked Darondill. Of the three he was youngest. If not for the youth in his eyes, he would have resembled Hálda and Aromé more closely.

"I trust that you have never been called to a meeting like this before," said Melinta, not unkindly. "There is much you will learn, my good Darondill of Delingmoor. Your father was dear to me, and a much-welcomed guest at my table. Now his son takes up his seat in an hour of most need."

Melinta's hand touched Darondill's shoulder gently, then he turned his attention to the entire gathering. "I have called upon the three of you, as you know, for your council . . . "

But Didrebelle was the first to speak. "Forgive me for imposing, Father," he said, beginning to rise from his seat.

"No, no, my son," said Melinta. "You may stay. I will have words with you after." Didrebelle sat, mourning his failed chance to leave.

Melinta focused on the three councilmen once again. Hálda, Aromé, and Darondill looked to Melinta, perplexity present in each set of expectant eyes. "Do you know the losses this Morok has cost me?" Only now did Melinta's voice assume its true impish quality. "Do you know the damage his sword has caused? He should not have even survived the Minotaur, which cost a hefty price in its lonesome. But he bested the most terrible creatures this age has ever seen! I refuse to compute the sum of the coin that was wasted on obtaining them, let alone the men that perished on the expeditions. If anything, the Morok will see his debt restored before the end."

There was a wildness in the king's eyes as he spoke this last part. When he had begun speaking to his councilors, his voice filled the spacious room with verve. Yet as he progressed his tone grew softer, but somehow more menacing, and when he finished it was as if he was speaking only to himself from behind gritted teeth.

Darondill broke the silence, and inwardly shuddered as Melinta's gaze fell on him. "If I may be so bold, Your Grace," he said, making an effort to keep his voice steady. "I am failing to see an offense the Morok has committed. His charge in the arena is to best whatever opponent is presented to him. Is he truly to be punished for killing those that tried to kill him? Is it not the nature of us all to do so?"

Darondill received reproachful looks from Hálda and Aromé before any words were spoken in response.

"Your tongue is rash, young Darondill," said Hálda sternly.

"No," said Melinta, with a tone of calmness that disquieted Didrebelle. "The young Darondill offers a valid point. It is precisely the duty of a fighter to kill who or whatever challenges him, as it is the nature of us all to undo whatever tries to undo us. And that is why the Morok lives to fight another day. For I think I have found an opponent worthy enough to match him. A champion the Morok cannot kill."

27

The Moonstone Hammer

There was much ado in the Great Hall when Lucian sauntered in. Stopping for the first time since he broke from Ursa, rational thought began reclaiming the reins of his mind from his sudden impulsiveness. *The way I must have come off,* he thought to himself. *Just when you ought to be drawing attention* away *from yourself . . .* The steps he had taken had indeed been spurred by purpose, yet the new bustle within Ehrehalle distracted him from whatever it was he had hoped to so rashly accomplish.

It was a good thing, too. For a moment or two he thought himself audacious enough to fly toward the stables and cross the plains of Reznarion on horseback. But now, with every knight present, he was beginning to realize how foolish a plot that had truly been. *You've never been one for good ideas, though.* Aside from the twenty-five knights it seemed all of Eap's order was present as well—whether in human form or bird—though he was unfamiliar with all the grim-faced messengers and their alternative shapes.

It was soon difficult to see much of anything amidst the thickening throng. The villagers, wary and wide-eyed, roamed about aimlessly, conversing with fellow townsfolk about one thing or another. The main topic, if not the only one, seemed to be the sudden evacuation that Orion ordered before the mid-morning hours.

A man within earshot of Lucian was quibbling on, "Would've yanked me from my bed if he had the chance, I don't doubt," he said. "I'll say, I don't know what the meaning of all this . . . *calamity* is, but I'm gonna be looking for some answers if they don't find me first."

"You can say that again, Kíl," said the other. "Had that colossus over there come and fetch me from my garden." With his eyes he alluded to Streph the Summit, who was helping three older women to an empty table while carrying all their crates and luggage. "Wouldn't leave until my pitchfork was down, I tell you," he continued. "What's more, I had to round up the wife and kids, and *she* wasn't none too happy, if you can imagine. Don't think too highly of these boys from Ehrehalle, the old lady. Had to practically bribe her to come to the feast as it were."

Moving onward and eavesdropping all the way, Lucian found that anger and confusion were widely shared feelings among *all* the villagers. *At least they're taking every precaution, though,* he thought to himself, sidestepping his way through the gathering. *No wonder there was a training schedule posted. But so few against so many?*

There were about as many tables lined up as there had been for the feast. Knights were leading packs of villagers to empty spaces so that they could sort their belongings and gather themselves. He heard many of them inquiring as to the meaning of their sudden evacuation, but the knights' responses were practiced shrug-offs at best. "You'll know when we know," he heard. " . . . precautionary reasons," some said. " . . . just want to be safe," others assured.

As he shrugged and slipped along, he tried to find someone he recognized. He would have preferred that person to be Jadyn, but there was yet to be a sign of her or even her father. It was not long, however, before he bumped into the edge of a long table at which Aries and Leo were sitting. Placed in front of them were two long sheets of weathered-looking parchment and a glass jar of black ink. Several men from Dwén Marnié had formed a line across from them, all hard-faced and of relatively decent build. The foremost of them was leaning over the table and signing one sheet of parchment with a raven-feather quill.

"That's it," Aries was saying jovially. "Your contributions are well received!" He might have been a peddler praising one of his paying customers.

Lucian sat as signatures scratched and the sheet of parchment gathered names. "What's all this?" he asked Aries.

"Bit of recruiting," Aries answered plainly. "Can't rely on steadfast hearts alone if it's true what they say about the force that is coming. A hundred of Dridion's finest isn't a thing to take lightly, mind you."

Try five hundred, maybe a thousand. "Can I talk to you for a minute?" He tried to ask this as plainly as possible, as not to draw attention to any sort of trouble, but his words came out strained.

Aries looked at him warily. "Is everything alright?" he asked. "Let me assure you, a little dispute like this is rarely serious. Often times the two forces can come to terms on some agreement without it leading to bloodshed. That's what we're hoping for, at least."

Lucian was silent for a moment, watching as a youth perhaps younger than himself took up the quill and signed away his life. "That's not what you'll get," he mumbled.

A quizzical look passed over Aries's face, and he opened his mouth as if to speak before closing it again. In his eyes the question of how Lucian knew this loomed, an inquisitive glare that was soon replaced by one of recognition. "What did you see?" he asked under his breath, turning his attention back to the flowing line and feigning smiles at the new recruits.

Lucian opened his mouth to speak when Orion emerged from the crowd around them. "Lucian!" he exclaimed, slapping a hand on his shoulder. "Good to see you up and about. I know you had a long night." He passed a glance over the sheet of parchment that was now almost completely filled with wispy signatures. "Ah, good. It truly is inspiring to see so many men having volunteered. Our numbers have almost doubled! In time we may be able to match Dridion man for man."

A strange silence passed between them, broken only by the general hum pulsing throughout the hall. There came a time or two when Lucian resolved to speak plainly to Orion about what the Luminos showed him, but he thought better of it. He neither wanted to draw attention to it in front of an already-riled crowd, nor listen to Orion drone on about his plan—duty—to fetch the Netherlings from Ren Noctis. He could only imagine what he would say to that, or do. After all, it had only been a matter of hours since he threatened to chain him up in his room.

"I'm going to go walk around," said Lucian at length. Standing, he scanned the hall once more for Jadyn, and when his search came up empty he passed through the crowd toward the high doors open to the gray-blotched afternoon. A chill wind rose up through the jagged crags, yet still the villagers came by the flock up the foothills, led by knights and surrounded by packhorses.

He could only watch them walking up the skirts of Azgoth for so long, could only withstand seeing men and women weep for a matter of moments as with each step their home passed further out of reach. Some dared a second look and were urged on by others. Yet there were those who openly stood in place staring down into the golden vale, upon the thatch-roofed homes and little alleyways over which their feet may never pass again. A feeling like this had overcome him once as well, a sad flame of his own that their grief rekindled.

Turning away morosely, he ambled over to the post upon which the training schedule was fastened. "Aries and Leo, Room One," he said to himself, scanning the list down to the postscript. "Before breakfast and after dinner . . . " He paused a moment to think. Dinner would probably be held in a matter of hours, and training perhaps an hour or so after that. If anyone would listen to his account of the Luminos, it would be Aries. If anyone would understand his duty, however farfetched and ill-advised it might seem, he had no doubt that it would be him. "I'll see you then," he muttered before cantering back up the corridor.

Whiling away the rest of the afternoon in his room, Lucian thought up several different ways to address his experience in the Chamber of Baths. "Aries," he practiced.

"So, I—er—took a bath today . . . "—*Stupid*, he reprimanded himself. "I got a little bored today, so I went up to look into the Luminos,"—*No!* "Hey, guess what—I'm a Sage . . . " *You can't just lead with that, idiot.*

The fact of the matter was that he was finding much difficulty coming to terms with the information the Luminos presented him, thus explaining it to someone else seemed impractical at best. To say that he was a Sage out loud was admitting that very fact, and the admittance of that fact was as surreal to him as claiming that he was a cat or dog. Yet somehow *I feel like that would be easier to explain . . .*

When he grew tired of rehearsing his conversation-starters he took to packing for his trip across Reznarion. *I* am *making it,* he told himself. *I have* to make it. An old leather sack lay in a clump beside the chest at the foot of his bed. In this he packed a change of clothes, extra socks, and one of the thickest fur blankets he could fit. Aside from these modest amenities, he was unsure of what else to bring. It was the first time he ever packed for a journey he meant to take on his own. *I suppose I could take some extra cakes from dinner,* he surmised. *And I'd love to see if I could get my hands on some of that jerk . . .*

Standing idly by his bed thinking of last minute additions to his luggage, he suddenly remembered Excebellus, leaning in its scabbard by the balcony doors. "I won't be forgetting *you*," he said, taking up the blade and setting it on the bed beside his pack. *Anything else I'm forgetting?* he asked himself, patting himself down as though looking for his wallet. That was when a sudden thought came into his mind. *The Key!* He had not laid eyes on it in many days, it seemed, but he could plainly see the glow of blue and green lights from beneath his pillow.

Taking it by the silver teeth he brought it up to his face. "All this for you," he mumbled, studying it as though this was the first time he ever saw it, and feeling his pupils constrict in the light of the gems. "I think it's best if you stay here." With that he tucked it firmly back under the pillow and patted it down for good measure.

"That'll about do it, I think," he said to himself at length, sighing. He did not want to go to Ren Noctis any more than he wanted to go to Nundric. In his mind his recent run-in with Amarog played all too vividly. A fear he had never known took hold of him then, despite having every knight present with their weapons drawn. The thought of confronting him alone and in his own domain . . . *I have to,* he told himself. The Luminos showed me what would happen if I refused . . . It's the only way. It has *to be . . .*

A gust of wind swept through the folds of his attire as he opened the balcony doors. It seemed a storm was indeed on its way. The smell of pent-up rain hung densely in the low and graying clouds as he stood peering far across the dreary road he would soon take. In his visions he remembered seeing the City of Night at its end, as if it were close enough to grasp. Yet in the waking world it was lost beyond the dismal horizon, far away where a relentless darkness loomed.

So it was the hours passed until dinner, and hours they were of deep contemplation on Lucian's part, accompanied by a slew of second-guesses. By time the low dong of the dinner bell sounded, he had almost entirely forgotten what an appetite was or could have possibly been. During supper he sat at Aries's and Leo's table, finding that there were now divisions amongst the diners. Most if not all of this table were of the same training squad, and would report, as Aries mentioned between mouthfuls of pork, to Room One after the meal, which was not far down the central corridor. Several villagers were present also—recent additions to Aries's and Leo's platoon. There must have been thirty altogether, not including himself or the dozen wives and children that sat amongst them. *Still not enough,* Lucian thought urgently. *Not by far . . .*

When supper was ended, those whose signatures still hung wet upon the recruiting parchments followed their regiments to their respective training locations. Nearly a hundred men passed into the deep-blue shadows of the central corridor, which lofted over them to a tapering point. Biding his time in the Great Hall, Lucian sat idly at the now-empty table. He made sure to hoard some extra cakes from the desert line; the jerk, however, remained to be seen. Most of the women and children had dispersed to whatever rooms had been assigned to them, but there were some who still lingered.

Silently he wondered how long would be adequate enough to wait until approaching Room One. *An hour, maybe,* he decided. *I don't think I should wait longer than that.* An hour sounded right. It would allot him enough time to go up to his room and retrieve his pack and sword. A sudden wave of incredulity blindsided him at his resolve to depart after speaking with Aries. *I can't believe I'm actually doing this,* he told himself coldly as he proceeded up the chilly corridor to his room. *If Mary could see me now, or Jem . . .*

When he opened the door to his bedroom he was greeted by an icy draft that sifted through the slightly-ajar doors of the balcony. Shutting and latching them tightly, he shivered before taking to build a fire in the hearth. Some dry kindling and shingled fragments of thin timber were stacked neatly beside it, and on the tip of one he caught a small bulb of flame from a hanging torch and set the pot ablaze.

Suddenly, just as the fire took on life and lit the room with its flicking glare, there came a knock at the door. Upon turning he glimpsed the blue glow of Jadyn's eyes gleaming amidst the firelight.

Great, he thought to himself. *Just what you need. Another incentive to stay.* "Hey," he muttered just loud enough for her to hear.

Shuffling against the doorframe, she crossed her arms. "Hey," she said, just as softly.

"Er—how did you find my room?" he asked, suddenly wary of the demanding tone of his voice. "Not that—" he stammered, "—I mean, it's fine. It's just . . . I didn't know—"

"I saw you walk by my room," she interjected coolly, brushing a soft strand of golden hair out of her eyes. "It's just down the hall."

Lucian nodded, acknowledging. It was Jadyn's voice who fluttered into the hanging silence that followed. "Going somewhere?" Her bright eyes passed a glance over the leather travel-pack on the bed and the glittering pommel of Excebellus that lay beside it.

"*Me?*" said Lucian without much suaveness. If he was going to attempt a lie, his ploy was botched by the utterance of that single word.

Jadyn meandered in from the hanging shadows around the doorway, taking in the minor details of his bedroom as a realtor's client might survey a potential residence. Lucian noticed she donned a lavender gown similar to the one she wore the night she yanked him into that dance. There was something about the way it sparkled in the firelight, the way it fused perfectly to her every slender curve so that it seemed a natural part of her body. Stopping at his bedside, she reached out for Excebellus. "This is your sword," she remarked, a statement that flirted with the borders of a question.

"Yes," Lucian said, trying not to make his gulp audible. A girl had never been to his room before—not in Amar or *any*where for that matter. Mary had always warned him against it. Some of his friends around town used to gloat about how *they* brought girls to their room . . . None of them were like Jadyn, though.

She unsheathed Excebellus as a dancer might draw a flowing ribbon over her head. The hilt was long enough for her to grasp two hands around with room to spare, and she twirled it up, down, and around with seamless elegance. "It's a good one," she said, bringing it down and sliding it back into its scabbard. "Double-edged. I don't have much practice with these kinds. Rosie is single-edged, after all, and until now I fancied her the lightest blade in the world. Yours has her beat, I think, though I thought it would have taken all my strength to wield it."

If you only knew . . . "It *is* a good sword . . . " he answered, but of that subject he would say no more—and didn't have to, for Jadyn's attention was now on the leather pack. Lifting it from the sheets, she curled it several times before setting it back down.

"You're leaving, aren't you?" she said at length, her

question filled with the tone of one already knowledgeable of the answer.

Well, it's no use to lie. You're no good at it anyway. "Yes," he muttered drearily.

Standing with her back to him, he could only imagine the look upon her face when he said this. He saw her shoulders slouch ever so slightly, and the ridges of her exposed shoulder blades protrude within the frame of her dress. In the silence that fell, only the soft crackling of the hearth was heard.

The first voice to issue through the hush was Jadyn's. "None of the others know, do they?" she asked knowingly. "That's why you're being so secretive. That's why I haven't seen you at all today."

"I've been looking everywhere for you," Lucian retorted quickly. "I couldn't find you either. I wanted to—"

"Say goodbye?" she snipped softly.

Lucian opened his mouth and closed it again before answering. "Apologize," he said. "About the way I acted last night. About what I said. I didn't like the way we left things."

It was a moment before she answered. Her back still facing him, she turned her head slightly so that he saw the beautiful profile of her soft face, however melancholy it appeared. "Neither did I," she mumbled. "I was angry with you—"

"I pushed you away—"

"I should have listened—"

"I shouldn't have said those things—"

She was looking at him now, tears twinkling in her glossy eyes as she locked her pleading gaze with his.

You might as well tell her, he resolved inwardly. *Who knows if you'll see her again after tonight?* "As a matter of fact," continued Lucian at length, "I couldn't have been more wrong. You saw through to my core before I even saw it myself. I guess I was scared to admit it, what I can do—scared of what it meant not only for me but for those around me. I guess I wondered how it would change things. I didn't ask for this. As it happens I'm still trying to come to terms with it, though I'm not sure if I'll ever be able to."

A moderately startled look danced momentarily across Jadyn's face. "It's true then?" she said calmly, though it was evident to Lucian that she had struggled to suppress her incredulity. "You *can* . . . do things? Heal things? Make them better?"

"I'm a Sage, Jay," he answered plainly. It seemed to take an extra ounce of strength to propel the three monosyllabic words off his tongue. As they hung back within the chasm of his throat they felt leaden, a stubborn weight that would not budge. But once the words were uttered a sense of openness washed over him—a sense of freedom and acceptance that of all things in that dark hour worked to lift his heart. "I don't know how," he continued faintly before sharing his account of the Luminos. It was difficult to describe its proper function plainly, and he found that his words tripped over one another as he tried. He did manage, however, to lay the basics out for her, so that at least she developed a general understanding of what it was and what it did.

Describing what he saw was perhaps his most difficult task. He omitted his earliest visions—those of Ation's several confrontations with Sceleris and Sceleris's eventual banishment—and offered a great deal of detail on the nursery and the account of Hilda and his three . . . siblings?—*Well you might as well start calling them that* . . . —before telling of the night he was placed on Mary's steps. And though he did not want to frighten her, he shared much about his visions of Ehrehalle and the demise that would come to fruition should he not retrieve extra forces—should he not call upon the Netherlings of Ren Noctis. To his surprise— and slight relief—Jadyn did not look at him as though he had somehow morphed into Beelcibur before her very eyes. Instead the look she wore was one of interest, if not intrigue. Whether or not fear lingered in her heart he could not say, but no trace of it was apparent on her face or in her eyes.

"Good thing I brought Rosie with me," she said idly. She might have been referring to an extra pair of socks.

Before Lucian knew it he took a step forward and held out a firm, reprimanding hand. "No, Jay," he said in earnest. "You can't be anywhere near the fight when it comes. You need to be—"

"Locked up?" she interceded, more mockingly than unkindly.

Lucian's shoulders slouched. *You know who you almost sounded like?* "It's best if you stay up here," he continued. It was now more of a meek suggestion than anything. "I'd like it if you did. I don't want anything to happen to you."

"Well, Lucian," she answered, playfully coy, "if I didn't know any better, I'd say you kind of . . . *like* me."

He had been setting his arms through the straps of his pack when she said this, and nearly stopped cold as he was slinging his right one through the loop. "Maybe a little," he answered, though the playfulness he hoped to employ did not match Jadyn's. Instead his words came out forced and timid, and he soon felt himself blushing.

That was when her lips fell flush onto his. There had not been time to think, let alone react. In a wave of lavender and gold her touch was on him. Wide-eyed and incredulous he gaped as her lips guided his own through his first kiss. *Close your eyes, idiot. She's got hers closed in good faith . . .* It eased him somewhat to see how silly even someone as beautiful as Jadyn could look when kissing. As he closed his eyes all his frigidness melted. His arms which at first hung stiff like a scarecrow's wrapped around her and pulled her close. He allowed the sweetness of her fragrance to fill him, the loose tendrils of her golden hair to tickle his cheeks . . .

And then it was over, and soon seemed as though it had never been. As she stepped back from him he saw that she wore a somewhat dubious expression. *Did she really think I'd be a terrible kisser?*

"What?" he ventured to ask. It was a sheepish plea, but he didn't care.

The edges of her thin lips curved into a faint smile. "Nothing," she said as absently as if she had been shaken from dream. She was silent for many moments, though at various intervals it appeared as though she was about to speak. Standing across from her, Lucian let his blood settle, though he was finding difficulty doing so. The very sight of her was beginning to unhinge his wits. It was as though he had been given a morsel of a most delectable treat, a scrap just small enough to make him yearn for more.

It was his voice that first whispered through the silence. "I have to go," he said faintly, summoning every last ounce of resolve that would fight for him. *Make me stay,* he silently begged her. *Just say the word. Tell me to stay behind and I will. For you . . .*

Filling herself with a slow and disheartened breath, Jadyn cast her eyes to the floor. "I know," she said woefully.

It was hard for him to figure out exactly why—despite the numerous spells of adversity that had befallen him—turning from Jadyn had been to that point the hardest thing he had ever done, yet somehow he found himself in the doorway. Before advancing down the corridor he made as if to turn and say a final word, but instantly thought better of it. *Don't say it,* he told himself. *Don't make a promise you're not sure you can keep.*

And thus for a final moment his eyes met hers, and to him the look they shared held more meaning than any words he might have spoken. It would have been enough for him had her image been the last thing he ever saw.

It just might be, he thought warily as he waded through the corridor's chill.

A sizeable crowd was issuing out of Room One as Lucian wandered down the *central* corridor. Knights in sweat-drenched, casual attire were among them, their skin glistening and their muscles swollen from having been recently worked. He noticed Eap amidst the throng with other flyers, their locks damp, matted and pressed against their brows. Several villagers were with them also, all grim-faced and burly, much like Yinsed. They passed by Lucian without so much as a word, all engaged in conversations about battle maneuvers and fighting combinations. Some were practicing moves slowly without swords, and somehow reminded him of the children he once saw fighting with sticks.

He waited until the crowd flooded past him before pushing further. As he approached the doorway he could hear the din of wooden swords still clacking, and when he stepped through the arching entrance he saw Leo and Aries sparring fiercely. Like most of the rooms within Shír Azgoth, Lucian was not sure how Room One came to appear the way it did. A cavernous room, it seemed to stretch on forever, much like the Chamber of Baths. Sources of pale blue light rose up from the walls and tall stone pillars, reaching into the shadows high above. And in the belly of that boundless domain Aries and Leo cracked their practice swords. Leo's appeared to be an exact wooden replica of Lionsbane. He held a wooden shield as well, though it was a generic, circular device and a poor substitute for the one he called upon in battle. Aries fought with two smaller double-edged swords, though he kept his hammer nearby, balancing on its ram's head not far away from the center of the ring.

Much like the performance Lucian remembered them display in Ravelon, Leo's ally was brute strength, while Aries's was a combination of both strength and agility. Though Aries bombarded him with waves of rapid combinations, his advances only seemed to wash off Leo's shield. Then with a deft shove of his shield-arm Leo would throw Aries back into a rolling somersault before advancing himself. It was very much like a game they were playing, both combatants trying to break through the other's defenses, trying to verify each other's weaknesses and strengths. For a long while Lucian stood there watching, taking mental notes of their maneuvers and tactics, wondering if he could summon the skill to mirror them even slightly should the need arise to set Excebellus to purpose.

Leo turned away Aries's next advance, and after a moment of locking their swords Aries went tumbling all the way to Lucian's feet.

"Is that all you've got?" he said, picking up one of his swords that had gone flying as he toppled. He sat up and scratched his head.

"Just a taste," said Leo, walking over to him. There was a moment when the two looked on each other with gazes of fire before the sound of their laughter filled the room. Extending a muscle-roped arm, Leo helped Aries to his feet.

"I almost had you that time," said Aries, dusting off the lower folds of his tunic.

Leo grunted. "Whatever helps you sleep tonight—ah, Lucian," he said, noticing Lucian standing in the doorway for the first time. "Come for some pointers, I take it? Couldn't have sought out a better instructor—"

"Not quite, actually," answered Lucian. "Just doing a bit of—er—walking around. Never been down the central corridor before; thought I might take a look. And here I find you—"

"Besting Aries yet again," Leo filled in, taking a swig from a sack of water he had lying close by. Lucian chuckled slightly at Aries's expression, which was a concoction of confusion and frustration. "Look all you want," Leo continued after another drink. "Plenty of things to see in this mountain. You could search for years and still not find all there is to behold. As for me, I think a victory bath is in order, and maybe a cake or two before bed." After sliding his practice sword back into a nearby rack, he scooped up his water skin and headed for the door. "Sleep tightly, friend," he said as he passed. "Oh, and Aries, don't beat yourself up over this," he turned back to say. "I think I've done enough of that for one night." With that he left, but his laughter stayed with them even as he passed down the corridor.

"Right old git, that one," muttered Aries as he turned away and shoved his own practice swords in the rack with the others. "Taking a little evening stroll, are you?" he said without turning, though his tone housed a twinge of knowingness.

"I am," Lucian said after a moment.

Taking off his tunic and picking up a clean one from a bench close by, Aries began changing. "That girl," he said from within his new shirt, "from the village—"

"Jadyn—"

His golden head popped out from the ring of his collar, and he began sliding his arms through the sleeves. "She was looking for you earlier," he continued, wearing a somewhat wry smile. "Came in with the first wave of villagers—"

"I've already spoken to her," answered Lucian, shortly but not unkindly. "Our rooms are actually pretty close."

Aries smiled. "She's a pretty one," he said. "Seems to have a thing for you, if I do say so myself—"

"Aries, I—"

"But you're not here to talk about *girls*, are you?" he continued. "No, I daresay you're here for something far more pressing."

"There's someth—"

"I know what it is you'd ask of me, Lucian. And I would make it so, if I could. But you have to understand. Orion would never—"

"I'm not asking to fight," Lucian interjected somewhat hotly. "Well—I am, but that's not truly why I'm here."

Aries turned then, and his brow furrowed at seeing Lucian dressed for travel with a pack slung over his shoulders and his sword dangling off his waist.

"You mean to . . . to *leave*?" he said, aghast. "In the dead of night? On foot? With no guide?"

"I mean to—"

"Where would you *go*?" he continued worriedly. "You don't know the—"

"Aries," said Lucian, and the utterance of his name caused the stammering Aries to settle down enough to listen. "The Luminos—it showed me things . . . terrible things." Aries's eyes gazed at him intently now, blue shards of ice on the verge of melting.

"What did you see?" he asked, in a whisper that was barely audible.

"Death," said Lucian with sharp candidness. "Orion thinks Melinta has dispatched an army of a hundred. He couldn't be more wrong. Five times that amount will leave Dridion to fight at Ehrehalle, maybe more."

Aries gaped for a moment, though his gaze was largely

one of stone. "Five hundred strong," he muttered to himself.

"Against what?" asked Lucian with a hint of disdain. "Fifty? Sixty? The men who have devoted themselves to your cause are noble, sure, but their loyalty won't help them last the night of the storm."

"Then what are you suggesting?" he asked, a fierce iciness claiming his voice. It was the first time Lucian heard him somewhat frantic, the first time doubt made itself present in his voice.

"You're going to need help," Lucian answered firmly.

"And who will we call upon? The women next? We might as well—they've as much experience as the men. Or maybe the children? I've seen them practicing with sticks a time or two; no doubt *they're* ready—"

"Amarog," said Lucian staunchly.

Aries guffawed.

"He's your only chance," continued Lucian hotly. "And I'm going to find him and bring him here. Along with his following."

"His following? You wouldn't make it three steps within Dredoway's ruins, and even if you did, their oaths hold no value. It's been long since they risked their lives for a noble cause. You'd have better luck summoning the Sages to fight for us, dormant as they are."

"*Are* they dormant?" Lucian asked coyly. If there was ever a time to voice his true making, it was now. "Are you sure of that?" Just then he paid close attention to Aries's hammer resting five paces beside them.

"Of course I'm sure," Aries answered, watching as Lucian sauntered over to the ram-headed weapon balancing idly on its curved horns. "They're massed upon Zynys trying to rejuvenate the Great One. Their gaze is turned from our plights—what are you doing?"

Lucian was now standing beside the hammer, slowly making as if to grip the shaft. *My hammer is only able to be wielded by me,* he remembered Aries having said, *and Sages of the Mountain, of course, for it was they who forged it.* It was a detail Lucian had all but forgotten until now, and perhaps the only way to convince Aries that everything he was sharing with him was true.

He found that the hammer was lighter than anticipated when he lifted it from the ground. He felt as though he could wield it with one arm if he chose. Instead he took it over to Aries, who gaped at him incredulously before taking it by the shaft.

"Dormant indeed," he stammered almost inaudibly. "*How*?"

"I don't know," answered Lucian. "But I have to go. Ehrehalle can't afford my delay any longer."

Aries knelt to one knee in front of Lucian. "What would you ask of me?"

"Get up, first of all," Lucian answered. "This doesn't change anything. I'm still me. Just—I don't know—*cooler*, I guess."

Aries chuckled as he stood.

"You need to tell Orion what I've told you," continued Lucian. "But don't tell him where I've gone. He can't know. If he asks how you've come to know about Melinta's force, tell him you saw it in the Luminos."

Aries nodded firmly. "Done," he answered.

"I have to go now," said Lucian hurriedly. "I have all of Reznarion to cross and not much time to cross it."

He was nearly out the door when Aries trotted up behind him. "Follow me," he said. "If you must journey through the darkness, you'll need the aid of one who treads the night."

28

The City of Night

Night-Treader bounded through the gathering darkness, a fleeting shadow over the dreary plains. It would have taken much more than a mere passing glance to perceive him. At one instance he might have been a brief rustle of nightly wind over the sad and withering fens; at another he could have been a bulge of dense shadow where the meager light of the veiled moon was held at bay.

It was impressive to Lucian how soundlessly the stallion's hooves passed over the yellowed flats of Reznarion, especially for one so fleet of foot. The impacts of his footfalls were not only barely audible, but scarcely felt. An hour into his trek it had begun to rain—not heavily, but consistently enough to at least be irritating. Added to the speed by which Night-Treader ran, he soon found his attire damp enough to send a shiver or two through his bones.

A putrid stench began to fill the air. Maybe it was the rain that intensified it, though a vague hint of it had indeed been present beforehand. It was a sweetly sour smell, more wrenching than that of spoiled milk. Lucian first thought that they crossed over a bog, though as the rain strengthened it became difficult to differentiate between marshland and simple moist earth.

With the lower folds of his cloak, now heavy with gathered dampness, he tried his best to shield the light of Excebellus's gemstones. They seemed to shred the rich darkness like colorful spears, fervent enough, he feared, to be seen for miles, especially if viewed from higher ground.

Like an old tower, he thought to himself, *or the ledge of a mountain.* He was thinking, of course, of the ruins of Dredoway—the remnant of the once-prevalent Mortal realm. Not knowing how far he was from there, he made sure to take every precaution when it came to stealth. This much, at least, he had the ability to control. But little else.

As the darkness became heavier it seemed Night-Treader's pursuit only intensified. Thinking back to when Aries had handed him the reins, he remembered him mentioning something about the stallion's background. He was of a breed the ancient men named the *Lunos Noc,* which—loosely interpreted—translated to *Night Beast* in most of the world's tongues. They were creatures who saw best by night, though that is not to say that sunlight impaired them. It certainly had not impaired Night-Treader on their flight from Ravelon, though the speed by which he pressed now was noticeably more rapid.

It was strange to Lucian how the stallion seemed to know exactly where to bear him. After all, the only thing he had muttered in his twitching ear was, "To Ren Noctis." Those were the last three words the stallion heard on their journey—the *only* three words for that matter. From that point it had been a seemingly effortless race, around crags and down the steep slopes of Azgoth and further still across the plains.

Stealing hard into the gloom, Lucian bent a thought or two upon the City of Night. He wondered if it would indeed appear as it had in the Luminos—jagged towers standing like propped-up shards of glass; chipped roads of weathered cobblestone littered with bones and ash; the fire-eyed Netherlings lurking amidst the ruins. Yet that soon became only a passing thought, a grim realization his mind would revisit when it was done pondering other things. Better things. Things more dear to his heart.

The foremost of those things was Jadyn. Though his face had been sprayed cold by rain, he somehow still felt the warmth of her lips on his. Dismally he wondered if his first kiss would also turn out to be his last, but that was only a brief worry. *They're going to listen,* he told himself,

354

however childish an expectation he felt it might have been. *They have to listen . . .*

It did not take much thought to imagine how the scenarios would play out if they accepted or denied his proposal. If they accepted, he would rally their entire number and return to Ehrehalle with an army. If they declined, well . . . There was *that* possibility also, he supposed. While the Luminos revealed to him what would become of Ehrehalle should he not seek out the Netherlings, it never truly showed him how he would fair persuading them. Just because it was Orion's and his knights' only chance to outlast Dridion's advance did not necessarily mean Amarog and his men would join his cause.

It occurred to him every so often, however, that the fear he thought would surely grip him during his flight was present only scarcely. Perhaps it was simply the company of Night-Treader that set his mind at ease, or the newfound discovery of his . . . Sage-hood? *What* would *you call it?* His greatest fear, strange though it was to him, was not confronting Amarog again, but the Netherlings' potential rejection. Should they decline, all would be lost. Aries, Leo, Orion . . . Jadyn.

A tall glass of Eveland Cherry, he felt, could have served him well now. But the truth of it was he had scarcely enough water to last him two nights. He could have drunk the rainwater, he supposed, but he had no way of containing it. He could always sit there with his mouth open to the sky, and might have resorted to that had he not optioned to conserve the contents of his water-skin as best he could manage. Too hampered by worry to eat anything, he left the cakes he took from dinner alone. *They're probably nothing but crumbs now anyway,* he guessed, judging by the way his pack bounced erratically on account of Night-Treader's haughty pace.

There had not been a moment, come to think of it, when he could have groped for a scrap of food even if he desired it. He told himself repetitively that he would be certain to eat something once Night-Treader broke stride, but every time he thought his pace was slackening the stallion seemed to trigger another gear that sent them bounding even faster.

For hours he carried on this way, barely lifting his sleek black head to whinny, making no noise louder than a brief snort here or grunt there. But there came a time when even his steadfast pursuit let up and became wary. Though his trajectory continued headlong, there was now noticeable caution in the stallion's steps that worked to discomfit Lucian greatly.

Lucian leaned in to whisper in Night-Treader's ear. "What is it, boy?" he asked, patting the stallion's firm, damp neck.

Night-Treader only shook his head briefly and grunted. The stallion's gait was careful now at best, his reluctance to go forward all too palpable.

"Are we there?" Lucian asked, as though he half-expected the stallion to answer. "Is this it?" He fought to penetrate the pitch night with his gaze but failed. "I don't see anything."

It took a flash of lightning for Lucian to be afforded a proper look at what lie in front of him, and several before he could see it in detail. The veins of light splitting the sky worked to paint the very portrait of woe before his eyes. There, not fifty yards away, loomed the high walls of Ren Noctis. From the earth it rose, stained and gray and beaten. It was bent in some spots, leaning one way or another from whatever force had rent it from its roots. Rigid, gaping holes had been borne into it in several areas, charred rings encircling their circumferences from the fiery projectiles that had blown through. Some were wide enough to send an escort of twenty horsemen through abreast.

Beyond the wall he saw the spoke-like shapes of ruined towers standing like the jagged crests of terrible mountains. Night-birds perched upon their summits, their sheens gleaming faintly when the lightning flashed. Some of their number croaked or cawed when they saw the horse and the rider approaching daringly. Confidently. Stupidly. With reluctant steps Night-Treader inched forward, as if yearning for Lucian's command to turn back. To his own surprise, he did not issue one.

On beneath the lightning the horse and rider passed, into the bleakness of Ren Noctis more ghostly than a graveyard. A sense of foreboding gripped Lucian as they slugged warily along, the disquieting feeling that he could be snatched out of his saddle at the slightest turn of a moment. It was raining heavier now, or at least he was just now noticing it. Beneath his legs he could feel Night-Treader, bred to weather the darkness, trembling.

A discomforting hush hung over the land of ruins like a stifling blanket. It was not the silence of peace, but that of hiding, waiting, lurking. Though he could see nothing but shredded homes, cloven towers, and cracked roads, he knew that there were those within the darkness who could see him. He hated it, this game of seeking—hated the way it made him feel as though he wanted to shed his very skin and not stop running until miles lay between him and the place from which he fled. But somehow, heart racing and blood thumping, he remained as still as he could. And Night-Treader meandered slowly on.

It was difficult for Lucian to picture this place, dismal and disheveled as it was, as the grand kingdom it once had been. Whenever Orion had spoken of Dredoway it was with the same verve as when Gamaréa had spoken of his king's city of Adoram. There was nothing of note now, except of course how ruthlessly the giant megaliths had been shredded, as if they had been bales of hay beneath a scythe. Great crescents had been blown out of some towers' sides so large in certain areas that it was a wonder they remained standing.

What happened here? he marveled in dismay, gaping at the destruction all around him. As Night-Treader crept further it seemed the damage only became more extensive. Ation had done a number indeed the day he brought the towers down, the day he crumpled the roads and slew the houses. *How vile could they have been to deserve such an end?* But then another flash of lightning brought light to the world around him, and in its glare he saw the amassed shapes of all those who had been forced to live—cursed with life. Like a black sea they stood before him, a rank of a hundred, maybe two, barring his way. Some huddled over him upon the jutting ridges of old towers, staring down upon the road.

Flanked by Netherlings, and without knowledge of what else to do, he removed the folds of his cloak from Excebellus's pommel and allowed the blue and green blaze into the gloom. Those among the front lines cowered in its glare, snarling, scowling, and cursing, but there were those who held firm, letting its fire fill their already-gleaming eyes and roaring challengingly at the sword-bearer.

Their cries and shouts meshed into an inane confluence of hoarse sounds that lifted all around him. From the tower ledges on both sides of the road, beasts were shouting and hissing. Some leapt down and joined the ranks in front of him, ranks that were slowly beginning to close in. Night-Treader became restless and sifted nervously this way and that, finding all ways blocked by wolfish men. Letting up a desperate cry, he brayed and pranced as the Netherlings flocked to within reach. That was when Lucian drew Excebellus fully, and in the lightning it seemed as though he held aloft a strand of fire. Its ring hung within the deepening midnight like the shrill toll of death's bell. Those who were closest fell back into the throng of fur and fangs, too hampered by Excebellus's light and Night-Treader's wild kicking to dare an assault on the rider. Turning Night-Treader into a quick rotation Lucian saw that a black ring of Amarog's cronies had now fully closed on all sides, but there were none who pressed. Not with Excebellus's point revolving and standing between them and their target.

A clap of thunder shook the night, a force that—to the Netherlings, at least—Lucian seemed a part of. As it quaked the already-battered road they fell back further, creating sufficient space between themselves and Lucian that Night-Treader felt comfortable enough to return composedly to all fours. The black ring expanded as they slouched into the shadows, their never-straying eyes not only glaring at him, but wary of him, brimming with something like fear. He felt it too, sitting atop Night-Treader. They feared him. Feared who he was. What he was. They knew. Perhaps they did not know in Ehrehalle, but they knew now. Knew that he was of the same stock that unmade them. And he knew he had them right where he wanted them. He knew above all else that they would bend to his will, see done whatever it was he desired.

Thus he unleashed his voice into the night. "AMAROG!" It was a throaty blast, a call he did not know he was capable of making. All around him the Netherlings bore into each other with gazes of incredulity. How dare he summon their captain? How dare he call out the last king of Men? Though all were sifting uncomfortably, none moved entirely from the spot in which they stood, and so Lucian called again. "AMAROG!" It was a louder call, more like the golden trumpets of Zynys than a human voice. And it received only a meager clap of thunder in response.

As his second call died unanswered, one from amongst the Netherlings' ranks dared to approach. He was shaped like a man in every facet but his face, where a protruding snout akin to common wolves projected. There were many who looked like this, in fact—faces warring to appear either wolfish or human. The Netherling approaching was naked to the waist where shredded, stained material that might once have been breeches hung loosely. Fur sprouted off him in dense black thickets, but Lucian could tell that he was wrought with slender muscle beneath. He stared up at Lucian cautiously with yellow eyes. Wolf eyes. And were it not for the furrowing of his brow, he would not have known the beast's intentions at all.

Twiddling his clawed fingers he inched forward, afraid of either Lucian or Night-Treader or both. "Not here," he said hoarsely. Lucian had forgotten how strange it was to hear such creatures perform speech. "Amarog," he continued sheepishly, or however sheepish a wolf can possibly seem.

"Where is he?" Lucian demanded. He was surprised by his tone only momentarily. Genuine frustration was beginning to coarse through him now. He did not have the time to bandy words with anyone but Amarog. *He would be hiding,* Lucian told himself. *Like the wolf he is. He would be.* "I need to speak with him now." More like an hour ago.

At this very instant Dridion might have been swarming the hills at the feet of Shir Azgoth for all he knew. At this very instant Orion might have a spear through his belly, or Aries's hammer might have already been broken, or Jadyn . . .

"Where is he?" Lucian demanded a second time, this time with a thriving firmness that seemed to make the Netherling shudder. He was holding the creature at the end of Excebellus's point now.

"Throne," the Netherling answered without a moment's hesitation. "Sent us out to scout the disturbance."

The beast was barely finished speaking before Lucian spoke. "Take me to him."

Eyes glaring reluctantly, the Netherling passed an imploring glance to his companions blocking the road. Discomfited and hesitant, the black gathering shifted aside.

"I want all of you in front of me," Lucian ordered, mostly to those at his back. He would not risk an ambush from behind. Those comprising the ring of Netherlings behind him slowly made their way in front of Night-Treader.

When they were gathered—all two hundred strong, perhaps—Lucian spoke again. "Lead on."

Like lambs to the slaughter they crept along. Night-Treader walked cautiously behind them, but he seemed to have regained his composure. Skulking complacently, the Netherlings lead him on, down roads so dark not even Excebellus could bring them to light. A thick cloud of disturbing energy stifled the air, the ghosts of that realm's dismal past cluttering to choke him. Somehow Lucian felt as though he could hear the sounds of Dredoway's final hour, feel the strife inflicted upon the many, hear the towers collapsing and the civilians screaming . . .

Soon there were shapes in the darkness ahead. Severed pillars, rising high despite being mere pieces of their former selves, stood in a semicircle around a high well of decayed weed-wrapped stairs of ancient marble. There, in a throne of dim gold and dull crimson, slouched Amarog, sitting as though bored during a lecture. Above his head Lucian could see the ruby plainly, as Ursa had mentioned—dull like the beast beneath it. When he saw the gathering approaching he sat up, however, and became alert. He passed a confused—and angry—glance at his men before his eyes came to rest on the rider in tow, where they stayed.

Rising, he proceeded awkwardly down the stairwell. For the most part, he was a great shadow from where Lucian sat, and might have been a dense cloud if it were not for his glowering eyes in which he was held. When Amarog reached the base of the stair his followers stooped low to bow, but he seemed to ignore them. Instead he kept his gaze firm on Lucian, who despite his fear sat atop Night-Treader unwaveringly.

Amarog's voice was first to pierce the gloom. "Does Orion Highlord think himself so above us that he sends his pet to do his bidding?"

Apparently fancying this an above-average quip, he released a snarled laugh. To his obvious frustration, however, his followers did not share in his mockery.

"Orion doesn't know I'm here," Lucian called out. "I've come on my own. War is coming to Ehrehalle—a battle that will see Orion's force outnumbered fivefold, at least. And so—"

"And so you've come seeking us out!" said Amarog, beginning to shift his way through the throng of still-bowed Netherlings. "How generous of you to offer us a place to die, Keeper. But I think we're content where we are, thank you. Run along now, back to your sacred crags. The time will soon come to break our fast, and it's been ages since we've tasted the flesh of man and horse."

It was as he expected, but he figured it would serve him best to begin by asking nicely. He had developed contingencies, however, for the all-but-certain event that Amarog refused his initial proposal. *One* contingency, at least. Just one. And it would prove to either be the most foolish or brilliant thing he ever thought up. *He will never know a mortal wound, nor suffer his companions to feel the sting of death,* he remembered the midwife having said in his vision. It was a memory so pungent that it felt as though she was speaking the words directly beside him.

The Sage of Replenishment, some are calling him. The Sage of Healing. The Undying One . . .

Sighing, and watching Amarog swagger away toward his mount atop the stairs, he closed his eyes. *This better work . . .*

Eyes still closed as if praying, Lucian heard his voice spread through the hush that had fallen. "If you won't aid me willingly," he said, "then I challenge you to duel." Tension immediately gripped the surrounding area as if the very walls had begun closing in around them. For several moments, the only sound was the consistent pattering of rain. Lucian saw several heads darting this way and that as the Netherlings passed wary looks toward each other. Amarog paused his trip to the throne as if considering, the sheen of his thick, black fur gleaming in the darkness.

The more time that elapsed without an answer, the more idiotic Lucian felt. *Why? Just why? That's a bit drastic.* But then a different voice nudged away his negative thoughts—a strong voice, confident and steadfast. Whether it was his or not he did not know, but he listened to it all the same. *You can't die,* it said. *It's time you let them know that.* And so he waited in the saddle as Amarog considered, waited as the rain poured down and splashed off the slate and marble of what must have formerly been a great forum of kings.

Amarog's eyes brimmed with a feverish light when he turned, like little bulbs of sun-fire flaring in the night. The edges of his lipless mouth curved into a sinister smile, scantily showing the fangs that lingered within. "Name your terms," he said wryly.

Lucian dismounted then, and came forward warily. He was within five paces of Amarog when he answered. "My terms are simple," he said. "A fight to the death. If I win, Ren Noctis rides to the aid of Ren Talam. If you win, well, you can remain here, and bask in whatever solace this place gives you."

"And these are your terms?" said Amarog, as dubious as if a realtor told him he could buy a palace for a copper coin. There was definite glee in his voice, however; he might get to taste man-flesh again after all.

"These are my terms," replied Lucian at length. *If I kill you, I get your men. If you kill me, well, we'll just try again . . .*

Amarog's gnarling laughter filled the air. "Those pretties over in Ehrehalle must be in quite the bind for you to wager your *own* life for the chance to aid them. But if that's the way you want it, that's the way it will be. Let it never be said that Amarog is not just."

Just then one of the Netherlings ascended from his bow and stepped forward. "My lord Amarog," he said. "Would you give us orders in the event of . . . " The beast let his words trail off before slackening his posture at the look Amarog shot him.

"No need," he answered firmly. "I will make quick work of this jester, then perhaps I will be allowed some peace."

With that Amarog dropped to all fours. Even in this position he was of a greater height than common wolves, and perhaps double their mass. Lucian never heard or cared to ask about the figure Amarog once struck as a man, but as a man-made-wolf, he was a machine bred for destruction. "Now, Keeper," he said, as if through boredom—as if Lucian had woken him up out of a sound sleep to spar. "Where is it you prefer to die? Out in the rain?" The word *rain* still hung in the air when he charged, a darting flash so rapid Lucian did not register that it had happened until the wolf was past him. He had managed—somehow—to dodge the blow, sidestepping with an alacrity that made him gape at his own reflexes.

The momentum of his charge sent Amarog well beyond Lucian, who turned to face him with Excebellus bared. Upon turning Lucian saw that he wore a look of frustration. He had not expected to miss. Claws protruding like black daggers from his paw-like hands he scratched the marble surface of the old throne room.

"Someone's been eating their vegetables, I see," he mumbled behind clenched teeth. With a burst more sudden than his first charge he advanced again.

When Lucian landed after his elusive flip, he tried to recall if there was one moment during his maneuver when he had control of his body. *How did I do that?* he inwardly gaped.

"How'd he do that?" he heard one of the Netherlings gasp.

If Amarog was confident his first charge would hit, he *expected* his second one to yield blood. Instead he found himself tumbling fifteen paces away, his groping claws having come up empty yet again; the Keeper of Fates standing unscathed and ready with sword in hand. He was not sure he was comfortable with his body acting almost automatically, but if it kept him out of harm's way, it was a thing he could get used to.

"What are you playing at, boy?" growled Amarog. Any chiding tones he had once used were gone now. The fury writhing within him was all too evident. Back arched and muscles flexed, he prepared himself to pounce. It was not headlong he bounded this time, however. Instead he leapt upon the midst of the throne's stairwell before redirecting himself and lunging at Lucian from above.

With his left hand Lucian caught him by the chest, fur and all, and used Amarog's own momentum to slam him upon the ground, where he drove Excebellus through his heart. Scattered gasps emerged from the ring of onlookers as they beheld their leader staked to the ground by the golden sword, the cross-guard's eagle eyes staring them down, begging for a second helping.

Struggling upon the slate, Amarog's fangs became stained with his own blood. In an oozing, wine-red pool it leaked down the contours of his chest and all around him. Propping a boot atop his scarcely expanding diaphragm, Lucian slid Excebellus out of the wound. For a moment Amarog writhed. The fire in his eyes was beginning to grow dim.

"You gave your word," said Lucian. "Ren Noctis rides tonight."

Amarog released a blood-gargling cough, and his voice came out scratchy and vile. "I will honor no pact between Ren Noctis and a peasant vagabond," he wheezed. Blood sprayed in red mists from between his fangs.

That was when Lucian stooped low and set a hand upon his chest. Amarog's blood was flowing freely now, and soon enveloped his hand like the tide consumes a beach. There was a moment when Amarog struggled, pain etched plainly across his face. On his back he squirmed, releasing involuntary yelps of discomfort. But in time he settled, and everyone around the platform thought him dead. Everyone but Lucian. He had seen this before, felt the life leave the body of the one he meant to save. But Nod woke anew. Replenished. Healed. Even now he saw Excebellus's bite mark closing, watched as the muscles, tendons and tissues reconnect and became whole. The blood would still be there, he knew, but the wound was vanishing before his very eyes.

As if from a nightmare Amarog's eyes widened and he sprung awake incredulously. On all fours he stood, hunched and shaking like the frightened dog he was. Crouching away he looked warily at Lucian, his blood-covered paw prints tracing his path from where he tracked through his own puddle. His eyes for an instant came to rest on Excebellus, the golden extension of Lucian's right arm still wet with his life's blood. Turning his gaze upon the dumbfounded gathering, he noticed that all were inching closer, their snouts airborne as if to detect something false, something wrong . . . But Amarog was as real as he had ever been. Before many registered what had happened, Lucian had killed Amarog and brought him back to life.

Several times Amarog looked from his hand—which rested over his heart where the sting of Excebellus might have still lingered—and back to Lucian. There was blood there, sure. Blood from an old wound, healed as though having never been inflicted at all. It seemed as though an hour elapsed before a voice scratched through the silence. It was Amarog's. *"How?"* he muttered.

But Lucian did not answer right away. Instead he looked out upon the road. The storm was intensifying. The black sea of Netherlings stretched on for a good distance, and at their back Night-Treader stood lonely and waiting. Beyond him he noticed the sky was brightening—that is to say becoming a lighter shade of gray. Dawn. With so many in tow it would take all day to cross Reznarion, if not most of the night. It was a journey that needed to be underway hours ago.

"I'll tell you on the way," Lucian said.

29

The Last Trial

Didrebelle dreaded the moments that he was left alone with his father. It felt as though Darondill, Hálda, and Aromé had been gone for hours, though given leave only moments ago. They sat in silence but for the soft patter of passing servants bringing plates of roasted pheasant and potatoes, along with a new cask of mulled wine for which Didrebelle was very appreciative.

Melinta delved into his plate as though the concept of food were new to him. Didrebelle's appetite, however, yielded in the light of the new information his father presented earlier to his councilmen.

How can there possibly be a champion more worthy than Ignis? The thought savaged his mind like wildfire. How indeed? Was there a sixth champion in waiting? Something fouler and more ancient than the Lord of Parthaleon himself? *Impossible.*

"The pheasant is delectable," said Melinta genially, wiping his mouth with the decorative cloth on his lap and setting it aside. His look became grave, however, when he noticed Didrebelle's plate was all but untouched. "Not hungry, Diddy?" he said, surprised. "I know that crud you eat in Cauldarím is vile. I was certain you would take this opportunity to indulge."

"Vile indeed," answered Didrebelle, laying a hand atop his stomach. "In fact I think breakfast may have gotten the best of me." He knew Fairies were not susceptible to disease or illness, but he had known certain foods to make him feel at least somewhat uneasy. Mostly bacon.

"Strange," said Melinta, considering. A silence that seemed to drag along fell between them. Then Melinta said, "Well then, no pressure. More for me, I suppose!"

Just how you like it. "Do you think it wise to call on the Morok to fight again?" said Didrebelle, not bothering with any build-up.

The abruptness of his question caused Melinta to stop mid-chew. "Yes?" he answered, stating it as more of a question than anything, as though inquiring if his son had other ideas.

"Despite his recent showing?" continued Didrebelle. "While undeniably admirable, his victory *did* cost you a great deal more than it was worth. Yet you are quick to subject another to his fury." *And I don't know how much longer he can last.*

Melinta wiped his mouth again, considering. "That is precisely why I must call on him again. Despite his lineage, he has become a spectacle. Folk will pay large sums to see him fight. Forgive me, my son. I thought I had been clear enough."

Oh, I heard you just fine.

Silence fell again. Melinta tapped into the wine cask and refilled his cup. After a lengthy drink he said, "I can say this though: I fear my debt to the Lord of Nundric will never be repaid. Ignis was dear to him, as a dog is dear to its master. The sorcerer's wrath, I fear, will be terrible, whenever he is brought up to speed. It required ceaseless persuasion on my part for his delegates to even *consider* loaning Ignis to me, thinking it for the betterment of the war. After all, what good would he have done guarding the gates of an unbreachable realm while his master's war wages above him? But now the creature lies in ruin."

Because of your stupidity. "And the errand runners—"

"Have been in motion for days. Hálda, Aromé, and Darondill—confounded tongue though he has—addressed them at the beginning of the week. I expect the roads to be littered with caravans of nobility in two days' time. All with heavy pockets!"

Didrebelle feigned a smile and simply raised his glass as if in salute. *I need a drink anyway.* When he set his cup aside he said, "And who will oppose him this time?"

Melinta laughed. "Now where is the fun in that?" The playfulness in his voice only set Didrebelle more on edge. "It is a surprise—and a great surprise at that, if I may be so bold."

I love surprises. "Well then," said Didrebelle, not entirely feigning his curiosity, "I am eager to see who is chosen to challenge him."

"It will be an event to remember indeed. But, my son, do forgive me. I have much to set in motion. Even now there are things I must see to in order to get this spectacle moving."

"Say no more," said Didrebelle. "I have business of my own to confront in Cauldarím. Until next time, Father."

And good riddance.

When Gamaréa was escorted back to the fields of Cauldarím, he resumed his usual stonework with his usual company. Daxau, however, was not present. *Perhaps he has not left the barracks just yet?*

He knew this was a silly thought. The routine by which the captives were led into the fields every day was as unchanging as the coming of dawn and dusk. As he walked to his work station, he scoured every corner of the camp for all his sight was worth, employing all his effort to catch but a glimpse of his neighbor. But there was not so much as a trace.

At his work station there were three Moroks whom he had seen before. They had always worked nearby, but Gamaréa had never shared words with any of them. As he approached, the Moroks' mannerisms tensed, and they carried on about their business with the anxious air of men who did not wish to be seen.

Gamaréa set his stone down, making it a point to shake the workbench as he did so. He knew these three were afraid. Part of him fed off that fear. Even now his shadow covered them in shade. Cauldarím had made them pathetic.

The camp had swallowed much of their muscle, leaving only skin-covered bone for them to boast. These were his countrymen, though they may not have known it. Thus it was unclear, even to Gamaréa, why he felt such disdain towards them. Perhaps it was due to the fact that they were standing in the place where Daxau usually stood. Perhaps it was because Daxau's absence meant only one thing, and these prisoners only added finality to the truth.

"Pass the blueprint," Gamaréa said impassively. As he stretched out his hand, the Morok nearest him flinched as though he had raised a knife.

It was truly astonishing how powerful his mere presence had become. But the tension in the air lifted momentarily as the Morok did as Gamaréa had bidden.

"You're that fighter, ain't you?" said the Morok who had handed it over. "The one they've all been talking about."

Here we go. Gamaréa issued only the clanging of hammer on chisel in answer.

After many moments of silence, the Morok beside the one who had questioned him said, "Don't think he's much fer talkin' 'bout it, Pip."

"I didn't mean no offense there, err, Gammer . . . if that's your name."

"Gamaréa," he corrected shortly. "And there is no offense taken. But your friend is right. I would prefer to let it be."

With that, Gamaréa continued chiseling at the stone. It must have been a piece of Melinta's neck, for aside from some kind of embroidery on his robe, there was nothing much to craft. Yet his mind felt parted from his body. He saw himself modeling the stone in front of him, but it was as though he was watching someone else. All his thoughts bent on Daxau. What was that feeling in the pit of his stomach?

"Tell me," said Gamaréa after a while, unable to turn his thoughts away from the vexation of Daxau's absence. The three Moroks were instantly brought to attention. Pip flinched again, though Gamaréa had not even gesticulated this time. "Where is the man who normally worked this station?"

Gamaréa dreaded asking the question, afraid of hearing the answer he believed he already knew.

"That mortal feller?" said Pip.

Gamaréa nodded. The three Moroks looked at each other apprehensively.

"'fraid he's dead, lad," answered Pip heavily, perhaps afraid to be the one to relay the news to Gamaréa.

The hammer and chisel clattered upon the ground before Gamaréa realized he had dropped them.

It can't be true.

"Sorry to say it is, son," said the Morok nearest Pip. Only then did Gamaréa realize he had spoken aloud. "Saw his body carted off myself. Took him from his cell an hour or two past midnight. Just gone cold. Sometimes this place gets to folk like that. And him being mortal and all—"

"I saw him too, Kibb," said the third Morok, who spoke as though he had only just now summoned enough gall. "Took three of 'em to carry 'im away. Didn't even bother to close 'is eyes, the mongrels."

"Dead." It was the only word Gamaréa could muster. He was no longer looking at them. Staring off into space, his eyes were unblinkingly open, though he saw nothing.

The rope burned a little more that day. He and his contingent made two trips into Deavorás, leaving little time to spare before dusk. So it was he took to the mess hall, though he barely even looked at his dinner. Across from him was the empty chair that Daxau usually manned. A warm sensation overcame his eyes. At first he thought it resulted from the steam rising out of his bowl, but before long he understood it to be the buildup of tears.

Slowly but surely the night trudged on. Once he returned to his cell he lay in the corner absently, avoiding the little moonlight that reached in through the bars. The small sounds of the captives down the walkway were constant, but did not distract Gamaréa's mind from exploring the possibilities of what may have befallen his friend. Though for every vision his mind concocted, every circumstance he imagined, only one word remained consistent. Sometimes he said it aloud.

Dead. He closed his eyes as if doing so would erase the truth—

And opened them hours later. Had he really been that weary? But his arousal was not unprovoked. There had been a sound. What was it? A scratching noise. He remembered the sound of scratching. Or had it been a dream? . . .

Just then he heard it again. It was a sound like falling dust sprinkling to the floor. His attention was drawn to the alcove of the small window in the upper corner of his cell. Soon pebbles flooded through the bars in waves. The familiar voice of Didrebelle accompanied them.

Doing the best he could to peer out of the barred slit, Gamaréa found Didrebelle lying upon his stomach on the ground outside, his slender fingers clasped around the bars as though he were trapped himself.

"About time," he said. "I was running out of stones."

"What are you doing here?" asked Gamaréa in a hushed whisper. "You will be discovered!"

"I will be quick, then. I am sorry for the loss of your friend; I came upon his body not long before I left to come here."

Gamaréa dropped his eyes, nodding only slightly. Then Didrebelle said, "Are you prepared to fight again?"

Let's see. Lucian is probably dead. Daxau is dead. You're undercover as the warden and your father's heir. My body still feels like it went through Parthaleon and back . . .

But Gamaréa answered brokenly. "I suppose I am as ready as I'll ever be."

Didrebelle's eyes narrowed, as though he had read Gamaréa's sarcastic thoughts. "Good. I must warn you: foul things are abroad—things that may disrupt my original plan. If we are to be free of this place and make for Lucian, we must expect the unexpected. Your freedom can now be bought, yes, but how long that will take not even I can say. What is more, I find it hard to believe that I am the only one who does not think the king will keep his word."

"What do you know, then?" Gamaréa was surprised to hear how anxious his own voice sounded. "Have you been told anything?"

"Nothing that would be of worth to you. You know as much as me. In two days' time you will fight again. Your opponent is yet to be determined, but according to the king, it is something or someone that you will be unable to defeat."

A long, dark silence enveloped them.

"I must leave you now," said Didrebelle shortly. "I will be in attendance this time—in the king's suite."

Didrebelle made as if to push himself up from the ground, but Gamaréa clasped on to his fingers, still wrung around the bars, and held him in place.

"Promise me something," he said. He wondered then if Didrebelle had ever heard such desperation in his voice. "If my end is indeed upon me, I would have you go to Medric and take up sword with Mascorea. He will need an able captain at the helm of his force. See his hope restored, as I could not. Rid this land of the evil that now festers freely upon it. Help fulfill the errand I failed to."

Didrebelle's heart was tormented by the look in Gamaréa's eyes as he clung to the bars on tiptoe in plea. Though his figure was all but shrouded in darkness, Didrebelle could see how broken and disheveled Cauldarím had rendered him. It was the shell of a once steadfast spirit to which he spoke, and for the sorrow welling up inside him Didrebelle could issue but two words.

"I will."

Dawn of the third day came much too quickly for Gamaréa's liking. Many parts of his body still ached dreadfully, but he tried not to grimace as he was brought to the armory. There he was given a different sword from the one he had used to defeat the five champions, that blade having been spent beyond repair.

Gamaréa much preferred this new blade, however. It was lighter and much more compact, making one-handed attacks achievable with little strain, whereas his former blade was longer and more cumbersome. Indeed it was a worthy remedy for his aching shoulders and back, but nothing could ever replace Dawnbringer. He wondered briefly where it now lay.

On this occasion he was also given a shield the shape of a crescent moon, the face of which was tattered and dented from its years of service. It was a component Gamaréa had never become acquainted with, Tartalion having trained him to be quick enough that a shield would be unnecessary. *Speed is the true shield,* he once said. *Master it, and no blade will catch you.*

Before issuing through the doorway, into the grim corridor leading out to the platform on which he would rise to the sands, one of the guards set a large bronze helm over his head. It was certainly a clunky piece of equipment, and stifling to the extent that Gamaréa nearly began sweating instantaneously. What was more, it muffled any sound from without while managing to amplify the sound of his own breathing. With those two forces combating, it was nearly impossible to hear anything around him while drawing breath. The helmet obscured his vision as well. Between its brim and the upper lip of its mouth-enveloping cage, there was barely enough of a gap through which to see.

This ought to be interesting.

In the company of the guards he passed from the armory, clumsily at first for the weight of the helmet. Already the anxious crowd could be heard above like a great storm. On their way to the platform they met a small, scraggly slave carrying a tray with a small bowl of cold porridge and some water. Though he was bid to eat, Gamaréa made little use of the lumpy muck and drank only the water that was provided. When he refused the porridge a third time, they carried on until they reached the platform. There he was instructed to wait until Melinta announced him.

It took nearly half an hour for the king to reach his balcony. Gamaréa had become aware of his arrival by the abrupt decrescendo of the spectators. When they were settled, Melinta began his oration.

"Not a week past, a spectacle was beheld on these very sands—a feat that has never been achieved, nor will again. A flawed venture, it was called. A futile cause. A task impossible as fetching the moon from the heavens. Yet that venture was weathered. That cause was settled. That task was completed. And a task it was that matched this champion against five of this world's most rigorous creatures. Their herald, as you may recall, was none other than Ignis, Flame of the Underworld, guardian of Parthaleon's gates! Bested most cunningly by he who is about to enter. I give you, my fellow countrymen, the Champion of Cauldarím; the Slayer of Ignis: Gamaréa, son of Gladris!"

The platform was set in motion, and Gamaréa rose slowly as the screeching chains delivered him upward into the overwhelming sunlight. To Gamaréa's surprise, the crowd was cheering as though they had loved him all their lives. When his eyes became accustomed to the new light, he beheld Melinta gesticulating to the crowd to quiet once more.

When all were settled he spoke again. "Who is left to challenge such a warrior, you may be asking? Who upon the face of the West could present a worthy challenge to the Slayer of Parthaleon's Flame?" The crowd roared with angst. "Enter the challenger, nameless until fate's gavel falls!"

So it was the gate across the sand opened, and the challenger came forth to a deafening chorus of jeers. A vest of worn, boiled leather covered his chest and torso, but his massive, muscle-roped arms were left bare. At his side he brandished a sword similar in make to Gamaréa's, yet his shield was much less than savory. He too wore a cumbersome helmet over his head, masking his face to the extent that only his eyes breached the narrow gap between the brim and the cage's lip.

In height the challenger nearly matched Gamaréa, but was slightly broader of shoulder while covered in a bit more bulk. But the Morok was poised. Seeing flesh alike to his own opposing him filled him with promise. At least there would not be any fiendish creatures to deal with today. *A strange mercy*, Gamaréa contemplated.

375

Melinta signaled the initiation of the battle. The challenger immediately crouched into a fighter's stance, his sword raised above his head as he slowly circled like a predator. Almost simultaneously, Gamaréa did the same.

Their slow, dance-like prowl continued for a long while, each combatant taking turns at bluffing toward the other. But it was Gamaréa who made the first complete advance. The small sword allowed him to utilize quick strikes, but the challenger matched him stroke for stroke, parrying skillfully as though he was not so much as bothered by Gamaréa's attacks. He could not recall a time in recent memory that an adversary had matched him sword for sword with as much talent as this new opponent.

Tartalion's voice edged back into his memory. *Never underestimate your adversaries.*

Gamaréa, panting deafeningly against the cage of his helm, regrouped and started circling again. *A little late for that.*

Before he could formulate a different strategy, the challenger was on him, swinging his sword fretfully. Their clashing blades rang through the hollows of the arena. Those close enough to the sand's level stood with excitement. Some began cheering. The utter speed with which the swordsman advanced nearly knocked Gamaréa off balance, and he was lucky to maintain proper footing as he staggered backward fending off his opponent's strikes.

After several moments, the swordsman regrouped and they each stood panting. The muscles in the challenger's arms were bulging from the strain of his attacks and were a truly imposing sight even to Gamaréa.

An hour passed statically, one advancing upon the other only to be driven back. Not one drop of blood was spilled in that time. In fact, the only difference that Gamaréa noted was that the strength behind his challenger's attacks was starting to wane. The speed that propelled his prior advances was depleting. In light of this, Gamaréa knew that he would soon have a much easier time breaching his defenses. It was only a matter of when.

Suddenly, growing tired of their methodical rotation

around the sand, Gamaréa tore through the air like a stray arrow until their shields pressed and their swords sang once more. Then there was a moment when everything stopped, when the shields refused to give, and the swords latched as though welded together, and the warriors' faces were but a hair's-length apart. Through the shadows of his challenger's helmet, Gamaréa could see his eyes, and thought to see a hint of sadness dwelling there.

It was no matter. Refusing to register his adversary's emotions, he drove his own helmet forcefully into the other's and they immediately became dislodged. With the challenger staggering backward, Gamaréa sent a swift kick into his open chest, sending him tumbling with such force that his sword and shield came lose.

The crowd's excitement escalated in an instant. Melinta stood to attention, anticipating the climax of the spectacle.

"Kill!" exclaimed the thousands in attendance.

Removing his helmet, Gamaréa allowed the fresh air to wash over him, reveling in the majesty of a full and unthwarted breath. Stooping low, he grabbed his opponent and yanked him to his knees. Gamaréa's kick had knocked the wind out of him, and his breaths were labored. Gripping the shoulder of the challenger's sweat-drenched vest, Gamaréa looked up to Melinta's balcony inquisitively. There he saw the king wearing a long smile, and soon he stood and stretched his arms out to the crowd, which was imploring him to consummate his victory. On Melinta's signal, Gamaréa removed his opponent's helmet—

And stared directly into the pleading eyes of Daxau.

A wave of fear and doubt and rage-crested sorrow overwhelmed him. *Impossible!*

Ever more the crowd urged Gamaréa to kill, perhaps wondering what was keeping him from staining the sands with Daxau's blood, but Gamaréa felt as though he lost every sense except his sight. He could not hear the crowd's demands. He could not smell or feel the dust rising through the light breeze. His focus remained on Daxau alone. The thought of his death was part of the fuel he had used to fight so fiercely. The realization that he would never again share words with him motivated him to kill whoever came out of those gates to oppose him. A thousand questions warred within his mind, each fighting to be asked first, but all of them perished. His lips quivered as his tongue desperately sought words, one word, anything. *How? Why?*

He felt betrayed, fooled, sick to the lowermost chasm of his stomach. A hollow sensation flowed through him now, a tempest of rage and hate and vengeance so tumultuous it felt as though he was on the verge of exploding.

It had indeed been sadness in Daxau's eyes, which were presently filling with tears. They were eyes in which Gamaréa thought he would never look again. Now he was burdened with the task of closing them forever.

"Do it now," said Daxau lightly, as though it was some backyard game the two were playing. "Send me to my father and my son."

Time seemed to slow his words. Gamaréa recoiled in disbelief, stepping back and dropping his sword. As it fell upon the sand, the entire arena seemed to shudder at his feet. The crowd above grew restless, then vengeful when Gamaréa backed away from Daxau and looked up to Melinta's suite shaking his head in slow refusal.

"KILL HIM NOW!" shouted Melinta above the angry mob. "On with it!"

"You must do it, friend," said Daxau slowly. "Send me on my way, or both of us will die."

Then, as if Daxau was showing his own son a simple lesson, he handed Gamaréa back his blade and guided its edge to his throat.

"You know what you must do," whispered Daxau, his voice wavering yet brave.

"You're right," answered Gamaréa slowly. He heard himself speaking as if through dream. "I do."

There was no way out of this tragic circumstance. The crowd's intensity had assumed a life force all its own as they wildly demanded Daxau's life. This was what they paid to see. This was the spectacle they traveled far and wide to witness.

Daxau straightened his posture. If he was to die, it

would be with honor. Gamaréa stepped back to allow himself a proper angle. He would not force himself to swing more than once. Now he stretched out his sword to assure he was far enough away for a clean stroke. Tears filled his eyes, but he refused to allow them passage down his cheeks. Anger rose within his heart, but he stifled it with all his will. He knew what he had to do—perhaps he had always known it. It would come at the utmost price, but it was a price he was suddenly willing to pay.

Gamaréa's measurement was perfect. Though he had not intended it, his back blocked the sun and his own shadow covered Daxau in darkness. Gamaréa raised his sword; Daxau fought to keep his eyes open. Gamaréa's arm swung rapidly—

But the sword never even grazed Daxau's neck. Gamaréa had sent it flying directly toward Melinta's balcony with a great heave. Spinning out of control, the sun flashing off the steel with every quick rotation, its collision course with the king unfolded for all to see.

Melinta evaded the blade with perhaps a second to spare. When he stood, it was with the hesitation of one who had survived the breaking of the world. A look of bewilderment was strewn about his face. Gamaréa's sword was embedded in a wooden beam behind him, still bobbing enthusiastically. The entire world seemed to hold its breath as Melinta held Gamaréa in his sight. Then like a disgruntled child, the king gave a nod, and guards from every corner of the lower levels closed in around the Morok and held him at spear-point.

As they circled them, Daxau whispered over his shoulder. "You said you knew what you had to do."

"And so it is done," Gamaréa answered plainly.

He did not struggle as they bound his wrists and ankles.

30

Ill Tidings

Long after the sight of Lucian was gone, Aries remained looking out upon the road leading away from the stables. In time the dreary evening gave way to a blotchy, starless night in which even the radiant moon was hidden. *A storm is coming indeed,* he thought to himself. Several questions had been running through his mind since the moment Lucian left, but there was one more recurrent than the others. *Should I have let him go?*

It all had happened in an eye-blink, it seemed. One moment Lucian was the scrawny peasant from a village far across the sea, and the next . . . *But the hammer,* he reminded himself. *He lifted it as though it were a twig.* He knew only himself and a Sage of Zynys could raise the moonstone instrument from the ground, but he was still having trouble believing that Lucian was of their kind. *About as learned in the evils of the world as an earthworm,* he thought. *And much too skinny.*

But as they passed toward the stables, Lucian had shared with him the several strange experiences he had endured. There was the moment with the lilacs, of course, though Lucian spoke of that as if in passing—perhaps, Aries thought, out of embarrassment for showing his soft side. He could have sworn there was another thing Lucian had wished to share, though he seemed reluctant to do so, and thus kept it to himself. "Then there was something . . . I don't know . . . " Aries recalled him saying. As Lucian's words trailed off he seemed to pass a quick glance up the mountain before saying, "Forget it." And so whatever he had been about to say was yet a mystery that worked to add to Aries's vexation.

There had been the information Lucian shared about the visions shown to him by the Luminos as well. In great detail Lucian had recounted the orders of the midwife and his arrival in Amar. When he mentioned the names of his three siblings, Aries felt himself give a knowing start. Charon, Nepsus, and Nephromera were three of the most prevalent Sages in the old Dredowan practices. Warriors had once built monuments and temples in honor of Charon where they would seek his council in times of battle. Seafarers, traders, and naval officers often developed similar structures in praise of Nepsus, in hope that he would bring them good fortune upon the seas. But everyone seemed to pray to Nephromera most of all. Sagess of Love and Tranquility, it was to her men and women alike prayed for companionship in times of loneliness, love in times of hate, and peace in times of war. There had once been enough of all three to keep the prayers rolling in. He had prayed to her himself a time or two, though Charon was often the Sage he sought most. *And now I may have just sent their brother to his doom . . .*

Trying to cast such thoughts away was difficult for many reasons. Firstly, the thought of losing Lucian was hard to entertain in general—but the thought of losing him at the hands of Amarog was deplorable. Aries had grown fond of Lucian since he and his company came upon him in Ravelon. He had developed a special friendship with the boy that made him reminisce on days long past, when he was yet an eighteen year-old whom time had barely touched. The protectiveness he felt when in the boy's company had become as involuntary as breathing, and it pained him more than anything that he could not stand beside him on his peril-riddled errand.

A matter just as bleak was what would happen should Lucian fail to summon the Netherlings. Speaking with them as men was about as difficult as trying to chew your way through a brick wall; speaking to them now . . . But if the Luminos had showed him this was the only way, then the only way it was. It was their only chance at standing a chance. And if he failed—if the Netherlings refused . . .

Lowering his golden head, he turned from the path and continued up the road to the stairs of Ehrehalle. A hafted torch was alight upon every other step or so, though the rising winds threatened to snuff out their entire sum. When he reached the bottom stair he passed a long, wary gaze across the vale below. Dwén Marnié was quiet and dark, a mere patch of shadows across the lifeless, yellow folds. Beyond the valley, the adjacent arm of the Red Peaks rose black and without detail beneath the fallen night.

The silence was enough to strip a man of his skin. If what Lucian said was true, it would not be long before Melinta's force set Dwén Marnié to the torch and attempted to storm Ehrehalle in search of him. He could almost see them advancing up the skirts of Azgoth in their gold-plated ranks, brandishing their dagger-bladed spears and glinting swords. It was just a matter of when.

The messengers of Ehrehalle were assigned to answer that question, and every night they took to the skies and scouted the expanse between Dridion and Ren Talam. So far their searches had borne no fruit, but there was always tonight's. Aries could only hope Ehrehalle's numbers were swelled before the time came for battle. Could only pray.

Within the Great Hall, twenty-odd villagers were scattered about throwing dice or drinking. The hearth in Ehrehalle's belly was roaring, sending small orange embers up to the rafters. As he passed through, he glimpsed Leo in the far corner at a table with Halag and two other leathery-faced men of burly build. Leo's hair was ruffled, and black as the pit of night. He had taken it out of its braid and let it frisk freely down to his shoulders, affording him the appearance of a lion now more than ever—a kingly lion, in his green, silver-mottled tunic. Every so often he would scratch his coarse, bristly beard with a thick finger before flipping over a card and grimacing. "Rigged," Aries heard him grunt when he came to sit. "The folk of the valley are scoundrels. What's the matter with you?"

Aries had not meant to appear as vexed as he truly was, but it was difficult, all things considered. Leo scanned the four cards in his hand before flipping over another and cursing. Halag seemed to take particular delight in his outburst. Aries hadn't a clue what they were playing. It must have been some game invented in the little thatch-roofed alleys of Dwén Marnié.

"You're not still mad about before, are you?" Leo said between card flips. He grabbed another from the pile in front of him and added it to the slowly-growing collection in his hand. "Hasn't been the *worst* defeat you suffered at my hands," he added gruffly.

"I need ale," was all Aries said.

Leo slid his over, the brown-and-frothy head of which was still bubbling over the rim. "Take mine," he said. "One of these villagers' brews. Not to my taste."

Halag looked up from his cards. "You complain about as much as all these folk put together," he said, apparently offended.

"Too bitter, if you ask me," Leo defended dismissively.

"I don't think anyone did," retorted Halag.

Aries thought this would be a good place to interject. "Has anyone seen Orion?" he asked, taking care to keep his voice as neutral as possible despite the anxiety welling up inside him. He needed to break words with him—needed to tell him everything that Lucian instructed him to.

"Up in that office of his," said Leo, flipping over another card and cackling. "Take them all, you brigand." Much to his apparent displeasure, Halag groped for the pile of cards in front of him.

"But anyway," Leo continued with a bit of a wry smile peeking through the thicket of his beard. "He's up in his quarters, like I said. Been up there most of the night, ever since training ended."

"What's he doing up there?" Aries asked, his best attempt at feigning disinterest.

"Who knows," answered Leo gruffly. "Probably studying old parchment and moving around all those waxen pawns and rooks of his. You know how he likes to do that. Sent out

384

five more messengers tonight, he did. This whole Dridion situation is really starting to get to him. Let the Fairies come, I say! Let their pretty faces get mangled by our iron fists! It'll be the last time they bring war upon *us*, that's for sure—*damn* you, fiend!" The pile of cards was now Leo's, and Halag sat back roaring with laughter.

One of the villagers who happened to be watching the card game unfold brought everyone's attention to the great doors, yet open to the night. Rain was beginning to fall steadily, and the stone patio of the high stairwell was already damp as heavy droplets fell upon it in consistent torrents. With a bony finger he pointed, saying, "Looks like them bird-fellows is coming back."

And so they were, all in a flutter. Making no pause in the Great Hall to reclaim their human figures, a raven, hawk, and owl swept through Ehrehalle as if the greatest of all dreads was at their tail feathers.

Aries's eyes remained on the leftward corridor long after they passed from sight. "You said there were five that left Ehrehalle?" he said to Leo, who at no point even bothered a second glance at the hasty trio that had flown through.

He had just finished dealing out new hands when he sat back and said, "Yes. There were five. Eap was with them as usual—the scoundrel—and four others. Why?"

A flash of lightning seared across the night, and a moment or so in its wake came a very distant roll of thunder. "Only three have returned," said Aries.

This was the third time that Orion organized the waxen pieces along the parchment, atop which was a blotchy blueprint of Ehrehalle. He was only grateful that none were present to watch his temper flaring, to watch his doubt seep through his actions as he swept the stained sheets out from under the red and black pawns and sent them clattering across the floor of cold stone. There was not a strategy possible that worked to nullify the odds they would face, no alignment or formation he could think of that would work to abate the numbers that would march upon Azgoth.

A hundred of Dridion's finest, he kept telling himself. That thought was usually the one that triggered his emotions and sent the pawns flying. A hundred trained assassins— who could not only fight, but excel in any terrain—against a hastily-assembled band of commoners of various professions with a handful of soldiers dotted in. Such realizations sent his fingers through his unkempt auburn locks almost involuntarily. *There is no way,* a voice would whisper in his mind. At first there had been a combating voice, quelling the one of negativity that freely frolicked about within him. *There is always a way,* it retorted. But even the alacrity with which it spoke was beginning to dim, beaten back by its dispirited counterpart and cast almost entirely into silence.

"A hundred!" He was surprised to hear his voice reverberate off the walls, and even more so when the table upon which he had leaned flipped over and smashed into several sharp fragments. So long had he been cramped silently within his quarters that anything scarcely audible worked to send a tremor through his skin. *What has gotten into me?* he thought, though the fact that something had only built his anger up more.

Two wide-bellied hearths were roaring in the room's nearest corners, and thus he fed them pieces of the broken table absently. It was a crammed room to begin with—less crammed now, of course, with the subtraction of the table. Red tapestries hung in loose folds here and there, the edges lined with white embroidery and golden lions stitched into their midsections. The walls and floor were of dark gray stone, glossy in the light of the fire yet pitch as obsidian in the nether sections where the blaze could not penetrate.

More vexed now than any moment of his life he could remember, he sat on a nearby bench staring blankly into the flames. *As long as Lucian is protected, it will be a victory,* he told himself. *If it takes him leaving, I will send him away. I have lived a life worth sixty mortals', and I would gladly see it forfeit if it meant the prosperity of . . .*

Suddenly a figure drew his attention to the shadows in the doorway. Were it not for the gleam of her eyes, he might not have seen Ursa at all.

"Ursa," he said softly. Only a fragment of the word held the trappings of a question.

As she stepped into the light he gave a start. She appeared more dazzling than he had ever remembered her. The years of toil and grief since the Day of the Wizard had conspired to rid her of her once superior beauty, yet it seemed she reclaimed it all, if not more, in an instant. She wore a velvet, well-fitting gown scarcely mottled with white, as if she had stolen a section of the night sky and draped it around her. White jewels were lined along the low collar, out of which her nimble shoulders rose before rising up to her slender neck. He could not remember the last time Ursa's smile reached her eyes, but they brimmed now with a fervent light long before she stepped out of the shadows. A silver diadem gated her tightly pinned hair, hair like a raven's plume.

It had been long since she adorned her brow with that silver piece, the piece the daughters of kings donned in the days when Dredoway was strong. And it was longer still since her hair added anything but a dreary aura to her countenance. Now it proved a contributing factor in the awakening of her former glamour. Black hair like the pit of night atop a face as white as mountain snows, out of which peered eyes of lively green. They were eyes that scanned the floor longer than the man sitting troubled to the side. Wooden shards were all that remained of a once sturdy desk, and splayed sporadically across the stone were the small wax figures she remembered Orion troubling with among his captains thousands of years ago. And they represented only one thing.

"War will soon be upon us," she said, eyeing the pieces a bit more firmly. Her voice wavered just enough for Orion to know that she was troubled.

"Dridion will be upon us soon, or so I fear, if the accounts of the messengers are accurate," Orion answered. "We have not the men to quell the storm that is coming."

Ursa slowly laid her eyes upon her former husband, vexed and nervous upon his bench. "Many yesteryears have passed since the men of Dredoway faced the hosts of Dridion and prospered," she said.

"Yet with an entire force," Orion replied contemplatively. He stood then, and took the image of Ursa in for the better. When he realized she watched him do so he cast his head away as though he were ogling at some upper class stranger in a lower class pub. "Here we stand with but a fistful of men who have seen battle, and fewer still who remember combat," he said, beginning to pace errantly to and fro. "The mortal mind was not built to hold ages worth of memory. I yet find myself groping at the dregs of what I sometimes feel are someone else's thoughts and dreams. It is no longer in me to lead these men, except to their doom. There are simply not enough at my call."

The silence thickened before Ursa's voice penetrated through. "The man I knew never permitted such thoughts entrance in his mind," she said thoughtfully. "The husband I married once vowed to defend his keep if he stood but he alone."

I'm not the man you knew, he wanted to say, a wave of new anger boiling up inside him. *I'm not the husband you married.* It was the doubt that threatened to drive him mad. He remembered his former self as a spectator might remember the performance of an acclaimed player upon a stage. That man once had a natural swagger when it came to battle, a confidence that could not be earned even by years of experience. His war tents were often riddled with his captains, sometimes even captains from other squadrons. They bent their ears upon his council as a professor's pupils might take in a lesson. Wide-eyed, interested, yearning for the knowledge he awarded them by the moment.

That he could not reclaim even a fraction of that prowess made him wish there were more furnishings to topple. But there was only Ursa, standing firmly as she always had, once more finding herself beside him in one of his darkest hours. Thus he held her with his eyes, no longer caring how strange it felt to do so. He had closed himself off from her centuries ago, and she him. But however difficult it was for him to recall what it was to lead an army, it was just as simple to seize the feelings he once had for her.

"You must forgive me," he said softly. "You were a good wife, Ursa, and loyal as the sun is to the morning. If ever I have caused you pain, I apologize from the deepest well of my heart. You never deserved to be treated so."

With that Ursa glided toward him and set a comforting hand upon his. He could not remember the last time her hands were so warm. "You speak as though you won't return," she said, not pleadingly, but curiously.

Sadness and urgency warred upon his hard face, and it was many moments before he spoke. "It is likely I will not," he said finally. The finality in his tone caused her lips to tremble, if only momentarily.

Keeping herself reserved, however much effort it took, she nodded resolutely. But she could not fight back the build-up in her eyes, now green orbs beneath shallow pools. She made as if to speak, but it was Orion who spoke again. "You know this mountain better than anyone," he said. "Should they breach our defenses, you must rally all within and take the secret ways out of Azgoth. For all their cunning, I do not believe the Fairies of Dridion are learned in the ways of mountains such as this. Not as much as you are, at least."

"Where would we go?" she said. It was all too evident to him now that she was straining to keep up her strength, fighting to hold back the tears glistening in her eyes. And she was doing an admirable job.

Orion contemplated a moment before answering. "Make for the plains of Medric," he answered, as if a long-sought answer had finally just dawned on him. "There are horses enough in the stables to bear everyone, I think. Some might have to double, but they are able beasts. Weight never seems to burden them."

Ursa slid her eyes away as if in thought, though her head remained still. "The plain of Medric," she said, as if to herself. "We will have to cross Reznarion for a time—"

"A short time," Orion broke in. "It would only be a half day's ride before the plains of Medric are upon you. The

Moroks defend their outlying lands as thoroughly as their king's keep. It would be best for Lucian to bandy words with them, seeing as how he sailed west with one of their countrymen. They are probably already aware of his cause; I do not doubt they will be welcoming."

"And if they are not?" said Ursa, sharply, but not hotly.

"We cannot afford such thoughts," he answered at length. He was beginning to realize what he was asking Ursa to do. Mortals were thought to be three thousand years dead—he might as well have been telling cadavers to rise out of their graves and waltz into Medric unchallenged. Fifty horses worth of them—sixty . . . "We must rely on Lucian," he said finally. "His account must be the one shared. If necessary, he may have to brandish the Key, but *only* if necessary. Mascorea's is a noble race, one that resorts to bloodshed when all other avenues fail beyond the point of success. You will not be met with hostility."

"And Lucian—"

"He will not understand. No doubt he will think this another one of my attempts to subdue him, another effort to prove that he is less than worthy to engage in confrontation, but . . . "

"He was never yours to command, Orion," Ursa interjected softly.

Orion looked into Ursa's eyes knowingly before he bent his own eyes away. "He will want to fight. I know. But he cannot. This task was given to me, and I will not risk its failure. Lucian is destined for greater things than whatever this battle will bring. I would see him far from it. Please. He is very dear to me . . . "

It seemed to take a great amount of effort for those words to leave Orion's tongue, but when they were spoken his shoulders slackened somewhat, and whatever hardness he may have once possessed seemed to leave him.

"Then I will see to it," said Ursa finally, and it was as though the sound of her voice woke him from a daze.

Not a word was spoken thereafter. Orion latched his stare with hers again, and a slight smile twitched at the edge of his lips. *You would have made a lovely queen,* he wanted to say, though he kept those words to himself. Taking her other hand in his felt as though he had set it above one of the hearths. Warmly she looked into his crystalline eyes. Her countenance was one of both pleasure and despair— pleasure for this moment similar to those they once shared in marriage; despair for knowing it could well be their last.

Yanking her toward him Orion kissed her madly. Though taken aback at first, Ursa meshed into the embrace with seamless bliss. Lifting her from her feet he spun her once, twice, remembering her scent, sweet and organic like rain-washed flowers, as the way she smelled when he first laid eyes on her in her father's grotto over three millennia ago. It had been there, oddly enough, where they shared their first kiss. As he set her down he could not help but realize— understand— that their last might have just concluded, there in the midst of Shír Azgoth in an empty room of cold stone. Longingly she looked at him, with the dreary countenance of one just waking from a pleasant dream.

Straightening her diadem, she could not help but smile despite the circumstances. Parting her lips, more voluptuous than even Orion remembered, she made as if to speak when a trio of winged messengers flew in with such haste that both of them gave a start.

Eap was the first to materialize into his human likeness, and when he did so he doubled over as if having run ten leagues without pause. The two at his back had shifted shape before Orion could even determine what kinds of birds they had been. Urgently he strode forward in front of Ursa, looking hard upon Eap and his companions inquiringly.

"Highlord Orion," Eap panted, arms dangling from having been spent as wings. "The Fairy host is in the mountain passes."

In the silence that followed, only the scratching pants and wheezes of the messengers were heard. Orion passed a wary gaze to Ursa, who had become rigid with fear. "Where?" he asked.

"Eastern ridge," Eap answered. "Their army must have forded the Elarian on the outskirts of the town of Drír and made their way along the Icebarrow into Riverwood.”

"If they are already in the passes then we must prepare the men for battle. How far from Ehrehalle would you say they are?”

"Probably twenty leagues at most," answered Eap without much certainty. "Only half of their sum had made the full climb out of Redwood when we glimpsed them.”

"How many?”

It was then that Eap's sallow face grew sullen. Through his beady, black eyes he stared grimly, and he released a deep sigh before saying, "At least five hundred.”

Ursa's initial whimper hung only on the edge of hearing. All else was silent. The crackling hearths blazed on. From where Eap stood Orion appeared as though a lean shadow before them, his eyes glinting with flecks of despair. "Five hundred," he said to himself, so softly that even he wondered if he had spoken aloud.

"They climbed the mountain stairs in waves," Eap said. "At first I thought them to have completely emerged. That was before another wave came into view. And then another. In ranks of fifty they appeared; ten ranks in all. Five hundred black-cloaked Dridioners that I would not have even known were there were it not for the meager light that shown off their faces.”

"Five hundred." Eap might as well have sent the butt of a spear into Orion's chest for the wind his tidings had driven out of him. Looking at Ursa one last time, he found that her face had again grown hard, not with solemnity but with determination, like a fire fighting to burn despite the rain. "You know what you must do," he said to her softly. With a subtle reluctance she bowed her head, and her diadem glinted in the light of the hearth. With that she turned and swept off, leaving Orion and the messengers to their business. *Goodbye, my love,* he said in his heart.

He remained silent until even his far-seeing eyes could no longer hold her image. "Five set out from Ehrehalle, yet only three stand before me," he said to break the heavy silence. "Where are Bons and Yewn?”

"Shot down, highlord," answered a scraggly-haired

messenger behind Eap's right shoulder, with more white in his hair now than red. His name was Conn—a red-tailed hawk when in disguise; a scrawny, gaunt-faced man in human form who perhaps did not outweigh an adolescent girl. "Right over the Riverwood," he continued. "They always liked that place; I reckon it's fitting they met their end there."

"They will be missed," said Orion heavily. "I am sorry for your loss." He turned his gaze to Eap when he said this, though his condolences were meant for all three present. Néjer was the other messenger, his gray-flecked beard bristly and his equally gray eyes as grim as the great-horned owl as whom he masqueraded.

"We'll avenge them," said Eap. "I don't care if I meet my end trying; we'll avenge them. If I have to pluck out a thousand eyes myself I'll do it."

Conn and Néjer had become riled, and mumbled encouragingly behind Eap as he spoke. *Good,* Orion thought. *The men will need some inspiration, especially the inexperienced ones. Five hundred . . .*

"If they travel all day, they will reach Ehrehalle an hour or so after nightfall," Orion began at length, reclaiming as much of a reserved tone as possible. "But they won't. It is a tiresome trek through the mountain passes, and their numbers will no doubt hinder them."

"Yet you speak from the standpoint of a mortal," reminded Eap. "These are Fairies, remember. Feathers would make more of an imprint on those dusty roads than theirs. They will channel through those alleys like a legged wind."

It was a moment or so before Orion spoke again, and a moment it was in which his hard blue gaze seemed to sear through Eap as though it radiated some sort of hazardous light. He was not upset with the messenger, but the information he shared. He knew Eap was right. The soldiers of Dridion were a perfect fighting assembly. A journey through the mountain passes—however long—would lay as much wear upon them as a descent down a flight of stairs.

"We will be ready," he said at last, though he was blatantly unconvinced. *Five hundred . . .*

"What would you have us do, highlord?" Eap asked, his stare having grown hard.

"Warn all those in your order," Orion answered at length. "Alert whatever knight or villager to cross your path as well. Tell them to spread the word that Dridion advances through the passes, and to be ready by nightfall."

After issuing moderate bows the three messengers parted, and Orion found himself alone yet again, with nothing on which to take out his aggression but the lone bench along the leftward wall. Declining to destroy the only furnishing left to the room, he sat wearily. Nerves and anxiety were beginning to make him feel as though he had already fought a battle. Thinking of the one that was to come . . .

It was not long before the din of quickly shuffling footsteps sounded again from outside the doorway, preceding the arrival of Aries and Leo. Orion felt a faint hint of relief flow through him, but it was not enough to rid him of the despair wrought freely across his face.

"What is it?" he heard the gruff voice of Leo say before he could distinguish his features.

"My friends," said Orion. "Eap has brought me ill tidings. Dridion has been unleashed, and is funneling through the mountain passes as we speak with an army of five hundred strong."

Aries's and Leo's only reaction was the exchange of a brief glance.

"Five hundred?" said Leo, more curiously than anything. "Last we knew they numbered no more than one."

"We were sorely misled," Orion answered plainly, then added after a moment's hesitation: "They have already passed through the Riverwood."

"Then we have barely a day to prepare," said Aries.

"Less, I think," replied Orion. "They travel swiftly. We must be ready by nightfall. Eap, Conn, and Néjer are informing all who come into their path."

"We ran into them on the way here," said Leo. "The

way they're going about it there will no doubt be chaos in Ehrehalle long before the Fairies come. How do you mean to approach this? Have you reached any conclusions yet?" Though as he said this he was surveying the toppled pawns on the floor with his dark and wary eyes.

Orion contemplated for a moment. "We now have archers enough to line the causeway over the doors," he said at length. "Fifteen men can stand abreast along its length, as well as three in each of the two battlements. Twenty-one archers in all, all with full quivers."

"And more arrows are being shaped as we speak," said Aries. "It will take many volleys to spend our entire sum."

Orion nodded. "We must make every one of them count," he said. "The higher ground is ours, and so we are fortunate. But our advantage can be lost quickly if our arrows go astray."

"And the archers," Leo put in. "Are they trained enough?"

"They have shown promise during my sessions," said Orion.

"And ours," added Aries.

"Camien and Bravos have reported the same," Orion continued. "They are far from marksmen, but they are all we have."

"Will you not fire with them?" asked Leo. "Your bow-work is deadliest of all, your arrows made to strike whatever target you wish brought down. It would be sensible for you to stand among the archers when Ehrehalle is stormed."

"I have entertained that thought as well," said Orion after a contemplative moment. "Perhaps you are right, Leo. The ground forces will be in able-enough hands . . . "

As Orion's words trailed off, Aries spoke. "Will you not employ the horses?" he asked. "We could storm through their numbers like a wave over a beach."

"Our number is yet too few," said Orion, "and we would lose many good horses—losses that we cannot afford. To them I have employed a more urgent task."

The room fell silent. It was Aries who was first to speak. "You would send the others away without proper escort?" he asked, with only a flicker of incredulity.

"If it means sending them far from the battle, I would," answered Orion firmly. "Ursa will lead them. She is strong of will and heart, and knows the innards of Azgoth better than even the Sages might. It is now her charge to see to the safety of Lucian. As long as he is out of harm's way, there is hope. This fight in which we are about to engage is to protect that hope."

As if by a trick of the light Orion thought to see a faint pallor come over Aries's face, but it was Leo's voice that drummed first. "And where would you send them?" he all but barked. "Down the back-roads of the mountain, I don't doubt; but that would lead them into Reznarion. It would be unwise to send the Keeper into Netherling territory with no one to defend him but gardeners and the like."

"It is to Medric that Ursa will lead them," said Orion resolutely. "It was for Adoram where Lucian's course was originally set; it will be to there he strives."

Leo became silent then, and fell in beside Aries whose golden head was bowed. "My friends," Orion continued. "These are the hours for which we were spared. We have seen to our charge until now; let us not see it abandoned because of the odds we face." Setting a hand upon each of their shoulders, he tried to appear as determined as he could. The looks his companions returned were searching and despairing, yet flecked with courage. "Wake the others," Orion continued. "Send them to the armories to see there are enough plates and mailed shirts to fit all those who will stand against Dridion. Tell them to see every sword sharpened, every shield able to bear the tremors of impact."

"It's the middle of the night," said Leo. "You would have them woken now?"

"Every moment from here is precious," Orion answered. "See this through. There is much to be done before the moon looks over us again."

As Aries and Leo made for the doorway, Orion thought to hear Leo's voice mutter faintly: "Let's hope not for the last time."

31

The Battle of Ehrehalle

Lucian stopped the pursuit as the day drew toward noon. Since dawn he and the Netherlings had been crossing Reznarion like a dense thundercloud, black and rumbling. Night-Treader led the wolfish assembly as though he were bred for that purpose alone, and, oddly enough to Lucian, they had no qualms following him. In truth, the race should have been halted at least an hour ago, but Lucian urged on those at his back with much verve, stressing the need for haste so much that he began thinking up new things to say.

When the gathering came to a standstill many of the Netherlings collapsed wearily. Consistent panting rose up from two hundred fanged mouths, filling the empty, sodden plain with a sound like a pulsating wind. Night-Treader was largely unfazed; Lucian thought he could have galloped another league or two if he wanted, but he did not regret allowing him rest. Looking behind him now for the first time since sunrise, he saw that Ren Noctis and the mountains around it were now faint and gray on the horizon. He had to bend his eyes to the utmost end of their ability to see in order to tell that they were still in view. There was nothing ahead of them as of yet, and perhaps would not be for many more miles. Every second that passed might as well have been a minute for the angst building up within him. He needed to get to Ehrehalle before Dridion struck. They all did.

As he stood peering out across the empty plain he stroked

Night-Treader's silky black mane absently. The stallion's hide was only barely damp, and if anything he seemed eager to resume the chase. Yet, what Lucian thought was eagerness may well have been anxiety, for Amarog emerged from amidst the Netherlings and approached on all fours.

"A word," Lucian heard his rasping voice say.

Rolling his eyes, he gave Night-Treader a final pat before joining Amarog off to the side. Here Amarog stood upon his hind legs, and Lucian once again took in his true height. He might not have been eight feet tall, as he originally thought, but he had to have been at least seven—a tower of fur and claws.

"My men grow tired," he said, his small, slit-like nostrils taking in whatever scent they had caught and looking out on the pitch gathering scattered across a chunk of the plain. "It's many leagues yet to the Red Peaks."

"We have to keep going," Lucian said plainly. "We can rest a while longer, but we have to move on soon if we're to reach Ehrehalle before nightfall."

"We'd need wings for that," said Amarog sternly. "It's been rumored that your kind uses great birds of transport to travel around their realm. Why can't you call upon *them?*"

"Because I don't know how." He might have been explaining why he could not open a locked door without a key. "For now our feet will have to do. You made the journey once pretty quickly. I'm confident you can do it again."

"We're hungry too," said Amarog, a bit more wryly than Lucian liked. "That horse of yours is looking rather fresh. What say you let us munch a bit? You Sages are fleet of foot, I hear. You don't need to ride upon a beast."

Excebellus was at his throat before he finished speaking. "If you even look at that horse in a way that I feel threatening, I'll kill you again. And this time I think I'll let you stay that way."

It took a moment for Amarog's posture to slacken, and when it did Lucian returned Excebellus to its scabbard. Though Amarog studied him grimly for several extended moments, the fire that began to kindle in his yellow eyes subsided. Lucian was beginning to like this new power of his more and more. Amarog, however, did not. That was as obvious as it could have possibly been. But he respected it—or seemed to, at least. Lucian felt he could ask no more than that. What was more, it was becoming evident that many of the Netherlings not only respected his power, but *him* as well. As he walked about he noticed many of their wolfish eyes following him, anxious to see what his next move would be. In a strange way he liked that too.

"There will be food enough when we get to Ehrehalle," Lucian said, as if an afterthought. "You want flesh? There will be plenty of it, trust me. Five hundred Fairies will march into Ren Talam. That's enough for you and your men to even have seconds."

Lucian had not realized, but those nearest him had listened in, and the word *seconds* began rippling through the lazing crowd.

Amarog wore a contemplative stare. "*Seconds*, you say? *Fairy* flesh. They're skinny, but probably very tender." He was talking more to himself than to Lucian, bringing a clawed finger up to his chin and thinking deeply. "But they'll have teeth too, no doubt. Won't be an easy meal to come by."

After a moment Lucian said: "It will if you're hungry enough."

Their pause had not lasted half an hour before the trek was taken up again. Night-Treader sounded the chase with a prancing whinny, and once more the black host thundered across the width of Reznarion, need and hunger the jolt that spurred them on.

* * *

There was not one knight who took rest since the calls of Aries, Leo and the messengers roused them from sleep hours before dawn. Though moderate curses had filtered throughout their number, they were content enough once out of bed and set to purpose. At least a dozen of them saw to procedures in the armory. Streph the Summit was among them, judging plates and mailed shirts as a shopper might a patch of vegetables. There were indeed enough to be had by all who would fight—a number now close to seventy-five.

The villagers proved most difficult to rouse. Early wake-up calls had rarely sounded in the vale of Dwén Marnié, and many eyed Aries and Leo incredulously as they all but yanked them from their sheets and the touch of their wives. When those who would fight were gathered, all else were instructed to follow Ursa's lead into Azgoth's lower levels accessible beyond the rightward corridor. By those seldom-ventured paths could secret passages be taken into the bowels of the mountain, some leading to the rear entrances of Ehrehalle facing Reznarion—that only few knew existed—others to the stables and several other frequently-used quarters.

When the din of despair and confusion dwindled, the men longed for at least some form of sound. The later portions of the morning and the entirety of the afternoon passed on virtually soundlessly. Knights hurried in and out of the Great Hall discussing one thing or another. How to properly bar the doors and the assurance of Lucian's safety—his presence assumed, though not ensured—seemed to be the top two priorities, but there were other things as well. Leo's main concern was the protection of Ehrehalle's stores. "It would be a great shame if the ale and wine casks were destroyed," his rumbling voice was once heard saying, "or the meat racks looted." In truth it would have taken a great deal of effort to even find the stores of Ehrehalle, as they were hidden down the rightward corridor and entered only by those who knew their location.

Orion spent a large deal of the afternoon speaking with his fighters outside the great doors. The archers he employed were first to speak with him, and with them he discussed the importance of each separate volley, as well as strategies regarding how and where to aim their arrows. They talked about wind factor and its effect on such things. Luckily for them, the storm that had raged during the night had lifted, but there were yet gray skies above that did not work to alleviate his concern for the conditions. Thus firing arrows into and against the wind became a prevalent topic.

With twenty-two archers as mentally prepared as they would ever be, Orion met with the fifty-three men who would comprise his ground force. It was decided that shielded spearmen would man his front lines, and for this duty he employed only his most able-bodied soldiers, men who could withstand a collision as readily as a tree withstands a hurricane. Thus Streph the Summit was chosen for their number, and Leo, it was determined, would stand beside him, for his shield was strongest of all. He became adamant about not holding a spear, however. "Lionsbane is long enough," he barked. "If I die it will be with him in hand, not some knife on a stick." Six other knights were given the duty of standing amid the men of the front line, along with five villagers among whom would stand Yinsed and other leathery-faced men of strong build and thick arms.

Five lines of—roughly—ten abreast would stand before the stairs of Ehrehalle when Dridion came. Orion only prayed that the archers would be able to not only lessen their numbers before they struck, but thwart the speed with which they advanced. It was a steep rise to the steps of Ehrehalle from the valley of Dwén Marníe, where the paths of the Riverwood emptied. Their climb would be slow enough, he determined, but then again slow for Fairies was perhaps top speed for a mortal man. *Five hundred . . .*

It was encouraging to Orion, at least, that it all seemed to be coming to a head before mid-afternoon. Speaking of the tactics he planned to employ not only prepared his men, but him as well. Yet discussing how to fight a battle and partaking in one were two very different things. He knew this. While none were *truly* ready, he could sense that a content air of preparedness—dare he think *willingness?*—was beginning to ruminate among them. There was no time to be afraid, only attentive. Orion dictated strategies and formations like the general he was when he commanded armies of thousands. Now he stood before the fractional squad among whom he would likely perish, and saw only courageous stares looking back at him.

All seventy-five were armored and readied before dusk. Spear-points, blades, and arrowheads were sharpened. Mail-shirts were fastened, plates were latched, and gauntlets were strapped over one-hundred-and-fifty wrists. No shield would allow Dridion easy purchase, no piece of armor would yield willingly to a Fairy blow.

It was a silent dusk. A grim dusk. A dusk darker than any one of them remembered. And nightfall was darker still. Storm clouds were indeed settling over the Red Peaks for a second consecutive night, and the wind was already beginning to pick up. The clinking of plates, the jingling of mail and the rough stamping of iron-shod feet were the only sounds heard outside the doors of Ehrehalle as Orion set his men into formation.

It seemed they stood peering into the deepening night for an eternity, at the black shapes of the adjacent peaks thrusting up toward the sky like mile-high spear-points. Every so often a flash of lightning would bring them alight for a short-lived instant. The third roll of thunder to drum across the sky preceded the fall of rain, and it was not long before the shower became steady, clinking off their plates and shields like an endless torrent of floor-bound jewels.

No one knew rightly how long they had been glaring through the darkness when lights began to kindle in Dwén Marnié. For a moment the dull-glowing, orange embers brought nostalgia to the villagers among Orion's ranks. It looked as though the village was alive again, as though some residents sought to enjoy a quiet night of reading or pipe smoking. But it was not the blaze of hearth that brought the village alight. Soon mounds of fire licked up like miniature mountains themselves, engulfing the thatch-roofed homes and little gardens so that they were lost to sight. In their glow a slew of slender black shapes were seen emerging out of the shadows and racing into sharp-edged lines. Dridion had come.

"Archers at the ready!" Orion ordered from the archway. In one sweeping motion the archers upon the wall were knocked and drawn. Against the pale-gray backdrop of the valley's rising smoke, the silhouettes of Dridion's army could be seen swarming the rolling hillside leading up to the great doors. Banners wove like shredded fragments of clouds fastened to posts, though Melinta's sigil of the white talons could not be made out in the darkness.

The front line of spearmen straightened. Leo felt Streph the Summit's muscles tense beside him, heard his shield-hand tighten its grip. Behind Leo in the second line Aries leaned upon his moonstone hammer casually, as though debating between ladies to dance with. But all the while Orion's voice was heard over the stamping and the rain. "Hold!" he cried. "Hold fast. The eleventh hour is upon us!"

From in front of him Aries heard Leo mutter: "Who will see the twelfth?"

The low-toned grinding of the Fairies' march ceased thirty or so meters from Orion's front lines. There in lines of ten across, which in black coils snaked down the hillside and out of sight, stood the chiseled, bright-eyed faces of Melinta's horde. Black cloaks shrouded them all, though between the folds their thin golden plates could be seen glinting in whatever subtle light they could reflect. Golden helmets flanked their faces also, sharp and pointed, an emerald in the center of each rising brim.

For a long instant the two armies held each other in stern gazes. The archers' arrows yearned for flight, but Orion had to consistently remind them to hold their fire. There may be negotiations yet. Maybe . . .

Sure enough a soldier from amongst Dridion's ranks came forward, carrying his king's banner and setting the wispy flag into the earth where it swayed slightly in the wind and rain. Removing his helmet he turned his fair-yet-grim face upon all who stood before him. He would have seemed a year or two Lucian's senior were it not for the bitterness in his bright eyes. Though slender, those nearest could tell that beneath his armor and cloak he was shaped as most of the Fairies were: lean and roped with slender coils of muscle. His voice was shrill and carried over the storm. "Folk of the mountain," he called, though it was clear he did not know who to address, the existence of these mountain folk being as obscure as it was. "Allegations have been brought upon you by Melinta son of Viridus, Fourth King of the realm of Dridion, and Keeper of the Emerald Throne in Deavorás. It is suspected that you are harboring a fugitive in your mountain hall. A thief of high caliber who has claimed Dridion property for his own . . . " As the soldier's words trailed off the men of Ehrehalle exchanged hard stares with one another. Leo grunted. The soldier continued. "But the King Upon the Emerald Throne is forgiving and just. He understands you cannot have known whom you welcomed among you as an equal. Thus his terms are as follows: release the fugitive into Dridion's custody. You can yet save the lands that remain to you. The village that burns below will be restored by the finest artisans and masons our realm can provide. No further destruction will befall your realm. Refuse and see your keep stormed and the fugitive taken by force. What say you?"

Silence. A gust of wind howled on its way by, dragging the rain with it diagonally across the night. The soldier stood facing the upright spearmen, a jagged wall of steel and flesh—looked up upon twenty-two glinting arrowheads, their shafts knocked and ready to soar. And it was the momentary flash of Orion's arrow that proved to be the last image that soldier saw on earth. The ground forces only heard it sear through the rain before it came to a thudding halt between the soldier's eyes. The initial blow threw the Fairy of his feet before he came to land upon his back a yard or so away. He would rise no more. *Four hundred and ninety-nine . . .*

A wave of shrill and furious cries rippled through the host of Dridion when they saw Ehrehalle's refusal still bobbing out of their companion's skull. Brandishing their polished spears and swords, the night was filled with the din of their chants and the stamping of their feet. Orion's front lines readied. Streph, Leo, and the others locked their shields together and planted their spears between the crevices. It would be a difficult task to break that line, difficult even for Fairies. But once it was broken . . . Their shoulders hunched and their fury rising, the host of Dridion raced forward and closed the gap.

The battle had begun.

* * *

Lucian felt as though he could reach out and touch Shir Azgoth when the Netherlings determined they could go no further without a drink. He could not have been keen to how badly they needed it until the race was brought to a halt for only the second time. There upon the edge of one of the Riveron's narrow arteries they collapsed and struggled for air. Even Night-Treader was quick to break for the river, though the stallion gave no inkling of weariness.

"Drink," called Lucian, dismounting and looking further ahead. Shir Azgoth stood monumentally before them, but he could not recall where the pathways were that cut through to its face. Without those pathways, he would have to lead his men into an elongated horseshoe around the range—another day's venture in itself at least, maybe two. Orion did not have that long.

The Netherlings lapped their tongues in the stream as if they wished to drain it dry. Lucian watched them, hunched like panting dogs at a waterhole, then turned his focus to Azgoth, as if by doing so a passage through would be highlighted for him. Yet there was no light other than a vein of lightning that rent across the blotchy sky.

After several sips from the stream, Night-Treader meandered back to him. "I know," Lucian said. "It's almost time. Don't worry." The stallion grunted. Lucian stroked his mane a time or two before he called out to Amarog and his men. "Finish up," he said. "Ehrehalle can't afford one more minute of delay."

Groaning and cursing the Netherlings rose, the ferociousness of their glowing eyes enhanced by the darkness.

"Amarog," Lucian called. It was a moment before he cantered forward, doing so with the sullen air of a child due to take his medicine. It suddenly dawned on Lucian that the answer to his shortcut through the mountains may have been among him all along. "You once led your men to Ehrehalle from Ren Noctis," Lucian said contemplatively.

The glow of Amarog's eyes gave light to the fur along his brow, but little else. He was a monster in every facet of the word, and yet Lucian's only chance at coming to the aid of Orion in time. "I did," he said noncommittally.

"And what paths did you take? Did you circle around the range or cut through?" Lucian received only rain and wind in answer. "Well?" he demanded impatiently. He hadn't the time for this nonsense. At this very moment Ehrehalle may have been getting rained on by more than just water.

At last Amarog opened his mouth to speak, but clamped it shut. His attention—as well as his mens'— was drawn to the gray-black skies over Azgoth. Lucian noticed it as well: the black shape of a raven swooping down from above. Trotting forward, Lucian raced to meet Eap as he touched down in human form.

"I thought you were fighting?" Lucian said nervously. What could Eap have been doing there? Had the battle already begun? A retreat already ordered? Or worse?

"I was," he answered in earnest. A deathly pallor came over his sunken face when he noticed the gathering in whose midst he now found himself.

"They're with us," Lucian said, trying to quell Eap's obvious worry. It did little, however, to alleviate his nerves. "What's going on at Ehrehalle?" Lucian asked urgently. "Has Dridion come?"

Lucian's voice seemed to have woken Eap from a daze. "They have," he said gravely. "I took up a sword myself, but found that my ability of flight would serve the men best. Here I meet you on my helpless errand to seek reinforcements, yet the lot you have in tow are the ones I wished to find. You have persuaded many, it seems." Eap looked ever more curiously at the gathering scattered along the stream before returning a searching gaze to Lucian.

"We set out before dawn," said Lucian. "This group is hungry. All we need now is a way through Azgoth. There isn't enough time to go all the way around."

A smile—strained at first—split the gaunt face of the shape-shifting messenger. "There are many ways through Azgoth," said Eap, squinting against the rain. Passing another glance left and right at the curious horde around Lucian, his smile became even wider. "They are with us, you say?" he asked. Lucian issued a curt nod. "You must follow me at once!"

Mad hope begun to fill Orion as volley after volley found purchase in Dridion armor. Depleted Fairy lines clashed with Ehrehalle's as a result, and it was little trouble for the stout and steadfast spearmen to repel them. At first . . .

Orion could not have been certain how many Fairies fell to their arrows, but it was not nearly enough to weather the advancing storm. Relentlessly they raced up the hillside, trampling their dead, and in some cases using corpses to launch themselves over Ehrehalle's front lines.

Once Ehrehalle's formation was breached and split, the unified tactics Orion had once stressed fell to the wayside. Some preferred the thrill of man-to-man combat over the structure that unified fighting required, but the majority had relied on that now-broken structure for their own survival. Now there was no choice.

Arrows continued to rain from the causeway, though Orion eventually leapt down with his swords in hand. "Hold the stair!" his men heard him calling. He knew the lines were broken, knew his men were falling by the instant. He had almost forgotten what it looked like to see a man die— the spray of blood, their blank stares as the knowledge of their demise resonated. Some died so quickly that there was not even a chance for them to realize their throats were cut or their heads were cloven.

"Hold the stair!" he cried over the cacophony. It was almost involuntary now. His need to command consumed him as much as his need to breathe. The deaths of his men would not be in vain. If the stair was held, there was a chance. If the stair was held, their deaths could be avenged. If the stair was held, Lucian would be safe . . .

Knights and villagers alike met their end holding that

stair. Fighting in its midst Orion watched as his men fought to triumph over the golden-plated doom that sought to break them. Aries leapt and twirled like a dancer, commanding his hammer with a beautiful concoction of power and poise, batting Fairies away with deft, two-handed swings. He heard Leo's gruff voice barking over the maelstrom more than he actually *saw* him, but that was comfort enough. "Come, Lionsbane!" he was wailing. "Let ring the lion's roar!" Beside him the hulking Streph the Summit threw Fairies aside as though he were a man playing a child's game. In random sections of the battle he glimpsed Camien and Bravos, bloodied and bruised, straining to keep up with the rapidity by which the Fairy lines were replenished.

It was an endless struggle. For every two Fairies smote it seemed four replaced them, and their numbers yet swarmed upon the dampened swards of the foothills. In horror he soon realized their hold upon the stair was relenting as the surge of the advancing horde gathered force. He might have had forty men left at his call—thirty, even. It was over. *As long as Lucian is safe . . .* he told himself. Spurred by this motivation, he slew two aggressively advancing Fairies with the spryness of his earlier years. That keep would hold as long as he drew breath. As long as he stood defending Ehrehalle, Lucian would be safe. Lifting his sword he let his voice ring over the din. "TO THE DEATH!" he cried.

That was when, as if in answer, the doors of Ehrehalle burst asunder from within. Splintered shards of thick oak flew out into the wind and were swept away. Those upon the stairwell ducked as massive shapes flooded over them. Sounds like wolfish howls emitted from the Great Hall as a tidal wave of shadow raged out into the night. Snarling, roaring, biting, and clawing, the images of the Netherlings came into focus. *How?* Orion thought madly. He did not care. He hadn't the time to care. He hadn't the men. Falling upon his back he let their entire number stream forth into the bloody throng, bounding out of the hall and into the wall of Fairies, toppling them like a relentless wind. Only this wind had fangs, and claws like knives, and bellies that yearned more than ever for flesh.

In their wake a horseman thundered into the blaring chaos. As his horse leapt from the doorway and into the crowd, Orion felt his hooves brush the blood-matted hair atop his head. It was a horse as black as the night itself had become, its hide shining as though made of obsidian itself. The horseman and his mount struck an impressive figure against the backdrop of the fiery mountains rising up from the valley below. Holding aloft a gold-furnished sword, the pommel of which was emblazoned with shining gems of blue and green, Orion needed no hint as to who had joined the fight. For a moment his mouth worked angrily as Lucian brought Excebellus down upon any who advanced. *How?* he wondered a second time. *How could I have let this happen?*

Rabidly the Netherlings stormed down the hillside, dismantling the Fairy lines with reckless abandon. After a while the consistency of ringing iron and steel was replaced by Fairy screams and Netherling snarls as the small band that remained upon the foothills tried to scamper off to whatever place could hide them. They were run down much too easily.

A fractional amount still tried to claim the stair, but the number yet at Orion's call stood strong enough to match them. Dridion's effort was short-lived, however, for when the Netherlings returned from Azgoth's bloody skirts, the Fairies fled by the only paths open to them—directly up the mountain.

"Follow them!" Orion ordered, brandishing one of his slender swords in the direction they were escaping.

"No!" Lucian called from atop Night-Treader. Orion stared at him curiously, at his blood-splattered face, weatherworn cloak, and charred and shredded tunic. Excebellus was no longer in his hand or on his person, but he seemed largely unscathed. Knight, villager, and Netherling alike did not hesitate a moment in heeding him. "Let them go."

"Nonsense," said Orion. "We have them running. Now we must strike!"

"There are others who would fight for Ehrehalle's cause,"

said Lucian plainly, passing a subtle glance to Azgoth's high peak yet lost in darkness. "It would be a shame to deprive them their piece of the fight."

After instructing a slew of Netherlings to follow in their wake, the remaining soldiers of Dridion were chased to the very summit of Azgoth where even Amarog's men cowered before the image of Pike, Marcie, and Nod. Scampering away as plates crunched and Fairies screamed, the Netherlings left those unimaginable blue creatures to their destructive business. Far below, amidst cries and songs of victory, Lucian thought to hear the voice of Pike—or it could have been one of the others' (there was little discrepancy among bólg voices)—carry on the wind:

"BÓLG FRIEND AL-WAYS!"

32

Fretful News

Gamaréa and Daxau were led out of the arena and loaded into separate carriages, and for many dark hours neither heard word of the other. It was to the fortress that Gamaréa was delivered, where countless guards bustled this way and that tending to whatever business was theirs. He was led directly through their quantity and funneled down a dark stairwell that spilled into the dank bowels of the old stronghold. There, in a small, lonely, desolate room, he was chained to the wall by his wrists.

No word of protest left his tongue, nor did he issue the slightest gesture as the guards bound him. He knew such actions were pointless. Gestures would have been answered with violence; words would have fallen upon deaf ears. So it was he remained passive until the very moment he was alone and left to ponder the events of hours past in the dark.

The treatment the guards had shown him was no less harsh than that which is shown to animals, and he was no animal. Yet he was so accustomed to the torment that at times he thought of himself as a sort of dog. This moment was no exception. His strength, which had been a popular topic across the lands of Dridion, could not avail him here, and he soon abandoned writhing against his bonds. His vain attempts only wasted the little strength to which he still clung.

It seemed to him that he remained forever lost in the void between life and death, between hope and despair.

Thus it was he bowed his head in grief, musing on how there is no time darker than that spent waiting to die. *If I am to die, I wish it would just be done with,* he thought angrily and anxiously. *Enough of this blindfolding and jailing and waiting.*

Thoughts that had remained dormant for a long while suddenly crept back into his mind. Emmanuelle was among them. Suddenly he missed her touch as though he felt her warmth just moments prior. Now that darkness was festering within his soul, he yearned to see her smile one last time, that smile capable of illuminating even spirits most troubled. His sanity fading, at times he thought to see her wading to him, as though the darkness itself were a grim ford across which she bravely sought passage. Yet those visions were all too quick to dissipate, and her spirit, if in fact it had been there at all, was summoned back to Parthaleon in earnest.

"I will soon join you, my love," he whispered to the darkness. "It shouldn't be long now."

In the early evening hours of the same day, Didrebelle was summoned to Deavorás for a "discussion of utmost importance" with his father. So it was he saddled a horse and rode casually into the white capital, and when he reached his father's hall he found him sitting at his long table in the company of his three councilmen yet again. Several servants were scattered about as well, but were bid to leave upon Didrebelle's entry, which, if he did say so himself, came fashionably late.

"My son," said Melinta, with an odd hint of—was it sadness?—in his voice. "Please, sit."

So it was Didrebelle reluctantly took his place at the table. A strange sensation of tension began to weigh him down, and he felt that an ill topic was about to be broached.

"Father?"

Melinta turned his eyes downward, but the scrutiny of his councilmen was unfaltering. "I would have a word," he began. "There is a matter most pressing at hand."

"What grieves you?"

The king sighed. "Word of the Key and its Keeper arrived here just this morning." Then Melinta stood, and cupping his hands together began pacing back and forth at the head of the table. "Not long after your arrival here, I sent a scouting party on the boy's trail. By then, of course, time had all but withered his trail away, and my soldiers had little to go by."

Didrebelle became suddenly grateful for the wind and other mechanisms of nature. Melinta's scouting teams were comprised of some of his best soldiers. If they were unable to determine Lucian's path, he would be surprised if anyone could. Was Melinta abandoning the cause? The very thought propelled Didrebelle's blood into a rampant flow.

"However," Melinta droned on, much to Didrebelle's dismay, "not three leagues from the determined location of the altercation in Ravelon, they managed to find a motley scattering of prints. That of a common boot-print, no larger than a school-aged boy's, was discerned amidst three separate pairings of iron-shod feet. The path they covered was extensive."

"Extensive you say?" said Didrebelle curiously. "You mean to say they coursed further than the forest?"

"Much further," answered Melinta sharply. "Cormac here had to pick up the trail, for it was far too broad for my men to follow on foot." Only then did Didrebelle notice the white hawk perched upon the sill of the open window to the right. Cormac's beady orange eyes pierced Didrebelle hotly as he swept down from the window and assumed his human form. A scraggly, gaunt man stood in his place, with stringy white hair scantily arrayed around his speckled egg of a head. Didrebelle had heard of these men before; men with the ability to take on an inhuman form so that they may blend in with their surroundings. In time gone by, many had been employed as spies and paid handsomely. He did not doubt that Cormac had proved invaluable to Melinta's cause. He could only imagine what he had seen.

"I followed the trail across Enorméteren, prince," said Cormac hoarsely, glaring at Didrebelle over a long, hooked nose, "and further still into the Red Peaks. Yet there they were lost among the rocks."

"The search has failed then?" Didrebelle instantly wished he had not employed such an excited tone. He hoped that it had passed off as one of frustration.

A devilish grin came upon Melinta's face just then, but it was Cormac who spoke. "Not nearly," he sneered. "The paths of the mountains are winding indeed, yet one betrayed the foursome's route. Never before have I flown so far from Deavorás, to where the mortal lands once prospered long ago. Yet an inkling told me to do so—and what a sight I saw! A lost dwelling there was, built within the face of storied Shír Azgoth, high and mighty. Within was a host of mortal men, all great in stature and grim of face. A village was strewn below across the vale, where civilian folk festered. And amidst their number, the boy—this Keeper of Fates— was counted. Before my eyes he brandished Kal Glamarig."

Didrebelle looked to the floor, for fear the look in his eye might betray his true feelings. "The boy is alive then?" he said as coyly as he could manage, attempting to keep his budding excitement as concealed as possible.

It was then that Melinta reached into the pockets of his robes and revealed something smaller than a fingernail. Beneath his long finger, he slid it slowly across the table. Didrebelle grasped hold of it, and when he opened his long hand he saw that he held the herald of all rubies—one of the last existing Rubbilius stones, mined by the Wizardrim from the ancient bowels of Zynys itself; the very stone that wrought the crest of the Key.

"After Cormac delivered the reports, I dispatched five hundred of my infantry to that little crevice in the mountains," said Melinta. "Their orders were to kill all whom dwelt within, burn the underlying village to ash, and deliver the boy to me dead or alive. What you hold in your hand is all that remains of the Keeper."

Didrebelle's heart plummeted. "And your infantry," he said, his voice openly wavering, "what of them?"

"Dead—to the last soldier." Melinta revealed this information so casually that he might have been talking about a fictional tale.

"So many soldiers? What fate could have met them there, I wonder?"

"There was one who returned, he and his horse half dead. The captain Faldrus, my most trusted mercenary, delivered that gem to me. Said he struck it from the Keeper himself after he smote him. Such an account perhaps has never been delivered from off a tongue of any race. Mammoth wolves, he went on; men with twice the strength of Moroks. Bólgs . . . "

His words trailed off, and though he spoke with much reserve, they seemed to echo through the cavernous hall. *Bólgs?* Didrebelle wondered. He had heard about those creatures, giant brutes said to domicile the summits of high mountains. But they seldom mingled with earthly folk, if at all. Melinta continued: "When Faldrus arrived he collapsed in my arms, and when he revealed the stone he spoke these words: 'Two of the three companions entrusted to the Key have been broken. The other is at large and perhaps far from here now.'"

Presently Didrebelle's heart raced feverishly in his chest. It couldn't be. It mustn't be!

"Regret filled his heart to tell me," continued Melinta, "and death had nearly devoured him so that I could hardly hear him speak. But there was one word that I could hear plainly through his inane whispers. It was your name. *Dragontamer.* What do you have to say to this, my son? What answer do you have for this claim of treason against you?"

How?

Didrebelle feigned an offended expression. "You would trust the words of a dying soldier—whose senses have all but left him—over those of your own son?"

"I held Faldrus most dear!" Melinta scoffed madly. "He was like a son to me, and was once like a brother to you. He was not just any soldier."

"Yet his dying senses are alike to all. Now is not the time to be unreasonable."

Melinta's eyes filled with suspicion, as though he were

beginning to doubt that which he so fiercely believed. "But to name you above all others," he said contemplatively, and the anger once present in his voice nearly faded altogether. "You, whom he has not seen in years upon years."

Silence had fallen momentarily before anger flashed once more in Melinta's eyes. "Something does not add up."

Didrebelle thought quickly. "It is said that many images race through the mind as one dies. Faldrus and I were inseparable in our youth. Perhaps a glimpse from our past came to his mind as a final thought."

Melinta waved his hand dismissively, his expression as of one who has sucked on a lemon. "Enough of this talk of senses. The fact of the matter is that an issue of trust is at hand."

"An issue of trust indeed, but it should not include your trust in me or mine in you. We are one, joined not only by blood but by purpose. I would see the Key return to its rightful place, and the,"—a burning sensation coursed through his throat— "death of the Keeper has added practicality to its retrieval."

Uttering the very admission of Lucian's death nearly tore a hole through the entirety of his spirit.

Melinta stooped over the table, resting on two weary arms. Over his face, his pent black hair flowed. He seemed broken and disheveled, wrought only of pain and fear. In a strange way, Didrebelle almost pitied him. But when his father's eyes peered through the willows of his drooping locks, Didrebelle saw nothing but vengeance in them.

"Spoken like the true heir of Dridion," he said proudly. "Ever have I longed to hear you say those words."

Didrebelle beheld the gem in his hand one last time before clasping his slender fingers around it. "The Key, however, will not simply grow legs and stroll into Deavorás. I will be off, then, and try to find what is left of it."

"No," said Melinta quickly. "Tarry a while. There will be an event tomorrow that I would not have you miss."

Didrebelle returned a confused glance. "Event?"

"Indeed. The execution of the Morok, of course."

Again Didrebelle's heart ceased to beat for a moment.

"Tomorrow?"

"Yes indeed. Noon, I think. Why, the gallows is being prepared as we speak."

Concealing his anxiety, Didrebelle inhaled deeply. "Very well, then. I can postpone my venture until the following day."

"I would ask that you stay, though I admire the spirit you show in this matter. I had not expected my men to meet such adversaries. The others will be demoralized in learning of their demise, and time will be needed to raise enough resources to launch a full-scale campaign into the Red Peaks and ultimately into Medric. Besides, we must take time out of these troubled days for a bit of fun. Allow yourself some pleasure while there is pleasure to be had. At least the Morok's hanging will afford the men some excitement."

"As well it should. I must go, then, and tend to matters in Cauldarím. If the Morok is to be executed at noon, the guards must be properly instructed."

Melinta laughed. "Your father's son indeed! Always one step ahead. Will you be off now, though, or can you stay? They will be mounting beloved Faldrus on the pyre shortly."

"My prayers are with him, Father," replied Didrebelle. "He was an honorable soldier, who served his country loyally. But I must go."

"Indeed, indeed."

With that Didrebelle turned and stole away, blind to any method that would calm his thoughts. Yet no matter the cacophony raging in his mind, two thoughts held steadfast: Lucian was dead, and Gamaréa would be quick to follow if he did not take action. Quickly.

33

The Gallows

The rancid smell of death hung in the dust-filled air. From within the darkness beyond his cell, the low droll of solemn songs reached Gamaréa's ears. Too weak to take up a verse, however, he merely stared blankly at whatever portions of his cage not cast in shadow, and if a thought managed to cross his mind it was of his fairings in the arena. These thoughts, at least, deterred his mind from events soon to come, and offered him some fleeting solace.

The memories replayed for him in a whirlwind of images, but none were more vivid than his clash with Ignis. Like a fresh wound, the beast's touch seemed to linger on his body even now. As though ringing up just outside his door, Ignis's horrendous cries remained fixed in his memory with all the verve they once possessed: his hoarse, trumpeting wail as he ascended like a rocket; his tremendous dying bellow, sad and shrill.

At least I will be left with that, he rationalized in his chains. *At least I managed to rid the world of* some *filth.* Yet the feeling coursing through his soul was nothing like defiance, in spite of the thought that Ignis was killed by his hand. Throughout his person, it was anxiety and nervousness that reigned supreme.

Many questions began haunting him down in those low dungeons. Where was Lucian, and was he even alive?

Yes, of course he is. He is stronger than you give him credit for, said his heart.

You would be foolhardy to believe a son of eastern

villagers could weather the perilous roads between Ravelon and Medric, alone and unguarded, his mind retorted.

He is a brave boy.

Go on, it is well past time to apply the past tense. Lucian was *brave. He* was *stronger than you* gave *him credit for. You know he is dead. You cannot deny it. They broke through your defenses. The Fairy let him go. You failed. Failed. FAILED! Once a failure, always a failure. Have you learned nothing? They were right to scorn you. You are not worthy to be considered among Mascorea's people. He trusted you. He trusted you! They all did . . .*

"ENOUGH!" It was darker than he remembered, if that was at all possible. Outside he heard the sullen hum of the prisoners' songs cease abruptly as his voice echoed down the avenues of cell-riddled corridors beyond. Bent and filled with grief, he lurched forward in his chains and bowed his head atop his chest, weeping openly. "I'm sorry, alright? I'm sorry for everything . . . "

It hurt to cry. With his outstretched arms and his expanded diaphragm, every deep heave of breath sent a new wave of pain through him. Yet that was all forgotten when he heard a voice say, "There is nothing to forgive."

Startled to attention, he bolted upright. The voice came from directly in front of him, and in the near-pitch darkness he managed to see only the subtle shape of Didrebelle not two feet away, shrouded in a dark cloak.

Gamaréa began stammering. "How . . . when . . . "

"You were asleep," answered Didrebelle, his cracking voice betraying the moroseness he tried to conceal. "And dreaming of something dreadful, I imagine."

"I didn't even hear you come in."

"My stealth can be unprecedented when I need it to be." Even in the darkness Gamaréa could see the smug little grin on Didrebelle's face.

Having shaken off their wariness, the prisoners took up their sorrowful songs again.

"What comes of this mission now, brother?" asked Didrebelle quietly, his voice straining to keep the heaviness he felt at bay.

A glacial silence fell. Outside, the prisoners' songs drolled low yet true. Didrebelle's question opened Gamaréa's mind to the finality of this moment. This really was the end. It was a harsh realization, the thought that he may never see a sunrise again, that he may never take another sip of water. When only moments ago he believed there was nothing dear to him in Medric, the thought of not walking the little roads of Titingale filled him with anguish. His heart sank faster still at the thought of Tartalion, who knew nothing of the obstacles they faced since Elderland. How would he receive the news of his failure and death? And ever the thought of Lucian weighed on him heavier than the rest.

"You must go and do what I could not," replied Gamaréa sullenly and at long last. "Use that stealth of yours to get yourself out of Dridion, but never forget what happened here. You must find Lucian—"

"But—"

"Find him and lead him to Medric. He will be safe there, for as long as Détremon stands, though I fear war will reach Adoram sooner than Mascorea thinks. Carry my story with you. Tell them of the perils of Cauldarím and the destruction of Ignis. Mascorea must know the beast lies in ruin, and that the gates of Parthaleon stand unguarded. If Lucian's deed is to be done, it must be done with haste."

"My friend—"

But he would not hear Didrebelle. Purpose swelled within him like a great fire. The more he spoke of it, the more he realized that there may yet be hope after he was gone.

"There is no time for soft words, my friend! You must go, and keep my desires close. Never forget what happened here. Keep it with you always."

Didrebelle looked upon his friend one last time, who bound by his chains would have appeared broken and defeated were it not for the new determination in his voice.

"Gamaréa, there is something I must tell you," he began, when suddenly he heard the great door above slam open and the voices of guards coming down the towering stairwell.

"There is no time," said Gamaréa sadly. "It was an honor to have known you, my friend. Countryman or not, you have been more than a brother to me. If there is truly something called eternity, I will remember you for its duration."

A slow tear coursed down Didrebelle's fair cheek. His lips parted as if to speak, but whether for the sorrow overtaking him or the quick advance of the guards, he was unable to give any response but a sharp nod. Waiting until the last moment to make himself scarce, Didrebelle leapt into a high corner of the cell where he clung to the wall like a spider, and was devoured by the shadows. Then a force of five guards bombarded the cell, dressed as though they were going off to war. Some carried spears, though all approached him warily. Yet when they unbound him he crumpled to the floor, famine and thirst and utter weariness having taken hold. It took two of them to bring him to his feet, and more still to wrap him in an old cloak.

When it was done they passed with him through the cell and out beyond the channels of the dungeon. Once he was sure they were out of sight and range of hearing, Didrebelle alighted upon the ground like a feather, and followed at a careful distance. Upon the closing of the door atop the stairwell, the prisoners' again took up their hymn.

The carriage trudged slowly through the white-stone streets of Deavorás. The alleys were riddled with civilians. Those holding the front lines nearest the road stood unyielding, while those behind scratched and clawed for a better view of the prisoner as he stood chained in the back of the wagon on his way to the gallows. There were some who threw stones. Though the vast majority aimed poorly, there were some who managed to hit him. Sometimes residents of overlooking apartments chose to cast old pottery or other household items from their balconies. By time the carriage came to a halt at the foot of Gallows Hill, Gamaréa had suffered several lacerations to his face and chest, and his left eye was nearly swollen shut from having been struck by one of the heavier stones heaved at him.

When the march finally ended, it took five armed

guards to escort Gamaréa to the top of the hill where the gallows waited. The mob, which had to be thrown back and reprimanded several times—even in the short time it took to reach the platform—finally adhered to the guards' orders and allowed them narrow passage. Angrily and anxiously, the assembly of harsh voices rose like storm-tossed waves as the bannermen of Deavorás ascended with Gamaréa to the platform. There in a massive wooden throne—no doubt constructed by Melinta for purposes such as this—sat the king with his thin, gold band of a crown, waiting in his robes of emerald and white.

The guards who escorted Gamaréa to the stand parted, and as they fell back into the sea of onlookers, the hangman came to appear at Gamaréa's side. He was a harsh-looking Fairy, with a stern face and blank eyes, and he looked at Gamaréa as though he had caused him an immortal lifetime of pain. In two swift movements, the noose was applied and tightened. Then the hangman went to stand by the lever that would send Gamaréa to his death.

Melinta swaggered forward from his makeshift throne, unwinding a large scroll, from which he read to the anticipating crowd:

To be executed this day at noon: Gamaréa, son of Gladris, Morok of Medric (this received ear-splitting jeers), *resulting from the offenses of: Disobeying the king's direct order; attempted assassination of said king; and destruction of royal property* (Gamaréa could only assume Melinta was alluding to the beasts he slaughtered in the arena).

"Forgiveness has never been a cog upon which the wheel of Dridion turns," Melinta added, casting the scroll aside. "Ill deeds must be punished." Turning and heading for his seat, Melinta nodded to the executioner. "Proceed."

It seemed as though the platform gave way before Melinta finished uttering his order. Gamaréa plummeted rapidly, with enough time in that split second to hope for the mercy of a broken neck so that he would be spared the slow agony of death by strangulation. He closed his eyes—

And smashed hard upon the ground below. Had the

rope been flimsy? The noose was still tight around his neck, but only a three-foot strand of it was still attached. A commotion ran through the crowd. Confusion began to build. Melinta and all those still on the platform hadn't any clue what the fuss was about, or that there was even anything wrong.

The near twenty-foot drop knocked the wind out of him. He was surprised that he had even survived the fall in his weakened state, yet even more astonished to find that he was unscathed. Though his ears were ringing, one sound became clear: the thundering of advancing horsemen leapt over the din from somewhere to the east. Nervously the crowd began to separate as though the earth itself was shifting beneath them, and in time a hooded rider pummeled through their ranks with reckless abandon.

Suddenly he threw back his hood, and it was as though a sharp light had emerged into the gloom. Didrebelle peered defiantly from horseback, his great bow raised and loaded, though none were prepared to oppose him just yet. He was leading an empty-saddled bay at his side.

"Need a ride?" he called amidst the frenzy.

Melinta rose from his throne, cold fury in his eyes as he watched his son's betrayal unfold in front of them. "It cannot be!" he called incredulously. "It cannot be!"

Just then a swordsman raced to subdue Gamaréa, but Didrebelle took him down with an arrow to the throat.

"Now would be as good a time as any!" he called, locking in another arrow.

Gamaréa sprung up, and mounted the horse with all the strength he could muster. Together now, up and over the winding road from Gallows Hill, the pair of horsemen sped along.

Their flight was tireless, and once the hilly roads spilled out into the open plains beyond, their horses gathered unnatural speed. Gamaréa's bay raced beside Didrebelle's, and when the Fairy realized Gamaréa was looking at him questioningly, the smug grin for which he was famous crept back along the edges of his lips. He wanted to thank him, to say something. Anything. But he could hardly even hear himself think with the wind roaring past them as it was. Only one question remained. *How?*

Yet suddenly Gamaréa turned his mind to more pressing matters. Green-feathered arrows began raining all around them. Melinta's guard was giving chase as though it was the only thing they were born to do.

"Riders!" shouted Gamaréa over the maelstrom of the stampede-induced wind. "They are gaining!"

Didrebelle turned quickly to survey them, then spun back to face the road ahead. "Ten of the king's guard," he said. "We will not be able to outlast them."

"Then we must—"

But Gamaréa was unable to conclude his statement, for it was in that moment that Didrebelle leapt impossibly atop the saddle of his racing steed and began firing arrows of his own at the advancing guard, balancing himself as though the horse was at a standstill. Didrebelle's bowstring thrummed at will. Arrows whistled away in rapid succession. Rider after rider fell. And, despite the difficulty of his efforts, Didrebelle merely swayed as if balancing himself on a narrow ledge. Eight of the ten were shot from their mounts. The remaining couple fell back and simply watched as their quarry shrunk into the distance.

The look Gamaréa gave Didrebelle as he settled back into his saddle was one of incredulity, perplexity, fear, and awe, and all he could say was, "You missed a couple."

34

Aftermath

From atop the rain-and-blood-drenched stair, Lucian peered out into the gray predawn. Shortly after the men of Ehrehalle had declared victory, he dismounted Night-Treader and took to scouring the field of battle. There he saw terrible things, things he could never have prepared himself to behold. Regardless how daunting the Fairies seemed in life, in death they appeared as innocent and fragile as boys of his own age. A large portion of Dridion's dead were left featureless by the Netherlings, lying in mounds of crumpled plates and shredded flesh. Though many had fallen to the sword, it was evident whom Aries's hammer had undone; many lay with saucer-sized, ram-shaped craters in their golden torsos.

At one point he stopped halfway down the first fold of the hill delving into the valley. There the great amount of blood and rain that had been spilled made the ground marshy. Lucian felt his boot sink two or three inches into the earth a time or two, watched as a bubbly, pale-red substance oozed out and worked to engulf his toes. That was when he turned away. The thought of squishing through liquid that had once allowed a body to operate unsettled him to no end—the sight of one more pale-faced, wide-eyed corpse he was sure would unravel his innards.

It was silent now as he stood leaning before the great doors—or rather where the great doors should have been. Remnants of their steadfast, oaken faces still lingered in scattered areas near and around the stairwell, but the entrance to Ehrehalle was now a gaping archway that opened to a cold and empty hall. The rain let up to a mere drizzle before stopping entirely, yet somehow the fires in Dwén Marnié did not manage to subside.

The banners of Dridion were still planted in random sections of the battlefield, tethered emerald cloths on golden posts that flapped in the passing breeze, upon which the smell of burning wood and other things carried. Steam rose in wispy arms from where the blood was settling into the earth. Among the dead walked the sullen, gray-clouded survivors of Ehrehalle's ranks, along with the hunched and skulking shadows of Ren Noctis's wolfish brigade. Not a word was spoken for a long while. Occasionally Lucian heard Night-Treader's whinny somewhere close by, but he could not see him. There was too much smoke and steam for him to see anything that was not within a stone's throw of the stair.

But he could hear, and it was not long before he wished he had been stripped of his ability to do so. He had heard children crying before, older and younger than himself. In Amar he had even heard a grown woman cry every now and then. But to hear a man weep—to see a man doubled over and beside himself with grief—was something that worked to tear his heart from his chest. Men of the village comforted those who had suffered losses. Fathers knelt beside fallen sons, and sons their fallen fathers. Some clutched a dead friend or brother in their arms as if squeezing them would bring them back . . . This was part of the reason Lucian stayed as far away as he could. Had they been alive, or perhaps even moments dead, he might have been able to save them. But he had quickly learned the limits of his power. Ehrehalle's fallen were too far gone for even him to recall by the time he reached them. A sense of inadequacy this overwhelming he could not remember ever feeling before.

He could but lean against the stone siding of the upper stair with his arms crossed. It was not long before Orion found him this way. Lucian saw him in his peripherals since he first leapt upon the stairwell, but he never turned his gaze upon him until he was certain that it was he Orion sought.

"Are you hurt?" Orion's tone was much less severe than Lucian had anticipated. If he did not know any better, he might have thought he heard a touch of concern in his voice.

"No," Lucian answered absently. He had paid a quick glance to the field again before answering. Looking away and cursing his own curiosity, he bowed his head solemnly. To his surprise, he felt a gentle touch upon his shoulder. Orion's face hosted a bruise near his left eye, and was crusted here and there with blood that was not his own. The scaled shirt he wore beneath his still-shining breastplate was torn through just under his right shoulder, the folds of which were lined with blood that *was* his own. His auburn hair was frizzled and matted, as of one having just woken from a nightmare.

Lucian expected a lecture, expected a reprimanding filled with a list of all the wrongs Orion believed him to have committed. Instead Orion handed him something. "You dropped this," he said, as though he were returning Lucian's wallet. Excebellus was largely unscathed—dirt-smudged along the guard and blood-smeared along the blade, but unscathed.

"I crossed swords with a Fairy and lost my grip on it," Lucian answered, studying the blade as if seeing it for the first time. It truly was a gorgeous piece of weaponry—a work of art made gold and steel. Then his look became grave, for upon the pommel he noticed that the ruby was missing, an empty crevice remaining where it once had been. "That won't be easy to replace," he remarked in passing.

"Yet I think there are other things more difficult," said Orion as if to himself. Had his voice not drawn Lucian's attention to him he would have missed the sidelong glance he passed beyond the stair.

It was a long while before Lucian spoke. "What are we going to do about this?" he asked. Corpses littered everywhere from the stairwell to the very base of the foothills.

"The men work to gather our dead," said Orion stiffly, as though piecing together a complex puzzle while being handed the fragments. He was about to speak again when Lucian cut in.

"How many?" It was a mechanical question. He did not truly desire to know the answer. One casualty would have been too many. Looking out upon those left to roam . . .

"Thirty-three of our own." Orion's voice was hard, though a face more sullen Lucian had never seen. "The count is yet final, though."

Wind frisked through the solemn silence before Orion spoke again. "Dridion's dead will take longer to gather than our own." He was looking out to the field where men were searching the destruction. "We will use the fires of Dwén Marnié to burn them, I think. It would not be fit to build them their own mounds. We have men enough now to gather them, and some wagons in the lower levels of Ehrehalle, if I remember correctly. It will be hard work, but we will see it done."

Lucian almost asked where the others had gone, but he closed his mouth. The thought of Jadyn seemed to still him. If he could have had one wish it would have been that she was as far away from there as possible. But not knowing where she was disquieted him more than the thought of her being close by. "Where are the others?" he asked as firmly as he could. Trying to mask his quickly-mounting grief only made him sound weary. "Ursa and the rest."

"In the lower levels," said Orion. "Ursa had instructions to lead the rest to the Medran border should Ehrehalle be breached. Since no Fairy made it through, I trust that they are still there." And that was where Jadyn would be.

"All accounted for?"

"Unless someone snuck out they are all accounted for, to my knowledge at least. Though how am I to know, truly? It seems even my eyes have not been so keen to wanderers of late."

It was a jab, Lucian knew, though Orion's tone suggested that he was nowhere near as furious as Lucian had expected him to be.

"I will have my answers, Lucian Rolfe," he continued after a momentary silence had once again passed between them, though there was no wryness in his voice. "Soon enough. I knew there was more to you than I thought upon our first meeting, but I did not know I would be right. Never mind that now, however. We've quite a mess to clean, and dawn is near."

There were indeed a large stock of wagons stored within the lower levels of Ehrehalle—twelve in all, to be exact. From an opening not far down the rightward road from the stair they issued out in single-file. The depth and storage capacity of the keep never ceased to amaze Lucian. Magic mountains were indeed a phenomenon yet solved. Even those who dwelled within them accepted the characteristics of the mountain rather than understood them. Teams of horses were brought out from the stables and hitched to them before the stairs of the Great Hall, though their passage along the water-and-blood-logged foothills was not easy. Wheels often got stuck—the carriages beneath which they sat so loaded with armored Fairy bodies that they sometimes sunk two to three inches into the earth. The slow and hindered trudge certainly helped the descent down the hills, however. Otherwise the wagons would have gathered too much speed and worked to overrun the teams charged to bear them.

The Netherlings were more than helpful loading the carts; many were strong enough to carry two or three bodies at a time as if they were tidying a child's playroom. Fairy weapons that were not destroyed were taken from their persons. At one point Orion ordered a wagon designated to haul the loot alone. Golden swords, dagger-bladed spears, bows of strong make—perhaps yew, or something stronger—and hundreds of arrows were carted off to be sorted. They found little of worth as far as their armor went. Those who had crossed swords with Ehrehalle's ground forces had found their plates rent by sword, spear, and hammer. Those who met the Netherlings . . .

A score of Amarog's men stationed themselves amongst

the still-roaring flames of Dwén Marnié, where they took to unloading the wagons as they approached. There most of the wooden houses had already collapsed, burning in great mounds that sent up plumes of thick smoke. In time Dridion's dead fueled it further, fed by Netherling, knight, and villager alike. For a time Lucian was with them, standing amidst the carriages and partnering with a knight or a wolf in order to swing a Fairy body into the flames. But he could only sustain his wits—and the smell—for so long.

It was sometime around mid-day that Lucian returned to Ehrehalle. He had no way of knowing. Minutes and hours seemed to have jumbled themselves together since he set out for Ren Noctis a night ago. Folk had started to gather in the Great Hall. Torches had been lit along the wall, though the light they provided was eerie at best. A very distinct chill hung within Ehrehalle, a chill to which not only the fading seasons contributed. Pale and frightened faces turned to Lucian as he walked through. Women with red-brimmed, glossy eyes looked at him imploringly; children perked up their heads and turned them sullenly away just as quickly when they realized he was not their father or brother. All would keep their eyes fastened to the gaping doorway, though many searches would turn up empty.

His room offered little solace. Not even lighting the hearth caused the dreariness within to subside. *All those dead . . .* he thought dismally. He had never seen so many corpses in one place. *All because of me . . .* In the looking glass he was afforded a vivid picture of himself. By all rights he was a filthy, disgusting mess. The travel cloak he wore was still wet upon the lower folds and crusted with mud, blood, and the Sages knew what else in random spots. His hair was unkempt to such an extent that he was positive he would never be able to get it presentable again. A splash of blood—whose, he did not know—was smeared across his forehead in wispy tendrils, and some of his own was caked beneath his nose. It had been broken once, he remembered. Someone or something had hit him. It might have been the butt of a spear or the pommel of a sword. He remembered feeling two sharp, instantaneous jolts of pain:

one when his nose broke, the other when it had somehow repaired itself. *Oh yeah,* he remembered suddenly. *Healing and what not.* His green tunic was slashed across the chest, revealing the mailed shirt he wore beneath. His fingers were so bloodstained that a stranger would have found difficulty determining their natural hue. A mess. But he was a living mess, at least. Solemnly he remembered there were thirty-three who would not come home.

Unlatching his sword-belt made for somewhat easier breathing. He had not realized how tightly it had been wrapped around his waist. Stretching and grimacing, he brought a hand up to his mouth to stifle a yawn. *I could use a bath,* he thought longingly. He felt as though some heated water would work wonders for the aches and pains that were beginning to settle in. The only thing keeping him from taking a bath was the fact that he knew the whereabouts of none besides the Luminos. *And I'm not going anywhere near that thing again . . .*

His attention was drawn to the doorway where he heard the light shuffling of approaching footsteps. Ursa looked magnificent when she burst in, looking as startled to see Lucian as he was to see her; though they were no doubt startled for different reasons. Ursa's eyes fell upon Lucian as if she had half-expected his bedroom to be empty. Lucian's eyes took in only her beauty, beauty he never for a moment thought she possessed. In a well-fitted gown she stood before him, studded with jewels along the low-cut lining just beneath her shoulders. Sweat glistened off of her from chest to neck as if she had been running.

"Lucian," she said coolly, though a hint of surprise was definitely present in her tone. "I heard rumors that you had made your way into Ehrehalle, but I had to see for myself. Are you alright?"

"I will be," said Lucian, none too convincing. Somehow he felt nervous in front of this new display that Ursa boasted. He was taken so aback by how stunning she appeared that he barely passed her a look.

"Are you hurt?" she asked, gliding toward him and running a spindly thumb over his lip. She sucked her teeth. "A broken nose," she said, grimacing.

"It was," Lucian answered softly.

"You reset it?"

Lucian laughed silently. "You could say that."

A brief twitch of her eye suggested that she did not entirely know how to take that, but she left it alone. Looking away dismally, she said, "What of the others?"

"Thirty-three fell," said Lucian heavily. Ursa's eyes widened and locked with his again, her thin eyebrows raised to sharp points. "Orion survived," he hastened to add. "He's out beyond the stair tending the dead."

"Thirty-three," she repeated, speaking as though to herself. She opened her mouth as if to speak several times before finally asking, "How many of Ehrehalle's?"

Lucian's response was stiff. "I counted five knights. I think most of the casualties were villagers, I'm sad to admit."

Ursa's hand was over her heart in an eye-blink, as though the very words he had spoken stabbed her. Her lower lip trembling, she bowed her head sullenly. "The families," she said contemplatively. "The poor families. There will be many pyres built in the days to come; that is certain."

Lucian looked away himself then. The remorse he was already feeling began to grow heavier, and a sickness overcame his stomach so that he almost sought a chair. *All because of me* . . . He heard Ursa sniffle lightly, and when he looked he saw a lone tear trickle down the pale length of her soft cheek. "I thought you would be among them," he heard her say. "Orion ordered me to lead all those who would not fight to Medric. When I came seeking you . . . when I saw this room empty . . . "

"It's over now," Lucian muttered, though Ursa's voice carried over him.

" . . . I knew that you had gone," her voice was heavy and tear-broken, despite her best attempts at resolve. "I knew that you had left for the city."

"I did what needed to be done," Lucian said at length. "Without Amarog and his men, I don't even want to know what would have happened. There'd be a lot more than thirty-three dead, that's for sure. Dridion brought five hundred Fairies through those mountains."

He had seen Ursa's eyes flare with a blend of recognition and disdain upon the mention of Amarog's name. "Amarog is here?"

"Somewhere out there, yeah. His allegiance, along with those at his call, turned the tide of this battle."

Ursa tapped the tips of her fingers together in thought, though the look she bore was of grave anger. It appeared as though she had thought of something to say when Lucian asked the question whose answer was dearest to his heart. "Where are the others?" he said, though he was not truly certain if he wanted the truth. "The ones you were to lead to Medric. A friend of mine was with them, I think."

"Some stayed below," Ursa answered. "Most flocked to the Great Hall when we learned the fight was through."

He had not seen her there, nor she him. He was certain she would have gotten his attention had she seen him passing through. Nodding to Ursa and issuing a less-than-half-hearted smile, he turned away for the hearth.

"If you need anything—" Ursa began.

"I'm alright for now." He did not intend for his voice to sound as cold as it did, but the maelstrom of emotions he had warring within him stiffened not only his posture but his mood. He saw Ursa's shadow upon the wall issue a faint bow before she turned for the door.

She stopped there and idled against the doorframe. Longingly she looked down the corridor before saying, "You did a brave thing, Lucian Rolfe. The weight of the dead is perhaps the greatest weight of all; alleviate it with the knowledge that, because of you, they fell victoriously."

Lucian only blinked in response. He was too weary to retort or speak his mind—too hurt to tell her that thirty-three men dead was too many for his conscience to bear. He felt her presence vanish before he saw that she was gone. In the firelight he removed his tunic and mailed shirt and let them fall to the floor where he stood. There was nothing on him. Not a scratch. That is not to say he had not been struck. At one point he had been certain that a blow from a Dridion cudgel cracked a rib or two, but there was not even a bruise as evidence. To this he could only shake his head. At times he forgot what he was, mainly because it was too surreal for him to even fathom. A Sage. *And my instructors thought I would never amount to anything.*

More footsteps. Rolling his eyes, he looked toward the door. They seemed heavy. He thought it was Orion coming to look for him, and he had neither the energy nor patience to be interrogated at the moment. Opening his mouth and nearly ready to say so, he clamped it shut upon seeing the figure of Jadyn canter into the room.

She scanned Lucian's bare torso and chest briefly before looking into his eyes, seemingly a bit flustered. "Hey," she said, her voice wavering. It was only when his eyes fought through the dimness that he realized she was crying.

"Hey." He felt ten times more relieved than he heard himself sound, though he was confused at the way Jadyn was standing. Ever since she came to a standstill her chest heaved progressively harder. Tears welled up in her eyes and made them gleam despite not having much light to reflect. He had never thought someone could look as beautiful as Jadyn when crying, puffy, red-brimmed eyes and all.

In an instant she raced into him, nearly bowling him over as she wrapped him in a firm embrace. Lucian felt awkward for his half-nakedness only for a moment, only that infinitesimal point in time when their union seemed less than natural. Clinging to him tightly, she wept into the nook of his bare shoulder with all she had. At times her breaths were so sporadic that he thought she had stopped breathing altogether before she took up sobbing and wept the harder. It seemed a thousand consoling words fought to flee from off his tongue, and as a result he said nothing, letting the sounds of her grief fill the room as he held her blankly. Though at first he had mistaken them for tears of joy, he was all but certain now that something terrible must have happened.

"My father," were the only two words she managed, but

they were the only words Lucian needed to hear to know what grieved her. He had not seen Yinsed among Ehrehalle's dead, but being that there were thirty-three in all—as he continually reminded himself—he had not managed to see half of them. Still groping for a word—anything—he could but hold her close. A dryness had possessed his mouth to the extent that he thought he might never speak again. It was all he could do to maintain their embrace, what with Jadyn's shoulders heaving as though her lungs sought an escape route through her back.

"I'm sorry," he heard himself say. It was such an empty response to such a grave situation that he wished he had remained silent. His voice had issued hoarsely, he was not surprised to notice. It felt as though a ball twice the size of a standard marble was beginning to manifest in his throat.

After a time, Jadyn's grieving subsided. Lucian took this to be the result of weariness rather than the alleviation of her pain. In the small time she had been in his chamber, she wept enough for five women, and the moisture of her tears collected warmly on the border of his chest and shoulder and trickled down his ribcage like sweat.

Taking her hand, Lucian led her to a nearby high-backed, red-cushioned chair beside the hearth. "Sit," he said softly, drawing her down as though she had never sat before. "Get warm." She was indeed shivering. He had not seen it before, not with her chest bobbing as violently as it had been. The poor thing must have been freezing. Night was certainly drawing near by now, and the draft channeling up the corridor from the gaping doors was definitely stronger than usual. He had not realized it, despite being shirtless. His mail, tunic, and cloak had worked to warm him to the extent that he was a sweating mess by time he left the battlefield. The draft, if anything, had been a much-welcomed sensation. But Jadyn hugged herself as if relinquishing her grip a fraction would cause her to freeze over.

Fumbling through his bedside chest, he sought as warm a blanket as he could find. He found one—a thick, fur-lined monstrosity that required a two-handed effort to raise. Taking it to Jadyn—her teeth clattering and eyes still puffed and watery—he wrapped it around her as best he could. Even still she hugged herself, gripping the blanket from beneath in tight fists and clutching it around her. Lucian sat in an adjacent chair, feeling terrible about the fact that the only thing he could think of was the kiss they shared before he left for Ren Noctis. He wanted to kiss her again, to assure her that everything would be alright. Princes did that in the stories he heard as a boy. The maidens seemed to love it, of course. But Jadyn deserved much more respect than that. She needed someone to comfort her; someone to listen. And all he could think of was getting his lips on her again.

"You saw your father?" Lucian asked softly, yet as soon as he spoke he wished he had those words back. Jadyn seemed to finally be settling down, when at the mention of her father a spark flashed in her eyes and an errant tear trickled once more down her cheek. To his surprise, however, she managed to cling to her growing resolve.

Nodding her head subtly, she said, "Yeah. When I came up from the lower levels they were starting to bring in those who fell fighting for Ehrehalle." She had been speaking from behind tears for so long that he almost forgot how musical her voice sounded. "They carried them on wooden stretchers, a man holding each arm. One by one they brought them in. I thought it was a massacre when the fifth was carried through the Great Hall. But then I counted ten . . . fifteen . . . " She let her words trail off for a moment as she tucked her head into the furry folds of the blanket and gathered herself to continue. "My father was the seventeenth man in their procession," she said brokenly. "Orion was carrying him, and your friend Aries. Two friends of his from the village bore him as well. They wouldn't let me near him. It took three women to hold me back, and an older boy. They probably thought I was mad."

"With grief," said Lucian quickly. "And you had every right to be." He frowned slightly upon noticing that his words did not manage to put a dent in Jadyn's sorrow. "Where did they lead them?" he asked at length. "The d—

the men." He caught himself, though he felt as though Jadyn knew what he had been about to say. Though dead most of the day, it was still too early for some to refer to them as such. That would have been killing them for good.

"To a room somewhere in the lower levels," she answered blankly, speaking to the fire burning before her. The lower levels. Lucian had managed to hear a great deal about these lower levels since the battle ended, but he had never understood what was there or how to get there. He was not able to broach the subject, for Jadyn's soft voice chimed dully again. "I asked everyone if they had seen you," she said, a twinge of something like—was it anger?—in her voice. "No one could answer that they did. Some said you had come, but that they hadn't laid eyes on you. When I went into the Great Hall, I saw those brutish creatures roaming the field beyond the stair, and knew you at least had managed to lead them this far. As I was being held back I waited, half-expecting to see them carry your body into Ehrehalle next. I never want to feel that again."

"Jay—"

"I lost my father, Lucian." Her tone was more pleading than demanding, but it was firm nonetheless. "My father. He was all I had until you showed up. I loved him, and now he's gone. I never want to know this pain again, Lucian. Never. I never want to feel what it's like to lose everything before I even have a chance to defend it. I wouldn't be able to see you fall. Now you are all I have."

If he looked as wide-eyed and gape-mouthed as he felt, he would have appeared as though the herald of fools, but Jadyn only looked at him imploringly, anticipating the response he had no clue how to give. Much like their first dance together, Lucian's eyes scanned every bit of the room but her. He could have guessed she *liked* him; that much at least had been obvious upon their first kiss. But her admission of the fact that he was all that was left to her after the horror of battle stripped her of her father . . . It was too much pressure. Too much to ask.

"Jay," he said, surprised at how collected his voice sounded despite the thumping of his heart. "This was only one stage of my journey. I still have . . . important things to do." The blasted Key. It always came down to that blasted Key. Holding his tongue on that matter, he continued. "I'm going to have to leave Ehrehalle soon. They know where I am now, and they know that the Key is here. More will come when Dridion learns of its defeat. Thousands. Tens of thousands, I'll bet. To stay here would be to condemn this land to complete annihilation. I can't do that to Orion or the others. I have to get to Medric, and soon."

"Then I'm going with you," she did not hesitate to say. "Though I don't think I'm the only one who's going to want to make the trip."

Orion was the last to enter Ehrehalle, drenched and weary. The rain had resumed some hours after noon, yet he and all those who survived the battle toiled through the storm, loading bodies into the resilient flames of the village. If it had not been evident before, it was all but plain now: this was not a natural fire. It was a similar element, sure, yet much stronger and more efficient than standard flame. What its true name was he could not be certain, but no mere blaze—however large—could withstand the consistent rain under which it managed to strive.

It worked in their favor, however. Without it, it could have taken months to clean the field of Dridion's dead. Mounds would have had to be built on which to load and burn them, which would have required men to send wagons and axes into the Redacre to haul back stacks of wood. That would have been a job the men would have taken up halfheartedly. Orion's knights never raised a hand to nature unless at need, and even then after a second thought. So it was they welcomed this fire in a way. Even the villagers who stood among them remarked how helpful it proved. Homes could be rebuilt. Many of their valuables were now stored in Ehrehalle as it was. All that burned before them was what they could afford to leave behind and forget—Fairies included.

Though it was a tireless effort, their resources afforded them some time-efficiency. Many of the wagons were loaded three or four times over before a noticeable dent was made in the number of bodies that lay scattered about the folds unraveling before Shír Azgoth. By dusk they were nearly gone, the flames in the village sweltering to towering peaks.

It was only then that Orion turned back for Ehrehalle. By now the field was largely cleared, the survivors having taken to the cover of the somber Great Hall. Even a vast majority of his knights had retired by that time, all weary and grief-stricken as the next. They had lost brothers too; men with whom they had shared their home for millennium upon millennium. It was the first time in all those countless years that they would step into Ehrehalle without them.

There were those who lingered on the foothills, however. Aries was among them, his clear blue eyes studying Orion intently. With his legs folded he sat as though a child watching a campfire far below, his great ram-headed hammer lying across his lap. Blood-splatters adorned much of its snout, Orion saw, though it was—as expected—without a dent. Moonstone was a fantastic element indeed—horrible, but no doubt fantastic. Orion had forgotten the destruction it could cause; he had never seen steel plates so undone than when butted by that ram.

As he approached, Aries's eyes remained fixed on the fires in the valley, burning now more fervently than ever. "It's fully fed, then?" he said absently.

Orion nodded subtly before peering out to the flames. "Almost," he answered.

Aries stood then, his sight never straying from Dwén Marnié. "It seems the Sages favored us," he said. "I've never known tables to turn so quickly."

Orion said nothing. The reality of Lucian's deeds were beginning to register. How could he have been so drastic? How could he have risked so much by seeking Amarog? How could he not have told him? He could not help feeling a twinge—or more—of anger. Being defied was not something he was used to. The life of a highlord consisted of giving orders and having them followed. He had been fortunate enough to have always given the *right* orders, and to have the right men carry them out . . . But to be disobeyed deliberately—for Lucian to risk everything on a whim, on a hope that in an eye-blink could have been rendered false . . .

"You're angry with him," Aries observed, resting his hammer atop its head and leaning with his hands folded on the shaft.

"He could have been killed!" Orion was surprised to hear the wavering of his voice. Thinking of what Lucian must have gone through . . . Crossing Reznarion alone was a feat in itself—the marshes and soiled fields were poor lands for fires, and it was rumored that fouler things than Netherlings lurked in unseen places. But to do it twice, and once with Amarog's ragged crew in tow . . . *How could he have been so rash?*

"He could have been," Aries answered plainly. "But just imagine where we would be had he not taken that risk. It takes a great deal of bravery and sacrifice to take risks . . ."

Aries let his words trail off. A small wind passed them by, rustling their blood-matted hair and blowing the folds of their fur-lined cloaks.

"Unless he knew without the worry of a doubt that it would work," Orion said contemplatively. Out of the corner of his eye he saw Aries pass him a quizzical glance. "It all makes sense. He probably thought I would never figure it out. The Luminos. It showed him how the fight would end should Amarog not be sought. Perhaps it showed him they would oblige to his request as well."

"That could be true," said Aries, though his voice housed something strange that piqued Orion's interest— something almost undetectable. It seemed as though he knew something the highlord did not. That was when Orion thought back to the battle. The entrance of the Netherlings was something he had been poring over relentlessly. A sound like thunder had erupted behind him, a sea of black shapes had cascaded over his head. Lucian bounded through the doorway on a horse as black as the pit of night . . .

"He came to you." It was nowhere near a question. "You

knew of his journey. You knew of all this." He spoke as one talking himself through a maze. Aries's mouth worked into a tight smile. "You leant him *Night*-Treader . . . "

"He did," said Aries. "Come to me, that is. He seemed vexed beyond measure; something had been tormenting him that he seemed to have difficulty giving voice."

Orion squared up to Aries, crossing his arms and listening intently. "And what did he say? Did he reveal to you what he saw in the Luminos? Did he speak of his need to seek Ren Noctis?"

"He did. But he also showed me something I still have trouble believing." Aries bent his head then. His smile was one of incredulity. Looking up into Orion's eyes, wide and anticipatory, he said, "He handed me this," as he raised his hammer from the ground.

"Your hammer?"

Aries nodded firmly, that smile still lingering.

"Impossible." That hammer could only be lifted by Aries himself or a Sage of . . . His brow furrowing and his voice strained, Orion repeated, "Im*pos*sible."

"As was my thought when handed the hammer by whom I thought to be a meek mortal boy—a skinny one at that. It would seem as though the Luminos showed him many things."

It felt as though the wind had been taken out of him. A Sage? It could not be. That had not been his charge. Long ago Ation entrusted him the task of seeking the mortal seafarer who would cross the ocean from the eastern shores to those of the west. That man, whoever he was, was to somehow restore hope for the earthly realms of the world in the struggles they would face as Zynys and Parthaleon warred. Orion had been led to believe that through this mortal, the Ruby Throne would once again ignite. Somehow. Through this man, the Rubbilius gem upon the Key was to be reactivated, permitting it to once again unlock the Chamber of Fates and destroy Sorcerian for good. But it was all too evident now that Lucian was no mere mortal. He was someone stronger, though he might not have known it himself. Someone fierce. Someone not to be hidden, but unleashed. As much as he had difficulty believing or admitting it, lifting Aries's hammer alone was enough evidence to solidify the truth.

"I will not ponder this here," he said at long length. He was growing cold now that he had finally stopped moving, and the rain was beginning to pick up again. *A Sage* . . . "There is no doubt a great need for answers, but we will get them in due time. For now we must count our blessings, and be thankful that we may yet share more nights within Ehrehalle together. Yet for how long such luxuries will last, I cannot say."

They were the last to turn away from the burning village, yet even as Aries continued on into the hall Orion stopped to gaze out once more. A Sage in his presence—and Lucian at that! He could still hear himself threatening to chain him to his bedpost. *A Sage.* He knew there had been something special about him, something he could not quite lay a finger on . . . But not that. Sighing, and looking into the Great Hall where a large assembly of folk was gathered, he strode in with as erect a posture as he could manage.

The girth of Ehrehalle widened to accommodate all those present. The benefits of magic mountains certainly outweighed the oddities. Even still, it was crowded. Orion sidestepped through the crowd as best he could, seeing nothing but despair-filled faces. Women hugged their children, who blankly let themselves be held. For him, at least, there was no pain greater than watching theirs. But he felt he owed it to them to at least help them endure. If it meant hugging someone, or letting someone cry on him, he would do it. He almost broke down himself as he watched one particular daughter grieve as he helped carry the body of her father in from the field. He recognized her as Lucian's friend—the one whom parted from him that night on the mountain pass. It had taken a small village to hold her back.

When he finally had a moment to himself, he rounded up the cooks and anyone who could man an instrument, and instructed them to go about their usual business. "Bring some life to this hall, so that we may celebrate those we have lost," he told them. "Let us not wallow in despair." Though he was far from certain the grim gathering would welcome any kind of festivities.

An hour or so later the buffet tables were beginning to be dressed. Row upon row of golden platters were laid out, laden with sizzling meats or steamed vegetables. Flagons of wine and barrels of ale were brought in from the stores below and instantly tapped. It was not a lively hall, but there was certainly movement around the food and drink. If they were anywhere near as hungry as Orion, they would be on their third helping in no time.

He felt a tap on his shoulder as he manned a lonely end of one of the tables. Turning, he looked up into the gaunt face of Eap, whose beady eyes were staring at him imploringly. "The musicians want to know if it would be proper to begin," he said coolly.

Orion thought a moment. "Not yet," he answered. The atmosphere was yet too somber for music, he felt, and Lucian was not even aware that dinner was being served. He had perhaps not eaten in days. "Take wing and fetch Lucian, if you would. He is no doubt in his room. When he joins us we will see about music."

Eap nodded. "It will be done. There is one other thing, highlord. Those of Ren Noctis seek entrance into Ehrehalle. There are knights yet barring their passage, but I thought I might ask you. Will you permit them among you?"

Netherlings. It was yet as sour a taste in his mouth as any. "I will not," he said at length. So what if they committed a good deed for once? The lives they managed to save during the night were not enough to quell all those they managed to destroy as men. "I will not sup with dogs."

Eap tarried silently a moment before issuing a shallow bow. Turning then he strode away, and as a raven left the hall for Lucian's chamber.

A light-knuckled knock on the door preceded the muffled voice of Eap saying, "Lucian? Are you decent?"

Lucian and Jadyn had been taking advantage of a

comfortable silence. After a time he had drawn his chair alongside hers where she laid her head upon his shoulder. Having taken his hand, she brought his arm under the blanket so as to not let in the cold air, and there she stroked his hand with hers. Sitting this way made him more content than he remembered being, and certainly cheerier than he thought he would feel any time soon. Suddenly the room had become soothing. The sound and warmth of the hearth lulled him into a pleasant daze, the feel of Jadyn's soft hair on his shoulder eased his thoughts, the touch of her hand dispelled whatever worry he was housing.

Rolling his eyes, he answered, "Come in."

Eap, if anything, looked sallower than when Lucian saw him in Reznarion, before he had led him and the Netherlings through the hidden passages at Azgoth's rear and out into the battle. Against the loose, black folds of his cloak, his skin seemed ghostly. He bowed his head slightly, his slick black hair glinting somewhat in the glare of the hearth. Lucian did not like the idea of people bowing to him. Aries had bent the knee to him briefly, he remembered. It was beyond peculiar to be shown such respect. He did not want to be considered superior to anyone; especially Eap. Were it not for him, he would still be circling around the Red Peaks.

"Orion has sent me to inform you that the chefs have prepared dinner," he said, passing a quick glance to Jadyn as though he had only then realized she was present. To him she must have seemed but a large bundle of blankets at Lucian's side.

Only at the mention of food did he realize how hungry he truly was. Even Jadyn, who had not lifted her head for a long while, began to stir.

"Thanks, Eap," he said. "We'll be down in a minute."

The messenger bowed his head. "I do apologize for the disturbance." Turning then, he left them to their lonesome. Lucian did not entirely like the way Eap said that. He thought he might have gotten the wrong impression.

Jadyn yawned. "Was I asleep?" she asked, her voice soft and weary.

"A little bit," he answered. It was not as difficult to stand as he anticipated. His eyes were heavy, certainly, but the aches and pains that had been present when he sat had subsided to near-nonexistence. Reaching out his hand, he issued a scant smile. "Shall we do dinner?"

To his surprise, Jadyn smiled back, if dazed, and took his hand. "I don't think I've ever been hungrier."

They entered the Great Hall with their fingers locked. There a large crowd was gathered, seated at the long tables or huddled around the colorful buffets. He saw Orion plainly, seated at a table joined by Aries, Leo, and two other knights whom he did not recognize. There was no music, though fiddlers and flutists had their instruments astride their laps.

"Why don't you go and get something to eat," he said, leaning into Jadyn. "I have to see about something." She eyed him quizzically before breaking reluctantly for the buffet tables.

The "something" he had to see to was the fact that he could plainly see the Netherlings huddled beyond the mouth of Ehrehalle, sitting in the rain. Instantly he strode over to Orion. He knew it had to have been his doing. On his way to the Great Hall, he had been thinking up ways to avoid him, too weary to get into a game of hard questions and evasive answers. But now he had a mouthful to dispense.

"Ah, Lucian," said Orion standing and smiling as Lucian came up alongside him.

"Why are they outside?" he said sharply. Though Orion stood nearly two heads taller, Lucian drew to his full height and looked him fiercely in the eyes. "The Netherlings. Why are they outside?"

Orion looked around questioningly, as if imploring for someone to explain the question he was being asked. "What do you mean?"

"Is this how you mean to treat those who just risked their lives to save yours?"

Orion smiled. Smiled! Surely he did not think he was joking? "You cannot be—"

Striding away from him, Lucian made for the open

archway. Relieving whatever knights were stationed there, he allowed all those who waited outside entrance. *Ridiculous,* he thought. It was amazing to him how quickly things returned to normal. Once the Netherlings did their part to secure Ehrehalle's victory, they reverted back to the scoundrels they might once have been in the eyes of Orion and his knights.

Backs hunched, ears bent back, and tails nearly between their legs, Amarog's men entered Ehrehalle soaked and shivering. The smell of wet dog soon overpowered that of the freshly cooked meats and other delicacies, but Lucian paid that no mind. Plainly he heard men groan and women and children gasp as the overgrown wolves shook out their coats wherever they saw fit, as for many long moments the Great Hall endured a shower of its own.

Lucian returned to face Orion, his expression a thing that could have stilled a molten stream. "They're with us now," Lucian stated firmly. *The nerve!* "We'll treat them as such."

Orion opened his mouth to speak and Lucian braced himself for what was coming. Yet he clamped it shut as Amarog meandered in from outdoors. Like many of the others, his mouth was stained pink, as was the bottom of his dense coat—what would have been his chest hair had he not been moving on all fours. The general buzz that had been humming gradually quieted as all eyes fell on the largest of the Netherlings now making his way through. Had Lucian not known any better, he would have mistaken him for a bear. Such was his brawn. His eyes of fierce yellow glowered left and right as he slowly stalked along, hesitantly, with no less caution than his men had employed. Finding Lucian, he came to stand beside him. Even walking as a wolf Amarog reached as high as his shoulder, his snout raised so that it was nearly flush with Orion's chin.

"Highlord," he grumbled, his lipless mouth barely moving. Lucian could feel Amarog tense beside him, hear the water drip from his damp coat consistently to the floor. He stank of dog and blood.

"You." Orion's voice was muffled by disdain, but he stood as firm and unmoving as ever.

A tense silence fell between them before Amarog spoke again. "So nice of you to invite us in. As I'm sure you saw, we had quite an eventful night."

"You—"

"A race across Reznarion is no easy thing, though you wouldn't know," he continued firmly. "And with so many in transport . . . Bounding up those crags at Azgoth's back is no simple feat even for wolves, but we managed. Looked like your people were nearly overrun by time we got here to save your neck. Again, might I add—after all, who was it that brought warning in the first place?—And here we are treated like dogs. We may resemble beasts, Orion Highlord, but regardless of our make, I'd say you're indebted to us now."

Orion's face warred with emotions before he spoke. Lucian looked on attentively, if nervously. Amarog was within clear snapping distance. One wrong word out of Orion's mouth . . .

"Forgive me," Lucian heard Orion mutter. He had been watching Amarog for any sudden movements. Turning his eyes incredulously to Orion, he saw that his head was bowed solemnly. "Forgive me," he repeated, firmer this time. It was as if most of the air had been sucked out of him. Lucian thought he might have been suddenly realizing the cruel extent of his ungratefulness. "Sup with us. It was wrong of me to neglect you so."

He never thought Orion was capable of reaching sense so quickly. Perhaps it was the pressure of having all eyes turned on him, anticipating his response. Many of the folk present did not know the Netherlings from many of the knights, and so their deeds in their past lives were a moot point as far as they were concerned. What mattered to Lucian—and he did not doubt to all the others as well— was the fact that they had fought to preserve the present. Ehrehalle's present. Their present. And they had done a fine job of it. Amarog issued what Lucian felt could only be a smile, though it was a hideous expression.

"Now, that wasn't so hard, *was* it?" he said. Stepping back a bit, he arched his shoulders and shook out his coat, spraying Lucian, Orion, and all in their vicinity. The vacant expression Orion had been wearing before his shower was replaced by one of fury, but only momentarily. "We've had our fill, I think," the slightly-drier Amarog continued, sitting down and nearly kicking himself in the face with one of his hind legs to scratch what must have been the itch to end all itches. "Those Fairies are more filling than they look. Very lean. Good source of protein, if any of you meat-racks are ever interested. We'll welcome shelter, though, and fires enough to dry our coats. When the storm clears, we will make for Ren Noctis, with full bellies, warm fur, and hours of rest behind us."

Orion nodded. "You will have it."

"Ah, very well," said Amarog. Again that strange, terrible smile. "If you insist!" Coming to stand beside Lucian—this time towering on two legs—he gave him a light nudge with his elbow. "I'm starting to like this highlord better than the last one," he muttered just loud enough for Orion to hear.

The Netherlings did not prove the sort for celebrations, however meager Ehrehalle's was proving in light of the largely sorrowful results the battle had yielded. Fiddlers and flutists had taken up somber melodies that worked only to compound the grief that many still felt. Lucian did not know who was in charge of the song choices, but even he had to seek them out after "Bear My Soul to Thee" sent several newly widowed women weeping to whatever rooms they had been given. After ordering livelier tunes, the mood throughout Ehrehalle livened somewhat, if scarcely. Village men sat absently pricking meat or vegetables with forks that were never destined for their mouths. Knights sat back lazily with grim expressions on their hard faces. Women cradled children in their arms, many of whom had not once stood to play or dance.

Orion had not been present for some time. He had appointed himself to show the Netherlings their housing, which he said would be a large cavern of sorts deep within the lower levels of Azgoth. There they were to find ample shelter for their entire number, which was yet largely intact—Amarog mentioned something about having only lost three men. Fires would also be built there, enough for them all to dry their coats and lighten their weight before their return trip to Ren Noctis. As far as Lucian was concerned, he could not have asked for Amarog and Orion to get along any better than they were. He had expected some tension, even after the Netherlings' heroics. But to have it alleviated so quickly was the quelling of another headache he did not think he could bear.

Amarog walked aside Orion, in fact, out of the mouth of the rightward corridor when he returned from lodging the Netherlings. To Lucian's surprise, Orion was laughing. Laughing!

"They seem to be getting along," Jadyn's voice cooed in his ear. Lucian had almost forgotten she was sitting beside him. She had frequented the buffet tables so much since their arrival she barely sat at all.

Lucian sipped some ale from an oaken cup. It was fresh and cold, and—he was sad to admit—still slightly better than Eveland Cherry. "They do," he said, though all of his puzzlement was apparent in his tone.

"You did well," she said, resting her head on his shoulder briefly before continuing to eat.

Lucian took another drink, smiling into his cup. He did do well. It was a different sort of feeling to think so highly of one of his own deeds. Though he knew he did not act alone, and thus did not deserve all the credit, he knew he had played a crucial role in saving lives. No more hiding while others fought for him. No more cowering beneath the shadows of foes. At least not anymore. *I'm a Sage,* he told himself. And I'm going to act like one until the day I die . . .

He grinned into his mug, thinking all the while: *If that day ever comes.*

Orion leapt upon one of the tables so that he managed to face all those who were present. Amarog, who had come with him from the lodging of the Netherlings, had broken from his side. He saw him find a place beside Lucian, who

451

welcomed him openly. The girl at his side seemed a bit tense in his presence—and rightfully so, he thought—but she seemed to settle once Lucian's demeanor suggested that everything was alright. He saw that Aries sat across from Lucian with Leo at his side. Meeting both their gazes, they eyed him attentively. They knew what he was going to say. Better than anyone, they knew.

"My friends," he began, holding up his cup of wine and drawing all to attention. The humming of several conversations died down as all eyes turned to the man standing before them on the table. Among the crowd he saw Ursa's face and caught a glimpse of her smile before he continued. "I once thought, in time gone by, that a sword was the greatest weapon a man could wield. It made sense to me, once, that an amply aimed arrow from a bow of strong make could pierce truer than any words a tongue could ever yield. Yet when my time is done—if I am ever fortunate enough to have my image strewn across the stars—I will not have it said of me that my beliefs were as such.

"For you proved otherwise to me last night. A man's greatest weapon is not his sword, but his heart. Steel can be broken, but the heart is a thing as true as mountain stone. I look into your faces now and see the truth of my claim. Though sorrow wreaths us all, let it be sobered by the knowledge that our soldiers fell as heroes. Let it be known that these men fell with glory in their clutches. Though my words may not offer solace now, when you speak of your husbands, or your brothers, or your fathers, or your sons, it will be with pride. That they have sacrificed themselves for the hope of better days. It was once the wish of every mortal man to be so fortunate. And I promise you now, folk of Ehrehalle: though their deaths were not in vain, they will be avenged."

Then he raised his glass and looked hard upon the faces of all those before him. In their expressions he was encouraged to see only small glimpses of sorrow. The look they now wore—man, woman, and child alike—was one he had seen plenty of times before, most recently a night ago.

Grim determination. It was a hardened folk that dwelled within Shir Azgoth now. A sturdy folk. A folk ready for the trials that were to come. Almost in unison, those with glasses stood and raised them, shifting like a well-practiced rank of soldiers. It was almost frightening how eager they seemed for vengeance—how eager they seemed to carry on.

"To our honored dead," Orion said, draining a portion of his cup's contents before drinking. The crowd repeated his words and actions and before drinking themselves. It was a moment or so before he continued. What he had to say would be difficult, he knew. Stepping down had never been in his blood, not even long ago when he had a king to answer to.

"I speak now to my knights, those brave and valiant souls who have stood at my side all these countless years. It has ever been an honor to serve as your highlord. You have shared in my feats, and in many ways made them possible. But a new order must shape itself among us, for there is one in our midst not even highlords or *kings* of men are above. Come forward, Lucian."

He saw the whites of Lucian's eyes before he even looked at him. Several heads turned to stare at the boy standing between the hulking Amarog and the beautiful Jadyn, who after a moment of him blankly standing, nudged him forward.

It was perhaps one of the most awkward and nerve-racking things Lucian had ever had to do. All eyes were on him. He felt as though everyone was focusing intently on his every action. What was Orion playing at? He did not want this. He had not asked for this. A new order? Him in command? He was not above highlords or kings! Sage or not, he felt that even Macintosh MaDungal was more knowledgeable of worldly matters and leadership than he was.

Nevertheless he felt himself moving, watched as the image of Orion perched upon his table drew closer. Standing beside him now he looked at Orion with something like fire in his eyes, but it was not the fire of determination. It was the fire of "I would kill you if there weren't so many to witness".

Slapping a hand on his shoulder, and obviously ignoring the look Lucian bore into him, Orion pulled him close. "My friends," he continued, speaking again to all, "though dormant, we have prayed to the Sages on countless occasions, no doubt as recently as the eve of the battle. Yet all the while we had a Son of Zynys in our midst. Lucian Sageborn, I name him, and only to him shall I bend the knee. Only in his wake shall I follow."

Stepping down from the table, Orion stood looking up to Lucian before bending to one knee with a hand over his heart. Though gasping and murmuring amongst themselves, the crowd began to do the same. *Great,* thought Lucian. *Now I'll never have time to myself with Jadyn.* It was his only thought. By her side was the only place that he felt content. But there was something that began to fester within him as the crowd within Ehrehalle bent the knee one-by-one. Something like pride. Something like duty. Leo came forward, and propping Lionsbane in front of him knelt beside Orion. Even Amarog was kneeling as best he could, though he was the height of any man standing when doing so. When Aries came forward he brought his hammer along. Drawing Lucian down to him, he whispered, "Raise this to the people, just to quell any doubt. They know the story well enough."

Lucian smiled. As he held the hammer aloft the gasping and muttering became exhilarated shouts. Passing a look to Jadyn, knelt beside Amarog—her hair a mess and her face still red and puffy from grieving—he issued a small smile. These were his people now. This was his charge. An overwhelming sense of realization swept over him. As long as he lived, there was still hope. As long as he lived, the Chamber could be opened.

The march to Medric, he determined then, would begin at week's end.

35

A Rest in the Woods

Didrebelle and Gamaréa rode on through the outlying lands of Dridion until some time after nightfall, employing as much effort as they could to avoid scattered towns where foes might have been expecting them. They could not afford any obscure detours, however, and in some instances were forced to follow roads through populated areas. Fortunately, there were none who opposed them.

By dusk the last spur of Dridion towns were behind them, and they soon passed along a shoulder of the Red Peaks through a wide golden field. Before night had fully fallen, they sought shelter in a forest at the mountains' feet, finding an ample location by a slow-trudging stream that wound down from above. It was made cold by the ices that had melted into it, and proved a wonderful refreshment for Morok, Fairy, and horse alike.

"There is grass enough for them to feast," said Didrebelle contemplatively, though Gamaréa was more worried about a feast of his own. It had been too long since he enjoyed a hardy meal.

Glimpses of the lilac twilight could be seen through the forest roof. The veil of night would soon pass over it, dark and velvet and hauling the stars in tow.

"Would you be so kind as to start a fire?" asked Didrebelle. "There is something I need to do."

It was not long before Gamaréa had a fire blazing at their camp. Having been held captive for so long, he feared he might have forgotten how to construct one. The bold warmth it emitted was like a foreign thing to him, and he basked in it for a long while. Didrebelle returned in an hour's time, and came to sit beside him as though he had not left at all.

"Great night," he said. "Nice and clear."

"Where did you go?"

"This is quite a blaze! I daresay it is a much better fire than I would have made."

A silence fell during which only the crackling of the flames was heard. "What did you do?" asked Gamaréa disconcertedly.

"Nothing! Nothing. Never you worry. You have had enough to trouble about the past couple of months."

Frustration swept through Gamaréa, but he could not stay angry with the person who had just saved his life. "There is one thing I hope you won't be so secretive about: how is it that you managed my escape? I find it a farfetched coincidence that my noose snapped a second before my neck, and just in time for you to appear on horseback with an empty-saddled mount in tow."

Didrebelle guffawed. "I will be honest with you, it was the result of several botched plans. The best of my plots fell apart in the middle of the night before your scheduled execution—"

Just then Gamaréa threw up a hand, silencing him. "Do you hear that?"

Rising abruptly, he scurried to unsheathe one of Didrebelle's swords from his horse's saddle.

"Horsemen," he said, brandishing the blade so that it glinted in the flames. "They have found us."

In much too short a time, three hooded horsemen thundered through the woods and circled their fire. Gamaréa, tapping the minimal amount of strength he still possessed, was poised and ready for a confrontation. Didrebelle, however, seemed unfazed, expressionless but for an odd smile on his face.

One of the horsemen dismounted and came forward.

"Get back!" said Gamaréa pointedly. "Or this fire will not be the last you see tonight."

Then the horseman unveiled himself, and Gamaréa shuddered to see Tartalion Ignómiel standing before him. The hard, fair face of his former mentor sent a bolt of shivers through his spine, such that he involuntarily collapsed on his knees.

"Rise, child," said Tartalion smoothly, in the same collected voice Gamaréa had grown ever used to in his days as his pupil.

Gamaréa fought for words in the face of Tartalion, but all he could manage were, "It is impossible."

Tartalion smiled. "Not quite!"

Then the two others stepped forward, and Daxau came up to stand beside the Lord of Elderland. Just when Gamaréa thought his heart could drop no further, it plummeted again in one fell swoop. The two locked wrists with verve, tears forming in each of their eyes.

"I thought you dead!" said Gamaréa. "With all the calamity, I regret to admit that I—"

"There is nothing to forgive or explain," Daxau interjected. "Except the fact that I was told there would be food prepared."

This statement was directed more at Tartalion than anyone.

"It was the only way to get you out of that inn," he said sharply, before going to greet Didrebelle. "Mortals," he grunted.

Then Gamaréa came face-to-face with the last rider, whom he recognized as Darondill, one of Melinta's councilmen.

"I come in peace," said Darondill, eyeing the firm grip Gamaréa was employing on the hilt of Didrebelle's sword.

Gamaréa passed a questioning glare to Didrebelle, who vouched for Darondill with a nod of his golden head. But Gamaréa's hard stare remained unfaltering. "Your heart is easily swayed, then?" he asked, not kindly.

Darondill shuddered in the face of Gamaréa. Though his figure had depleted somewhat in Cauldarím, he was still a brooding presence, and even more so when complemented by Darondill's lanky frame.

"Toward just purpose, I assure you," the former councilman muttered, then held a bundle out to Gamaréa as if it were some payment.

Gamaréa's eyes hardened as he unraveled the cloth and laid eyes on Dawnbringer's sheath at long last. "You were quick to defy your king," he said, though in his heart he was thrilled at having the sword returned to him. "What is to say you will not do the same to us?"

"Day by day Melinta leads his country to slaughter," said Darondill, finding his bravery. "He is blind to it, though. The enemy has lodged in his house in the guise of a friend, but will throttle him in the night. Once his part is played, he will be all too easy to dispose of."

Though Darondill had not realized it, all ears had turned to him, and none more alert than Didrebelle's. "I have sought you out because, if I am to die, I would do so bearing the banners of justice," he continued. "To you I pledge my loyalty."

"And we accept it," answered Didrebelle, who had made his way to Gamaréa's side. "Welcome, brother."

"Good!" called Daxau from the fire. "Now that we're all friends, who's hungry? Our food's not going to catch itself."

The darkness made it difficult even for the three Fairies to find anything worth hunting. Darondill, who had a mind only for words and indoor-doings, did not factor much in the efforts, and in time returned to "watch over the camp." After a time Tartalion joined him, claiming that he was much too old to partake in the "childish affairs of gluttons." Oddly enough it was Daxau who faired best, no doubt spurred on by his outrageous hunger, which seemed to affect Mortals more so than Moroks or Fairies. Thus he swaggered to the fire when he returned, and even offered to roast his kills himself. Gamaréa and Didrebelle soon followed empty-handed.

"Just do it quickly," said Gamaréa. "Now that I am so close to food I am beginning to realize how hungry I truly am."

"That is to be expected, having not eaten a nutritious meal in quite some time," said Tartalion, who had taken to smoking his pipe. "This brute, on the other hand"—he motioned toward Daxau, who was skinning the squirrels and rabbits with angst, ignorant to the conversation going on about him—"ate three meat pies in an hour's time at the inn we stayed at last night. How he is this hungry again, I have no answer."

It was some time before Daxau finished readying the small animals for cooking. After sticking them on makeshift spits, he passed them to his companions. Tartalion respectfully declined. Darondill was hesitant at first, but obliged once he saw Didrebelle take hold of one eagerly. Thus the four of them began roasting their meals over the fire. Gamaréa, more than anxious to eat anything other than the dreadful muck of Cauldarím, felt as though he held a steak on a stick.

For a time the only sounds around the fire were those of eating. Tartalion sat on a large nearby stone blowing smoke rings in the moonlight, while the others did their best to gnaw away the modest meat their meals once boasted.

Darondill was the first to speak. "My father was a virtuous Fairy," he said at random. Speaking of the memory seemed to weigh down his heart. "I followed his pursuit of joining the King's Council. In fact, I think I may have only gotten a seat because of my relation to him." He took another bite of his squirrel, grimacing somewhat as he nibbled on the meat.

"In another time," said Didrebelle, "pursuing a seat on the council would have been a noble goal. But there are now too many of them who have followed the king into darkness. You entered politics at the wrong time, it seems."

"Which is just my luck, mind you." Darondill's attention then turned to Gamaréa. "When you left Melinta's hall that day, I defended your position. For some reason or another, the king neglected my argument: that the natural state of any living creature is to kill lest be killed. In times of peril, when our lives hang in the balance, we resort to our primitive roots. Claw and bite and lash—whatever it takes to survive. He disagreed, as you can imagine. My allegiance to him, which had been altogether dwindling, vanished in that moment. I knew then that if an opportunity presented itself, I would flee Dridion, though it was my greatest fear that none would arise."

Daxau snorted, and said through a mouthful of roasted squirrel, "*Your* greatest fear?"

"My apologies," answered Darondill. "I did not intend to belittle your sufferings in Cauldarím. I was merely speaking of my own."

"I think it is best to put all talk of that place behind us," said Gamaréa. "Let's turn to a more interesting subject." He took another bite and turned his gaze to Didrebelle. "You were talking about how you managed the escape earlier?"

"Ah, yes!" answered Didrebelle. "Before I was so rudely interrupted. As I was saying before: I had a great idea thought up, but that of course unraveled the night before your execution. I had not planned on them moving you from the barracks to the dungeons of the fortress. Imagine my surprise when I found your cell empty. I had planned on storming the barracks by force. At that point there were only ten guards in your wing, a small enough contingent for me to dispose of in my lonesome. From there we would have fled under the cover of night with nothing more than a second look from anyone.

"It took longer than I care to admit to gain enough secrecy to even go down to you in those dungeons. Soldiers who had retired for the evening swarmed about the fortress in great numbers, and my disappearance into the dungeon would certainly have raised suspicion. Wardens have never been known to venture to the stronghold's lowest levels. I would have been followed, if only for my own protection. When I came upon you it was just before sunrise, and my original plan was lost."

"How was it that you formulated the new plan?" asked Gamaréa.

"This seems a lot more interesting than *my* escape," added Daxau, still chewing.

Didrebelle smiled. "I had to improvise, of course! I knew Melinta would only be accompanied by his guard at your execution. The vast majorities of his numbers would still be in the city, or in Cauldarím beyond. So I found two of the most able horses I could find, and kept a fair distance behind the mob on the heels of your carriage. When the rope broke, I wasted no time in racing to fetch you. I knew it would take a moment or so for the king's guard to register what had taken place, and even longer for them to ready their horses to pursue us. By then I knew we could put a great distance between us."

"And how did you know the rope would break?" asked Gamaréa. "Did you sabotage it?"

Didrebelle drew a look of confusion. "I shot it."

The faces of Gamaréa, Daxau, and Darondíll, all of whom had taken to listening attentively, became wrought with awe.

"But . . . shot? . . . " said Gamaréa. " An impossible feat! What if your timing was off? What if you . . . what if you missed?"

"I must say that question offends me. *Miss!*"

Daxau had taken to picking his teeth with his empty spit. "So, if I'm hearing this story correctly, the noose is about to go taut, and in the nick of time your arrow splits it in two."

"Indeed," said Didrebelle. "It must have been flying with vengeance too, for you not to even notice it skimming the top of your head."

"Forgive me," said Gamaréa. "I had a little bit more to think about than a crazed archer shooting my noose. I merely thought the rope was faulty."

Just then Tartalion strolled over and dumped the contents of his pipe into the fire before taking a seat beside Gamaréa.

"And where do you come into this?" asked Gamaréa, not unkindly. If anything, he was still taken aback at Tartalion's presence.

He could not help but notice unmistakable despair in Tartalion's face. The Lord of Elderland had seemed glum since he revealed himself hours before, and had been passive and quiet while the group conversed and enjoyed their modest form of merriment. Laying a gentle hand on

Gamaréa's shoulder, he said quietly, "It grieves me to tell you this, child, but Elderland has fallen."

His voice was bleak, and the suddenness with which he shared the news made Gamaréa's stomach lurch. "It cannot be!" he cried.

Tartalion was silent for a moment. "This is a night of many things that cannot be, it seems. But Elderland, sadly, is no more. The white towers and moon-beacons have tumbled, hacked down by Morgues and Fairies of Dridion. The citadel has been raided and left bare. The clearings within that forest were still ablaze when I boarded the last ship west. Those of my people who survived are in pursuit to Adoram, perhaps even as we speak. It is there I hope they may find shelter and means for recovery for the time being, though I fear war will reach there next."

As much as Gamaréa's spirits raised when he first saw Tartalion, they had fallen tenfold as he relayed his sorrowful news. "How did you know where to find us?" he asked distantly.

"It would not have been easy, mind you—though it was not a leisurely errand by any means—without the aid of the Aquilum. Their chiefs alerted me as to your whereabouts. They shared your tale of Beelcibur with much verve, and said that it had already grown famous among their people far beneath the waves. Aquilus, their king, steered our course in the direction they had taken you many months ago. Knowing you well enough, I assumed you would have taken the road through Ravelon, though I would have suggested otherwise. There I found your tracks, which led me to Deavorás.

"I proceeded to sprinkle myself throughout the city, never lingering in one lodging longer than three days. Finally I managed to get Didrebelle's attention as he was traveling to Melinta's hall one night. Once I learned of your predicament, I kept a watchful eye on the goings-on in Cauldarím from the outlying borders of the forest. It was I who aided you in your most trying hour. After all, how could Ignis have been stripped of his defenses without a bit of Sagely magic?"

"That was you?" said Gamaréa incredulously. "I noticed the light coming from afar, though at the time I mistook it for an arm of death coming to seize me."

"I played my part, yes," answered Tartalion. "But the Light of Zynys was made ever more potent when Dragontamer came to my aid. Together we breached Ignis's black-magic defenses, but it was you who brought him to ruin."

A sullen lull fell over them, and none spoke for a long while. Slow tears coursed down Gamaréa's cheeks, and Tartalion's eyes, despite reflecting the flames before him, were dim.

Then Daxau said, "I would have liked to see the land you called Elderland, my friend. From what you told me of it, it seemed like a wonderful place indeed."

Tartalion could only nod his thanks before he turned his attention back to Gamaréa. "I came upon this fellow the same night Didrebelle met with you, though our flight out of Cauldarím was much more discreet." Didrebelle could not determine whether or not that was a dig at him. "He told me he was dear to you, and that it would grieve you to abandon Daxau to his fate. Thus it was I stepped foot in Caludarím for the first and final time, travelling in secret to Daxau's cell and freeing him as Didrebelle once plotted to free you.

"It was young Darondill here who discovered us. At that moment I thought my plan undone, but he proved to be a friend to our cause. He begged me to let him pass with us, and so I did. Had he been in the company of hundreds I would have encouraged all of them to do so. None should suffer the fate Melinta is driving Dridion towards.

"Thus it was we fled as a threesome to the small town of Drír, which was most accommodating. Being so far from Deavorás, I knew we would be safe enough for one night. It was to be long yet before Didrebelle's plan came to fruition, and longer still before you reached the forest."

"How did you know where to find us?" asked Gamaréa. "It is a small forest, but big enough in which to get lost if you don't know where you are going."

"We followed the lights," answered Daxau plainly.

It took a moment before Gamaréa understood. "The lights," he said, as if to himself. Then he turned to Didrebelle. "That was where you went."

"Indeed," answered the Fairy. "Against the night sky, the Light of Zynys can be seen for miles."

"Though I daresay it was a risk," added Tartalion. "There are those among Melinta's ranks who would recognize it if they saw it. Let us hope it went unnoticed, though I don't doubt he has set battalions on our trail by now."

Gamaréa stood abruptly. "Then we should waste no time in setting off again," he said earnestly. "These are precious hours. We should not spend them taking rest."

Tartalion could not help but issue a slight smile. "You have forgotten your weariness, apparently."

On the contrary, it's proving hard to forget. "Weariness can be remedied," he said. "But now we have to find Lucian. He has wandered in his lonesome for too long, but I have hope that he may yet be alive."

Breaking for his bay, he began applying the saddle eagerly. It was not until he was nearly ready for a new journey that he realized he was the only one to have moved. Even more disquieting were the solemn looks on each of their faces, either looking away into the fire or to places beyond.

At length Didrebelle stood, his face pallid and his eyes dim with sorrow. "My friend," he said sadly. "I am sorry that I did not give you this message sooner. Lucian . . . is dead."

Gamaréa's eyes watered instantly, and his brow furrowed at the news. Didrebelle continued. "One of Melinta's final tidings was of Lucian's death," he said despairingly. "He had made it to the Redacre Wood, or so it was said, and from there proceeded into a dwelling called Ren Talam with a small contingent. Who they were I cannot say, but I believe them to be friends—"

"The Protectors, some call them," added Tartalion glumly. "A band of an ancient breed of men, the last remnants of the country of Dredoway, granted immortality by Ation during the Mortal Damnation."

"The fall of Mankind," said Gamaréa. For some reason, Daxau's ears perked at this, and he became newly attentive.

"They were employed to fulfill the prophecy of rekindling the Rubbilius stone. There were those who mistook them for myth, and I regret to admit that I was once among them. But it is evident now that they existed, albeit proven much too late."

"Some *protectors* they were," said Gamaréa angrily.

"Do not speak so harshly of them, however troubled your heart may be," replied Tartalion.

Gamaréa looked away and contemplated. Fury rose within him, such as though he wanted to grab hold of something and fling it or smash it. "I will not believe it!" he screamed at last. From above, some night-dwelling birds scattered frantically away. He motioned toward Didrebelle. "How could you trust the words of a serpent? Melinta wants us to believe Lucian is dead. He probably suspected your lack of loyalty the entire time."

Soon Gamaréa's rage could not be controlled. It took both Didrebelle and Daxau to subdue him and sit him down. The horses had grown restless, and in their panic brayed and pranced, their cries piercing the night. Then Gamaréa was weeping openly, the violent heaves of his chest nearly propelling Didrebelle from his embrace.

When at long last Gamaréa settled, Didrebelle reached into his pocket and revealed the ruby. "You know what this stone is," he said sadly.

A new sorrow welled up within him—the like of which he had never felt. It was as though he held the death of the entire world in his palm. His cry was bone shattering—a horrible collection of rage and grief as he wilted to his knees. From above, the heavens opened, and rain delved through the forest roof in quick torrents.

Then Tartalion was at his side, and extending a hand offered to help him from the ground as he had so many times before. "Come, child," he said gently. "There will be no ride tonight."

It was long before Gamaréa reached for him, and when he did the company made for some shelter in a denser part of the forest nearby. Wrapped in their hoods and shrouded in darkness (the fire had been extinguished by the rain), they sat still and silent long into the night.

Some hours later, the rain subsided. The entire company had fallen asleep. Everyone, that is, except Daxau. Gamaréa's outburst had nearly driven him to tears. As he sat helplessly watching, he could remember only one time he saw a grown person so inconsolably grieving. *Oliver,* he thought to himself. The nearby stream only strengthened the memory, but he could not put it out of his mind.

Gamaréa's bravery had spared him from death in the arena. His love for him caused Didrebelle to plot his rescue. Yet he could do nothing but sit and watch as one of his dearest friends grieved openly before him.

"I am sorry, my friend," he said softly to his sleeping companion. "I owe you my life twice over, and I will restore my debt on the road from here."

Gamaréa snored in response.

It was an amazing sensation, being able to sleep outdoors after being caged for so long. The air was sweet and crisp after the fresh rain, and even in the middle of the night it seemed brighter than it ever had in his cell.

It is a pity about that Lucian boy, he thought to himself. *I would give anything to avenge him. For my friend.*

Just then he noticed Gamaréa's outstretched hand, in which the ruby still lay.

This must be a thing of great importance.

Out of curiosity, he retrieved it from Gamaréa's light clutches.

Nothing remarkable, he thought. *It's not even shiny . . .*

Suddenly something like a bright red jolt of lightning illuminated the forest. After a moment or so of darkness, it happened again. The ruby was becoming hot in his hand, but he could not cast it away. It flickered a third time, then a fourth. After the fifth flicker—when it finally shook itself from weariness after a millennia of dormancy—the forest came alive with its unfaltering, blood-red gleam.

Daxau became frightened. What was this in his hand?

Could it have been dark magic? He was so used to simple things that something this magnificent seemed foul to him. It was so abrupt and frightening and miraculous that he gave a yell, and the other four woke thinking they saw the light of morning.

"What is this?" he exclaimed, pain and fear evident in his shaking voice. Somewhere by their camp the horses whinnied. "WHAT HAVE I DONE?"

He held up his hand in which the ruby gleamed more fervently than ever. It felt like it was trying to weld itself on to his skin, burning like cold flame. Blinded by the power of its radiance, it was long before any could hold it in their sight.

Then Tartalion came forward, shielding his eyes, for even they were straining against the blaring jewel. Awe and fear warred within his voice. "You, my boy, may have turned the tide of this war," he whispered incredulously.

ABOUT THE AUTHOR

Nicholas T. Daniele was born on June 9, 1988 in Norwalk, Connecticut and discovered his passion for writing in the second grade. In 2013, he made his debut with The Jewel of the Sorcerer, the first volume in the three-volume series The Keeper of Fates. Since joining the world of authors, Nicholas has toured the New England area promoting his action-packed series, speaking in libraries, schools, and small venues, and looks forward to continue interacting with readers and fellow authors.

He earned a Bachelors degree in English and Secondary Education from Framingham State University, and hopes to produce future classics while teaching those from the past. A dedicated writer, avid reader, and die-hard Yankees fan, Nicholas currently resides in the New England area close to his close friends and family.

Follow him on Facebook (Nicholas T. Daniele), and Twitter (@NTD_Pub).

The City

of

Night

Shir Azgoth
Erehalle
Ren Noctis
Morin Mountains
Medric
N
W
E
S
The Red Peaks
Glooms Wood
River Wood
Icebarrow River
Red Acre Wood
Springcrest River
ELARION
ENORMÈTEREN
Hrothgale
Dridion
The Moaning Wood
Kazakmuir
Deavorás
Ravelon
Cauldarím
Arena
Nundric